SLAYER OF
EVERMORE

SLAYER OF EVERMORE

James M. Lipuma

To order additional copies of this book, contact:
Xlibris Corporation
1-888-7-XLIBRIS
www.Xlibris.com
Orders@Xlibris.com

CONTENTS

Thank you to everyone who helped with Slayer of Evermore. Whether you are one of those who has role-played, read, edited, listened, talked, or just was there with me, I appreciate it. You know who you are—thanks.

INTRODUCTION

We, the eldest race on Moniva, are known as the Azurine. In a small well-protected valley on Corinan, Moniva's largest continent, we have secluded ourselves from the other races that shared our planet for many years. As the great chronicler of my people, it is my duty and honor to pass the stories of my world to our future generations. Though only one of many stories in our long history, the adventures chronicled here mark a turning point for our race. More importantly, these events touch the lives of all on our planet.

Corinan is separated into four major regions. The northern portion of the continent is a mountainous expanse containing active volcanoes, glaciers, vast plateaus, and deep chasms. The giants, beasts, monsters, and barbarians call this area home. The only settlement in the northern lands is Arrek, a giant stronghold constructed on the side of five mountain peaks near the eastern coast. None but the brave and the fool-hardy dare to travel there or adventure in any part of the northern lands.

The rest of Corinan is divided into unequal thirds by two mountain ranges which run from north to south—the Terrillians to the East and the Blackspine to the west. For longer than our records have chronicled, Dwarven hands and hammers have worked to transform the entire Eastern range and much of the surrounding lands into a maze of tunnels and chambers that they rule over. The Blackspine runs closer to the western edge of the continent and hooks along the coast as they meet Folksa, the southern sea. Hidden within the mountain passes of the range are lush, verdant forests where the elves built their villages. Stalliac, the only large elven city, is nestled into the southern coast. It serves as both a center of trade and a stronghold for the elven race.

Large verdant plains stretch from the base of the mountains to touch Asdorn, the great ocean that covers our planet. Human are spread across both of these great expanses. Between these great ranges lie vast plateaus and high valleys broken by jutting peaks and ridges. The great plains are split amongst kingdoms too numerous to count. By stark contrast, the central lands are controlled by the legendary half-fire-giant, half-human, known only as Redlin. The southern half is known as the Forbidden Lands, while the northern, where our kingdom rests, is called the Valley of the Dragons. Both earned their names for reasons too complex to explain here. It is here, at the edge of the Forbidden Lands where magic is still permitted that an old story ends and ours begins.

Almost seventy years ago, just after the last great battle to defeat the eternal dragons in the valley bearing their name, the Great Cleansing occurred. Jealous humans, over-zealous barbarians, and the fearful beast-like races banded together to try to eradicate all magic-users from the world. The barbarians hated magic and so it made sense for them to join the quest. The beasts could not learn its ways and so envied those races who were able to wield it. Though they were happy to use weapons imbued with the power, they killed all who had knowledge of its mysteries. Humans saw a way to seize power and control from the elder races of the world. In a short time, magic-users were a rare and hunted breed. The only place where the art still thrived was in hidden guilds and the magic school located in Phinn, the capitol of Redlin's kingdom. None dared assault Phinn or Redlin directly. Even so, enrollment dropped dramatically as new apprentices were found dead daily. The prices on wizards' heads were very high and the common folk were made fearful of anyone who might bring ruin to them by casting spells or using magic of any kind.

Of course, several human warlords had retained the services of their own wizards for the ensuing battle that they planned. Unfortunately for them, they had not planned on the wizards banding together to hoard the remaining knowledge and carve out a kingdom for themselves. After ten years of slaughter and internal struggle, little magic remained in the world. Anything or anyone who knew its secrets was hunted and prized as spoils of war. Any items imbued with magic became valuable and highly sought by all. Quests for legendary magic weapons were embarked upon and even the most mundane of magic items brought great interest when used and huge profits when sold.

It was then that a young ambitious wizard named Thrack Morgan came to power. Morgan, known to his beast allies as the master of demons, forged an alliance with the barbarians of the north. With their help, he has grown strong and bold enough to challenge the aging Redlin as his allies quarrel amongst themselves unknowing of the danger that lies in wait to the north. In the past several years, these two great forces have been gathering to face one another. Redlin has been preparing for the final battle with Thrack Morgan for control of Corinan as Morgan tested Redlin's defenses waiting for the moment he would attack.

We, the clan Azurine, were fortunate enough to have one of our most gifted scribes adventuring with those Redlin chose to help him at this pivotal moment in our history. Her story and the story of those who quested with her for the Slayer of Evermore begins now. All who gave their lives are honored by the telling of the story and will never be forgotten as long as one of our clan still lives.

CHAPTER 1

"Tommy, clear the place," Peter Zorich announced calmly but with force as he pushed through the door of the inn. Though it had been over a year since he had last seen human civilization, Peter confidently crossed the barroom of the Rusty Sword as if he was a regular.

A large burly man that acted as both bouncer and bartender, looked up to see who had made such a presumptuous statement. The bartender's mind worked as he looked Peter up and down trying to make out who was hidden under the dirt of the road and behind the long hair and beard obscuring Peter's face. After a moment, his eyes met Peter's and he said, "It's been a while since you've been in—something serious?"

"Redlin said meet a party at the Rusty Sword, so that's exactly what I'm doing. You decide if it's serious."

The few customers that were seated around the place did not care about Peter's proclamation. The small inn on the outskirts of Hamiltanville near the edge of the Forbidden Lands was often frequented by braggarts, blowhards, and drunks. This, however, was different. The bartender nodded as he moved to the far end of the bar. Raising his voice while pounding the bar, he exclaimed, "Time to go! Get up and get out."

Though his customers looked confused and not at all happy, they trudged slowly to the door knowing that they would not win an argument with him.

As the handful of people left, Peter surveyed the place reacquainting himself with its interior. The ground floor of the Rusty Sword consisted of a large room with a bar and a few tables surrounded by chairs. The bar ran along one wall and ended at a door that opened into the alley running next to the inn. On the opposite side was the door to the kitchen. In the center of the back wall was a set of stairs that led up to the rooms overhead. Peter found the place to be remarkably clean by his standards which made it passable for most others. Once the other patrons had left, he relaxed slightly and moved to a table.

The journey to town had taken almost a week of constant hard riding and he was weary from the travel. His first stop was the stables where he left his armor, weapons, and other equipment in the care of the stable manager whom he knew well enough to trust. Freedom from his weighty adventuring equipment allowed him to move effortlessly as he made his way across the room. Tucked under his left arm was a large sword-case made of Dragonthorn heartwood—a rare and valued commodity. As he reached a corner table big enough for six, he sat with his back to one wall and slid the case down to the floor between his feet. He liked having the door on his side and a wall to his back. It was a habit he had picked up years ago and one that served him well.

If not for the years of battle and journeying that cut the look of a seasoned warrior into him, Peter would seem average. The lean muscular build, hard features, cold eyes, and eerie calm that hung about him told most observant people that he was not one to be taken lightly. The only thing that seemed out of place was his cheery smile. It was somehow even more ominous than any of his other features.

"Good evening sir, can I get you something?" the serving maid asked politely as she came to the table.

With a wave of his hand and a shake of his head, Peter let her know politely that he wanted nothing.

Smiling she replied to his gesture, "If you change your mind, just ask."

He watched the girl move to the bar. Watching was something he did reflexively after so many years of adventuring. It was more attentive than edgy but either way, he was always alert. It took only seconds for him to sense trouble as it walked in. Two men, if they could be called that, came into the bar carrying swords and wearing Orcan armor. Each was as tall as Peter but at least double his weight. The dull look in their eyes coupled with their stench, marked them as half-orc mercenaries. Neither bright nor sociable, half-breeds like this always meant trouble. They had come in for business or a fight. From the look in their eyes, Peter figured both. Normally, he would just leave the trouble behind, but this time he had to stay and wait for the rest of his party. He had no choice.

In as much a grunt as intelligible speech the half-orc began to spit orders toward the bar as he walked to Peter's table. "Bring food . . . bring drink. We eat with this podrick human. Do it! Go, now."

Peter had heard many insults in his life, but podrick was one of his least favorite. Usually it was reserved for mating slaves and crippled beasts of burden. Peter thought to himself, "These two must be even more stupid than most of their kind."

He was sure of that when the second half-orc stepped up next to him and put a hand on his shoulder. The other half-orc spoke, "We saw case . . . give it to us or die and we take it, podrick."

Peter did not want to cause problems but neither did he like these beasts—especially the one touching him. Unfortunately, he was sitting and his view of the door was blocked by the first beast. Before he could answer, someone he could not see began to speak. "Sirs," the voice began in a melodic and elfish tone, "I think you need to leave him alone."

The two half-orcs turned to face the unseen man. Peter could only catch a glimpse of the one who had spoken. He was a four-foot-tall half-elf dressed in leather riding clothes from head to toe. What surprised Peter more than anything was that this small peaceful looking being carried no weapons and seemingly no fear.

The two half-breeds took a step towards the half-elf saying, "We kill you first . . . then deal with the podrick."

Peter stood as the half-elf began his reply. If nothing else, this distraction had given him a chance to stretch his legs before he would have to kill these beasts.

The half-elf clapped his hands together and began rubbing them back and forth as he said, "I think the two of you need to . . ." He placed one hand on each of the half-orc's chests as he intoned in a deep booming voice, "Back Off!" There was a clap of thunder as the two half-orcs were thrown as much through the table as over it. They hit the far wall leaving a jagged splintered impression where their heads met the wood. Their limp bodies slid to the floor where they laid motionless. Before they could regain consciousness, the bartender lifted them up onto his shoulders and carried them into the alley. Once both were deposited on the street like bags of garbage, he locked the side door and returned to the bar. After having executed his entire task in silence, the bartender raised a hand and waved to Peter as if to say everything was taken care of.

By the time Peter's attention had returned to the half-elf, he had reset the table, picked up a chair, sat, and made himself comfortable. As Peter sat, the half-elf placed the fingertips together and nodded his head slowly. "You may call me Gallis. The mage master sent me. I assume from your appearance and the case you carry that you are the wanderer."

Peter nodded his understanding of the statement that had just been thrust at him. While he spoke as clearly as he could, Peter tried to gather as much information about Gallis as he might be permitted. "Knowing how Permillion, the mage master, thinks of me, I must be the wanderer—call me Peter." He extended his hand in friendship.

Gallis shook his hand and then leaned back in his chair. "We have a great deal to discuss before the master arrives. I am sure the scribe will be here soon. The master will arrive later. Have you a room?"

"Not yet. I thought I would have a drink and relax first. I hoped that the party would move together to a better inn or maybe even onto Helexpa tonight. I'll know better once everyone has arrived."

Gallis laughed a hearty laugh and smiled. "You are more eager than most to get to Redlin's palace my friend. We have a long way to go still, but we will be moving soon I hope. We will wait together."

Though Peter thought that Gallis appeared genuine, something about his manners seemed forced. "Fine with me. First things first, though, I need to know that you're who you say you are."

Without hesitation, Gallis reached beneath his shirt collar and extracted a chain. Dangling from the end was a golden card and a small purple figurine shaped like a dragon. Lifting the chain and all off his neck, Gallis handed them to Peter saying, "These should be proof enough. Just the fact that I even knew to come here should tell you the rest."

Accepting the necklace, Peter examined it carefully. The golden card was engraved with a flaming *R*. This was to assure safe passage in territories governed by Redlin or his allies. The purple dragon was a sign that Gallis was part of the same adventurer guild as Permillion. Together, they proved that the half-elf could be trusted. Smiling, Peter handed the necklace back to Gallis saying, "Looks like we'll be traveling together."

Gallis replaced the chain around his neck and then pressed Peter. "So what about you? Do you have any proof other than my assumptions?"

Smiling, Peter produced a chain similar to Gallis' with one important exception—his card was made of platinum and veined with gold and a mystic black metal known as lythrum. Upon seeing it, Gallis' eyes gleamed with understanding and a bit of envy. This card was more than a pass through Redlin's kingdom, it was a gift from Redlin himself. Its bearer would be shown every hospitality and, in this case, signified that Peter was owed a favor by Redlin himself.

Gallis' tone became very deferential as he spoke. "I'm sorry if I did not show the proper respect to you earlier."

Peter shook his head. "Don't you worry, I've taken no offense. I rarely do. One thing though, I'd like to know what type of sorcerer is brave enough to use magic in the open. Only a master or a fool would do that."

As if on cue, the door to the inn opened with a creak and Vineta Azurine stepped through the opening out of the night. All eyes were irresistibly drawn to her presence. Vineta was at least as tall as Peter but very slight of build. Her pale bluish skin was highlighted by shoulder length soft golden blond hair. Most captivating of all were her emerald eyes that seemed to glow against the pale bluish-green skin of her face. Her only clothing was a one-piece black leather tunic with what appeared to be a matching quiver slung over her left shoulder. Oddly enough, there was no accompanying bow. She carried a small leather-bound book with only a few sheets of parchment and a quill pen wrapped inside. Around her neck was a simple silver chain with an intricately carved purple dragon and a gold card similar to Gallis' dangling from it.

No one spoke while she made her way to the table where Gallis and Peter stood silently staring at her. Vineta broke the silence as she sat next to Gallis. Her voice was melodic and so pleasing; all were silent as she spoke hoping not to miss any syllable. "Hello gentlemen. My name is Vineta. I am of the Azurine, and have come at the request of Androthy Permillion. He has told me of the two of you." Once seated, Vineta placed her book on the table, opened it, and picked up the quill pen that rested inside. "You may call me Vin. I am the scribe of the Azurine. I shall record all that happens on this, the greatest of adventures." Without turning her head to acknowledge his presence, Vineta spoke to Gallis. "Young elf, servant of Permillion. Have you news of your master's arrival?"

Not at all offended by this lack of respect, Gallis answered her immediately and with the respect and humility reserved for royalty. "No my lady. I know only that he is to be here some time tonight."

"Whom does he bring?"

"An apprentice, a warrior, and another . . . exactly who, I'm not sure."

"Very well." Her eyes had remained fixed on Peter through the entire conversation. Even as she wrote a few words in her journal, her gaze never left his face. It was as if she was absorbing his essence as much as studying his features. With one graceful motion, she placed the pen on the page and extended her hand towards Peter. "Hello and good day to you sir. You must have great stories to tell if Permillion asked you to adventure with us. While we wait, will you tell me of your life?"

Peter took her hand without conscious thought. He was surprised by its warmth and its apparent strength. "I am Peter Zorich. Gallis called me the wanderer. Androthy and my family are long-time blood friends. When he asked my service, I gladly gave it to him with no questions. Though truthfully, it was Redlin who sent for me." He was amazed at how his own words sounded foreign to his ears. Even as Vineta's hand slipped from his grasp, he could feel her magical presence linger a moment longer. It had been many years since he had encountered an Azurine yet his memories of the experience were still crisp and not entirely pleasant.

"I can sense your confusion Peter, let me tell you of myself. I am a scribe sent out amongst the races of the world by the Azurine—"

"Are you sure you should be telling him this?" Gallis interrupted.

Not bothering to dignify the question with a response, Vin continued. "We are a secretive race and few ever leave our protected valley deep in the mountains, guarded by the guilded horsemen and griffin riders. I, however, have been sent to roam the world and keep an account of all I see. As such, I have trained for what would be several of your lifetimes in many different arts. I had already been traveling the world of humans for many years when I first met Permillion. He was only an apprentice then." Peter consumed each word she uttered, still ensnared by her magical aura. "As I am sure you have noticed, I have certain innate abilities and my rank and station bring their own measures of respect. I have chronicled some of the greatest figures in your history."

"And now you have come to journey with us to find out more about Redlin and the great relics." Peter's statement startled Vin. "Did you think I couldn't sense your spell? I haven't lived this long without some measure of self-control."

"And much more I'm sure." Vineta smiled and gave out a little laugh. "I think it will be very interesting to hear what you have to say my friend. This is not going to be a dull adventure at all."

Gallis breathed a sigh of relief and eased back in his chair. It was very unusual for him to be at the bottom of the rankings in any room. At this table, however, he was the servant, the squire, and perhaps even the weakest of the three participants. When his master arrived, he was sure that this would not change. Even the apprentice who accompanied them would have higher station and better lineage than the others. Though he did not enjoy it in the least, he would have to quickly become accustomed to following rather than leading. "Is there anything I can get either of you?"

Vineta spoke first in a pleasant tone. "No thank you. I'm fine for now."

Peter was slower and more deliberate in his speech. "I'm all right—for now. Maybe later I'll need something. Don't worry, I'll let you know."

Gallis was sure that he had said this just to irritate him, but he could not take any chances. This wanderer and warrior had an important role to play. Even if he was unsure what that role was to be, Gallis was positive that the mage master had his reasons. Not letting any of the comments get to him, he stood and excused himself. As the chair under him slid back, the door to the inn opened and the unmistakable stench of half-orcs assaulted him. As he turned, he felt the bite of a crossbow bolt in his right shoulder. As he dropped to the floor screaming in pain and clutching at the metal point that was sticking out the front of his shoulder, he saw two of the beasts in the inn and two more just outside guarding the door. The two half-orcs in the bar each had a spent crossbow. Gallis had not, however, heard any other screams.

As Peter vaulted over Gallis' chair, he yelled "Stay down. These podricks are mine. Just make sure the case and the scribe are safe." Peter threw himself into the two waiting orcs as they tried to draw their swords. The force of his tackle knocked them to the floor. Snarling, they struggled to get up and retrieve their lost weapons.

After closing her writing book quickly, Vineta stood calmly and moved towards the back of the bar. From the side of her quiver she took a small case, opened it, and extracted a dart. As she tucked the case into a fold of her tunic, she faded from sight.

In the confusion and movement, the serving maid and bartender dove for cover and then made their way out of the small room. Peter had sprung to his feet and readied himself for the fight before the two guards outside had even realized what had happened. With one smooth motion, he lifted and then tossed one of the stunned half-orcs out the door onto the two guarding the escape route.

Though Vineta had completely vanished, she was still able to see and be impressed by Peter's display of strength and agility. A flurry of fists and elbows reduced the last beast in the bar to a mass of pleading half-intelligible grunts. While this pathetic creature crawled to the door, his three compatriots were gathering themselves outside. As Peter stepped to the door, he heard a thunder of hooves. Six city guards, wearing black chain mail, rode to the front of the inn from out of the darkening night and dismounted. Each wore a breast-plate with a flaming red *R* emblazoned on it. All recognized the symbol identifying these men as part of Lord Redlin's elite guard. Four of the guards took custody of the beaten orcs and two came to speak with Peter. One of the guards said, "Sir, you'll have to come with us, until we determine what happened."

Peter, Gallis, and Vineta all thought the same thing at once, "This was not supposed to happen."

CHAPTER 2

Redlin's castle, Helexpa, stood ominously alone atop a single peak overlooking the secluded and well-protected valley in the deepest recesses of the Forbidden Lands. Eight of Moniva's most powerful leaders waited in camps at the foot of this mountain that held Helexpa like a gem just out of their reach. Each leader had been invited to a conference inside the walls of Helexpa.

The castle had been built long before the great cleansing and was fabled to hold many secrets of magic not known elsewhere in the world. Though much of Redlin's greatness had since been forgotten, his legendary deeds and accomplishments warranted caution, if not respect, by all. Redlin was a mystery and a powerful wildcard in all affairs. For the last fifty years, his troops and envoys had made their presence known throughout Corinan. Long before that, Redlin had forged alliances with the rulers of each of the kingdoms and it was time to reestablish those ties. At one time or another, almost everyone had discussed dissolving the alliance with the aging half-giant. Redlin's personal armies and his many allies, coupled with the fear of the magic that he could unleash upon anyone who left the alliance, quieted even the most powerful of these dissenters.

As a result, when Redlin's envoys invited the most powerful leaders to come to his stronghold, none would refuse. To assure their attendance, he included a small gift of powerful magic with each invitation. To him these items were only trinkets, but to the invited guests, they served as irresistible calling cards.

Representatives of all the races had arrived as well. The dwarves, elves, and giants all knew and respected Redlin and had sent delegations to show their support. Most of the other invited guests were human and represented a diverse group of guilds and warrior classes that served the five large kingdoms and several smaller ones that flanked Redlin's holdings. It was rumored that a powerful Elven wizard and his entourage had been invited but no one had seen his party as of yet. Once everyone had arrived, they all would be allowed to enter Helexpa together.

Amongst the many delegations was that of a young king named Aaron Boewin. Aaron had inherited his lands, holdings, riches, and army from his father, King Darrius Boewin. Marcus and Raymond, his older brothers, had both died before their father, leaving Aaron as the sole heir. Luck more than skill had allowed him to keep it. Philip Cragmore, Aaron's most trusted advisor, was responsible for young Aaron's continued success as a ruler. Cragmore had pledged to be Aaron's protector and teacher when the boy was a newborn. He soon found himself watching over the continually frightened and unsure boy. As general, Cragmore had kept the army loyal and focused. With this, the entire kingdom remained under the young ruler's control. Aaron was not a poor king, just unhappy and ill prepared to be a leader. His mother had protected him for the first years of his life until she died. His father had tried to be there for his young son, but ruling a kingdom was not an easy task. Though Aaron had the body of a warrior, his heart was still one of a scared and easily daunted child. Cragmore had not been able to impart all his wisdom to the young king. Aaron never had the patience for lessons that did not pertain to arms and armaments. Book learning did not come easily and Aaron was quickly frustrated by anything he did not find amusing. Worst of all, as he grew older, he steadily became more hesitant to act decisively.

Aaron sat patiently at a make-shift desk in the middle of his tent reading a book. Nature had blessed him with a strong body and mind. Years of physical and mental training had hardened his body and made him a formidable warrior. At the tender age of thirteen, the weight of ruling a kingdom had been placed squarely on his shoulders and he had tried to carry it for the past four years.

However, fighting as a soldier in his father's army and ruling as a king were two completely different things. Despite his powerful build, the sense that he was always confused or afraid to make a decision was conveyed by the look that hung about his face and dwelled in his eyes. His own insecurities kept him from ever being considered a powerful warrior or an inspiring leader. Even in his most imposing of royal garb, his subjects saw him as a follower of orders or a pawn in someone else's game. Aaron had been thrust into many roles he had never really wanted. Besides, far too many of them needed to be earned and not granted. Rarely did he look comfortable or calm, and was never at ease. Everyone knew he was trapped in an uncomfortable position from which he could not extract himself. Until the untimely death of his siblings and father, most expected that he would be a soldier or perhaps a priest. Now he was a king.

When Cragmore, a man of four times his age and twice his stature entered his tent, Aaron was startled and seemed edgy. Cragmore feared what might have happened in his young lord's tent over the past few hours. It had taken weeks for him to build his young king's confidence enough to even make the impending meeting possible. Though Aaron knew very little about anyone in attendance, somehow just knowing of their reputations made him feel less important. The venerable general knew that there might be a huge confrontation in the morning when all were brought together in Helexpa's great hall. If this did happen, there was a good chance that Aaron would crumble under the pressure and flee. Though he was resting when he received the call, Cragmore had come to his lord's tent almost immediately. His boots and a sword had been thrust on quickly. Everything else was left behind. "Is there something you need Aaron?" His voice was filled with concern and caring, without any hint of annoyance. He was accustomed to being awakened at all hours, for all reasons.

"I need your advice. I'm worried about tomorrow's meeting."

"That's understandable. You're meeting a legend and will be surrounded by dignitaries from across our world." In a more forceful tone, he continued, "Remember, you're a king. You've been personally invited by Redlin himself."

"It's more than that. This is my opportunity to prove to everyone what I'm made of; what I can do."

"What do you mean?" Cragmore did not have to ask. He was almost certain of the answer.

"When will we ever have this type of access to the heads of so many powerful groups. I must make a lasting impression. Any sign of weakness could mean the loss of respect, or worse, the loss of the kingdom."

"I know it's important, but you're ready for this." The general sat next to his young lord. "It's not my place to tell you what to do, but you've listened to my advice in the past. By my accounts, I haven't done badly." Cragmore placed his hand on Aaron's shoulder, and spoke to him like his father had in the years long ago. "A king must rule with diplomacy as much as with might. You must choose your fights carefully and choose to fight reluctantly. I will gladly take my charge as your general and carry your standard into battle, but please, don't throw my life and the lives of your soldiers away. The people you'll meet do respect the power of your army but they'll be more impressed with how you carry yourself."

Aaron nodded his understanding and agreement as these words made their way into his mind. "I know, good friend. Perhaps, I . . . well . . . maybe, I just want to be rid of this royal charge. I was not meant to be king. My father had planned for Marcus to be the diplomat and Raymond to be the king. My future was to be nothing more than a soldier, a priest, or an apprentice. They were both so much older than me."

"But for these past years, you've been the king," Cragmore said reassuringly. He had heard Aaron complain this way many times in the past, and he hoped that this was nothing more than the young king venting his frustration.

"They never let me forget my future was not to be a part of the ruling class. For them, it was only a matter of time before I would be sent away, never to return." Aaron exhaled loudly as he shook his head. "I knew that eventually I'd be able to escape from them, but it didn't work out the way I thought."

"It was fate that your brothers would die. The duel and the riding accident made you heir to the throne," Cragmore interjected, trying to hide his distaste for this type of sniveling.

"Before I had a chance to . . . to even explore the world, I was given my role in it. I need time . . . time to make a name for myself . . . time to find myself . . . time before I am given a title to accompany the name." Aaron dropped his head and began to shake it slightly.

"I'm sick of your worthless whining! Show some backbone!" Cragmore thought to himself but did not dare say. He knew Aaron would just crumble at words like these. Instead, he said confidently, "We've talked of this before. You have the royal Boewin blood flowing in your veins. With time you will feel its power and be more comfortable in your position. As for tomorrow, the others are just people. You're as good as the best of them." Cragmore smiled and patted Aaron's shoulder. He knew that the words could do little to assuage the feelings of inadequacy the boy felt. Everything that Aaron needed had to come from within. "Is that what you're worried about? Do you think you won't measure up tomorrow?"

Aaron felt the hand on his shoulder and it helped him feel better. Cragmore gave him strength and helped push away the fears. "Not really, my father told stories about most of the kingdoms assembled here. I've even heard you talk of the many wars fought amongst them. More than anything, well, I worry about meeting Lord Redlin. Even my father feared him."

Darrius Boewin feared no one or, at least, he never let it be known that he did. Cragmore now realized why Aaron was so worried. If his father, the fearless warrior and king, had fears of Redlin, what hope could he have to conquer his own fears. Searching his mind for something encouraging to say took a noticeable moment. "Don't think of it that way. Redlin's a powerful and influential being. There have been few who could say that they could equal his accomplishments. He was a smith, a warrior, a wizard, and a king." Aaron's expression became even more concerned. This was not what Cragmore wanted to accomplish. "What I meant is, Redlin deserved your father's respect. It wasn't fear, it was just caution. You can't let that—"

Before he could say anymore, the guards outside the tent began to sound an alarm. As Cragmore stood and drew his sword, four of Redlin's personal guards entered. Each wore armor made of what appeared to be gold and silver strands braided together. Each carried a spear and wore a long sword and dagger at his side. Two guards flanked each side of the door and a fifth of much higher rank entered. This fifth soldier was at least a lieutenant. He was adorned in the same armor but with the addition of a solid gold breast plate. Entering confidently, he stared at Cragmore. His voice was clear and authoritative. "Lord Boewin, please have your man put his weapon down. We mean no disrespect nor harm to you or your men."

Aaron turned to Cragmore and gestured for him to sheath his sword. Surprised by his lord's seeming confidence, Cragmore did as he said. "If they wanted us dead, I'm sure they would've been able to do it much more effectively and with much less trouble than this." Turning to the lieutenant, he continued, "What is it you want with us? I thought we were all to enter Helexpa tomorrow."

"That is correct sir. This is an invitation meant especially for you from Lord Redlin himself." The lieutenant extended a scroll case towards Aaron. Once the boy had taken it, he continued, "We're to wait for your response, and hopefully, escort you to the palace."

Aaron was not sure if it was adrenaline or something else that gave him the confidence to act decisively, and he did not care. The castle atop the mountain had always struck him as a formidable icon of power and a fortress meant to keep Redlin safe, not a palace. Suddenly, things had changed. He was no longer an outsider. Rather, this invitation made him feel special. In a commanding tone, he said, "Wait outside while I discuss this."

The guards all nodded and left the tent. As Cragmore moved in closer to his lord, Aaron opened the scroll case and read the words written on the scroll contained within. Before Cragmore could even ask, Aaron had begun to explain. "I've been invited to a special meeting with Redlin tonight."

Cragmore was almost overwhelmed by all that was happening. Both the note and the sudden change in Aaron had taken him by complete surprise and he did not like surprises. "Can we trust the note . . . the messenger . . . any of this? I just don't think—"

"Don't worry. This is authentic. Look for yourself." Aaron turned the scroll to show its face to his advisor. Attached to the scroll was a ring with the royal crest of his family that had belonged to Aaron's uncle. It had been given to Redlin as a pledge long ago. Only a select few in the Boewin household had known about it. "This is a message from Redlin, or someone with enough influence, money, and power to make it appear so. Either way, I should meet with them."

With the impatience of a man late for his wedding, Cragmore stepped to the door saying, "I'll be ready in a few minutes."

"No, I'll be going alone. You were right, it's time I took responsibility. If I am to make mistakes, so be it."

Cragmore was pleased by Aaron's newfound assertiveness and confidence, but at the same time, he worried for the young king. This was going to be unlike anything he had ever known. Before the general could even voice concern or give advice, Aaron had thrown a cloak around his shoulders and stepped out of the tent into the night air. Even as Cragmore followed him out of the tent, he saw the five guards and his lord disappear into the night.

CHAPTER 3

Androthy Permillion and his young apprentice Twig stood talking in a clearing near a stand of oak trees next to a dirt road. As dusk approached, both were growing tired of the day's lessons, though neither would agree to stop before total darkness was upon them. Their camp was only a few minutes walk down the road, so traveling was not a concern. The lessons were more important than anything else.

Though Twig had been studying under the mage master Permillion for many years, she was only now becoming an accomplished sorceress in her own mind. It was not that she was a slow learner but rather that there was so much for her to learn. Only recently had she been allowed to work with the final class of magic in her course of study. Soon she would choose her name and be considered a true mage.

The Master of Magic, Androthy Permillion, was of pure elven descent. He stood less than four feet tall and always wore dark robes or cloaks. Living for over 2000 cycles of the seasons and practicing magic for more than 1500 of those cycles had withered and aged the small elf. His purple-white hair highlighted his grayish skin and eyes. Long before humans had ever considered the power of spell casting, the elven clans had perfected many of the mystical arts that Androthy now practiced. He was first a student, then a journeyman, and finally a teacher. Never did he have a taste for adventuring across the world. After 500 years of practice, he was deemed a skilled master mage and began teaching others. In the last 1000 years, by human reckoning, he had taught many of the greatest and the most infamous magic-users. Unfortunately, that all ended with the great cleansing. Though he was still very powerful, few of his students still lived, and even fewer new students wanted to risk learning. Twig was his last student. She had learned much, but still had a great deal left to work through. Humans were never the easiest or best students, but in this case, Permillion could not complain. She had done everything he asked and he had no regrets about accepting her as a pupil.

Named Daniella Monterack by her family, immediately upon becoming an apprentice that name was replaced with the much simpler Twig. Once deemed a full mage, she could assume any title she wished. For now, however, she was Twig or little one. This was rather ironic since she was tall and muscular. The chores and hard work of everyday magic-working as much as breeding were responsible for her physique. While with Permillion, she had grown to be an attractive woman, though few could see because the cloaks she wore hid almost all of her features. Contrasting her height and athletic build, she had a rounded face with gentle curves and golden-red hair that accentuated the fire that burned in her greenish-gray eyes. Most alluring of all her features was her friendly disposition. No matter what task she was given, she worked diligently, with surprisingly few complaints.

Danielle's parents were the lords of a small northern kingdom with five sons, all in line for the throne ahead of her. Her only chance to be of use to her family was to become a valuable resource or commodity. For her, this meant either becoming a marriage prospect, a magician, or an assassin. The magician seemed the least distasteful and so the most fitting choice. On her tenth birthday, Daniella Monterack was sent to one of Androthy Permillion's journeymen who delivered her to the mage master. Once there, Permillion began her studies.

Androthy had agreed to train Twig because of many favors owed to her family and their allies. As well, he saw a glimmer of magic in her eyes when he first met the young princess and knew she had potential. However, he knew potential and desire were never enough. In the time they had been together, Twig had proven herself worthy of being trained in the arts of magic. More than that, she showed him that with enough time and instruction, she could become one of his best students. Androthy's only concern was that she would never have the time.

"Come now Twig, try it again." Androthy said encouragingly.

"Yes sir." she replied obediently, for what seemed the thousandth time.

"Remember, imagine an arrow of light leaving your hand and striking the tree limb." As Androthy said this, he extended his arm and pointed at a dead oak tree at the edge of the stand a short distance away. "Once you have it in your mind, just release it. The magic will do the rest." As he said this, a crimson arrow of light leapt from his finger and impacted a low branch on the tree at which he had pointed. It had taken only an instant for the bolt to travel and hit the tree with a thunderous crack. The limb exploded into a thousand toothpick-sized splinters. The piece of the limb that remained smoked and smoldered where the magic arrow struck the doomed limb.

"You make it seem so easy. I don't understand why it is so hard for me to accomplish these simple spells when I can do so much more. You've told me that making myself disappear is much more advanced than this, yet I can't seem to make these spells work."

"All in time little one. You must understand that magic is not something easy. If it were, everyone would use it." He shook his head as he saw that she did not want to hear what he was saying. Continuing in a more forceful tone, he said, "How easy was it for you to learn to use a sword?"

Twig was surprised by the question. "Well, it was easy to just swing it, but when I really started to learn what I needed to do— that was hard. I was barely strong enough to lift it, and not nearly skilled enough to make it move the way I wanted it to."

"But with time, you are its master."

"Yes, but that was only a matter of strength not like magic."

"When you began studying magic, you needed to make your physical and mental strength work together to bend magic to your will. In the same way that you learned to train your muscles to move the sword, your whole being was trained to use magic." Twig might not like what he was saying but he saw that she understood he was right. "Even though you knew how to use a sword, did that help you learn to wield an ax?"

Reluctantly, she provided the answer that her master was looking for, "No, of course not. I was stronger, but it's entirely different."

The old magician did not let her say anything more. "And magic is no different. Just because you're a master of illusion, apparition, transformation, or any of the other arts, you cannot assume that the rest will come without work and practice. You must learn to use your will to channel each type of magic differently and at its own rhythm. That is why I taught this magic to you last. Far too many of my other students learned to use magic to attack and then learned nothing else. With you, it will be different." Pointing at the dead tree, he said in a kind fatherly tone, "Now try again."

A look of deep concentration consumed Twig's face as she worked on the spell. She raised her hand and pointed. Nothing happened. "Urrr," she exclaimed in disgust. "It's not coming. This magic is eluding me . . . maybe . . . it's that . . . I just can't use it."

"All magic is the same—only the skill of the artisan is different. The type of spell or the force you choose to put behind it is all a matter of practice and control. The same spell I just showed you can be shaped any way I choose—watch." Silently, Androthy raised his hand, extended a finger and then said, "Go gather firewood."

A bright white bolt emanated from his hand and hit the same tree as was hit before, but this time it impacted the center of the trunk. There was a clap of thunder as the once mighty oak was shattered into little more than chunks of firewood and kindling. Though she was going to say something before he had cast the spell, the apprentice simply dropped her head and walked towards the newly created wood pile. Androthy followed her.

The two stopped by the pile of wood and Twig began stacking the jumbled pieces. "I know, I know, it's just a matter of time and hard work." she retorted to his unspoken comments without lifting her head.

"No, I don't think you do. When it comes to magic, most humans have neither the patience nor the persistence to become spell-casters. Others only want to know the devastating spells of flame, fire, ice, earthquake, and such manipulation. You've worked this long to become a true caster of spells. It all takes time."

"With time . . . you mean maybe with two or three lifetimes of time."

Seeing his pupil's disgust, Androthy decided to stop for today. "Come now, let us go back to camp and work on your cooking."

"Very funny master, you know I've already mastered that. I haven't seen you complain once when I've offered seconds."

Androthy smiled, nodded his head, and turned to the road. "Come Twig, time to go. Send the wood on ahead."

Without another word, she obeyed. After stretching her hands towards the sky, she spread her fingers and brought her two hands together in a large sweeping arc that ended in front of her waist. She touched the pile of wood and watched as it vanished from sight. Turning, she jogged to her master's side. "All done."

It took only a few minutes for the two to walk down the road to where their camp had been set up. Neither spoke. While Permillion silently scanned the road ahead, his apprentice let her mind wander. It was rare for her to have a moment to herself and she wanted to enjoy it. She had been alone with her master for almost a week now and she longed for her bed and some conversation with someone her own age. Her first thoughts were of Jeremy, one of her master's servants and the only person her age at home in Androthy's castle. As much as she looked forward to returning to him, her thoughts quickly shifted to her true family and the prospects of returning home one day. It had been so long since she had known any company or family other than that of Permillion, she wondered if anyone else in the world even remembered her.

As the two topped a hill, they saw their tents pitched at the side of the road just far enough into the brush to camouflage them from untrained eyes. This sight brought her mind back to the reality of her everyday life. She searched carefully to see if the pile of wood had appeared properly. She spotted it next to the ring of stones that marked their campfire. Placing his hand on her shoulder, Androthy complimented her, "Good work. Teleportation is not a trivial matter and you accomplish it with such ease."

"Yes, but it's easy, there's not much to it at all. Maybe if it were living or moving or—"

Before she could finish, Androthy silenced her with a gesture of his hand. With urgency in his voice, he commanded, "Quickly little one, start a fire. It will be dark soon and I think we will need it."

Though somewhat confused by her master's tone, she obeyed without question. She piled several large chunks of wood on top of some kindling, reached her hand into the center of the mess, and lifted up slightly to form a tiny pyramid. After removing her hands, she snapped the fingers of her right hand several times until she made a clear loud snap. After pausing for an instant, she placed her hand in the space under the wood and snapped her fingers again. There was a spark followed by a fire that hovered just above her fingertips. In a moment, the entire pile caught and was burning well. Sitting back, she felt the warmth of the fire embrace her.

While his student worked, Androthy scanned the horizon, giving special consideration to the area where the road met the sky. As the fire roared to life, he saw what he was looking for. A boy in his late teens atop a fast moving stallion was galloping over the rise. It was Jeremy Devlin, his young stable-hand and house boy. This was not whom he expected. Turning to Twig, Androthy spoke in a sharp authoritative tone. "Little one, gather our things. Take only the essentials. Leave the tents and other traveling supplies where they are, we won't be needing them."

Hearing the immediacy in her master's voice made Twig move even more quickly than her usually prompt responsiveness demanded. "Yes sir." She sprang to her feet and ran into and out of the tents, filling sacks and satchels as she went. Before long, she had assembled all the things that would be considered vital to their life on a campaign. Only those things used for spell casting, fighting, or self-preservation were even considered. Many of those items were discarded after a moment of thought. In the end, she had a pile of things that could be carried by her and her master while still allowing them both to cast spells and her to fight with her sword.

By the time she finished, Jeremy had made it to the camp and dismounted. He was a few inches taller than Twig but had none of her grace or coordination. As a horseman, he could hold his own, but he had little of the training that was a prerequisite for fighters or mages. As he stepped towards Androthy, he tried to catch his breath and adjust his leather riding clothes at the same time. "Master, I've been sent with a message." He paused to take a deep breath. "Dirk Lancer . . . he was near death . . . when he rode into our courtyard." The exhausted and frightened boy immediately drew in and expelled another breath. "He sent me with the message. A stalker and two guar are behind me—less than a day's ride." The boy tried to compose himself. "I've ridden for almost three days. Sir Lancer told me where to find you. He would've come himself, but the guar, they tore him apart worse than anything I'd ever seen. I don't know how he was still moving." The terror of remembering what the knight had looked like when he first appeared at the stables overwhelmed the boy.

Androthy pushed for details in the pause. "What did Lancer say? Where is he? Did he survive? Who was after him? Did he reveal his mission?" Calming himself, Androthy continued speaking in a less hurried tone. "I know it is difficult for you, but I must know. Time is vital now."

Jeremy tried to compose himself by taking in a large gulp of air and releasing it slowly through his nose. "Dirk had me take him to a healer and then told me what to do. I took my fastest horse and made my way to this place where he said I would find you. I was to keep looking until I was successful. That was the easy part. He explained about those things that were following him so

I could tell you. He said that I should tell you that the messages were delivered . . . all the messages. And the ones you want to meet will be waiting for you at the Rusty Sword ." Androthy nodded as the boy spoke. When Jeremy paused, Androthy gestured for him to continue. "Dirk said speak, don't sleep just ride or it could mean my death. The monsters that had almost killed him would be close behind me—he made sure I was clear about that. The one other thing he told me to not forget was . . . was tell you Thrack Morgan has summoned Thazul." As the name crossed the boy's lips, Androthy lost the color from his face as though it had been frosted by a gust of cold wind. Not noticing, Jeremy continued speaking, "Though I couldn't see anyone or anything behind me, I know they were there. I only stopped to sleep and eat for a few hours each night. I hope I did well sir."

"He was right about everything and you did excellently. Thank you." The old wizard fell into deep thought as the boy relaxed.

Twig listened intently to what Jeremy had said even though not much of it made sense. She was familiar with Dirk but the rest was beyond her. Lancer was a knight in the service of one of her master's friends. He had been on a quest for the last year. Something must have happened. Exactly what that something was, she did not know. What worried her most was that two of the guar things had almost killed him, yet she had seen him defeat and utterly embarrass at least four knights at once in a tournament only two years ago.

With resolve in his voice and determination in his eyes, Androthy placed his hands on Jeremy's shoulders and spoke to him as more of a father than a master. "You've done well. Unfortunately, there is neither time nor opportunity to get you safely home. You will have to continue on our quest. If there is a stalker with two guar after us, they will track you down and extract any information you might have before they kill you. I can't let that happen—for your sake and ours." Though his words should have disturbed the boy, they seemed to calm him. "From now on, Twig is as much your master as I ever was. She will be able to care for you in the time to come. Heed her words and follow her instructions as best you can."

Having fully recovered his breath and his senses, Jeremy asked submissively, "What can I do to help? My horse is almost spent but I can ride her for at least a few hours before she collapses. If you need me to fight, I might be of some help as a distraction but I haven't been fully trained."

Androthy gestured for him to stop speaking as he turned to Twig. "You've done quite enough for now. We will talk more later. Sit by the fire and gather yourself for a trip like none you have ever taken."

Jeremy nodded his understanding and sat dutifully near the fire, absorbing its warmth and composing himself. Meanwhile, Twig wondered what her master had in mind as he gestured for her to come to his side. She obeyed and as she came closer she saw that a troubled look had come over his face. In a whisper, he said, "If Lancer was injured enough to send Jeremy, we're in grave danger. The stalker will be here very soon. Guar are ruthless and relentless especially when they are being driven by a high level tracker. I'm going to have to send the two of you across the world, but I'll need your help. Do you think you can handle it."

Without hesitation, she nodded 'yes.' Her voice did not waver and reinforced the conviction of her thoughts. "Of course. I am ready to do whatever you need."

"You'll appear in a town called Hamiltanville. Go to the Rusty Sword and find my journeyman Gallis—you know him. He'll tell you what to do. Your training is all but done. He can help you finish. The two of you will have to quest together to fulfill my obligation to Redlin."

"But what about you? Where are you going to be?"

"I need to slow down the people pressing us. Don't worry about me, I can take care of myself little one. I'll meet you at Redlin's castle, or maybe someplace after that. You have all you need inside you."

For the first time that Twig could remember, she did not believe her master. His confidence and wisdom were gone. He was worried and that worried her. "Please let me stay with you. I can help."

"Your place is with those on this quest. Once Gallis finishes your training, you can choose your name and become a full-fledged mage—a master. I have another path to follow. I'll be fine, don't worry." The thunder of hooves in the distance drew Androthy's attention. He knew it would be the stalker. "My little ones, come gather the things you will need for the trip. Twig, you'll have to prepare the boy too. He's never traveled this way. It will be difficult on him."

All discussion ended with this decree. Androthy began to conjure even as Twig moved away. It was time to act. The boy looked confusedly around the camp as Twig moved to the heap of belongings piled near one of the tents. In a calm but forceful tone tinged with urgency, she instructed Jeremy as she handed him things to carry. "In a moment, the master will be placing his hands on you and then casting a spell. You'll probably feel very sick and disoriented for a few instants. You might vomit or faint—that's normal. If you have to, sit on the ground and wait for the dizziness and nausea to pass. Other than that, hold on and let yourself float for the time you're being transported. I can't help you more than that."

Jeremy listened and followed her directions as she handed him things to carry. "Yes, I'll do my best. I understand."

Androthy broke his trance and stepped up to the two. "Hold hands. I don't have much time." Three riders clad in black armor and wearing dark robes came over the top of the hill as the mage master thrust his hands into the air with his fingers spread widely apart. Twig grabbed Jeremy's hand as he looked at the three riders in terror. Two had the head of a jackal on the body of a human. These must be the guar. The third was shrouded in darkness. It's eyes glowed with a pale purple tinged with fiery yellow. This must be the stalker that was tracking him.

Androthy muttered in a low voice something meant only for his own ears. Twig strained to say goodbye as she concentrated on the spell that was being cast, trying to add her strength to her masters'. The mage placed a hand on each of the two travelers as the guar dismounted a hundred yards from the camp. Their time was quickly running out.

Jeremy's mind clouded as he and Twig slowly faded from sight. The last thing he saw was the lightening quick movements of the two guar streaking towards the old elven mage as he turned to face the three monsters.

CHAPTER 4

The master of Helexpa had chosen a small out-of-the-way place to meet his young and important guest. Though not often used for entertainment, Redlin's palace did have every comfort that could be expected or imagined by even the most demanding guests. The select few who might call the Lord of the Forbidden Lands their friend knew the place as Helexpa. Though Phinn was the capital city of Redlin's empire, Helexpa was his palace and his personal fortress from which he oversaw his kingdom. Phinn, less than a days ride to the west, served well as a staging area, a place of commerce, a home to the magic school, and a place to conduct the everyday business of running a kingdom. However, no matter what others might think, Helexpa was the true seat of power in this kingdom. The fortress itself was constructed from enchanted stone hewn from far inside the Dwarven kingdoms and metals forged in the volcanoes of the fire-giants. A garrison of thousands was always on guard while a staff of mages was fabled to have spent their entire lives within the walls.

Redlin himself was as imposing as his palace. His human half softened many of his giant features but could do little with his fiery red hair, crimson eyes, and sheer bulk. Though small compared to most pure-blooded fire-giants, he still stood over eight feet tall and was as broad as any two healthy men. Years of adventuring, magic use, and ruling over his vast and unequaled holdings had cut deep lines into his face and scarred most of the rest of his body.

Worry accentuated the hardness of Redlin's features as he sat uncomfortably in a chair near a fireplace in one of Helexpa's small antechambers contemplating what was to come the next morning. A couch and two chairs were the only pieces of furniture in the room but because they were all large enough to accommodate the half-giant, they filled it adequately. Tapestries depicting battles of years past covered the walls. Most conspicuous of all was the lack of protective space. No guards or even guard posts were anywhere to be found. This was one of Redlin's private areas not meant for entertaining.

Soon, the young Aaron Boewin would arrive and the destiny of his and many other kingdoms would be placed in the hands of this young boy. What he had to say to Aaron would surely confound and intrigue the boy. Redlin hoped that young Aaron would take after his uncle and mother. If not, all might be lost before it ever had a chance to begin.

A knock at the door signaled the arrival of his guest. Redlin spoke in a quiet yet commanding tone. "Enter," was all he said.

One of the guards that had accompanied Aaron entered and bowed. "Lord Redlin, sir, we've brought King Boewin to you as you requested."

"Very good. Show him in and then leave us."

The guard stepped to the doorway and gestured for Aaron to enter. Like a man about to see his lifelong hero for the first time, Aaron entered and tried to project confidence even though he was overwhelmed. Since the moment he entered Helexpa, he had felt the magic coursing through its walls. He could see and almost feel the power that Helexpa signified. Redlin was even more powerful than he had imagined. A million thoughts flooded his mind as he tried to prepare what he would say. Now that the moment had come, his mind was blank. His mental picture of the most powerful being he might ever meet was nothing like the true sight. If possible, Aaron thought Redlin was more imposing than he had imagined. He was looking at a true warrior, a true magician, and most of all, a true king.

As Aaron stood in the doorway, he heard Redlin's voice and it seemed to move him as if it took him by the hand. "Come Lord Boewin, please have a seat. Make yourself comfortable."

Without much conscious thought, Aaron sat in the chair on

the other side of the fireplace from Redlin. He looked absurd in the giant chair as if he was a child of three sitting in his father's easy chair.

With great effort, the young king uttered some pleasantries. "Thank you for . . . for the . . . Invi . . . for the opportunity . . . to see . . . see . . . meet with you. I am truly, truly . . . truly honored." As these words sputtered out, Aaron could feel moisture gathering on his forehead and back. Never had he been so nervous.

"Thank you for coming. We have much to discuss and very little time. I wish we could have met under different circumstances, but at least you are here now." Redlin shifted in his chair as he took a small pouch from a pocket in the cloak the entirely shrouded his body. "I need to repay a debt and, at the same time, ask a favor of you."

Aaron struggled with what Redlin said as he worked to conquer his fear of this overpowering being. "What can I possibly, even remotely, hope to do for you? You have everything."

Redlin shook his head as he spoke like a father marveling at his sons admiration. "What I have can easily be swept away and all I have accomplished quickly forgotten if people like you do not decide to help me. I have asked all the many leaders of the various realms to come together to form an alliance to fight Thrack Morgan." As Redlin paused, he could see that his young guest did not recognize the name.

Though Aaron had never heard of Morgan, he tried not to look ignorant. Unfortunately, he had never been skilled at hiding his thoughts especially when he was so lost in a sea of thoughts and feelings. Before he could say anything, Redlin raised a hand as if to dismiss the young lord's confusion and bring light to the darkest areas of his mind. Slowly, Aaron's mind cleared and he became more relaxed and attentive. "Please go on. I understand and I'll be quiet." The smallest piece of the young boy's mind was aware that some spell had been cast upon him. As there was nothing he could do, he relaxed and let the spell take effect.

"Morgan is one of the last great magicians. He has organized the barbarian hordes of the west and the beast races of the northern wastelands into a powerful force. He hopes to overthrow the various kingdoms of the civilized world and eventually destroy me and my kingdom. I fear that without cooperation from the kingdoms that have assembled here, I will not be able to stop him. He has already begun an assault on some of the border towns across the world—testing the defenses of the weaker outposts. Even with our alliance, there is still much that needs to be done."

Before he had even realized he was speaking, Aaron was asking a question. "Why did you call me into Helexpa? I'm the least of all those gathered."

Surprised by the question, Redlin took a moment to answer. "That's a simple question with a complex answer. No one has entered Helexpa because the five major kingdoms all wished to enter together so that none would be seen as favored. Lord Rana, of the coastal dominion, is expected on the morn. Then all will be invited in. Though I'm sure you can't remember, you've been here before. Your grandfather had done me a great service during the battle with the Troll Dringnun. Some years later, less than a year after your birth, your mother came to tell me of his passing. The two of you were my guests. At that time, I pledged to watch over you and offered you a place in Helexpa whenever you might visit. Thus, there was no dilemmas with protocol when I let you enter."

The boy's mind reeled with this revelation. No one ever told him that he had been so honored. He tried to keep listening as his host continued to speak. It was of little use as he struggled to wrap his mind around this concept. All these years, he had an open invitation to enter Helexpa freely. His family had belittled him and made him feel worthless for most of his life. After all that, he was actually the most favored of all. Redlin paused to let the young boy digest what had been said. Aaron turned his attention back to the conversation saying, "Please continue. This cannot be why you asked me here tonight."

"Unfortunately, no. There's something much more important I need to discuss with you. Your lands lie far to the south and are not of great strategic importance to Morgan. However, eventually he will take them from you once all the other kingdoms have fallen. I need your help and, in turn, I can help you."

For the first time since he had entered the room, Aaron felt some strength and personal pride. He was needed and that meant he had power. "I'm happy to give my troops, but you would need to outfit and train them." He smiled as he thought of his army being trained and outfitted by Redlin and his allies.

"You don't seem to understand. I don't want your men or your resources—I need you. More correctly, I need you to undertake a quest with a party of adventurers to retrieve several items. The other leaders would not trust anyone but nobles and members of the ruling families to undertake the quest."

Aaron's face drained of color and his jaw dropped as if he had been hit over the head with a club. He could not believe what he had just heard. In a shaky and cracking voice not used since puberty, he asked meekly, "What did you have in mind?"

As he leaned in toward the boy, Redlin said in a fatherly tone, "I'll help you become a man, a warrior, and a king. You, and several others, will be entrusted with the task of getting the Slayer of Evermore—the most powerful weapon I ever forged and imbued with magic. In order to do that, however, you will need to first acquire three other items. This quest will not be easy and there is a very good chance that those who travel with you, or even yourself, may die."

Though he heard all the words spoken, none stuck with him as much as Slayer of Evermore. From his childhood, he had heard songs about Max Konicker and his fabled ax. It was unparalleled as weapons went. As a young boy, Aaron had insisted on learning to fight with the battle ax because of the stories he had heard. Dragons had been cleaved in two by its blade. Castle battlements shattered with one blow. Armies defeated by one man wielding the all-powerful weapon. Any risk would be worth the opportunity to hold it and any price would be too small to possess it. As he was about to speak, Helexpa shuddered as if the palace were a person feeling a frigid wind blow across its back. There were several low rumbles and Aaron immediately thought that the foundation below him would give way under what must certainly be a huge earthquake.

Redlin sprang to his feet more agilely than Aaron thought possible. A guard burst through the door as the boy made it to his feet. "My lord, three Silver-vein dragons have appeared from out of nowhere. Each had a darkling rider. They decimated the camps and then tried to assault the palace. We've killed one and drove the others away."

Though he tried to keep his emotions in check, Redlin had to fight hard not to show his concern. "What of the nobles and their camps? Were there assassins?"

The guard nodded his affirmation of his lords fears as he spoke. "Guar, stalkers, and some others we couldn't identify. Some think they were demons. There are not many survivors—mostly women. All are badly wounded. King Rana's delegation had not arrived so they are safe."

Redlin broke in, "If he makes it here at all." Shaking his head in disgust, "If he ever intended to be here."

Aaron looked around stupidly in disbelief as he muttered to himself. My men can't be dead. Cragmore wouldn't let that happen." Then a wave of apprehension overtook him as he continued trying to reaffirm his own beliefs. "Cragmore must have survived. He was always ready, always thinking . . . always on guard. He must be all right . . . has to be . . . must." Like a man slowly sinking into a quagmire, the significance of what had happened penetrated Aaron's mind. As the realization that his most trusted friend and advisor was most likely dead cemented itself into his mind, he fell silent. Though he tried, he could not form words anymore. His voice had abandoned him as well.

Redlin's face showed his concern transforming into rage with each word the guard uttered. "Find any survivors and bring them into Helexpa. I want any information you can find about what happened brought to me immediately. Warn the footmen that are retrieving the wounded to be weary of invisible assassins. They'll ambush or attempt to infiltrate the palace. Morgan likes to use that trick. Now go." Turning to Aaron, Redlin continued, "You can stay or go with them to find your men. Whatever you decide, let the guards know. I need your help now more than ever. The rest of those who will quest for Slayer should be here within two days. If Morgan hasn't killed them already. You're the only noble I can trust and the only warrior I can spare right now. You've more reason to go now than ever. Decide quickly." Redlin did not wait for a reply. The guard stepped back to let him leave the room.

Aaron sank back into the chair and let his head drop into his hands. In an instant, his entire life had changed. He needed to decide whether to risk his life or return home and pray for deliverance and mercy. For the first time, he had no one to turn to for help. The time had finally come for him to be the king he did not want to be. The words, "Why me . . . oh, why me?" echoed hollowly in the small room. He repeated the words over and over like a holy chant as he felt the weight of his loneliness and despair crush down upon his shoulders.

CHAPTER 5

As the two town guards approached Peter, he relaxed slightly, letting himself come out of his fighting crouch. One guard stopped
at his side while the other passed him and entered the bar. Neither
said anything. Meanwhile, the four half-orcs had been helped to
their feet and corralled by the other four town guards. Something
about the way the guards moved bothered Peter. A question began
to form in the back of his mind as he slowly moved his hand to the
chain around his neck. His card from Redlin would clear him and
his party without delay.

Before he could say or do anything, he heard Gallis' voice inside the bar. "What do you think you're doing? Leave that case
alone." His voice grew more forceful and pained at the same time.
"Ahh . . . put it down." Peter turned just in time to see the guard
hitting Gallis with the Dragonthorn sword case. There was a loud
thwap as the case contacted Gallis' head followed by a dull thud as
the wizard struck the floor.

Before Peter had a chance to even think, the guard next to him
said in a clear crisp voice, "We need that for evidence. Don't worry
about it at all." Immediately, he felt magic pass through him.
Grunting, Peter shook his head to clear it and grabbed the guard
nearest to him yelling, "They're not real." He tossed the stunned
guard into the bar towards the one carrying the sword case. The
four guards and the half-orcs on the street drew their swords and
moved towards Peter without hesitation.

Peter found himself in a very poor fighting position, but needed
to keep the doorway blocked so he could protect Gallis and watch
the case. There were only seconds before he would be rushed and
he needed to even the odds.

A small grayish stone fell into view from off to Peter's right. It came to rest a few feet in front of the advancing guards and exploded with a burst of white-yellow light. All the guards were knocked back into the half-orcs. As hiss eyes cleared, Peter could see that Vin stood just outside the door. He guessed that she had tossed the magic stone. More importantly, the light had dispelled whatever illusion had been cloaking the so-called guards. Now he could see that the four guards outside were actually knarves, human-like beasts bred in the northland as warriors. They were slight of build with a face that resembled a raccoon. Peter knew them to be intelligent enough to carry-out complex missions but not skilled enough to use magic. One of the other two guards had to be something else. He hoped Gallis could take care of them. Four knarves and four half-orcs would keep him busy at least for a little while.

Luckily, Vin's magic had bought him enough time to arm himself. Moving his hand forward as if to shake someone's hand, he said in a loud voice, "Justifier, come to my hand." The instant he uttered these words, a bastard sword appeared in his hands surrounded by a brilliant white light. The sword itself was jewel-encrusted and engraved with an intricate pattern of runes. On both face's of the blade was carved the word JUSTIFIER. Both the half-orcs and the knarves were less anxious to attack as the sword came into view. All eight seemed to know about the weapon and were more wary because of it.

The knarves attacked while the half-orcs waited to see what happened. They watched as the knarves moved forward. Using two hands to wield the sword, Peter cut large sweeping swatches out of the air. This kept the knarves at bay while he glanced in to see what had happened to Gallis. One of the guards was running towards the side door. A knarve waited to deal with Gallis who had recovered and had gotten to his feet. Though he could not tell, Peter guessed that the one that was fleeing must be the magician. There was no time to play with these beasts. He needed to stop the one with the case. In one fluid motion, he moved forward and to the side of the doorway closest to the alley. The knarves pressed the attack. Bringing Justifier down with a short chop, he struck the closest attacker in the hand, severing it. The next two slices of Justifier shattered the sword of one knarve and decapitated a second. As Peter moved back to gain better position, Vin threw a dart into the neck of the fourth knarve attacking him. As the dart struck the back of its neck, the knarve crumbled to the ground like a sack of rocks.

While Peter adjusted his fighting position, a hazy, blue cloud billowed from the barroom through the space he had just vacated. The two knarves still standing and three of the half-orcs were caught in the spell. As the cloud touched each one, they fell to the ground shuttering as if they had been dunked into a frozen stream. In a low voice only he could hear, Peter said, "I guess that means Gallis is all right."

The last half-orc charged Peter. With short quick slashes, Peter blocked the onslaught of unskilled thrusts and slices. Once the half-orc tired, Peter thrust into its chest and followed with a slice to the throat. In an instant, the mercenary was dead.

As the half-orc fell limply to the ground, Vin yelled, "Wanderer—behind you!"

Spinning, Peter saw the guard carrying the sword case running away down the street. Lifting Justifier above his head, he said, "Strike to the heart of my enemy." Without aiming for more than a moment, he threw the sword at the fleeing man. With unerring accuracy, Justifier buried itself deep into the chest of the guard, splitting his breast plate into two pieces as it entered. He was dead before he hit the ground still clutching the case. Both Gallis and Vin were in awe and said nothing.

Wasting no time, Peter went to retrieve Justifier. Placing his right foot on the man's back, he drew out the sword effortlessly. Next, he turned the man over to examine him. As he did, a pale gray human face with deep-set dark black eyes was revealed. Peter recognized this man to be a mind warrior like the dying can recognize the grim reaper. Mind warriors were a special breed of magi-

cian trained in illusion and charms. At their highest levels of training, some were able to use their will to change the way others
perceived reality. Rarely did they travel in small groups and never
without another mind warrior, usually an apprentice, close at hand.

As soon as Peter saw the face, he spit on the dead man's pale
gray forehead and turned towards Gallis and Vin saying, "It's a
mind warrior. Get the guard's horses—we're leaving now." The
cold instinctual look of battle that had consumed his face during
the fight was now replaced with hatred and determination. Quickly
examining the mind warrior's hands, Peter saw he was wearing a
ring on the index finger of each. Squatting down, he took both
and placed them in the waistband of his pants. Once the rings
were safely tucked away, he bent, picked up the Dragonthorn case,
and turned towards the Rusty Sword.

As Peter walked back, Gallis came out of the inn and looked at
the scene. Though the bolt was gone from his shoulder, the arm
hung heavy and bothered him as he moved. Seeing him, Peter
yelled, "Get Vin and the horses. I'll take care of the rest." In
response, Gallis moved to where Vin calmly stood waiting and
watching. Taking her by the arm, he moved with her to where the
horses had stopped.

Meanwhile, Peter surveyed the street to determine which of
his attackers were still alive. Like a man picking up litter in a park,
he made his way to where each of the incapacitated knarves and
half-orcs were laying and drove the tip of Justifier into their throats.
After ensuring that each was dead, he quickly examined their bodies and moved on. After killing the last knarve, he left the sword
sticking in its throat so he could use his free hand to dislodge the
dart from the back of its neck. Having done this, he drew out his
sword and joined Gallis and Vin.

Gallis was drained from the fight. Though he had many
questions, he was sure that Peter knew more about what was
happening and decided that it would be best if the wanderer led
for now. Vin, however, was less agreeable with the idea.

Like a disapproving girlfriend, she began to question Peter.

"What do you mean we're leaving? Where are we going? What about the others? And why did you kill them all? They were no threat."

Without saying anything, Peter dropped the dart on the ground at her feet and then mounted one of the horses. Once atop the horse, the look of determination softened slightly and a hint of the smile he usually wore returned. "I don't care if you come with me. I'm going to get my equipment from the stable and then move on to Helexpa. As I see it, the adventure has begun. Our first task is to get to Redlin. There are others already waiting for us there. As for the ones who were supposed to be coming here—we can't wait. They'll catch up, go home, or die. Right now I don't really care. My job is to get you through the Forbidden Lands and then begin the quest." He pointed sharply at the dead beasts that littered the street. "As for those podricks, I don't leave any of my enemies behind, especially when they're with mind warriors—I hate those bastards." With that, Peter turned his horse and headed out for the stables at a slow saunter. He did not want to leave them behind, but he would if they did not decide to follow.

As Peter turned his horse, Gallis mounted another horse with some difficulty. His right arm was barely functional. The fight had hurt him more than he wanted to let on. "Come on scribe. The wanderer is right. We need to go now. He's our leader now. It's not safe here anymore."

Vin groaned her dislike of the treatment she received as she bent to pick up her dart. Once it was safely back in her possession, she mounted a horse and turned to ride towards the stables with her two adventuring companions. It was not clear what they would be doing together, but she was not going to miss this story— whatever it might be. If nothing else, she would be able to see the inside of Helexpa.

CHAPTER 6

As the haze cleared from Jeremy's mind, he felt nausea overcome him. His vision was still clouded from the magic trip he had just made. Using what little strength he had left, he fought the urge to vomit. He surprised himself, as he stood up effortlessly from the crouch in which he found himself. Slowly, the nausea eased, his eyes adjusted to the darkening night, and his mind focused. Looking down, he realized that his efforts were in vain as he saw his riding boots adorned with his lunch. As his head cleared more, he felt a firm but friendly hand touch his shoulder.

"How are you feeling?" Twig said in a concerned tone. "Do you think you'll be able to move soon? We really should get out of this alley."

Jeremy took deep breaths and swallowed hard several times to help quash the need to vomit again. He did not feel well, but he would survive. "I'm not great," he said weakly, "But I can follow you." As he looked at her, he was amazed to see that she was apparently unaffected by the travel.

"Stand still. I'll ease the travel shock." She smiled and said in an approving voice, "You've done quite well for your first jump . . . especially since we've been sent so far." After placing her hands on his temples, she rubbed them gently. Closing her eyes, she concentrated and cast the spell.

As the magic passed into him, Jeremy felt better than he had since Lancer told him to ride. "Thanks," was all he could say.

Twig turned and moved to the end of the alley that met the main street. Though daylight was waning, she could make out three figures on horseback just a few feet away. The street was lit by something one of the figures was holding but exactly what that something was, she could not tell. Her face brightened as she recognized that one of the figures was Androthy Permillion's journeymen, Gallis. In a hurried voice she yelled, "Gallis, over here." She waved her arms and repeated her call more emphatically. "Over here!"

It took him a moment to register who was speaking. All three riders turned to examine the young woman who had called attention to herself amidst the aftermath of the battle. Even Peter took a moment's pause from his determined departure to see who was so oblivious as to call to Gallis in such a familiar way.

Turning towards Jeremy, Twig extended her hand and said, "Come on, we're leaving."

Taking her hand, he dutifully responded to the order. As he reached the end of the alley, a look of shock overtook him as he saw the remnants of the fight. "Oh crap!" He looked around in amazement, as Twig saw for the first time what should have been evident when she first reached the end of the alley.

"Who the hell are they?" Peter asked with authority. "I don't trust anyone, especially when there are mind warriors around. Gallis, we need to leave." Turning his horse, he surveyed the street. "We'll have more trouble to deal with any minutes now. We have to go." Everyone could feel the force of his words.

Gallis replied to Peter's concerns. "She's Permillion's apprentice; the one we're waiting for. I don't know the boy."

Before anyone could comment, Peter drove for answers. "Where's Permillion? Where've they been. What're we doing now?" The anxiousness in his voice betrayed his distrust and concern. He had expected to see a mage master and at least two other fighters, not a boy and an apprentice.

Gallis turned to Peter. "Go to the stable and prepare yourself. We'll be right behind you."

Peter snapped out his response, "No. I'm not leaving you or anyone here. Get the two of them on horses. We'll all go together."

Dumbfounded, Gallis' gaze bobbed back and forth between Peter and Twig. Taking the initiative, Twig said. "Jeremy, get us horses—we're going with them." Still enthralled by the knarves, Vin, and all the other strange things on the street, Jeremy did not respond. Twig tugged at his hand, and repeated more emphatically, "Jeremy." After he turned his attention to her, she continued, "Get us horses.

Like a dutiful stable-hand, he quickly glanced over the three unspoken-for horses and chose the best two. Leading them to where Twig was standing, he presented her with the reins of one and gestured for her to mount. After she took the horse and climbed aboard, he mounted and turned to follow the others, saying nothing.

"Stay together. I don't trust anything now. Mind warriors are near and they know us," Peter said in a grave tone. Taking the lead, he spurred his horse forward down the street towards the stables at the outskirts of town. Twig took up right behind him saying, "Jeremy, follow behind and be careful." She put extra emphasis on the last few words, stressing them like a teacher instructing first grade students.

Gallis and Vin brought their horses into formation by flanking Twig. Jeremy waited for all to ride a short distance down the street and then followed a few feet behind Twig. As the group rode towards the edge of town, the three in the middle exchanged introductions and related their stories. Jeremy soaked in all that he could see and everything that was said about the scribe, the wanderer, and especially the half-elf wizard. Though Peter said nothing, he listened to Twig's stories with the interest of a spy. By the time the group reached the stable, they were all acquainted.

Peter dismounted in front of the door to the stable where his war horse was being kept. Placing the Dragonthorn case on the ground, he opened it carefully. All watched hoping to see its contents. Inside were fitted slots for two bastard swords. One slot contained a sword identical to Justifier except that it had the name VINDICATOR engraved instead of JUSTIFIER. The other slot held only a scabbard. Peter placed Justifier into the empty slot and closed the case. Once this was done, he broke his silence. Lifting his gaze to Twig and Jeremy, he said in a cold matter-of-fact tone, "Gallis and Vin have given me reason to trust them, so I do." Gesturing to Twig while he spoke, he continued, "I don't know you. I don't trust you or anything here. For now, let's say I'll tolerate the two of you because the others seem to believe you." Turning his head to look at Gallis and Vin questioningly, "Is that right?"

They both nodded their agreement. The group dismounted in silence. While the others began walking their horses towards the open stable door, Vin moved toward Peter saying, "Why are you being so distrustful? They must be part of Androthy's party. They don't look like anyone who could—"

Peter interrupted sharply saying, "Don't tell me what you think . . . what you see . . . what you even know. Mind warriors can confuse anyone or anything. That was just an apprentice I killed. It had us confused. His master is still nearby . . . just waiting for the right time. If I can't believe my own senses, I won't believe anything." Calming himself, he took a deep breath to ease his frustration and continued. "As long as they're willing to follow orders and help, we'll be fine. From now on, question everything you see and assume we are fighting for our lives at all times." Releasing the reins of his horse, he reached his hand out towards Vin. "I don't mean to be so damned forceful with you, but we need to act quickly. Let's go in and talk to the others."

Smiling, she took his hand and let him lead her. "You're a unique man, Peter the wanderer. I will enjoy learning your story."

While Vin and Peter spoke, Jeremy had brought the rest of the horses into the stable. As he looked around, he saw that there were five other horses already inside. Four were not worthy of note. The fifth, however, was a beautiful war horse that he assumed belonged to Peter. Seeing the horse, he immediately knew that its owner must be a man of wealth, power and station.

Meanwhile, Gallis and Twig discussed their situation as privately as the surroundings would allow. "What should we do?" Twig asked in a low, secretive voice.

"Get to Helexpa as quickly as possible. If the master's been captured or killed, Redlin needs to know. I think Peter, the one we followed here, can guide us through the Forbidden Lands to Helexpa."

The statement hit her like a hammer to the chest. "You think he's been killed?" she asked with horror in her voice. Swallowing hard, she worked to control her emotions.

"It's possible." He shook his head in disgust adding, "Somehow, Thrack Morgan knew we were at the Rusty Sword. Anything's possible."

"What about the two you're traveling with—can we trust them?"

"Permillion trusts them, Redlin trusts them . . . we have no choice but to trust them." Pausing to look at Vin and Peter, he said, "Peter's a warrior and loyal to the cause but I don't know about the Azurine. What about your companion?"

"He's the master's servant . . . since before I came to study. I only know the master said for him to follow me and he's done well so far."

"What about the jump. How strong are you?

Twig looked surprised by the question. "I can cast whatever you need. More importantly, how are you and your group. After a fight and that wound, you must be exhausted." She pointed at Gallis' shoulder hesitantly.

"I'll be fine. What about the boy?" Having finished with the horses, Jeremy approached the two magicians as they held their conference. He stopped and listened intently when he heard them reference him.

"I don't know how he'll do with more abuse—It might kill him. We'll have to wait a few hours at least. I eased his pain but did nothing for the actual damage the jump might have caused."

"We don't have time to wait. He'll have to chance it or stay behind. Either way, he'll probably die. This adventure isn't for the weak." As Gallis said this, Twig sighed with sadness.

Though disturbed by what he heard, Jeremy did not want them to know he had been listening. "We're all ready," he said confidently.

Peter and Vin entered the stables to join the other three members of their party. Peter spoke first. "We need to figure out what's next. We don't have time to heal or even wait here."

Twig and Gallis began speaking simultaneously until she yielded. "Permillion is captured or dead. We need to move on to Redlin's and tell him about this. Morgan must be planning something. Why else would he try to stop our meeting?"

"You're right . . . let's go." Peter said impatiently. "I'll get my things from the stable-master. It should only be a few hours ride to the palace but we'll need to move fast. Darkness is setting in and we'll have the other mind warrior to deal with very soon."

Twig turned to Jeremy with concern in her eyes. "This is not going to be easy on you. I don't know if you'll make it."

Trying to hide any trace of self-concern, he said, "Don't worry, I'll be fine. I'm not being left behind."

"It's settled then. Get your things together and we'll leave." Peter barked the order with such authority that no one even thought to disagree or continue discussing the matter. As Peter moved to his war horse and checked his belongings, Vin and Gallis each moved to one of the horses that were stabled there as well. While the three seasoned adventurers checked their mounts, Jeremy brought two horses to Twig and helped her mount.

"Thank you," she said with a smile and a blush as if he had just given her a bouquet of flowers.

"I'll lead you outside. Duck as we pass through the doorway." Taking the reins of her horse in one hand and those of his in his other, he led the two out of the stable. As he emerged, he was met with a hail of crossbow bolts. His side was riddled like a practice target. Two bolts cut across his abdomen as three others dug deep into his left thigh and calf. Even as his leg crumpled under him, he snapped the reins of Twig's horse sending it walking back into the stable quickly. As the horses stomped backwards, his head hit the ground sharply, dazing him.

Twig screamed, "Oh no, they're already here! Jeremy's been hit!"

By now, the others had mounted and moved close behind Twig. Peter vaulted from his horse, pulled the boy back into the stable and looked around. Twig jumped down off her horse and tended to her wounded companion. After removing the bolts, she cast a spell to stop the bleeding and ease the pain. While she worked, the others dismounted and Peter surveyed the street. At least eight hooded bow-men stood across the street waiting to take a shot at them. Amongst the attackers was a taller figure in a red cloak that he immediately identified as the mind warrior. As if to confirm his suspicions, a semicircular ring of bluish-orange fire encircled the stable door. Peter moved back saying, "What can you people do? I can't get close enough to them right now and our horses won't go through the flame." His eyes fell first on Gallis.

"I'm too weak to cast much more than something simple like a magic arrow."

Twig broke in. "That'll be enough. If you can hit the mind warrior. Breaking his concentration should be enough . . . as long as the fire is only an illusion."

Peter had not thought of that. "It better be. What do you want to do?"

"If Gallis hits the mind warrior and the flames drop, we can all ride through. I can protect us from the arrows and them cast a spell to stop the others from following us until we're long gone."

Peter looked at the rest of the group questioningly. "I can't make this decision. I don't know enough about any of you to know what you want or what you can do." Looking at the others, he added, "But I'd try it."

Vin concurred, "Yes, it sounds good."

Gallis nodded and mounted his horse carefully. "Let's do it."

Everyone except Twig followed suit. Peter picked up Jeremy and draped the boy's unconscious body over the back of his horse. With that done, Peter mounted his war horse and took the reigns of the Jeremy's horse. Once everyone was ready, Twig raised her hands and cast a protection spell that made everyone's skin tingle. Having finished, she mounted and watched as Gallis rode to the door. As he emerged, a series of bolts flew towards him and his horse. Just as they should have made contact with him, they seemed to fade from existence and reappear just behind him. With a thwap, they hit the stable door. Raising a finger and pointing it at the mind warrior, he said, "Fly." A glowing red arrow of light leapt from his finger and hit the cloaked figure in the middle of the forehead. The mind warrior's head snapped back and the wall of flame died as he did. All five adventurers moved out of the stable and down the road away from the pursuers. Twig stopped as all the figures carrying crossbows moved to the middle of the street to take aim and fire.

With a roll of her wrist and a fling of her arm, she cast the spell. The street behind her turned to thin soupy mud. All the bow-men sank down to their hips as they flailed about trying to move. In a moment, the mud turned back to solid dirty trapping all eight. As the bolts from their crossbows whizzed through the air, the five adventurers rode out of town and off into the night. In a few short hours they would be through the Forbidden Lands and at Helexpa.

CHAPTER 7

Redlin's guards brought the wounded into the main hall of Helexpa which was transformed into a triage area. Priests, doctors, and other healers tended to those few who had survived the attack as best they could. All were dressed for battle and bore the flaming *R* insignia on their chests. Of the thousands assembled at the base of the castle, only hundreds still lived. All who had survived would bare the scars of this attack for the rest of their lives, however short that might be. At best, fifty were expected to recover enough to participate in the war council Redlin was convening.

Amongst the disarray, Aaron searched for any sign of his men—particularly Cragmore. After a short time, he came upon two of his guards standing near a table. He recognized one of them as Mark Deans, one of his more capable lieutenants. As Aaron approached, he prayed that Deans would know what happened to the general. Once he reached the table, however, he did not need to ask the question. Laid out there, covered in the charred remains of his armor was the young king's advisor. "What happened?" Aaron pressed his men before they even had a chance to register his presence. "How can you be standing here and he's in such a state?" He glared at his men with contempt. "Where were you when it happened? Why aren't you wounded?" Aaron paused the inquisition to press for a reply. "What do you have to say for yourselves? Talk to me—tell me now."

Recoiling from the onslaught of questions and accusations, the guards cringed away from their king. After a long silence, Deans spoke hesitantly. "We're sorry. We don't know what happened or why we're not dead. Lord Cragmore sent us to follow you. We were to wait by the castle until you returned."

The other guard broke in with his testimony. "It all happened too fast for us. The flame and smoke engulfed our camp. We tired to help—what were we to do? It was over before we even got close. We're sorry, my lord—we're sorry."

"Very sorry, my king. We brought the general here as quickly as we could. Everyone else was dead," Deans added in the humblest tone that could be found. "The healers did what they could."

Cragmore shifted on the table and moaned. In a barely audible voice he said, "Aaron . . . urrrrr . . . Aaron." The young king leaned in to hear his mentor's words. Once his ear was close to Cragmore's mouth, he continued. "You're on your own, now.—trust no one." His body convulsed violently.

Aaron turned to his two guards. "Get a healer. We can't let him die."

Cragmore pulled Aaron close. "Your kingdom comes first. Protect it as I protected you." His muscles tensed momentarily as he drew in a deep breath. Then, just as suddenly, his body went limp and the air escaped from his lungs in a long, low hiss.

Aaron screamed, "I need help here." Looking around frantically for his men, he saw them coming with a priest. Gesturing frantically at Cragmore's body, he said, "Help him—do something."

The priest walked around the table to Aaron's side saying, "There's nothing we can do now." He placed a hand on the young king's shoulder. "I'm sorry, my son. We eased the pain from the dragons' fire and slowed the assassin's poison. Unfortunately, both have taken their toll."

"Do something more. Use your magic," he commanded them like a boy ordering his parents' servants.

"I'm sorry, there's nothing more we can do. Only time, if anything, can heal him now." The color drained from Aaron's face as the words sank in. He stared blankly at the priest as he left to help others. Tears formed in Aaron's eyes. His sadness could not be contained and he did not care to keep up appearances. Awkwardly, the two guards took up positions on the opposite side of the table from their weeping king and watched as his head dropped. Time passed slowly as the three stood silent vigil over the body of their fallen general. The entire time Aaron prayed for the guidance and strength he would need now that Cragmore was gone. The only words he heard in his own mind were, "Avenge Cragmore. Take up the quest. Make all those responsible pay for his death."

The solemn scene was broken when Aaron felt a powerful arm come to rest on his back. As he looked up, he saw that his soldiers were struck with awe. It was Redlin's hand. The half-giant and one of his palace guards had come up behind him without making a noise.

"I know this is a difficult time for you, but I need to know what you have decided. Are you questing for Slayer?"

Without hesitation Aaron replied coldly, "Yes," while nodding his head. Wiping the tears from his face, he continued, "When do I leave?"

"All in good time. The rest of the adventuring party is here. My guards will escort you to them. Now, I need to address the crowd." Redlin turned to the palace guard saying, "When King Boewin is finished here, take him to meet the others. Attend to any of his needs."

Hearing Redlin call him king made Aaron smile ever so slightly. Turning to his men, he said, "Stay with the general and see he has everything he needs. If he awakens again tell him I'm questing for the Slayer of Evermore and I have pledged myself to Lord Redlin."

Deans and the other guard said simultaneously, "Yes my lord." Their faces revealed their shock at this news.

"If he dies, give Lord Redlin whatever help you can. All I have is at his disposal now."

Without waiting for a response, Aaron turned to Redlin. "Thank you. I'm ready to leave now." Gesturing for the guard to lead Aaron away, Redlin took his leave.

Redlin watched as Aaron was led from the room. Once he was gone, Redlin raised his hand and motioned to the trumpeters at he top of the entrance hall. A blast of horns echoed through the hall. It was followed by a chant of "Redlin, Redlin, Redlin, Redlin," from throughout the hall that continued until the lord of the castle had walked to the front of the great hall. Once there, he raised both his hands. Immediately, the chant stopped and the hall fell perfectly silent.

In his powerful and commanding voice, Redlin addressed the crowd. "Today marks a dark day in the history of our land. If any of you thought that Thrack Morgan was not a threat or might leave your lands alone, you now see his true nature. I had called you here to forge a new alliance. That alliance has already been forged in the fire of the dragon's breath, the heat of battle, and the blood of your fallen comrades in arms." He paused a moment to let the words sink in as he looked over the crowd. "The fight is now at hand. I can give you and your kingdoms gold, weapons, magic, and my help. Only you can fight the battle. If you fight with me, I will do all I can to help. We will be together as equals. If you stand neutral, Morgan's armies will flow over you like a black tide, destroying everything it touches. If you join him and stand against me, you and your descendants will be marked as traitors and deemed my enemy for all time." The last few words bit with the cold sharpness of a blade. "Thrack Morgan has underestimated us. If you can hold your lines at the front, I can destroy his armies. What I need from you is time."

A voice from the crowd yelled, "What are we to do against dragons and monsters of the north?"

Others joined in yelling "Yes, what can we do? Look what happened against just a few tonight."

Raising his hands for silence, Redlin said, "I myself have killed many dragons, many beasts, and fought in many battles. Together we can defeat anything. As long as we stand as one, Morgan cannot win."

The same voice yelled, "You had magicians, heroes, and the great weapons with you then. All that's gone now. You're but one, and they are many."

Redlin did not wait for the words to sway the crowd. He spoke in a booming tone. "I have much magic at my disposal. Androthy Permillion, the elven mage, is coming to fight by my side."

"Two isn't enough. What will we fight with?"

Realizing it had been too long since these humans had seen the power of magic, Redlin quickly changed his tactics. "Haven't you heard the stories of a man slaying hundreds with only a single weapon?" The crowd paused thoughtfully, as some began to nod their heads in agreement. "How could you forget the tales of how one man rid the world of Trolls? Didn't Elmo Patsy banish the dragons back to their valley?" All those in the crowd began to mutter yes as they recalled the legends. "What of the incredible deeds of Max Konicker wielding the Slayer of Evermore?"

All of Redlin's guards in the hall yelled, "Yes!" in unison.

Redlin raised his voice to incite the crowd even more, "Why do you doubt these great men and their deeds now?"

A lone voice protested, "Because they're all dead."

Smiling, Redlin said in a loud striking tone, "No, they're not. My death has been proclaimed three times already, and yet you see me here standing before you, alive." The crowd fell silent at this revelation. It had been a hundred years since anyone has heard of any of the great heroes. It had been assumed that they had died and their weapons lost. In a smoother softer tone, he continued, "I have assembled a party to bring me the many relics from the time before the Great Cleansing—including Slayer of Evermore." Before anyone could doubt his words, Redlin gestured to a guard standing near a side door. The guard opened the door and Peter stepped through. He wore a skin-tight leather suit of armor and was clean-shaven and bald. "This is Peter Zorich, of the family Zorich. He is the keeper of the swords—Justifier and Vindicator."

With a bounding step, Peter assumed a position next to Redlin. Raising both hands to the ceiling like a preacher, he took a deep breath and waited a moment. Opening his hands he proclaimed, "Vindicator . . . Justifier . . . come to my hands." Once the words were spoken, a bright white glow appeared around both his outstretched arms. Justifier appeared in his right hand and Vindicator appeared in his left. A murmur ran through the audience. All were impressed or scared by what they saw. Peter continued, "These blades have been in my family for generations. The house of Zorich has always helped the cause of justice. I am pledged to help Lord Redlin and his cause now. Justice and honor can give us all strength as my swords provide me during battle." The crowd watched with amazement as Peter stepped forward saying, "Give me strength. Give me fortitude." As he said the words, his body grew visibly. The leather suit strained to the braking point as his muscles bulged.

Redlin said, "If you don't believe my words, believe your own eyes. He speaks the truth and has shown you one of the many great warriors I have brought to quest for Slayer. When they return, they will bring with them the ancient weapons so long lost that even their tales don't truly recall their awesome power."

Peter added, "You all know that the one who wields Justifier does not lie. Believe me. I trust Redlin. So should you." As his voice boomed through the hall, all began to cheer. Turning, Peter bowed to Redlin and began the chant, "Redlin . . . Redlin . . . Redlin."

CHAPTER 8

Six relative strangers waited impatiently in a meeting chamber deep in the bowels of Helexpa. Vin, Gallis, and Twig stood warming themselves near the lit fireplace that provided both heat and light to the room. Gallis and Twig talked intently as Vin surveyed the room and listened with only a piece of her attention. She was both curious about the others in the room and impatient to see what had happened to Peter. The room itself was rather mundane. A large oaken table surrounded by twelve chairs consumed the middle of the chamber and was the only furniture to be seen. A large muscular human and a thin wiry man with an elvin look to his features sat at the table discussing the day's events. From the look of their leather suits and worn faces, she marked them as adventurers. The only passage in or out of the room stood at the opposite end from the fireplace. A lone person, concealed by a black cloak, stood by the door as if to guard it. Vin felt that person silently watching everyone and everything in the room. From what she saw, she was certain the figure was not a guard, but could determine little else.

Twig and Gallis spoke in low tones as much to be private as not to disturb the others. "How's your shoulder?" Twig asked as she examined it with her eyes.

"Feels wonderful. Redlin's healers know what they're doing."

"I hope they can do something for Jeremy."

"You really care about that stable-hand, don't you?"

Twig's face reddened. "Well, yes . . . we're friends and the master put him in my charge. I . . . well, I . . . I'm to look after him."

Gallis smirked. "Sure, I understand."

Twig blushed a deeper red as she lowered her eyes and tipped her head down. "The master said that you need to finish my training and, well . . . that I'm all but done. Just a little more work on some attack skills—ice, flame, lightning, and all of that. Once you feel I'm accomplished . . . well, uhm . . . I choose my name."

"That makes sense. Very good, I'll do my best. Once we're on the road, I'll start right away. I've always been good at that brand of magic. I teach differently than the mage master, but you'll learn quickly."

She smiled at the idea of finishing. The end had been so long in coming, it felt strange now that it was so near. "How long do you think it will take?"

"It depends on what the master has already shown you. It might only be a matter of days—no more than a few weeks of hard work I'm sure."

The door to the chamber opened and Aaron entered, led by one of Redlin's elite guards. As he walked into the room, the shrouded figure near the door stepped back and closely examined the newest member of the group. After a moment's pause to survey the room himself, Aaron sat in a seat near the fireplace. Vin moved towards him but before she could say or do anything, the doorway was filled by two more of the elite guards. They stepped into the room and in unison said, "All who are gathered, please rise and give your attention to Lord Redlin. He will speak with you now."

The three who were sitting complied with the firm request as all those in the room turned their attention to the door eagerly. Redlin stepped into the doorway, filling it. He said in a cordial tone, "Welcome. I must be short as there is little time for formalities. Please be seated." Taking one step into the room, Redlin took his place at the head of the table with his back to the door.

A stifled chuckle came from behind Redlin, as Peter entered the room. "Funny that you should say short my lord." Without waiting for a response or comments from the assembled group, he sat at Redlin's right hand.

Vin, Gallis, and Twig were shocked as much by Peter's comment as by his appearance. As Peter moved to a seat, Vin moved around the table dexterously so that she could sit next to him. Once seated by his side, she placed her journal on the table, opened it, and began writing. Gallis and Twig sat next to one another at the end nearest to the fireplace. Without thinking, Gallis sat at the foot of the table directly across from Redlin. The others moved to seats that were close at hand and sat. The hooded figure waited until all were settled before taking the chair nearest the door on Redlin's left hand side. None said anything, even as Gallis presumed to sit at a place of honor.

Once all in attendance were seated, Redlin began, "I have called you together for a very special purpose. I had hoped that Androthy Permillion and several others would have been able to meet with us. Unfortunately, that was not possible. Before I tell you why you have been called together, I want to give each of you the opportunity to introduce yourself, in your own words. Please be brief. You can elaborate later." He gestured towards Peter saying, "I have asked Peter Zorich to lead the expedition. As such, he can begin."

Nodding, Peter said, "As you've heard, my name is Peter Zorich. I am keeper of the swords of judgment—Vindicator and Justifier. My training, however, has prepared me to be a complete fighter with all the classic arms. In the past twenty years, I have adventured throughout the world. Many of those years have been spent at Redlin's side. My life has been devoted to maintaining balance and justice throughout the world. I am honored to be one of the chosen few to embark upon this quest." Stopping, he looked to his right at Vin and gestured for her to speak.

After silently placing her pen on table next to her journal, Vin told of herself in a melodic tone that captivated the audience. "My name is Vineta Azurine of the clan Azurine—you may call me Vin. My people chose me as their adventurer and scribe. Redlin has called me friend since his first kingdom was carved out of the Forbidden Lands and the city of Phinn was built to be his capitol. Now, I am here to quest for Slayer of Evermore. My skills are varied and too numerous to mention. Trust that I will be a valued part of any expedition and easily able to care for myself . . . in any situation." After taking a moment to run her eyes over everyone in the room, she added, "I look forward to learning all of your stories." With that, she passed the speaking floor over to Aaron with an elegant gesture of her hand.

Sweat glistened on Aaron's forehead as he saw the fingers of Vin's hand point towards him. Even as he opened his mouth to say something, he could feel his throat drying as if he were running in a race. "I'm Aaron . . . err . . . Aaron . . . uhm . . . Boewin." He fidgeted in his seat as he hunted for words like a man feeling for something in a pitch black room. "Well, ahh . . . I look forward . . . I mean . . . I'm, well, happy to be on the quest." His face glowed a bright shade of crimson as the last few words blundered out of his mouth. "Not happy . . . well, err . . . honored. I'm honored to quest with you for Slayer." He looked dumbly at Gallis who was waiting patiently for the boy to be out of his misery.

Rescuing him from the spotlight, Gallis said in a cool formal voice, "I am called Gallis. Androthy Permillion trained me and I am now a named mage of the eighth order. As he is not here, I shall take his place in all things until he arrives." Pausing briefly, Gallis nodded his head at Redlin before continuing, "My magic, my knowledge, my belongings, and my life are at your disposal my lord." Running his eyes over the other adventurers between himself and Redlin, he said, "This quest must be successful. Morgan must be defeated and his forces destroyed." Everyone thoughtfully nodded their agreement of the statement. Turning his head to look at Twig, he placed a hand on her shoulder saying, "This is Twig. She is another of the mage master's pupils. We are fortunate to have her with us." Turning his hand over and withdrawing it, he gestured for her to continue the introduction herself.

"Hello . . . as you've heard, I'm Twig . . . a spell caster." Smiling, she let out a nervous titter. "I'm not sure what to say. I'm questing for several reasons . . . more reasons than most of you . . . I think." Looking around at the others, she shrugged her shoulders. "I guess that's it." She directed her attention to the elvin-looking man next to her. "It's your turn."

The man received the speaking role with a smile. His words betrayed his dislike of formality and his periods of solitude. "Thank you dear. My name's Shane Forester. Redlin . . . Permillion . . . me . . . we're like old drinking buddies. I've served em well and they've been there when I needed em." Placing his fingertips gently on his own chest, he continued, "As for what I am . . . I guess . . . well, you'd call me a ranger or maybe, well."

The burly man to Shane's right clapped him on his shoulder. "Don't believe that bullshit. He's an assassin just like me."

Shaking his head 'no,' Shane turned his head to look at the man. "I was going to say bounty hunter. Well, I guess assassin works too. That's enough for now. Let the others know about you, Mr. Beam—big man."

The large man leaned back in his chair and laughed a hardy belly laugh. "You're all too serious. What's going to happen when we actually start this quest? Somebody's gonna snap." While shaking his head in feigned disgust, the large man brought himself back even with the table. "Seriously now. My name's Jack Beam. I'm a bounty hunter or assassin or whatever you'd call a man who does what I do. I'm not a sell-sword but for a price, I'll find anyone or anything—then return it to you."

"Or dispose of it," Shane chimed-in sarcastically with a smile.

"Or dispose of it, if that's what's been paid for." The smile disappeared from his face. "Whatever else you say about Shane and me, we're Purple Dragons and ready to die for the quest."

Shane nodded and added without hesitation, "In the flick of a dragon's tail."

Nodding, Jack said, "Though I never expect to die."

All eyes turned and watched the cloaked figure as a noise that was as much a rattle as a laugh emanated from under the hood. In a deep, raspy voice that ground the ears of all in the room, the figure said, "Few expect to die . . . most do before their time." The figure slowly reached up and lowered his hood, revealing a worn face covered with scars and burns. Twig and Aaron both stared with awe as the human-like creature leaned forward and ran his deep-set purple and yellow eyes over them. Neither were sure that he was human but both showed their uncomfortable feelings in the disturbed looks that covered their faces. "I see some of you have never seen an Ultar Stalker—that's a good thing. I'm called Darvan by those not part of my race. All of you may use that name." Letting his gaze fall back to an empty space somewhere on the wall behind Peter, he continued speaking slowly and methodically. "I dislike magic and distrust those who would wield it unnaturally. I am on this quest to see Morgan dead and his demons banished." He paused to let the words sink in. "Other than that, I have no interest in any of you." Turning his head towards Redlin without fixing his focus on him, he continued, "I respect you Lord Redlin, so I'll . . . well, let's just say, I'll be part of the quest. I want nothing to do with Slayer or the other relics. I just want Morgan's head." Darvan replaced his hood and settled back into his chair.

Even as the stalker was replacing his hood, Redlin began to speak. "Since everyone has accepted the quest and you've all been introduced, I'll tell you what must be done." Everyone in the room fixed their attention on him taking in each word as if they were more vital to life itself than air. "First, you must go to Phinn and retrieve several magic items from people gathered at the Grand Coliseum for the pit battles. All of the combatants are mercenaries or sell-swords with no loyalties to me. Moreover, most dislike my rule and would be happy to capitalize on the disorder Morgan would bring. Peter has the list of items you need to obtain—use any means necessary." Redlin watched the crowd, judging their acceptance of his statements. He saw that Aaron and Twig both beamed with curiosity and anxious anticipation as thousands of questions ran through their minds. Vin wrote every word said like a secretary taking minutes. The rest just stared blankly as he spoke, absorbing what was said like dutiful soldiers. "Once you have the items, you must make your way north to Thwardscall where the Forbidden Lands and the Valley of the Dragons meet. Once there, you'll be taken to Max Konicker and find out the whereabouts of the Slayer of Evermore. You must retrieve Slayer and then return here." Placing a hand on Peter's shoulder, Redlin continued, "I've explained everything to Peter. He knows all of you, and will be in charge of the expedition."

Peter broke in. "I'll tell you all I know on our way. Time is short."

Redlin said, "I've done all I can to help. The rest is up to you. I can provide each of you a horse, gold, and supplies for the journey ahead. Other than that, you must rely on one another. You leave in the morning—prepare yourselves." His eyes scanned the room. "Everyone is relying upon your success—good luck."

As Redlin stood to leave, Twig said hesitantly, but firmly, in a questioning voice, "Before you go Lord Redlin . . . well, ahh, I was . . . what about Jeremy . . . the young man. The one who came here with us. I want to know if I could . . . if, can I see him? I want to see if he's all right."

A flash of sudden insight flared in Redlin's eyes as Twig spoke. While he stood at the end of the table nodding his head knowingly, a plan of action formed in his mind. "Of course you can. I'll send someone. Just wait here for them. Once you've all finished your business, you'll be taken to him."

"Thank you very much."

"If there is nothing else, I—"

Aaron said in a shaky voice, "Excuse me. Uhm, I . . . I waned to . . . to ask about . . . to know about the Purple Dragons. Ahh, well . . . what are they?"

Everyone in the room except for Twig shifted uncomfortably in their chairs as Aaron stuttered through his question. A frustrated groan emanated from Redlin's chest as he stared at the boy who was to be a king and a vital part of the quest. Shaking his head in disgust, he placed a hand on Peter's shoulder. In a firm voice, he said, "My friend, take him in, explain what it means to be a Purple Dragon, and teach him to be a man, an adventurer, and a king." Softening his tone, he continued, "Please, I have neither the time nor the patience right now." Redlin lowered his eyes to meet Peter's upturned look. "Teach him as you were taught. He's important to our success."

"Why did I say anything? They think I'm an idiot now," Aaron thought to himself as he squirmed in his chair. "Just shut up."

Without looking at Aaron, Peter spoke. "I'll do my best, Lord Redlin but now we both have other things to tend to. Go . . . let us prepare ourselves."

With that, Redlin left. Once the door had closed behind him, Shane said, "Hey Peter . . . try and teach the youngster to be, well, not so nervous." He followed the comment with a laugh. "I'm just kidding son. You'll be fine."

"Just listen to the bald guy. He knows what he's doing. Oh, but watch out for the Azurine . . . she bites," Jack added with a chuckle.

Slowly turning her head to look at Aaron, Vin pulled back her upper lip to bear her teeth. She narrowed her eyes making her face look like a cat about to strike. Seeing this, Jack let out a boisterous laugh. Gallis and Twig joined him with a stifled chuckle.

Peter stood stone-faced like a drill sergeant saying, "Enough. We have no time for this!" Taking a deep breath to calm himself, he continued forcefully, "Go ready yourselves. Meet me at the stables at first light. If you need me before then, ask a guard to bring you to my quarters." Not waiting for a response, he marched out of the small room. Once outside the door, he barked, "Guards, come with me to the stables." He passed the three men waiting outside the door as he moved down the hall. All three followed him obediently.

Aaron stood spastically and hurried after him like an embarrassed apprentice following his master after making a mistake. In a hurried voice, the boy pleaded, "Wait . . . please wait . . . I want to come with you. I need to ask you some questions." He ran from the room and turned down the hall after Peter.

"Damn, kid—don't be so eager. You sound desperate . . . like Shane," Jack said sarcastically.

Shane smacked him sharply with the back of his right hand.

"Don't be a troll's ass. The boy just wants some help. Not all of us are like you—big man." Jack smiled and laughed a belly laugh as his friend hit his arm again.

Vin leaned forward as the two men laughed together. "Gentlemen, if I can call you that, I'd love to hear about the two of you . . . especially how you came to be part of this adventure."

Shane grinned as if he had just been given a nugget of gold. "Of course . . . well, let's go back to our room. We'll be more comfortable there."

Jack nodded his head knowingly and stood. "That sounds like a wonderful idea. Let's go."

Shane and Vin stood simultaneously as Jack moved past Darvan to the door. All three met in the hall and moved off in the opposite direction from Peter and Aaron.

Saying nothing, Darvan stood and seemed to glide out of the room, not making a noise as he moved. Gallis watched him closely as he left. As the stalker turned the corner to follow the other three, he faded from sight, slowly blending into the background. Shooting to his feet, Gallis said, "Will you be all right by yourself Twig? I need to go."

"I'll be fine. I'll go see how Jeremy's doing and tell him we're leaving in the morning."

Even as she answered, he was leaving the room to follow Darvan. As he was out the door, she said, "And I'll see if he's strong enough to come with us." Her voice trailed off to a whisper as she continued, "As long as you don't mind." Pushing her chair back towards the fire, she turned and warmed her hands. In a voice that filled the empty room, she said, "Well, I guess that means it's all right for Jeremy to come then." More to herself than to anyone, she continued, "I just hope he's strong enough to make it."

CHAPTER 9

With effort, Jeremy forced his eyes open and saw Helexpa for the first time. The last thing he remembered clearly was praying he would survive as he felt the bite of the crossbow bolts. After that, everything was a mix of pain and delirium. As he came in and out of consciousness, he was consumed by shooting pains that ran from his toes to his head like flames consuming a tree in a forest fire. Each rush of pain was punctuated by stabbing thrusts that hit his chest like punches. Everything else was a blank. As he regained consciousness in Helexpa, he felt a throbbing in his temples. When he first awoke, he found himself lying on a table unable to even open his eyes or lift his head. He had spent the last few minutes resting with his eyes closed, trying to deal with the throbbing.

A large hand jostled his shoulder, rousing him from his rest. "Are you awake enough to speak yet. I need to speak with you."

In a lazy sleep-laden voice, he said, "Yes, I'm up." His jaw felt tight as if it were covered by a crust. Licking his lips, he tasted the horribly distinct flavor of his own dried blood. Slowly, he lifted his hand to his face and felt the mask of blood that covered his mouth and chin. Apparently, at some point while he was unconscious, his nose had been bleeding profusely and no one had taken the time to clean it.

"Is your name Jeremy? Did you come with a young wizard named Twig—an apprentice of Androthy Permillion?" the voice pressed.

Jeremy turned his head, hoping to see who was speaking to him, as he said, "Yes, I . . . I . . . I'm . . . I'm, I'm, oh crap!" Jeremy exclaimed as he saw Redlin standing next to his bed. He promptly fainted.

Redlin shook the boy gently but firmly to rouse him again. Once the boy seemed coherent, he said, "Calm down, Jeremy. I won't hurt you. I'm Lord Redlin. You're my guest." The words did little to ease the shock that Redlin saw in the boy's eyes. "I know my appearance might be frightening and overwhelming but, believe me, I mean you no harm. Twig asked me to see how you were doing."

"I'm sorry sir . . . I mean, my lord. Forgive me, please. I'm fine." Few children had grown up without hearing the stories of Redlin and his adventuring parties. Jeremy was no exception. To him this seemed like a dream. "What do you want from me?" he added reverently.

"I need to know if you're well enough to quest with Twig and the others."

Jeremy was even more shocked by this question than he was by Redlin's appearance. So many thoughts ran through the young boy's mind, he could not even keep track of them. Mostly, his thoughts jumped back and forth between, "I need to stay with Twig," and "How did I get involved in this?" Forcing himself to a sitting position, he said in a low voice, "As long as I can move, I'll be going with them . . . if they'll have me." Lifting his face to look at Redlin, he added, "I just don't know what good I'll be to true adventurers."

Redlin nodded his head. "You have a good heart boy. It will serve you well. Oh, and don't worry about the others, you'll do fine. Stay with Twig. The two of you will help one another."

Jeremy did not really understand what the half-giant was saying. All he knew was that he needed to prepare for another long trip that he was sure his body was not truly ready to make. "Yes sir," he said obediently. This answer always seemed to work when he did not understand someone.

"I need you to do something for me but it needs to be kept secret. Only you and I can know about it. Can you keep a secret?"

The question made him nervous but he tried not to let it show. "Of course, what is it?" he said in a low tone without hesitation.

"I need you to carry a message with you to a town called Thwardscall. The adventuring party is headed there."

"Sounds easy enough, what's the message?" he said with feigned confidence.

"All in good time but first, can you read?"

Somewhat embarrassed, he said "Yes, well, master Permillion taught me."

"Don't be embarrassed. Just be honest with me. Many great adventurers know little more than how to speak the common human tongue."

Pushing back his fear and uncertainty, Jeremy fumbled to explain himself. "No my lord, you misunderstand. It's not that at all. I began studying to be a mage but then . . . I had to . . . I stopped. I've read every book in master Permillion's library and some more than once."

Nodding and smiling a knowing smile, he said, "Excellent. That's enough for my purposes." He reached into a pouch concealed on his belt and extracted a plain looking metal chain. Dangling from it was a small carved purple dragon charm and a small flat star with a flaming *R* intricately carved in the center. "Put this around your neck and tell no one I gave it to you."

"Not even Twig?

"Not even her. It's vital that you deliver this to Thwardscall." Handing Jeremy the chain, he continued, "Turn the star over and look on the back."

After receiving the chain, Jeremy did as he was told and examined the back expectantly. It was blank. "There's nothing there," he said confusedly. "Am I supposed to see something?"

"Just wait." As he said this, Redlin passed his hand over the face of the metal star. Slowly words began to appear. "This is the message you must deliver. Only you will be able to see the words. To everyone else, this is nothing more than a worthless trinket. Do you understand?"

"Yes, but what if something happens to me?"

"Trust me, you'll be safe enough. Can you read the words?"

"Sort of . . . yes. I'll study them. Just tell me how they sound once. I'll be okay after that. I remember things., especially words, no matter the language."

"Good, the words are from an ancient tongue used by beasts and many of the elder races. They sound like this—thrack, arrato, mambo, and delivan."

Jeremy repeated them as best he could. "Thrack, arr . . . arraty . . ."

"Arrato," Redlin corrected.

"Arrato."

"That's it. Now mambo and delivan."

"Mambo and, and."

"Delivan."

"Delivan."

"Once more," Redlin prompted.

"Thrack, arrato . . . mambo, delivan."

"Good, you don't need to know what they mean. The party you're meeting will understand. Say the words first, before you show anyone the amulet. They'll respond to you with the words 'good day messenger' and everything else will carry on from there. Can you handle that?"

Shrugging his shoulders even as he tried to be positive, he said, "Yes sir, no problem my lord." Letting the star fall through his fingers, he played with the dragon charm. "What about the dragon? Only the most worthy adventurers can become dragons of the guild. I'm not even an apprentice much less a warrior or a wizard or an adventurer of any type."

Redlin chuckled. "You're an adventurer now." His humor was not appreciated by Jeremy. "Don't worry, everything will be explained to you as you travel. You'll train on the road."

"Train to be what? I'm not strong enough to . . . well, to do anything. What will I be? The adventuring failure; the wandering stable-boy?" Without conscious effort, his words took on a bitter and sarcastic edge. "Ooh, watch out or he'll brush your horse. Look out, it's Jeremy the servant. Oh no." The words came from deep inside him and rang with the harshness that they had once hit him with. Hearing them a thousand times as he was growing up had emblazoned them like a brand on his being. His family had pledged him to work for Androthy Permillion from birth to death. He was not a slave, just the property used to repay a costly debt that Jeremy himself knew very little about. Long ago, he had accepted his position in life. Master Permillion treated him well and made him feel as if he were part of the household, but everyone else saw him as only a servant. Though he hoped he had put these feelings behind him years ago, these unchecked thoughts showed him he was wrong. "I'm sorry my lord but I . . . since master Permillion stopped training me, I've been."

Redlin placed his hands firmly on the boy's shoulders and said, in his most inspiring kingly voice, "Whatever you were, you're now an adventurer—a Purple Dragon—and, most of all, one of my men." Pausing, he lifted his hand slowly and cast a spell. After a moment, he removed his hand, letting the words sink in and the magic take effect. "The others can teach you any weapons you want but I think you should learn the bow. Haven't you hunted before?"

Jeremy felt a tingle in his shoulders and back as Redlin spoke. A tiny light of rediscovered self-esteem flickered in his eyes. What Redlin had said was touching him. "Yes, of course. I'm a good hunter and tracker too. I always watch Twig at lessons or at practice, when I can." He smiled a half-smile as he placed the chain around his neck.

"That's a good start but you'll need to work hard in the days ahead."

With determination and a newfound purpose in his voice, Jeremy said, "I will. You can count on me now that I'm one of your men."

"Good, I'm glad to hear that. Now I have one more gift for you."

Jeremy's eyes lit up like a child waiting for a birthday present. Even though he was thinking a million other things at that moment, he said, "You've given me so much already. I don't deserve anything more."

Redlin raised his hand to stop the boy's chatter. "I'm giving you a bow and a very special one at that. Like the star, it looks ordinary but actually holds much magic. It belongs to the star and the star to it. Together they can make you an archer." Redlin lowered his hand and leaned closer to the boy as he continued, "Just touch the star before drawing an arrow. As you shoot the arrow, direct it to the target with your mind. The bow will make you a champion marksman. Eventually, you won't need its assistance but until you've finished training, these will be a great help."

Jeremy tried to hold back his excitement unsuccessfully. He had never really been given anything and now he was the recipient of three amazing gifts from Lord Redlin himself. With a shine of confidence and happiness glowing on his face, he said, "Thank you . . . thank you, so much. I can't say it enough."

Redlin patted the boy on the side of his arm and held his other hand up to stop Jeremy's outpouring of thanks. "Rest now. Just before first light someone will come to bring you to the stables so you can be prepared for the journey. I'll give you the bow then." In a gravely serious tone, he added, "Remember, tell no one about any of this until you've made it safely to Thwardscall. If anyone asks, I made you a Purple Dragon pledged to Twig. You'll do what she says."

"As long as she doesn't ask about the chain."

"Exactly. You'll be fine." Redlin was pleased with the boy. Speaking more to himself, he repeated, "You'll do just fine."

Suddenly, from off to Redlin's left, Twig said, "What was that, I thought I heard my name?"

Both men turned to look in the direction from which her voice had come. She stood next to one of Redlin's elite guards, a short distance away. Neither was sure how much she had heard or how long she had been standing there. Redlin said, "Yes, I was just telling Jeremy that you were coming to see him. I wanted to know if he was going to be traveling with you."

While walking towards the two, she looked at Jeremy saying, "And what did you say?"

"As long as I was breathing, I would follow you anywhere."

"I believed him," Redlin added quickly.

Twig stopped next to the table where Jeremy was sitting. "How do you feel? You looked horrible when we first arrived."

"I'm better now. I guess I needed a rest."

"And healing, too, I'm sure." As she said this, Twig popped herself up onto the table and sat next to Jeremy. A grin ran quickly across his face before he had time to quash it. Pointing at the chain around his neck she said, "What's this? Are you a Purple Dragon now?"

Redlin broke in before he had a chance to say anything. "I was hoping to ask you that when you arrived. Since Androthy's party was short of adventurers and you seemed fond of young Jeremy, I thought you might take him on as a trainee. I took the liberty of making him a fledgling dragon. You'll need to teach him all about it. I hope that's not a problem."

"No, not at all," Twig said quickly without really thinking what she had just agreed to. At least this meant that Jeremy would be coming with her. "I have to look after him anyway. The master put him in my charge." As she said this, she wet her finger with her tongue, raised it to his mouth and brushed away some of the dried blood. "See, I'm already taking care of him." Jeremy smiled as her finger played near his upturned lips.

"Very good. I'll leave him in your care."

"I was hoping that I could ask you some questions about my family, Lord Redlin. I haven't seen them for so long. Recently, I haven't even been able to hear about them from travelers or master Permillion's friends and journeymen. I was hoping you knew something."

Redlin's head dropped and his eyelids half closed. "I'm sorry, I thought Androthy would have told you. Morgan began his invasion from the north, at least a month ago. You're family's lands were some of the first to be seized by his armies and their allies."

"What happened to my parents . . . my brothers? Were they captured? Did they put up a fight?"

"I'm sorry, no one knows what happened to your parents. Most likely . . . they've been, well . . . killed. If they're still alive, Morgan would have sent them to his dungeons deep inside his mountain fortress to the distant north."

The color drained from Twig's face as he spoke. Now that she was almost free to return home, she had no home to return to. Almost afraid to continue asking questions, she said, "What of my brothers?"

It was painful for Redlin to continue. He hated being the bearer of bad news, especially like this. "Your four oldest brothers died trying to save the kingdom. The youngest was sent to me for help."

A glimmer of hope lit her face as she asked expectantly, "Where is he? Let me see him."

Redlin's head shook solemnly as he spoke in a low mournful tone. "He was caught in the attack just outside of this castle to-night. I am sorry. We tried to heal him . . . an assassin's arrow, coated in poison, struck him in the back of the heart. He was dead before he hit the ground. No matter how much we tried . . . there was nothing we could do."

The color completely drained from her face. Burying her head in Jeremy's shoulder, she began to sniffle, trying to hold back the tears. "I feel sick." Her efforts failed as the sniffling quickly became weeping. "First I lose the master; now I find my whole family has been killed. I have no one."

Jeremy wrapped his arm around her shoulder trying to console her. There was nothing he could think to say. He had always been alone. As tenderly as possible he said, "I . . . I'm here . . . I'll be here for you." He had never really known a family and so did not have one to lose. Even so, he felt her pain and wanted to be able to make it go away.

Redlin said in an apologetic and sorrowful tone, "I'm sorry." Lifting his eyes to Jeremy, he said, "Stay with her. I'll meet the two of you at first light. Take care of her until then. She needs you now." He gestured to the guard that was waiting dutifully a few feet away. "Stay with them and tend to their needs. When they're ready, help them back to the young lady's quarters. Bring them whatever they ask for." Patting Jeremy's shoulder he said, "Remember what we talked about. You're not Permillion's anymore. Be strong and make me proud as one of my adventurers." With that, he left.

CHAPTER 10

Though Aaron had followed Peter out of the room, he had not been able to keep up with the determined leader of the expedition. After a few quick turns, the young king was hopelessly lost. After almost an hour of searching, he finally found a serving girl who helped him make his way through Helexpa, to the courtyard with the stables. Torches were lit every few feet to give enough light for the many workers to finish their preparations. When Aaron finally arrived at the stables, Peter had chosen all the equipment for the expedition. The three guards, along with the stable-workers, were outfitting the horses for the journey. Peter was preparing to return to his room as Aaron entered the stable frustrated by his own inept pursuit. In his most forceful tone, Aaron said, "We need to talk. I have some questions for you," as he stepped up to Peter pointing his finger.

Peter was tired and his patience for conversation with one of his underlings was almost nonexistent. Allowing the pointed finger consumed much of what was left of his self-control. "Can't this wait until tomorrow or at least until I'm back in my room?"

"No, I need some answers now."

Rather than fight pointlessly, he capitulated. "Make it quick boy. I'm tired. There's only enough time for a few hours sleep before we have to be back out here. I'm not even going to have time for a decent meal."

Neither Peter's words nor his tone penetrated into Aaron's mind. The whole time he had been looking for Peter, he was replaying Jack's words in his head. "Don't be so eager . . . kid . . . desperate . . . damn kid . . . kid, kid, kid," The words replayed over and over. As the serving girl led him outside like a lost boy, he resolved not to be a kid anymore. He would make people, and especially Peter, treat him like a man. "First of all, explain what Redlin meant by Purple Dragons and why you need to teach me anything. I'm an accomplished fighter with rod, sword, and ax—not to mention, quite good with a bow."

Fatigue made fighting back the urge to slap the boy difficult but Peter held back his hand. Gesturing towards the courtyard, he said, "Let's go outside into the night air and talk. I can tell you all you need to know about the Purple Dragons." Peter walked out of the stable certain that the young king would follow right behind. After walking a few paces past the doorway, he turned to see Aaron still standing inside. As Peter turned, Aaron started walking out slowly. Peter began his explanation in a somewhat aggravated tone, "The Purple Dragons are an adventuring society started by Redlin, Androthy Permillion, and a few others. It's a way for people to find others who like to undertake expeditions as well as give everyone involved a measure of trust in those in the party. There are only a few rules. If you're a Dragon and you take on a quest, you have to finish it or die trying. The only ways out are to have more than half the party die or get everyone to agree not to continue. If you desert the party, you're banned from the society. If you betray your party, you're marked for death."

"You mean life, don't you?"

"No, I mean death. All the other Purple Dragons who find out about what you did are obligated to kill you. If you are not killed within a year, they arrange a quest to hunt you down. Needless to say, few people betray the Purple Dragons and none who have are still alive." Peter poked Aaron's chest to punctuate the statement. "Anyone can be a Purple Dragon as long as someone in the society inducts them, usually there's an apprentice period for new members."

"That's what Redlin meant. I'm to be your apprentice?"

"You could call it that. He wants you to be my student. I need to teach you so you can survive the quest. I guess he thinks you're going to get yourself killed. That means you have to do what I say. If you want to be a Purple Dragon, you'll follow my rules."

"That shouldn't be a problem. I'm good enough to hold my own now. I've been training my whole life. I shouldn't have much to learn."

Peter laughed a hardy laugh that bothered and embarrassed the young king. "If you say so, kid. Just follow me and do what I say. You'll do fine."

The word kid rang in Aaron's ears like a battle cry. "And if I don't?"

The boy's tone annoyed Peter. "I'll leave you behind, beat you down, or kill you myself. It depends on what you do."

"What gives you the right to talk to me like that. I'm a king . . . an honored guest of Redlin . . . am accomplished warrior."

Shaking his head in disdain, Peter laughed in disbelief. "What gives me the right? I'm in charge of the expedition for one . . . oh yeah, that's right, you're a king, so that doesn't apply. Grow up. You'll do what I say. Start by shaving your head."

"I will not. Why should I?"

"You will because I said to."

"I'm not going to make myself bald just to let you feel like you're in charge."

"You do it to signify the beginning of the quest. It helps you mark time and show your commitment. If you don't want to, I can do it for you."

Aaron growled saying, "I don't think so—little man." In an instant, he sized up his opponent. Peter was still wearing his leather fighting suit, bracers and boots. In his favor, Aaron was a head taller and many pounds of muscle heavier than his opponent.

Peter sensed the fight in the young man's words. He did not have time or energy to waste on this scrap. "Look Aaron, I'm tired. Let's not get into this now. We can—"

Before he could finish, Aaron had thrown himself at Peter. A grab, a twist and a side-step by Peter sent the charging boy reeling onto his back a few feet away. A cheer came from the workers who had stopped to watch. Peter yelled to them, "Get back to work."

As he yelled, Aaron exclaimed, "Yah, take this old man!" He

rolled twice and pivoted at the hips to send his legs sweeping through Peter's lower body.

Peter deftly stepped back. Aaron's sweep caught one of Peter's legs which he lifted like a flamingo to let Aaron's attack pass. "That's enough boy. Stop before I have to hurt you."

Aaron sprang to his feet enraged by his inability to do anything. The jeers and cheers from the gathering crowd only fueled his anger. "It's all that magic that's helping you, old man. I saw what you did in the great hall. Why should anyone follow you. You're all tricks and illusions."

This insult was more than Peter could stand. He was more than just annoyed, he was angry. "Okay boy, you want a fair fight— here it is. Go get a sword, or an ax or whatever you want. I'll strip down to nothing and still kick you around this courtyard." He held up one finger to punctuate what he was saying as he continued, "Ahhhh, but when we're done and you're broken and bleeding, then you do exactly what I say. Are we agreed?"

Aaron was incensed and could not imagine saying anything other than, "It's a deal." Walking over to where the three guards where standing, he asked "I need your help to put this heap of troll dung in his place." All three were more than happy to help him. One of the guards, who was about the same size as Aaron, offered his chain chest piece. Gladly accepting, the ever-more-confident boy's head swelled. All three guards worked like squires to prepare their newfound knight for the fight.

Meanwhile, Peter stood in the middle of the courtyard stripping off his armor and other possessions. He began by motioning to a serving maid who was watching. "I want you to hold my things so the little boy doesn't think I'm cheating him." First, he handed the girl his bracers and boots.

"Don't forget the belt and armor, too," yelled one of the guards helping Aaron.

Peter growled, "Don't worry, it's coming." He stripped off his leather fighting suit and handed it to the blushing girl placing his sword belt on the top.

"What about your necklace and jewelry?" yelled the guard again, this time with biting sarcasm in his voice.

Angrily, Peter stripped off everything else he was wearing other than a small loin cloth. As Aaron turned to look at him, Peter said, "I trust you'll let me keep on my cloth . . . women are present."

Seeing Peter infuriated Aaron. He charged while answering, "Uhhrrrr, you're dead."

Pushing the girl to one side, he said "I'll take that as a yes." While she moved back, he stepped forward, crouched, and prepared for the fight.

While the two prepared themselves, the crowd had talked amongst themselves. Some laid wagers while others just cheered on one or the other combatant. It had been a long time since anyone had fought a duel in Helexpa. All were going to enjoy the entertainment. As the boy charged, the noise of the crowd grew steadily louder. Most were yelling for Aaron to take Peter's loin cloth while others wanted him to go for a clean cut of Peter's head. All noises were lost on Aaron who only saw his target. No longer was he trying to kill Peter, he was trying to slay all the bad memories of his past. Everything bad that had happened to him in his life was now embodied in this bald warrior whom he had met only hours before.

Aaron's charge towards Peter stopped abruptly when Peter caught the incoming sword-hand with one arm and thrust to the boy's chest with his other. At the same time, he pivoted sending Aaron spinning off randomly. Once Aaron regained his composure, he realized the sword he had been holding was now gone. He heard Peter say, "Looking for this?" as his nemesis held the sword aloft and then tossed it off to the crowd harmlessly.

Aaron approached again, more cautiously this time. "I was too angry . . . too rushed. This time . . . this time I'll pound you down." Aaron trudged forward with an ever maddening expression overtaking his face.

"Don't lose your head boy," Peter jeered. As Aaron came within three feet of him, Peter sprang up at a point just over Aaron's head.

Though Aaron ducked, Peter was able to snatch off the boy's helmet. Rolling as he met the ground, Peter righted himself and turned to face his stunned opponent. The helmet joined the sword in the crowd. "Have you had enough or am I going to have to actually hurt you?"

"You're just afraid to stand and fight—one hit and your finished," the boy said confidently.

Peter laughed and soon it was echoed by the crowd. "Come get me." He stood upright and placed his hands at his sides.

Aaron approached tentatively having learned quickly not to take Peter lightly. He jabbed once, and then again. Both whooshed passed a dodging Peter as they hit nothing but air. There was a smack as the third punch made contact with the open palm of Peter's hand. As he tried to pull his fist back, Peter's hand closed on it like a vice. It was now trapped. Aaron tugged twice but made no progress. Then, in and instant, his hand was wrapped behind his back. His body bent back involuntarily as Peter's free arm wrapped itself around his exposed neck.

A cold voice whispered in his ear, "A broken arm and then a broken neck." He increased the pressure on the boy's arm sending a ribbon of pain all the way up to the shoulder. "You wouldn't have even felt the pain—you'd just be dead." Flexing his biceps to cut off the blood supply to Aaron's head, he said, "Concede."

"All right, you win." Aaron murmured hesitantly.

Peter let the muscles in his arms go slack so the boy could free himself. Aaron jerked spastically throwing Peter to the ground. Peter landed face-down a few feet to his right. Once the boy had taken a deep breath, he moved towards Peter trying to pounce. Peter growled his distaste for the boy, lifted one leg and drove it hard into the boy's exposed abdomen. In response, Aaron doubled over in pain and crumpled to the ground moaning.

After standing up, Peter stepped up to Aaron, saying, "Serves you right. You need to learn honor and when to quit, my young king." He drew back his foot and measured the space between it and Aaron's head. Two swift hits with the back of his heel knocked the young battered and embarrassed boy unconscious. Bending down, Peter checked to make sure he had not killed Aaron and then hoisted the boy's body up onto his shoulder like a large sack of gold. "Everyone get back to work. The show's over." He pointed to the serving girl, saying, "Bring my things and come with us. We need to shave him and then put him to bed. He has a great deal to do tomorrow and he's going to have a headache to deal with besides."

Dutifully, the maid fell in behind Peter as he walked towards the passageway back into Helexpa. The crowd slowly dispersed and everyone returned to their jobs as if nothing had happened. As they walked, Peter said, "If anyone asks, nothing happened. We were sparring—that's all."

CHAPTER 11

As the western edge of the mountains shone with the glow of first light, Peter entered the courtyard from the stables. Leather riding clothes covered his body from head to toe. He had come to check his war horse and the supplies that would be needed for the journey. As head of the expedition, it was his duty to arrive long before any of the others would think to come to the meeting place and be ready for them. After checking his own horse, he inspected the horses that were for the other members of the party. He was pleased to see that everyone had given their personal equipment to the servants who packed them on the mounts. This would save time and avoid confusion later. Once he was reassured that everything was in its proper place, he decided to stroll in the courtyard. Waiting was something he did not like but was very accustomed to and, by now, quite good at. This quest would not allow him much time to himself and almost no peace once the party was traveling on the open roads. He knew this next week would be gone in a flash. Hoping to savor his last few moments of solitude, he took a deep breath of the sweet, cool, morning air and tried to enjoy the momentary respite from duty. His stroll did not last long.

Vin emerged from the castle entrance into the courtyard, writing in her journal as she walked towards him. It was as if her hands worked independently of her mind, recording what she saw instinctively without her direction. She lifted the pen to wave saying, "Good morning, how are you? Are we ready to begin?"

"I'm fine. Everything's ready. We're just waiting for the others to arrive."

"I'm sure they'll be along soon. I left Shane and his bounty hunter friend in their rooms several hours ago. They wanted to sleep. How can anyone sleep when we're about to go on this exciting adventure? I just can't fathom it."

Surprise covered Peter's face as Vin mentioned being with the bounty hunters. He thought to himself, "Why does that bother me?"

Before his thoughts could continue any further, she wrapped her arms around him and hugged him saying, "I hope you got some rest. You seemed consumed with worries last night. Even now you seem distant. Is there something?"

Hugging her quickly but fiercely, he said, "I'm fine . . . just preoccupied by the preparation. There's so much to anticipate and so little time. It doesn't help that I really don't know all the members of our party. Redlin tried to tell me what he knew, but that wasn't much."

"I'll tell you what I know. Maybe that'll help." She smiled and let her hands slip from around his waist.

"I'd like that but right now we have other things to attend to. When we're on the road. We'll do it then."

Just then, Gallis and the two bounty hunters entered the courtyard together. Peter waved to the group and gestured for them to come his way. Once all three had come across the courtyard and exchanged salutations, Jack said, "So where's the eager little kid who all but chased you down last night. I would've thought he'd be here first . . . licking your boots and all."

Shane slapped at Jack's arm with the back of his hand saying "You really are a troll's ass sometimes."

"All the time. Good thing no one hunts trolls anymore."

"You better watch out or Tyrone the Shooter will come after you . . . he's still looking to kill trolls."

Vin added to their bantering by interjecting, "Actually, not all the trolls are dead . . . some still live far to the north, in the deep mountain caves. I followed Shooter on an adventure only a few years ago."

While the two bounty hunters and Vin playfully talked amongst themselves, Gallis moved to speak to Peter. In a guarded voice he said, "I want to know if you think we can trust the stalker. I saw him disappear after you left the meeting. I tried to follow him but he vanished without a trace that I could follow. I couldn't hear as much as a whisper or see a ripple in the air . . . no matter what I did, including magic. No one has seen him since."

Peter nodded and was about to speak when Darvan appeared right next to Gallis. It was not that he was invisible and had reappeared, but rather, he just seemed to materialized a few feet from the spot that the two men occupied. Gallis stood straight up with a start. Since he was normally cautious and observant, he did not understand how he could have missed a person approaching him, even invisibly. Without removing his hood, Darvan said in his gravelly voice, "Good morning all. Hope I didn't startle you . . . huh huh ha." The breathy laugh faded to nothing. This dark cold demonic laugh was more disturbing to Gallis than even the stalker's voice or appearance. "Where are the rest?"

Ignoring all the others, Peter responded to Darvan's question. "The last two will be here soon enough I'm sure. The boy, Aaron, he had some things to do for me. He might be a little late. Redlin himself told me he would send someone for the mage apprentice Twig. If you want to know more about her, ask Gallis." Clapping his hands to get the attention of the others, he said, "Redlin will be here in a few moments to present us with guides, gifts, and well wishes. I suggest you all prepare yourselves. I made sure everything you gave to the stable-hands was packed on the horses. Take care of last minute business now. We won't have time once we leave Helexpa."

As he said this, Aaron came into the courtyard. All the hair on his head, including his eyebrows, was completely removed. A black oblong bruise stood out like a birth mark on the side of is head near the temple. He wore black leather riding clothes just like Peter's. With his head down, the beaten boy crossed the courtyard and reported to Peter. "I've done as you said, sir." Though the words were formal and respectful, the look in Aaron's eyes betrayed his dislike and distaste with having to say them.

"Very good. Go check your horse . . . see if you can help the others when you're done."

"But I thought the guards and stable-hands did that. Why do I—"

A cold stare from Peter stopped the words in Aaron's throat. He dropped his head and walked to the stable. Heeding Peter's advice, everyone took a moment to examine themselves. Once each was satisfied with their preparedness, they began talking amongst themselves again.

As Aaron walked away towards the stables, Jack slapped Peter on the back. "You've gotten him trained well," he said with a grin. "Does he shine armor and oil swords too?"

Ignoring the comment, Peter yelled to Twig who had just entered the courtyard. "Over here Twig." Lowering his voice to a level to be heard only by himself he said, "Finally, we're all here . . . just need Redlin and then we're off."

Twig moved at a quick but unhurried pace to join Peter at the place where he was standing. To his surprise, she was dressed in a mix of riding and fighting armor, suited best for wilderness survival. A sword hung at her hip and a bow and quiver of arrows was slung across her back Though he was not accustomed to having wizards or young women with him as part of the adventuring party, it was the way she carried herself so confidently that he found particularly strange. No more than a step behind her was Jeremy. A far cry from the young bedazzled boy he had met in Hamiltanville, the young man who approached looked poised and ready for the quest. He was clad in a thin metal mesh suit of armor like none Peter had ever seen. Slung across his back was an ordinary-looking bow and a quiver filed with an assortment of arrows. Together, the two made an impressive sight, especially for such young and seemingly inexperienced adventurers. Even so, Peter thought to himself, "What's the boy doing? He can't be coming with us, can he?"

Before he had a chance to voice his questions, a trumpet blared to signify the arrival of Redlin and his entourage. Twenty guards, squires, pages, and other nondescript servants slowly processed into the courtyard ahead of their master and lord. The noise from the horns drew Aaron out of the stables. Quickly, everyone gathered around Peter's position and waited for Redlin and his procession to approach.

Gallis was dismayed by the appearance of Jeremy. He worked his way next to the boy and in an accusative tone he said, "What are you doing? Why are you dressed like that? Where do you think you're going?"

In a matter-of-fact tone he said, "I'm questing with you. I'm pledged to Twig."

"You're not coming with us. What gives you the right? This quest is only for experienced adventurers. We can't be bothered watching out for you."

The two had kept their voices low as the entourage entered. At this, however, Jeremy held his voice low no longer. "In the last three days I've gained more experience than most might have in as many years." Vin's ears perked up as she overheard the two speaking. "My quest started the moment Dirk Lancer arrived beaten and half-dead. He sent me to find our master. I knew nothing, but I went—it was my duty. I was chased by things . . . guar and a stalker. They . . . well, they belong in nightmares." As he spoke his voice steadily grew louder. "That was just the beginning. When I found the master, he pledged me to Twig and sent us across the world. Then I was shot and brought here. In a matter of minutes, I was swept up and made part of the quest."

By now all were listening to the boy. Gallis said, "Calm down. Lower your voice."

"You knew me as a servant. Since then, I've watched and learned. Just in the last few days . . . I met Lord Redlin . . . I . . . I'm, well, I'm."

Redlin finished Jeremy's statement. "Going on a quest." Everyone's attention immediately shifted to the lord of the castle who was now standing a few feet in front of his assembled entourage. Fixing his gaze on Peter, he continued, "Is everything in order?"

Nodding, Peter said, "We just needed to divide the party and give everyone their missions."

"Very good. I just came to wish you luck and see you off safely. I wish I could send healers and warriors with you, but I can't spare them." Turning to his entourage, Redlin gestured to an old dwarf standing amongst the guards. His body was covered by iron chain plates that were the same color as the reddish gray hair that covered his head. "This is Meldrin. He'll guide you through a secret pass in the mountains to the west. It will allow you to be in Phinn by tomorrow." The dwarf stepped forward, bowed, and stepped back without making a sound. "He's an excellent tracker and knows these mountains better than anyone. His people helped to build my castle and Phinn as well." Redlin shook his head. "Other than this, there's little I can do. Now, it's time for you to begin. Good luck." Redlin gestured to the servants who immediately moved to the stables and brought out the horses.

As this was being done, Peter spoke to the group of adventurers. His tone was so authoritative, everyone listened to him by virtue of its sheer force. "As leader of this expedition, I have decided to separate us into two parties. One will make it's way with Meldrin to Phinn. I'll lead that party. Redlin has arranged for us to meet with agents who can help us secure the items we need. We'll pay for, barter for, or take what we can find. Then, we move on to Thwardscall." He paused to watch as what he said sank in. All had an anxiously curious look on their faces. "The other party will be led by Shane Forester. Redlin has told me he has traveled to Thwardscall before. That party will head directly there and meet the giant's emissaries."

Shane shook his head 'yes' as he said, "Uh huh, he's right. I've concluded many a bounty for the giants there. They like the place . . . feel safe there and that makes them comfortable."

"My party will head there as soon as we've finished in Phinn. The whole quest shouldn't take more than a week, I hope. Once we are back together, we'll push on to wherever Max Konicker and the Slayer of Evermore might be found."

Vin said eagerly, "I'll go with you, Peter. Phinn sounds more interesting."

Peter looked at her disapprovingly. "I'll split us up according to how our skills might best be used and what the journey requires." Softening the bite of his words with a gentle touch of his hand on her forearm, he continued, "As it happens, you are coming with me but that's still my choice, not your decision." Turning his head to look at his new apprentice, he said, "I'll take Aaron and Jack too." Looking around as he pointed at Shane, he added, "Shane'll be in charge of Gallis, Twig, and, I guess, Jeremy. The boy seems to want to stay with the girl." As Peter spoke, the servants brought all the horse out into the courtyard.

"Well, ah, that's fine with me, as long as the boy can fend for himself. I don't have time to play nurse-maid to a fledgling adventurer," Shane said without prompting.

Removing the bow from his shoulder, Jeremy said, "I know I'm a better rider than most and can survive in the wilderness. As for fighting, I'm good enough with a bow to take care of myself."

"Caring for yourself and being in a party are two different things." Aaron said condescendingly.

Redlin was about to intervene when he saw Shane take the initiative. "The boy's right," Shane said, as he moved to the horse carrying his things. After retrieving a large mechanical crossbow, he said, "Let's have a little test." Lifting the crossbow and taking aim at a nearby tree, he pulled the trigger twice in rapid succession. Two bolts struck a low-hanging branch two hand-widths apart. "Well young archer, put an arrow between those two, and you're good enough to ride with me."

"Ho ho, that's no easy test," Jack said with a half-chuckle.

Saying nothing, Jeremy touched the star that hung at this chest, drew an arrow, and knocked his bow. Taking a deep breath and holding it, he let the arrow fly. With a thwap it hit dead center between the two crossbow bolts.

Twig smiled saying, "That's great. He's coming with us."

Aaron said cynically, "Anyone can get lucky. That shot doesn't mean anything."

Before anyone could make an argument, Jeremy proclaimed, "Left or right—you choose."

Aaron looked around speechless for a moment and then said "Left, I guess."

Touching the star once again, he drew out a second arrow. This time he looked at Twig. He raised the bow, and shot it in one swift arching motion. The arrow flew straight into the shaft of the bolt that was on the left. Twig clapped as the others looked on approvingly. Aaron dropped his head and retreated to a place behind the others to sulk.

Vin and Jack said "Nice shot," in unison.

"Good job," Peter said as he grinned.

"Good job," Redlin echoed as if they were of one mind and voice.

Shane said, "Wow! That's better than good enough. Besides, Twig seems to have become fond of having you around. The last thing I want with me is an upset wizard. I'm glad to have you."

Gallis seemed too preoccupied with watching the stalker to have bothered with the archery display. Once the commotion had died, he said, "What about the stalker? You haven't said who he's traveling with."

Peter's smile faded quickly as he returned to the job at hand. "Of course—he'll travel on his own. Darvan can work best if he's apart from the group. I've spoken to him already about it. He knows what he needs to do. Don't worry."

An uneasy looked filled Gallis' eyes. He neither trusted Darvan nor wanted the stalker traveling unattended. "Are you sure that's the best thing?"

Before Peter could answer, Redlin stepped up to the group saying, "Enough discussion. You all know your duty. It's time for the quest to begin. We have all put our trust in you. Now place your trust in one another and go. Remember, time is short. Be safe but be quick. All of you have taken an oath as Purple Dragons or their pledged apprentices. That should be good enough." Like a father telling his children to stop bickering, all arguments and discussions ceased. Redlin called to Peter, "Bring over Twig and Aaron. I have something for them."

While the others mounted their horses, Peter escorted Twig and Aaron to Redlin. "Here they are my lord."

Gesturing to a pair of servants holding large Dragonthorn cases, Redlin said, "I have a special gift for the two of you . . . axes once used by Max Konicker himself." The servants stepped up and presented the two young adventurers with one case each. "They are not nearly as powerful as the Slayer of Evermore, but they are magical and very excellent weapons in their own right. May they help your quest be successful."

Twig took her case and said, "Thank you so much. I will treasure it and wield it proudly." Without opening the case, she moved to her horse and packed the case on its back. Once it was secured, she mounted.

Aaron took his case greedily, placed it on the ground, and knelt over it. He started to open it like a starved man opening a sack of food. "Thank you very much Redlin. I can't wait to see which of Konicker's axes it is. I know them all."

Peter stopped his new apprentice before he opened the case. Placing a hand on the boy's back, he said, "You have a lot to learn boy. Yesterday, you didn't know when to stop. With Jeremy, you stopped too soon. In time you'll learn." Aaron did not want to hear anything Peter had to say. "Give me the case. You can look at it later."

"No! I'm a grown man—a king. I can do what I want and what I please, when I please." Aaron's fingers felt for the latches that held the case closed.

"You're nothing more than a boy. After some training and some time, you'll be a man. Then a warrior if you're lucky. Eventually, you might be a leader. Kingship isn't something you're given. You have to learn to be a king and earn the kingship." Aaron felt the shirt of his suit tighten as Peter gathered it in his fist. As his fist closed, he leaned in to whisper in the boy's ear. "Don't do it boy. I'm in charge and you're my apprentice. I can be your teacher or your master—your choice."

Aaron immediately stopped feeling for the latches, picked up the case and tucked it under his arm. "My teacher has reminded me we are short of time. I will examine my gift later. Thank you very much once again Lord Redlin. I'm in your debt. I'm sure it will serve me well."

Peter let his hand relax and said, "Very good, you're learning."

Aaron moved to his horse and secured his case. Once he was certain it would be safe, he climbed aboard his horse and brought it into line behind Jack. Peter mounted and took the lead next to Meldrin.

Redlin bid them farewell as they headed to the gates leading out of Helexpa.

CHAPTER 12

Upon leaving Helexpa, Peter let Meldrin take the lead. The party rode in twos behind him until they reached the foothills that led into the Blackspine. Vin rode next to Peter while Aaron rode beside Jack. The dwarf guided them up into the mountains along a path seen only by his keen dwarven eyes and, perhaps, some mountain goats unfortunate enough to wander through the area.

After only a few minutes of riding, Vin moved forward to speak with Meldrin. As she made her way towards the dwarf, Aaron called forward, "Peter . . . I wanted to know . . . to ask if I could, well, look at my ax now?"

Peter turned and replied coldly, "No."

"But why? I just want to—"

Peter interrupted, "Because I said no. That should be reason enough. Learn to control your emotions . . . deny yourself some things. Curb your curiosity."

Aaron dropped his head and said, "Yes sir."

Like a venerable instructor speaking to a new pupil, Peter said, "You'll have time enough to look at it once we've stopped. It'll still be there. We're having enough trouble riding without you worrying about opening a case and playing with an ax. Be strong. Be patient."

Aaron resigned himself to what he was sure would seem like an eternal wait. "I'll be strong; don't you worry."

Jack leaned over and slapped Aaron's left arm to get his attention, saying, "Why is the ax such a big thing for you? I know it's magical and all, but it can't be that great."

"You don't understand. It was one of Max Konicker's axes. I know everything about him and his adventurers. He was one of the greatest warriors ever. I've trained to be just like him. Magic is only part of it. I think magic can make me more powerful but to have one of Konicker's axes . . . that's special."

"Okay, I can see that. I heard a little about the Slayer of Evermore. You know, the basics."

Before Jack could finish or invite a conversation, Aaron was already speaking. "It's magical. It can heal. It can give you strength—plus other special powers known to Redlin, Max, and the thousands that have died by Slayer's blade."

Jack broke in, "But I never really heard about any of Konicker's other weapons. How great can they be? I thought he got Slayer early on in his adventuring career."

Aaron's voice raised as his face brightened. "No, he had two other axes at least—Splinter and Cleave. Both were very powerful in their own right. I would love to have either."

Jack began to become interested in what the boy had to say. "Do you know what they could do—the magic and all?"

"Not really. Cleave was given to him by a mysterious smith that lived in the Valley of the Dragons. It had magic and was supposed to be able to protect the wielder from the magic of all dragons. That would be nice. He used it while he was questing to recapture three of the eternal dragons that escaped from the Valley."

"Some say they were released. That was over a hundred and fifty years ago, so it's hard to know. What about the other one— Splinter you said, right?"

"That one was his ax just before he was given Slayer. He had it custom made less than a year before but then came Slayer, directly from Redlin himself. Anything else Max had was going to be put aside. Since it was rarely used, Splinter wasn't really spoken about much in any of the stories I heard or read. Once Max used it in a pit battle in Phinn and again to kill orcs; he loved killing orcs."

"Of course, everyone knows the Konicker maneuvers and the death toll."

"Some say he killed over a thousand orcs while he was adventuring."

Aaron shook his head incredulously. "More like ten thousand.

I've read accounts of battles in which he killed five hundred in a day. While he was wielding the Slayer, it's said he could kill eight at a time with just one slash."

"Damn!" Jack was genuinely impressed with both the legend of Max Konicker and the amount of detail his young companion could remember. "So you know a lot about Konicker and his ax."

"Like I said, He's my hero. I know all there is to know. I've studied his life's story."

The two exchanged more stories of battle until their attention was drawn away by the task of following the trail. Eventually, as the trail became almost impossible to follow, all conversation stopped completely. Meldrin's silent followers focused their attention on the task of keeping their horses in line and on the mountain side as the path grew harder to see and the angle on which they rode increased. In a short while, the party was riding single file along a dipping and swerving path through the mountainside. As their ranks had spread, Meldrin slowed to let everyone gather together.

After six hours of riding in silence and listening to the others, Meldrin began to speak. Though small in stature, the dwarf's voice seemed to boom off the nearby rocks. "Stay close. This entire region is aptly named the Forbidden Lands. Nothing grows except for a few shrubs and scrub grasses. Neither are good for horse nor man nor even fires. Hidden valleys, underground streams, and secret magical gardens are rumored to exist. No one has ever found them and lived to tell about it though. As far as anyone knows, Helexpa's the only settlement in the entire valley and it's surroundings. Redlin likes it that way. Well, you see, my people live east of Phinn. The elves live far to the west in the mountains on the other side of the city. It works well to have Redlin's capitol in the middle. My people were brought here by him hundreds of years ago to help construct Phinn, Helexpa, and many other things, including the magic school. We stayed. Now the eastern range of the Blackspine is as much ours as anybody's except for Redlin, of course." Just as abruptly as he had started speaking, the dwarf stopped. As he crested a hill, he reined in his horse and raised a hand for the rest of the party to stop as well.

Peter brought his horse up next to Meldrin and then dismounted. Meldrin joined him. The two scrutinized the horizon near the place where Meldrin pointed. Signaling for the others to dismount, Peter said, "It looks like an orc patrol hunting for something. There's at least six of them . . . maybe eight. We can't let them discover us."

"Or leave either," Aaron prompted. "We should use a modified Konicker maneuver. I've studied it. It's perfect for orc patrols."

"This time you're right boy—that's what we'll have to do," said Peter encouragingly. "Does everyone know what the Konicker maneuver is?"

The three other party members gave their affirmative silently. "Good, but we'll need to modify it for the terrain and the fact that there's only five of us."

Vin said, "I'll be an archer and stay invisible until I have to attack."

"I have my crossbow and can camouflage well in this rocky terrain. If I have to though, I don't mind being the bait or the runner. Just let me know what you need," Jack added in a professional tone.

Peter pointed to Meldrin and Aaron. You two will be the anvil. I'll be the bait. Vin will be the driver. Jack, you pick up the strays and help with what you can. The walls of the next cut are steep so I don't think we'll have a problem as long as Vin can stay behind them. Are we agreed."

Everyone quietly said "Yes," together. They all moved to their horses and drew weapons. Like a field general, Peter said, "Meldrin, when we've finished, tether the horses over the rise behind us and take up a scout position for me. Vin, once you have your bow, make your way to the other side. Jack, get as much cover as you can and wait until we needs you. Hopefully, we'll put these beasts down before you even se them."

Aaron tapped Peter's shoulder and hesitantly asked, "Since I'm part of the anvil, can I use Konicker's ax—the one Redlin gave me? It might help."

After thinking for a moment, Peter replied, "Okay, but be careful. You really don't know what it can do. That can be dangerous, especially since it's magical and once belonged to Konicker."

The boy's face beamed as he quickly opened the Dragonthorn case and drew out a large magnificently forged and engraved two handed battle ax with one cutting blade and a spiked top. The word BLOODLUST was emblazoned vertically on both faces of the blade in a silverish metal that stood out from the flat gray of the rest of the ax. As he examined his gift, Meldrin moved the horses and returned holding two large iron war hammers. The others took their positions. Vin disappeared as Jack made his way to a cluster of rocks on the right side of the path near the top of the next rise.

"Which one is it? What does it do, boy?" he heard Meldrin say as the dwarf returned to the crest of the hill. Peering over the crest, he watched for the orcs. They were moving slowly. Peter waited for Meldrin's signal before beginning the maneuver.

"I don't know. I never heard anything about this ax. It's not in any stories I been told but I'm sure it's an excellent weapon," Aaron said quietly as he waited anxiously for the battle to begin.

Dropping back over the hill, Meldrin said, "They're just coming over the rise now. There's seven of them for sure. They look like they're from the mountains near the north end of the Valley of the Dragons. Wait a minute, then go."

Though Aaron did not say anything, he was amazed at how specific the dwarf had been. He thought to himself, "I thought all orcs looked like husky humans with bad teeth and a pug nose. How can he tell the difference?" He inched his way to the crest of the hill to sneak a glimpse of the approaching orcs.

Peter walked over the top of the hill. He gauged the distance from his end of the valley to its lowest point. The other side was a steeper slope that made almost the same rise in only slightly more than half the distance. He began his slow walk down his side with his head down. As soon as the orcs saw him, they began to lumber to the bottom, eager for a meal. Though stupid, orcs were fierce fighters that loved the taste of human flesh. This group would not miss the opportunity to feast on fresh food in the Forbidden Lands. The Konicker maneuver was in motion. Everything was just a matter of skill, timing, and luck. Once at the bottom, Peter looked up and acted stunned to see the seven orcs charging down the hill. Their heavy armor made it difficult for them to move in any direction other than straight down the slope. Two ran ahead of the rest drawing their swords as they approached. Peter waited a moment for them to be within striking distance and them flung himself at their heads. One of his hands hit each of the two orcs square on the chest thrusting their torsos backwards. In the next instant, the orcs hit the ground with a thud. Immediately, Peter turned and ran back up the hill he had just descended. As he turned, the other five orcs fell over their fallen companions. By the time he was half way up the hill, the orcs had regained their feet and were following, joined by the other five. They scrambled up the hill after their dinner.

As he crested the hill ahead of the orcs, Peter turned and yelled, "Now!"

The near exhausted orcs were shocked to see Aaron and Meldrin charge down the hill at them. Upon seeing the orcs, Aaron could feel a hatred for them well up from within. He did not care about what the others were doing; he wanted to kill orcs. With one swing, Bloodlust removed the head of the orc nearest him like it was the top of a dandelion. Using his hammers in tandem, Meldrin incapacitated the other lead orc. As the next rank advanced up the hill, Aaron drove into them with a fury. He chopped with the ax into any orc that was near enough for him to reach. With each successive hit his hatred intensified. At the same time, his strength seemed to grow and the ax became easier to wield. By the time he had reached the bottom of the hill, all but one enemy had been slain. Even the orcs battered by Meldrin had not escaped Bloodlust. Aaron ensured their death with a quick sharp chops of the blade.

This last survivor tired to flee up the hill. Arrows and bolts rained down on the orc. As they impacted his chest, he was stood up and his progress stopped. Without thinking, Aaron brought the ax down on the helpless beast, splitting him like a log. Though he was covered in the blood of his fallen enemies, the ax itself shined. The dull gray had become a bright gleaming silver that reflected the sun like a mirror.

Even as the two halves of the orc hit the ground, Aaron was climbing the other side of the hill in search of more victims. He yelled as he climbed, "I know there's more around here. I can feel it."

Vin moved towards Aaron as he approached. Peter yelled to her, "No! Let him go for now. We'll follow him. He's in a battle rage." He barked to the others, "I'll get the horses. Keep an eye on him, if you can." While Peter ran and brought the horses, the others climbed to the top of the next rise and scanned the distance for their companion. He was already gone. Once Peter joined them, everyone mounted and they began to ride off after Aaron. In the distance, they heard the sounds of battle and the cries of orcs falling under the blade of Bloodlust. The whole party rode as quickly as they dared to join Aaron.

"What do you think happened to him?" asked Vin.

"Battle rage," Jack replied quickly. "He's young and impetuous. I hope it doesn't get him killed."

"I don't think so," Meldrin said thoughtfully. "It might be that ax he was using. I didn't like the look of it."

Peter said, "I didn't think Bloodlust would cause problems; though I probably shouldn't have…"

Vin broke in, "Bloodlust! He's wielding Bloodlust against orcs? We need to get there fast."

"What the hell does that mean?" Peter asked like a man that missed the first half of a secret plan.

"Yeah, what's that all about?" Jack concurred.

Vin raised her voice and spoke hurriedly as she pushed her horse faster. The sounds of battle grew louder as they moved up the rise. "Bloodlust is responsible for the Konicker maneuver. I thought you would've known that. It craves orc blood and drives its wielder into a battle rage if orcs are anywhere nearby. It feeds on the their blood. The more it tastes, the more it wants; but the better it is at killing."

"Who the hell would make a weapon like that? And why did Redlin give it to the boy?" Jack asked incredulously.

"A powerful wizard who hated orcs but who didn't like warriors much either." Meldrin said. "The blade is cursed."

"Actually, it wasn't meant to be a curse but it seemed to work that way. Bloodlust will keep Aaron conscious and fighting until he dies or the orcs and their allies are totally destroyed."

Jack broke in saying, "Why did Redlin give him the damn thing?"

As the party came over the top of the rise, all conversation stopped. Aaron stood in the midst of a troop of orcs numbering no less than thirty. All but three had already been killed. These last survivors protected the opening to a cave. As Aaron slashed the orcs with Bloodlust, they held their ground. In a futile attempt to draw the assailant away, two ran past slashing at him as they went. With a large circling blow, Aaron shattered the skull of one and then split the head of the other like a melon. It was only a matter of seconds until Bloodlust was buried into the last orc's chest, killing him instantly. With his death, Aaron's blood-soaked body went limp as he fell to the ground unconscious.

The others moved in to investigate the scene. Peter took charge, saying, "We need to check the cave and then move on quickly. Meldrin, you're best suited for that type of work. We're short of time and I don't want to be here when more orcs show up." Dismounting, he wrested Bloodlust from Aaron's clenched fist and returned it to its carrying case. The others dismounted as well, keeping watch while the dwarf scouted the cave.

Vin said, "Why do you say others?"

Peter replied, "These that we've killed, they're just scouts and footmen. There should be a leader amongst them . . . a sergeant at least."

Jack added, "And this cave must be something important. They wouldn't have stayed to protect it. Ahh, but, none of them ran away."

Meldrin walked cautiously out of the mouth of the cave. As daylight hit his face, the others could see that the color had drained away. "It . . . it's . . . it's, it's a dragon. Small, hurt, and asleep, but definitely a dragon. One of those that struck at Helexpa in the night. Its rider must have died recently . . . I don't think the young thing knows about it yet."

All at once the comments flew at Peter. Vin said, "We need to find out what happened."

Jack said, "We best kill it while it's sleeping, before it knows we're here."

Meldrin just continued speaking through everyone. "The thing is going to be needing food soon, so we had better figure out what we're doing fast."

Peter ended all discussion. "We're not going to kill it, not yet. Let's give it something to eat, other than us of course. Toss in five orcs. That should be enough for now."

"Better make it ten. Don't what it hungry or looking for food," Jack said as he picked up the nearest orc.

"What about the dead rider?" Vin asked as she dragged an orc closer to the cave entrance.

"I'm hoping that the dragon's like a horse. Once it eats and heals, it will just fly home. If it's not our enemy, hopefully, it won't want to attack us without a rider forcing it to. The food offering should help with that too."

Jack shook his head in disbelief. "I never thought I would have a chance to kill a dragon and decide to feed it instead. I hope you know what you're doing. Remember, horses don't breathe fire, slice people in half with claws, eat entire cows in one bite, or knock down walls with their tails."

As Jack and Meldrin tossed the seventh orc deep into the cave, there was a grumble from inside. Sounds of the dragon shifting on it's pile of discarded bones made Vin shiver uncontrollably. After a moment, there was a flash of firelight from inside the cave followed by the crunch of bones. One, two, three, the orcs were devoured. There was another growl that shook the walls of the cave. The dragons was on the move.

Peter gestured for the others to move back. "Get ready, it's coming out."

CHAPTER 13

Shane's party of adventurers left Helexpa as Meldrin's horse disappeared into the Blackspine. Though they were not in a hurry, Shane knew it would take at least a day of steady riding to make it to Overton. He addressed his three companions as they began their journey. "Well, I guess I'm in charge but we're all in this together. I thought we'd go to Overton first. It's a good stop on the way to Thwardscall. If we head north along the side of the valley we'll pass right through it. Well, there are a couple of other little stops between Overton and Thwardscall but, well, they're not really towns. I figure we could take it easy and get to Overton tonight. We'll be in Thwardscall three days later."

"Whatever you say. You're the leader now." Twig said quickly. "And you know where we're supposed to be going."

"I'm just following her," Jeremy added. "Where she goes, I go."

Gallis watched the others and frowned as Twig giggled at Jeremy's comment. "I'll need to start Twig's training as soon as possible. As long as you can guide the party while we work, I'm happy to let you take us where we need to go."

"Then it's settled." Shane said as he scanned the horizon. "I'll scout ahead and return every-so-often to check on you. Well, just follow the curve of the hills as they work themselves up towards the mountains. Jeremy, you'll be in charge of leading the others while I'm gone. Can you handle that?"

"Yes sir," he responded without a hint of deliberation.

"Well then, we're set. Be back soon." Without waiting for a reply, Shane spurred his horse up the hill and rode off out of sight at a trot. Jeremy walked his horse forward to a place several feet in front of his two companions. Watching the path closely, he matched their pace, keeping the distance between himself and them almost constant. Once the three were settled into a steady rhythm, Jeremy listened silently as Gallis spoke to Twig about her magic.

With one eye on the trail and the other on Twig, Gallis began the final piece of her training. In a cold formal tone, he said, "Little one, it is time to start your magic again. Close out all other stray thoughts and focus on me."

"Yes master Gallis. What is your wish?"

"First tell me what Master Permillion has taught you. Then I can know where to begin."

"I've learned all the arts there are to know . . . finished most, except for the use of the offensive spells. He made sure to keep them for last." Gallis stroked his chin as she said this. "Even as this quest began, I was working on this last art and having some difficulty."

"Don't worry, I can fix that. Permillion was afraid to teach you. Afraid you'd leave. I am particularly good at this brand of magic. We shouldn't have a problem. From what I've seen so far, you have more than enough skill and training—only too much control. It's just a matter of the correct instruction, that's all." Gallis thought silently for a moment and then turned his head to look at her. "I don't usually teach on horseback, but we can begin. Can you make a fire in your hand?"

"Yes, I learned that when I was only eleven."

"Impressive, show me."

Twig lifted her right hand, snapped her fingers and extended her thumb upwards. A bluish orange flame licked up off of it as if her thumb where a candlewick. "Is that what you wanted? Or perhaps, more in the palm." She slowly unfolding her fingers so that her palm faced up. As the flame died about her thumb, it grew in her palm. "How's that?"

"Better than I would have expected. From what I've seen, you know more magic than I do and probably have more power behind even your most simple spells. Do you know the art of illusion and invisibility?"

Nodding, she closed her hand and extinguished the fire. Blushing slightly, she said with a grin, "Yes, when I was fourteen. Would you like to see?"

"Yes, I'd like that. How about an illusion?"

Cupping her fingers, she placed them over the bridge of her nose. After a minute of intense concentration, she touched her horse's main. After an instant, the air around her shimmered as the horse was transformed into a baby griffin. Extending her hand towards Gallis' horse, she spread her fingers. His horse faded from sight.

After he glided along in midair for a few moments, he raised his hand and said, "Be gone." Both horses returned to normal. "Excellent, but you don't use words. It's all gestures."

"Master Permillion says that words are a crutch for the weak and slow-minded. If I am to learn, I must learn correctly. If I am to finish my training, I must train correctly."

Gallis laughed aloud. "That sounds like the master. He's just afraid you'll go adventuring like so many others."

"What do you mean?"

"Several students left him before they finished their training. Most just wanted to learn the attack skills you're lacking. I guess that's why he wanted to make you a mage before he even started teaching you those things. As far as I can tell, you know more than most journeyman."

Blushing more, she said, "Thank you for the compliment, but I don't think that I'm ready for my name yet."

"No, but you're very close—closer than you realize. As far as I can tell, you know all the other magical arts, and most of them very well. By keeping you in training so long, you have had time to perfect them without having to fend for yourself. As an unnamed mage, you did everything I did as a named mage except learn one thing."

"And now you'll teach me that one thing?" she said with anticipation.

"Before we reach Thwardscall if you train hard."

Twig's face beamed. "Anything you want. I'll even forgo my sword and ax work if you think it will help."

"No, you're mind will need a rest. Physical activity will be helpful but just don't wear yourself out. Most of what you'll be doing can be done while riding or sitting."

"Whatever you think is best."

"I'm going to start you as if you'd never cast a spell before. That's usually the case. You've probably been over-thinking everything and that's been your problem."

Confusion filled Twig's mind as she asked her new teacher, "But I thought . . . well, you know . . . willpower, strength, concentration. That's the keys to spells—always have control."

Gallis shook his head as he responded, "In general yes, but this last art is easier to master when you have no control and no power behind the spells and it's less dangerous as well. I'm sure you're worrying too much and trying to force things." She nodded her head as he continued, "Okay, here's an exercise for you. Just imagine an arrow flying through the air. Choose any target you see and hit it with the arrow that's in your mind. Don't even bring magic into it at all. Just use your mind's eye. Work on that. Once you can imagine the arrow, see it flying through the air, and hitting your target every time without distraction, we'll continue."

"Yes master. I'll start right away." Closing her eyes, she started to imagine an arrow.

"No, you can't close your eyes. How will you see the target? You have to do it with your eyes open, while riding."

"Ugh, yes master Gallis." Now she felt like she was back in training with the mage master. It took some time, but she was finally able to imagine an arrow in her mind's eye with her eyes open. It took even more time to be able to send it off and have it hit a target.

While she worked at this task, Gallis played with the magic of making a fire appear on his finger the way Twig had. Though he could make a fire, it was difficult for him to conjure it without speaking. Even more difficult for him was forcing the flame to obey his command to remain at the tip of his thumb. As he lifted it skyward, the flame jumped from finger to finger flitting about like a moth. Throughout the entire lesson, Jeremy listened and absorbed what was said. He had no problem conjuring an arrow in his mind and having it hit any target he picked.

All three were consumed by their individual distractions for hours. It was only when Shane returned periodically that they realized how much time had passed. All continued to ride even when they needed to eat or drink. As the sun moved across the sky and began to fall towards the eastern edge of the valley, small clusters of trees began to appear on the roadside. The first few trees they came across seemed small and underdeveloped. Soon, grasses began to cover the bare rocks of the hillside. As they continued north, the party saw fields of lush grasses and denser clumps of healthier trees appear on the mountainsides in the distance.

Jeremy let his horse fall back so that he was next to Twig. "How are you doing? Do you need a rest from the saddle?"

Though he spoke loud enough to make it seem he was addressing everyone in the party, Gallis and Shane could tell his comments were meant mostly for Twig.

Shane said, "Well, I think that's a good idea. Now that we're out of the Forbidden Lands, Overton is close by. A few minutes rest might be a good idea." He led his horse off the path and dismounted near a small sapling. Hitching his horse to the tree, he stretched and walked around. The others followed his lead.

Once everyone was dismounted, Gallis took Twig by the hand, saying, "Let's see if what you've been practicing has helped." Leading her off to a nearby clearing, he said, "Now we'll add in the magic. Are you ready?"

"Absolutely."

Jeremy edged his way towards the two mages. He made sure he was close enough to see and hear everything without disturbing them.

Gallis said, "You'll be doing just what you've practiced, but this time, you'll be casting the spell along with it. Release the magic the way you do any other spell. Instead of forcing it through the gesture, use a word; any word that seems appropriate."

"I'm not sure I understand. I can put magic into the arrow but what is the word?"

"It's just a tool to help you right now. I'm sorry if this doesn't seem right or how Androthy was teaching you, but it's the only way I know. It's how I learned. Eventually, you might not even need or want words. Right now, it's just whatever helps you cast the spell—watch." Raising his hand to point to a rock in the distance, he said, "Fly." A glowing red arrow of light leapt from his finger and hit the rock with a crack, shattering it.

"I see but I don't know if it will help."

"Try it." Closing her eyes, Twig raised her hand. "No, don't close your eyes. You should be able to do it without that much concentration. Let go. Let the magic flow."

"Okay, if you say so." Staring at another rock, she pointed her finger and said, "Arrow." An arrow of white light leapt from her finger just as she saw it in her mind's eye. The rock disintegrated into thousands of small pieces as the magic arrow impacted it. "I did it! I did it!" Turning to Gallis she said, "That was easy."

"The words make the casting simpler. Gesturing magic is the hardest and the most powerful. Try it again but without saying the word."

Twig pointed and cast the spell. Nothing happened. "It didn't work."

"I know. That's the thing. The words have to be spoken. If you cannot speak, you cannot cast the spell. That's why the master has avoided teaching you all but the purest forms of magic."

"Will the words work for all the other spells too? Can I cast them this easily?"

"Of course not, little one. They must be mastered like any of the other spells you've learned. This came so easily because you've been working on it. I just showed you a shortcut you did not know you already had. I have a book of magic to help you cast other spells and perfect this art."

"The master has shown me many other spells that I've worked on as well. Will you teach me to cast them, too?"

"All in good time. Now work on this spell. You need to be able to control all the many facets of it's casting. When you can cast it without the words—in any way I choose—then, and only then, will I move on."

"Time to go," Shane said into Jeremy's ear.

The boy jumped back as he heard the words. "Oh!" Clutching at his chest, he turned to look at Shane. "I didn't know you were there. I didn't even hear you."

"That's the idea. Quiet's good if I'm hunting someone. Besides son, you were too busy watching the lovely lady do her magic. Did you pick up anything useful?"

"Not really. I'm not a wizard. Just a normal person."

"I hear that son, but they're normal people too. It's just they've worked at it for a long time. Hell, do you think I became a bounty hunter in a day? Did you become an archer overnight?"

Jeremy laughed unexpectedly at this comment. "No, it took a little longer than that I suppose. But magic isn't for me anymore. I'll stick to my bow."

"Whatever you say. Go get them and tell them we need to be going. I'm going to scout ahead. Get them moving and I'll meet you down the trail."

"Yes sir." With that, Shane moved to his steed, mounted it, and rode off down the path in the direction they were traveling. Jeremy moved to where the magicians were practicing. "It's time to go. Shane went ahead to check out the trail. Once he returns, we're moving on to Overton."

Gallis said, "All right, that's enough for now. You seem to be tired anyway."

The three mounted and started down the trail. After riding for no more than five minutes, they heard Shane's muffled scream from just over the next hill. As Jeremy came over the rise, he saw Shane heading back in his direction. A guar lay on the ground behind him. Jeremy imagined an arrow flying from his outstretched hand impacting in the middle of the guar's head. He said "Zoom," and pointed his index finger emphatically. Nothing happened.

Shane yelled, "Get back boy. It's an ambush," as he rode passed Jeremy. Once he was on the other side of the hill, he exclaimed, "Twig, Gallis, let's go." As he said this, he reached down to the side of his horse and retrieved his mechanical crossbow from its sling.

Jeremy wheeled his horse around and headed after Shane. Before he could do anything, he saw another guar drop out of a tree. It landed on Twig's horse behind her back. He jumped from his horse and dropped to one knee. In one smooth motion, he drew the bow off his shoulder and then touched the star. Taking an arrow from his quiver, he took aim at the guar. The shot would have to be perfect. He let the arrow fly. It pierced the left eye of the creature and buried itself deep inside the guar's head. Even as he was drawing another arrow, the guar behind him leapt up and pounced. He was knocked down the hill and sent sprawling without his bow. As he skidded to a stop at the bottom, he blacked out.

As Twig saw Jeremy fall, she cried, "No!" Raising a hand, she pointed at the guar. Without a word, a glowing white arrow leapt from her finger and hit the guar's head. It had no effect. The creature crouched, preparing to spring.

Gallis yelled, "That spell won't work—they're immune!"

Dexterously, she slid off her horse and used it for protection. Reaching up, she grabbed for the Dragonthorn case. Throwing it to the ground, she flung it open and took out a large but simple-looking two-headed ax with a large spike extending from between them like a javelin tip. The word SPLINTER was engraved across the face of the two blades on both sides. Though she was a large person, she needed to use both hands to wield it effectively. While she retrieved the ax, another guar had dropped from the trees behind her. As graceful as a ballerina, she spun around leading with the ax. Before the guar could even cry out, Splinter cut it into two halves. The split was so clean and the blow so forceful that the blade continued its cut until it had buried itself into the tree behind the creature. The ax sliced three quarters of the way through before it finally stopped. Pulling Splinter from the tree, she turned to search for another target.

In the meantime, the last guar attacked Gallis. Two slashes with its razor-sharp claws drew blood and hurt him severely. By this time, Shane had been able to dismount and take aim with his crossbow. He fired three times in rapid succession at the guar attacking Gallis. The shots buried deep into the creature's back but did not kill it. As it turned towards him, Shane dropped the crossbow and twisted his left wrist to release a spring-loaded dagger into his hand. As the guar sprang at him, he thrust the poison coated dagger into its abdomen. The guar clubbed him with the back of its right hand, as it swept his legs with its left. Together, the two blows spun him around in midair like a cart-wheeling acrobat. His head hit the ground hard, knocking him unconscious. Even as he hit the ground, the poison did its work. The guar screeched and collapsed. After writhing in pain for a moment, it was dead.

The only guar that was still breathing sprang at Twig. As the creature glided through the air, Twig raised Splinter and struck at the beast. The guar's head split like a piece of fire wood. The force of the springing creature knocked her backward as Splinter wedged itself between the monster's shoulder blades. Twig stood and drew her ax out of the guar's shattered body. Once she had composed herself, she looked around. There was a groan from Jeremy as he tried to get up. She ran to his side saying, "Take it slow; you've been hurt."

Trying to be strong, he said, "I'll be fine, what about the others?" Even as he said this, he stood and brushed himself off to show her he was all right.

"I don't know. I was about to check them. Go see how Shane is. I'll check on Gallis." She moved towards him. While she walked, she kept a concerned eye on Jeremy to make sure that he was really all right.

As she did this, Jeremy checked on Shane. He was alive but

unconscious. No matter how much he shook the bounty hunter, he could not be woken. After several minutes of trying in vain, he joined Twig at Gallis' side to see if she could help. Though not trained in the ways of healing, even he could tell that Gallis was hurt badly. As Jeremy knelt down beside her, she placed her hands on the wounds, concentrated, and cast the spell. The bleeding slowed but did not stop entirely.

"How's Gallis?" he asked.

Startled by his appearance, she turned to look at him with a gasp. "I think he'll survive, but I'm really not sure. I don't know enough about those beasts . . . guar. All we can do is wait." Jeremy nodded his head. "How's Shane?"

"Knocked out. I don't think we'll be able to wake him." Placing his hand on her shoulder, he continued, "How are you?"

Twig placed her hand over Jeremy's as if to say thank you for the concern. "I'm okay . . . well enough, I guess. But I'm too tired to cast spells, especially anything that might heal."

"What should we do?"

"I don't know, go on I guess. What do you think?"

"Whatever you say, you're in charge."

"I never thought of that. I really don't want to be in charge." As she said this, the tree that Splinter had hit fell with a crash. "Well, I guess we'd better get moving. Can you get us to Overton?"

"I hope . . . I think . . . I can do it."

Standing in unison, they worked together to put their fallen companions on the horses. Once Gallis and Shane were secured, Twig replaced Splinter in its case and mounted her horse. Jeremy handed her the reins from Gallis' horse. After taking up the reins from Shane's horse, he mounted his own and headed towards where he thought Overton should be. Neither looked back nor thought of what might be waiting for them in the forest just ahead. Sunset was rapidly approaching and both knew better than to be caught in the forest after dark.

CHAPTER 14

Crunch, crunch, crunch, the bones of the orcs were turned to powder by the jaws of the dragon. Suddenly, in the midst of a crunch there was a terrible roar from the dragon. Fire licked out of the mouth of the cave like a tongue wetting lips. As the flames receded, there was another crunch followed by an agonizing roar of pain. The dragon cried, "Drak, Drak . . . Est Drak met enina."

Everyone looked around scared and bewildered except for Vin. In a loud voice she called, "Met enina . . . nin parters human." Lowering her voice, she said to the others, "He's speaking in an ancient tongue. Asking for his master. I think he's hurt and needs help."

"Ahhh . . . what happened to my master?" the dragon growled. "He's to fix me . . . feed me . . . bring me home." As the dragon spoke, he slithered through the tiny opening at the front of the cave. "I don't know what to do." The dragon's head popped out the mouth of the cave like a groundhog searching for its shadow.

As the others backed away, Vin stepped forward saying, "Here, let me see what's wrong . . . I'm a healer." The dragon wriggled further out of the cave so that's its front paws were now also exposed. A heavy chain encircled the dragon's neck and ran back into the cave. As Vin came closer, she saw a series of arrow-marks in the dragon's right foreleg. "That looks bad; it must hurt."

The dragon shook its head, saying, "Yes, it happened last night when I was flying away from a castle. Can you fix it?"

"I think so, but I need my friends' help. Just wait here." As she turned and walked away, the dragon rested its head down and sighed. Vin motioned for her companions to come together. "The dragon's hurt but not too badly. It seems Redlin's archers were using arrows that could penetrate the dragon's scales—probably Dragonthorn. Even so, I can stop the pain and might even be able to get the barbs out of its leg."

"Oh damn," Jack exclaimed, "I never thought I'd pass up a chance to take down a dragon. Now, not only have I tried to feed it, she's gonna heal it. This is insane."

Peter lifted his hand to silence him. "From what I know about dragons, this one is too young to predict much. Assuming we can heal the thing, why should we? It might just turn on us?"

Vin replied swiftly, "No, dragon's are not deceitful, especially when they're this young. He's been a slave to his master . . . his rider and trainer . . . who's now dead. If we help him, he'll leave us alone and might even help. Besides, he's chained down."

Meldrin broke in, saying, "If we don't do something, once the orcs are all eaten, he'll just go hunting for himself. That means all of us, including my kin, would be in danger. I say we help. I remember what a rogue dragon's like. It's not a pretty thing at all."

Jack groaned in disgust. "Ugh, I guess you're right. Why make enemies when we can have friends. I'd rather kill anything I don't trust but nothing says I'll be able to kill that thing even with it being hurt and tied down."

Peter thought silently for a moment and then said, "Okay, say that you can fix it up, what then? I mean, we might have a baby dragon who wants to follow us home. If we just let it go, it might wander back to Morgan's men and be used against us later."

"Send it to Redlin's," Jack suggested.

"No that won't work. Even without a rider, the guards would kill the little guy before he was close enough to explain." Peter responded.

From off to the side, Aaron suddenly started screaming, "What am I doing here? What the hell is that?" As everyone looked over towards the boy, they saw him slowly making his way to his feet.

Peter rushed over saying, "Stay quiet and take it slow. We'll explain everything once you have your wits back about you. You've been in a battle rage brought on by Bloodlust. Right now, we're trying to help the dragon." Still confused, Aaron confirmed his obedience with a nod and remained quiet. As he made his way to his feet, he rubbed his eyes with his fingers as if he had just awoken from a long sleep.

Vin said, "I'm going to see how I can help. We'll worry about what to do with him later." Marching defiantly to the dragon's side, she said, "Do you have a name? What can we call you? I'm Vin."

Turning his head slightly to face her as she approached, the dragon said, "Hello Vin, my brothers call me Quinx. My master calls me Drakina."

"I'll call you Quinx." The young dragon smiled as much as the teeth of a dragon can be called a smile. She knelt next to Quinx's injured leg. In a melodic and soothing voice she said, "This may hurt. I want you to be brave. Let the pain disappear. Imagine you're soaring through the air with no cares at all. Can you do that?"

Nodding, he said, "Of course. I fly all the time."

"Good, then picture it in your mind." Vin kept reminding herself that this great hulking beast was little more than a child. No matter how intelligent it seemed, Quinx was no more sophisticated than a human of five years old. Though he would be very innocent and trusting, any mistakes could be fatal for her. After a quick examination of the arrow wounds, she stood and spoke in a motherly caring voice. "I'll need some help to get the arrows out and I want to give you something to stop the sting. Is that okay?"

"Yes, I guess . . . well, if it's going to help me, okay."

Vin removed a small vial from a pocket concealed in her waistband. Removing the cap, she extended the bottle towards the dragon's mouth. "Let me put a few drops of this on your tongue. It will make this easier." Quinx extended his forked tongue towards her. Once it was within a few inches of her outstretched hand, Vin let four drops of the potion fall onto it. Even as the tongue was withdrawn the potion began to work. Quinx's eyelids became heavy and closed. His breathing relaxed and his head came to rest on its side. In a moment, the young dragon was in a deep sleep.

Jack shook his head in disbelief as he took two steps towards the now sleeping dragon. "My god, that's powerful stuff." The others looked on silently as he moved even closer.

After replacing the vile in her waistband, Vin gestured to Jack. "Come here, I need your help." Once he was at her side she continued, "Pull the scales apart so I can dig out the shafts of the arrows and any tips that are still lodged in there."

Without hesitation, he did as she asked. "So can you heal him? Do you have that kind of magic."

"No, but I know more about his race than he does. All dragons heal quickly. They're magic by nature. Some are even immortal."

"Is Quinx?"

Vin chuckled. "On a first name basis, are you now? Actually, I think this young one can be killed. He's not a grand dragon like those in the valley. He's some sort of cross-breed or hybrid."

"If you say so. Why did you say you could heal him then? "

In a sincere tone she said, "So he'll owe me a favor and think we're on his side. A dragon on your side can always be an asset."

Jack smiled widely and said, "Right you are, right you are." Curiosity tinged his voice as he continued, "But then what did you do?"

"I cast a charm on him to make him trust me and help him forget the pain. He's too young and inexperienced to know how to stop it. An older dragon with training would have been immune to anything I could hope to try. I was lucky with this little one." As she removed the last two arrowheads from his flesh, Quinx stirred. Placing her hand on the side of his snout, she said, "Just relax. You'll be better soon enough. But you'll need to rest." The dragon put his head back down and fell back to sleep. Having finished her work, she stood and gestured for Jack to walk with her to where the others were waiting and watching.

Peter stepped forward and began to speak. "How did it go? I saw the dragon start to move while you were still working."

"It's fine. All the arrows are out and he's resting."

"The question is, what now? We need to keep moving and I don't want a dragon tagging along."

"No matter how nice he turns out to be," Meldrin added.

"Let's just leave him chained here. It doesn't look like he can get away." suggested Aaron. The others looked at him disapprovingly and he knew there were too many reasons why that plan would not work for them to even bother letting him know. "I'll be quite now," he said dejectedly.

Jack said, "Like I said before, can't we send him back to Redlin? If we tell him what to say, he should be fine."

A decisive look consumed Peter's face. "All right. We cut Quinx loose and one of us flies the thing back to Helexpa." He pointed at Jack, saying, "That's going to be you Jack."

"Me!" He stepped back from the others in protest. "I went from killing the thing, to helping fix it up, to baby-sitting it? I don't think so. Let the girl or the dwarf or even the crazy kid do it."

Peter's voice was cold and forceful as he spoke. "You're the only choice. I need to be in Phinn and Aaron stays with me. Meldrin needs to guide the rest of us there, so the choice comes down to Vin and you."

"Let her do it then. She can handle the joyride."

"No. First of all, Redlin knows you. Second, you can find your way to Overton without a problem. I don't know if she can do that. Most of all, what if the dragon is just playing us for fools. You'll have to kill it. I don't trust her to do what's necessary if it comes to that."

Realization crossed bounty hunter's face as the potential for adventure became part of his mission and the likelihood he would change Peter's mind continued to decrease. At the same time, Vin recoiled as Peter brought up this potential outcome. While nodding his head, Jack said, in a resigned voice, "I'll do it. I'll cut him loose and we'll head out as soon as the rest of you are cleared out, just in case."

"Good," Peter said as he turned towards the horses. "We need to get moving. We've lost too much time already. Once you've delivered him to Redlin, get to Overton or even Thwardscall. We'll meet you on the road. I'll leave word in Overton letting you know we came through if you've not made it there yet."

Jack said, "Okay, I know how to get to Thwardscall. It might be best for me to go right there as long as you can do without me."

"We'll be fine."

"Just let me get some things off my horse and you can take it with you. I'll be flying the dragon back, I guess." Jack moved to his horse and took a backpack, a mechanical crossbow, and a sword from the items packed on its back. As he did this, Vin protested vigorously. "We can't just leave him here. He might kill Quinx or the other way around. And what about trying to fly. Who knows if he can even do that. There's so many things we don't know we should—"

Peter interrupted her stream of comments. "Too bad. Our quest lies in Phinn and then Thwardscall. We need to go. Are you coming?"

"Just give me a minute." She motioned for Jack to come with her. "I just want to let him know what's happening. If we're all gone when he wakes up, there might be problems." He followed her to Quinx's side. She gently touched the dragon's snout and shook him slightly to waken him.

There was a sudden snort as his eyes opened. "Huh . . . what? What is it?"

In a sweet pleasant voice Vin said, "It's time for us to go. My friend Jack, the one who helped heal you, is going to stay here and help set you free. When you're healed enough to fly, he's going to take you to someplace safe. Is that okay?"

Quinx groaned slightly and said "Yes, I guess. Can't you stay too?"

"No, I have to go. There's someplace I have to be. Jack can take care of you. Rest now. When you're strong enough, he'll set you free." She rested her hand on the side of the dragon's head and rubbed it softly.

While she spoke to the dragon, Peter made his way to his horse and mounted. Aaron and Meldrin followed his lead and mounted their horses as well. Aaron tied Jack's horse to his and took up a position behind Peter. When they were ready, Peter called to Vin. "We're leaving."

Reluctantly, she moved towards her steed. As she prepared to mount, she called back to Jack, "Be careful with him. He's just a child."

Jack grinned and said, "Don't you worry, I'll take care of him. You'll hear all about it in Thwardscall." He waved goodbye as if to help her leave.

Vin turned to Peter. "Can we trust him. Will he really take him back?"

"I don't know but I really don't have time to care. The dragon is of no consequence as long as it doesn't get in our way. We need to get to Phinn as soon as possible."

"But what about Quinx? He's just a—"

"It's just another distraction. Keep focused on the quest. If you don't want to continue, you can stay with Jack and accompany him back to Helexpa. We're moving on." With that, Peter spurred his horse forward saying, "Meldrin, get us to Phinn."

"Wait, I want to . . . we should . . . oh . . . wait." Before Peter's horse was over the next hill, Vin was riding after the party. She looked back once to watch what Jack was doing. Before Quinx had moved from his resting spot, the party had moved on over several hills and the dragon's cave was long gone. As they rode, Peter could tell Vin was displeased with him by her pouting face and lack of conversation. She moved forward passed him and began a conversation with Meldrin. Since there was nothing he could do about it, he just let her go.

Before long, Aaron built up enough confidence to speak to Peter. In a timid voice he said, "I'm sorry about everything. I guess . . . I'm not, well, ready yet."

"Don't be sorry. You're alive and in one piece."

"Yeah, but, I . . . I don't even remember what happened. Everything's a blur. I'm confused about everything. I even think I remember seeing a dragon in that cave—a dragon!" He shook his head in disbelief and then continued. "I've always dreamed of wielding one of Max Konicker's axes and when I do, look what happens. I'll never be a great warrior like him or you. Why did Redlin even give it to me? I'm not worthy of having anything like Bloodlust. Why me?"

"So you could learn about magic for yourself." Peter thought to himself, "Now the lessons begin. If this boy's to be mine, I best get started with him." In a proud and praising voice, he said, "You did well today."

Aaron's face brightened at this unexpected compliment. "I did?"

"Yes, especially considering that you survived Bloodlust. Many lesser men would have been killed just trying to wield it." Peter put particular emphasis in his voice as he added, "Oh, and forget about the dragon. It must have been a remnant of your battle rage. You know, brought on by Bloodlust. The important thing now is for you to learn from this encounter."

"I will." Aaron said with supreme confidence. After a moments pause to think, he added, "Learn what exactly?"

"To deal with power. Anyone can wield an ax, or have gold, or be a ruler. The trick is to do it well and wisely. Magic is one of the most powerful things that you can ever possess. More than a kingdom or treasure, it corrupts you at the deepest levels—especially if you're weak or unprepared. You've survived and can learn from the experience. Next time, you'll have more control."

"If there ever is a next time."

"There will be. Whether you're battling with Bloodlust or faced with some other decision, remember to think. Always stay in control. Keep your eyes open and your wits about you, so you know what's going on."

"How can I do that? I mean practice it?"

"You can't. It comes from experience. It's not like training with a weapon . . . it's all experience. I'll work with you in Phinn."

Aaron's face showed his anxiousness and impatience to learn. "How long until we're there?"

Peter raised his hand and pointed with his index finger at a light in the valley ahead of them to the north. "That's Phinn—Redlin's capital city. We should be there in less than an hour." Aaron looked in the direction he had pointed. "We're coming out of the pass now. Meldrin will leave us soon. Then we'll ride into the city where we'll spend the night."

Aaron could make out very little as dusk approached and the light ran away from the valley floor. Even in the dim light he could not miss the huge, well-lit coliseum that stood many stories above all the other structures in the city. As he stared, he asked, "Is that the pit?"

Peter smiled, saying, "Yes, that's the Grand Coliseum. Isn't it impressive? It never ceases to amaze me."

Aaron could not contain his excitement as the realization of where he was began to fully hit him. "Is there a pit battle scheduled? Can we go inside? Is the city really magical? Do you think they'll have anything that once might have belonged to Max Konicker?"

Peter cut him off sharply by raising his hand to gesture for Aaron to stop. "Don't worry about all that. Try to keep quiet when we're in public. Stay alert and study the things around you. I'll answer all your questions when the time's right and we're in private."

"Yes sir." Aaron answered respectfully. For the first time, he really felt like he had a purpose. He was not just pretending to be important or in control. It was as if Cragmore was teaching him again.

Meldrin raised his hand as he pulled his horse to a halt. "This is as far as I go. The rest of the journey to Phinn is easy. Just head up the valley and you'll find what you're looking for."

Peter said in a cordial and sincere tone, "Thank you for your services. Safe journey my friend."

Vin added, "Yes, thank you for sharing your story with me. Be safe."

Meldrin turned his horse along a trail that none other than he could see in the failing light of dusk. As he rode off, he said, "May you find your quest a fruitful one. Good luck." With that, he rode off leaving the three adventurers to find their way to Phinn.

CHAPTER 15

Jeremy shifted in his saddle as he rode in what he hoped was the correct direction. Part of his uneasiness was due to his uncertainty but most was directly related to being with Twig. This was the first time he had really been alone with her. Though he worked hard to hide his thoughts, his mind raced. "Why am I so nervous? I've been close to her before. We've eaten at the same table. I've watched her work at chores, practice her magic . . . do lots of things. This is no different. What am I saying? This is totally different. We're adventuring together. We're alone and the people who are supposed to lead us are unconscious or dead." He let out a long breath while shaking his head.

At the same time, Twig's mind was busy as well. "What are we going to do if the others don't wake up? I don't know If we can do this alone. Jeremy is being so strong, but I don't know If I can or even should make him take me to Thwardscall . . . then further. But I do like having him near." Jeremy's sigh broke her from her thoughts. She asked, "What's wrong . . . are you worried?"

He was startled by her voice. He blurted out, "Yes master . . . ahhhh, it's nothing."

"Master? Why do you say it like that? I'm not your master."

"Master Permillion left me in your charge. He said to treat you like my master."

A slight blush reddened her cheeks. In a flustered and uncomfortable voice, she said, "Well, let's put an end to that right now. I'm not your master. I've done nothing to earn that title and don't deserve it. Besides, we're . . . well, equals and friends, I hope."

This time he blushed. "I don't know about equals, but I'd love to be friends."

She half-smiled in an awkward way she hoped he could not see. "At least friends and maybe more but why do you say we're not equals?" Her head shook involuntarily as the question left her lips.

"Ehum em, ah well, I've watched you practice. You're a master of magic . . . of fighting . . . of so many things. I'm just a stable-hand."

In a modest tone, she said, "Is that all? You just need to practice and you could be as good as me in no time. I've seen you ride and shoot that bow."

He shook his head. "I was there when you arrived at Permillion's house. You're a princess. You're just better than me."

For the first time in a long time, Twig saw herself in a different light. All the years she had spent with Androthy, she was surrounded by people who treated her like an apprentice or a servant not a princess, a warrior, or a magician. Her master had tried to protect her from the enemies of her family and those who would be fearful or jealous of her magic.

Leading her horse up next to Jeremy's, she put her hand on his elbow, and pulled her horse to a stop. As he felt the pressure of her hand, he halted his steed as well. His head turned and their eyes met. Her voice was filled with honesty and caring that even magic could not rival. "I might be many things, but I'm not better than you. I watched you too. I always wondered why you rarely spoke to me. I thought I was doing something wrong. I was always so busy but I . . . I never looked down on you. You have to believe that. I would have made time, if I knew." Her words trailed off as she heard a noise from the horses that trailed behind.

Jeremy's mind was overwhelmed with thoughts and feelings like a rowboat caught in a hurricane. He tried to say something but his thoughts did not translate into words. "I've spent ten years watching . . . wasting time. We could have been . . . I should have . . . oh."

He was so distracted, he did not hear the noise or register the fact that Shane had begun to speak. "What the . . . where am I?

What's going on?" Shane asked as he reached up and rubbed the side of his head where he had been clubbed. As he shifted his weight, he slid down off the back of the horse and hit the ground with a thud. Twig dismounted and tugged at Jeremy to break him from his thoughts. Though surrounded by trees, the faint orange glow of sunset still hung over the barely visible edge of the sky. In the dim light, it was difficult for them to see how Shane had landed as they made their way to his side.

Both Twig and Jeremy said with relief, "Oh, you're awake."

Jeremy fell silent, letting Twig continue. "The guar knocked you out. We tried to wake you but it was no use, so we started moving. We're on the way to Overton, I hope. I think we're headed the right way. Jeremy has been leading us."

Groggily, he said, "Yeah, this is . . . it's real good . . . it's good . . . we're headed the right way. To Overton . . . yeah." He shook his head to clear it. "Just give me a minute to compose myself." Shane put his hands over his face, closed his eyes, and drew in a breath through his fingers. Exhaling as he ran his hands around the side of his face, he put his fingertips on his temples. "From the looks of it, Overton is just a short way ahead. We're real close. You two did a good job." Both his companions smiled widely at this praise like school children receiving a gold star. "Where's Gallis?"

Jeremy pointed at Gallis' body draped over the horse as Twig said, "Right there."

"What happened?"

"The guar slashed him and knocked him out. Just like you. We didn't know what to do so—"

"He's been cut!" A sound of terror filled Shane's voice as he ran to examine Gallis' body. "Make a light and bring it here."

Jeremy rummaged through his equipment trying to locate a lantern and a tinderbox. "I'll try and find something."

While bending down, Twig said, "Don't bother." She picked up a rock that fit in the palm of her hand and closed her fingers around it. After squeezing it for a second, she opened her hand

and the rock was glowing with a radiant white light that drove back the dark in a broad circle that extended out beyond the trees in all directions. "Will this work?" she asked as she handed the glowing rock to Shane.

"Perfect. Hold it near the wounds so I can see them." She complied. Jeremy came over to watch as Shane probed each of the slashes working like a detective looking for some unseen sign of a killer hiding in the shadows. After examining each wound thoroughly, he stepped back from the body saying, "We have a problem."

"What is it? What's wrong with him?" Twig asked with panic in her voice. She stepped closer to Shane to press for the answers.

"I can't be sure how it works with half-elves—especially magicians—but if a guar draws blood, it's only a matter of time."

"Before what?" she asked impatiently.

"He goes crazy and tries to kill himself or us."

With a mix of fear and desperation in her voice, she said, "Can't we do something?"

"Well, unfortunately, the one who would know best is Gallis, and he's not talking right now."

Twig looked around like a frightened mouse that senses a nearby snake. "We can't let him die. We need him. I need him. We have to do something."

Shane responded calmly, "There's not much we can do. Hopefully, he'll come around before we get to Overton. Otherwise, well, we'll have to finish the job the guar started."

"You mean kill him?"

"Yes. That's exactly what I mean. We have no choice. Our quest lies beyond Thwardscall. We can't allow anyone to jeopardize that mission."

"But we can't just . . . he's important too."

Through the entire conversation, Jeremy stood silently watching and listening. Now he broke in to help Twig save her friend. "Why don't you take him back to Redlin's palace? The healers there can fix him up I'm sure. It's less than a day's ride. Once you've gotten him back, you can meet us on the road to Thwardscall. How hard can it be to find a city?"

Shane thought about the idea for a moment and said, "If that's what you both want to do, I can try it. Thwardscall isn't hard to find from here but you'll have to fend for yourselves on the road. Do you think you'll be able to handle it without me?"

Twig answered quickly, "Yes, of course. That's the only answer. We'll be fine. I've traveled. I can handle it."

Jeremy was slower and more deliberate with his answer. "Honestly no, I can't say I think we'll be safe or even handle ourselves in a fight. But we can't let him die. We'll have to do it. Obviously, we weren't safe with the two of you with us either. We might be less conspicuous if its just the two of us."

"You might be right. We'll have to give it a try. I'll tell you how to get on the road to Thwardscall and what to look out for. I should be able to catch up with you in two or three days. The journey isn't really that tough."

"Except for the guar and other monsters following us." Twig added to finish what he was saying.

Jeremy ignored her comment hoping not to undermine his dwindling self-confidence. "Just tell me where to go and what to look for. We'll deal with any problems when and if we run into them."

Shane smiled at the assertiveness in Jeremy's voice. "Sit here. I want both of you to hear this. Remember what I tell you. All of it's important." Shane motioned for the two of them to sit side-by-side in front of him. They obeyed his orders as he sat down across from them, cleared off a flat spot, and began to draw in the dirt. When he was finished, there was a crude drawing of something resembling an hourglass with a rock caught in the neck. Twig and Jeremy leaned in to study the sketch as Shane spoke. "These lines represent the mountains on either side of this valley. The Terrillian on east side and the Blackspine on the west." Shane ran his finger along the sides of the hourglass and watched as his two students nodded their heads in unison. "I'll do everything from your perspective as if you're walking up the valley heading north. Near the bottom is Helexpa—where we came from." He dropped a stone at the bottom of the drawing nearest Twig. Running his fingers up the left side of the sketch, he said, "This is how we came . . . along the edge of the Blackspine." He dropped a rock on the edge. "Overton is here, near a break that can be crossed with little trouble most of the year." Moving his finger to the block in the neck of the hourglass, he continued, "This is Thwardscall. It's on a plateau at the narrow opening to the Valley of the Dragons. If you follow the mountains natural curve, you'll run right into the city. It's at the closest point between the two ranges." He paused to gauge the looks on his two pupils. "You have enough food and water so that you can head around Overton without stopping. Go to the east a few miles then head north until you come to the foot of the Blackspine. Once you see the mountains, just follow them north and east until you're in Thwardscall." He traced the path in the dirt. "Stay away from towns and caravans as much as possible. The less people who know that you're traveling the better. More importantly, be suspicious of those you meet—Morgan's agents are everywhere."

Jeremy spoke first. "It sounds like an easy thing to find the city but can we make it there?"

Twig added, "Won't we be conspicuous? Morgan's mercenaries will be able to find us easily."

"Not really. Thwardscall is a good place for travelers and traders to blend in and get lost. Getting there will be the problem. Just keep a low profile and avoid trouble."

Jeremy asked, "How do we do that? It always seems to find us these days."

"Here's the rules. Remember them well. Avoid contact—even small towns can give you problems. If people give you trouble, leave. Don't let anyone pick a fight with you . . . run away." Pointing to Twig, he said, "Most of all, don't use magic. It's not commonplace in the outside world, especially in small towns. If you do anything or show anyone that you have magic, they'll kill you for it . . . out of greed, or jealousy, or just stupidity. Be careful and realize you can't trust anyone except one another." Both nodded as they studied the map. Shane put his hand on Twig's shoulder. "You're in charge until I join you again. Is there anything I can give you before I leave? Your supplies should last but, well, I have no idea what Gallis might have with him that might help. I overheard you talking abut lessons and books and magic things. Is there something of his you can use?"

For the first time, she realized that her training might come to an end before it was finished. With Permillion dead and Gallis on his way there, she would have no one who could teach her what she needed to know. Concern tinged with anxiety colored her voice as she said, "Let me see if he has his books of magic with him. If I'm lucky that will be enough for me to finish my training."

Shane gestured for her to check Gallis' horse. She got up and searched through the packed items. Even as she opened the first saddle bag, she jumped back with a scream. "Ahhh! Oh no!"

Shane leapt to his feet and twisted his wrist to trigger his dagger. It was not there. "What the hell? Where's my knife?" Though momentarily halted, Shane recovered from the surprise, grabbed Gallis from off the horse, and tossed him to the ground. The body fell limply like a dishrag, hit the ground face-down, and did not move.

Meanwhile, Jeremy scrambled to his feet as well and was a few steps behind Shane. He ran to Twig's side and put himself between her and Gallis' horse, trying to protect her. "Is he awake? Is he insane? Is he going to kill us? Stop him."

Twig yelled, "No! Stop! It's just a snake . . . his familiar's in the bag. He's still unconscious. It's okay."

Shane approached Gallis carefully. Using his left foot, he flipped the body over. He was still knocked out. Shane checked the half-elf's pulse to make sure the fall had not killed him accidentally. "He's still alive and unconscious. Good work. Remember, trust nothing." He picked up the body, put it back on the horse, and lashed it down with ropes. When he was finished, Gallis looked like a prized deer being brought back as a trophy. Once he was finished, Shane said, "What happened to my knife?"

Jeremy looked perplexed as Twig thought for a moment. She said, "I guess we left it behind. Hope that's not a problem."

A grave look of concern came over his face. "Never leave anything behind that can identify you. Take everything and leave no one alive."

"But what—"

"Leave no one and nothing behind to let them know you were there. If I can't go back and get it, they'll have my scent and we'll never lose them. I don't even know if you killed them all."

"They were dead. I'm sure of it."

"Did you cut off their heads? Cut them into little pieces? Burn them . . . disintegrate them . . . utterly destroy them? They're magical creatures, not easily destroyed or deterred."

"I'm sorry."

"Don't be, but learn from the mistake. Take no chances. Now get the things you need and move on. I need to get back even quicker now." He mounted his horse and led it up next to Gallis. "Hand me the reins so I can get going."

Twig said, "All right. I'll just be a minute." With dexterous fingers, she searched through the items on the back of the horse like a thief.

While she worked, Jeremy took the reins and handed them to Shane. "Is there anything else we should know? I can find Overton and even Thwardscall . . . I think."

"Be careful of Morgan's minions. The further north you go, the greater the chance you'll run into his men. It's not just guar you'll have to worry about."

"What else?"

"Orcs, knarves, stalkers, and a host of other creatures . . . not to mention humans . . . probably the worst." Jeremy nodded but had no clear idea of what he was being told. All this was new to him. "Just remember to stay with Twig and run away. If you can, make up a story about the two of you . . . you know . . . pilgrims headed to a festival . . . going to find family . . . just married, searching for a lost friend, whatever."

Jeremy grinned at these thoughts. He looked over at Twig who was just finishing her examination. After searching, she had found two books she thought would be useful. Tucking them under her arm, she said, "You can go. I have what I need." She placed the things she took in her saddle bag and mounted her horse holding the glowing rock in her hand so she could see. As she moved to join Jeremy, Shane turned his horse back towards Helexpa.

Extending his hand towards the two, he said, "Good luck. I'll get back as soon as I can. Keep going to Thwardscall. The others will meet you there."

The two young adventurers waved to their guide as he rode off with Gallis' horse trailing behind. Jeremy put his hand on Twig's forearm and said, "Now we're on our own. I'll do my best to get us to Thwardscall safely but . . . I'll . . . I'm gonna need your help."

She smiled as she put her other hand on top of his. She giggled with nervousness, as she said, "Just, uhm . . . tell me what you need. I'll ah, uhm . . . do what you want."

"First, well, I think we should get to Thwardscall . . . I mean as fast as possible. Avoid Overton all together and other towns too."

Brightness filled her eyes as she looked at her traveling companion with confidence and assurance. "That's a good idea. As long as . . . well, you can lead. I'll follow, but I'm not good in the woods . . . on a horse I mean."

"Give me the glowing . . . the rock, ahh . . . the light. Try and follow along closely. If you get tired or too far back, call and let me know. We'll stop." She handed the stone to him. Once he had it securely in his hand, he headed due north as best as he could determine.

Night fell quickly. The blackness joined with the ever increasing thickness of the bramble and underbrush to slow their progress. Off to the west, they could see the lights from Overton. Though not a large city, its position on the side of the mountain made the lights of its fires visible. The forest soon thinned as the valley floor became the grazing lands and farms of the inhabitants of the nearby city. The two travelers rode for several hours until the lights of Overton were gone and nothing but the oppressive darkness of a night sky absent of stars remained. As they rode silently, both strained to keep their eyes open. When both were too tired to continue, Twig called to Jeremy, "We need to stop. I can't focus anymore."

Jeremy scanned the surrounding area for a place to set up camp. He pointed to a stand of oak trees saying, "Let's go there and set up the tent . . . then, ah, well we'll need to sleep . . . together . . . to be safe."

"Yeah . . . you're right. We'll have to stay close . . . I mean sleep with one another . . . I mean, near one another." Blushing, she changed the subject awkwardly, saying, "We'd better hurry. The light's magic's fading."

Both dismounted and set to work erecting a tent and gathering wood for a fire. By the time the light had completely faded from the rock, the camp was ready and they prepared to light the fire. As Jeremy searched for a tinder box amongst the supplies, Twig said, "Wait a minute . . . maybe we shouldn't light it."

"But it'll be cold tonight."

"Better to be cold than dead. The fire will attract all sorts of things. It's better if we just stay close. We'll keep each other warm."

He hoped that she could not see his smile in the dark. "If you think it best . . . Shane did put you in charge."

The darkness made it difficult for him to see anything. With some effort he made his way back to her and the tent. Neither removed any clothing as they slid under their blankets and found the warmth of each other. Though the first few minutes were as uncomfortable as a blind date, they soon relaxed. The exhaustion of this first day of traveling on the quest took its toll and soon both were fast asleep. Even so, neither slept deeply or soundly. Every noise had the potential to be one of Morgan's men hunting for them or some other disaster waiting to befall them. Their first night together was one they would remember for reasons they wish they could forget.

CHAPTER 16

Vin, Peter, and Aaron were all lost in their own thoughts as they slowly descended into the valley that held Phinn. Dusk quickly approached as they turned towards the city a mile or so to the north. None of the three travelers seemed to notice the others until Vin shattered the silence. She wheeled her horse in a way to stop the progress of Peter's mount. In a determined tone that shocked both of her companions, she said, "I think it's time to find out a little more about what's happening, wanderer. You've kept far too many secrets from us already, Peter Zorich of the family Zorich. I know we've only been together for a few days but . . . well, that's usually more than enough time for me. I usually find out everything I want to know and more in that time or at least something. I've tried to be pleasant, cordial, servile, charming, magical, and even seductive. Nothing has worked so, now I'll just be blunt. I'm an equal partner in this expedition. I want to know what's going on. It's fine to keep your apprentice in the dark but not me." Thrusting her pointer finger at Peter, she continued, "You need to answer me some questions now."

Peter shook his head, acknowledging the inevitability of this moment. It seemed the time had come for him to reveal some of the many secrets he carried. "What did you want to know?" he asked innocently.

Aaron walked his horse up close to the others so he could hear the conversation more clearly. As they began, his first thoughts were, "She tried to seduce him?" followed by, "Am I his apprentice? I guess I am." This realization made him feel better. Then, as the rest of the conversation sank in, he thought, "He's got secrets, what secrets?" While the two spoke, he became aware of just how much he had been missing. Focusing his attention on the conversation at hand, he worked hard not to miss anything.

Vin began like a mother interrogating a child who came home late. "First, where are we headed once we've entered the city and what are we looking for?" She paused for a moment and then continued, "And who or should I say what are you? I've never met a man anything like you. You're no ordinary sell-sword or adventurer. There's much too much to you Peter Zorich."

Peter raised his hand as if to stop the flood of questions that was pouring in his direction. "One thing at a time. I'll answer all your questions—just give me a chance. Let's keep riding; we'll talk while we go." Peter put the tip of his boot into his horse's side, moving it forward between Vin and Aaron's horses. Aaron brought his steed up next to Peter's and kept pace.

Peter's half-dismissal of her questions perturbed Vin. "Urrrr," she groaned while moving her horse up to flank Peter. "Fine. Where are we going?"

"Stay calm."

This irritated her even more. "Don't patronize me."

Peter exhaled a long breath and said, "I'm sorry. I'm just trying to tell you what you want to know without your getting more angry. I honestly don't know that much more than you. I do have to be careful for your own sake and the sake of the quest."

Vin's body relaxed as she sensed he was being truthful. "You're right. I'm sorry. Go on."

"We've got rooms reserved at the Dragon's Head Inn. It's just across from the Grand Coliseum." Aaron's face lit up though he said nothing. "We're to meet a man named Vanness. He's ahhh, how can I put this?"

"Thief," Vin finished his statement. "I've heard of him."

"In Redlin's territory, people call themselves other things but you're right, he's a thief."

"Why are we meeting him?" she asked with honest curiosity. Her tone moved away from interrogation towards conversation.

"He has some of the items we need and knows where the others can be found. Once we've finished with him, our quest will be much clearer."

Aaron spoke up. "At least we'll know what we have to do and who we'll have to deal with."

"Exactly," Peter said approvingly. "So until then, I don't know much more than either of you."

Vin smiled and nodded her head thoughtfully. "Okay, but I still want to know more about you." Raising her index finger, she shook it as she pointed it at Peter.

He laughed a breathy knowing laugh. "Ha hahha . . . I'm just an ordinary man, on a quest. An experienced adventurer perhaps. Nothing that special."

"No ordinary men can walk the halls of Helexpa like it's his second home. Not even most experienced adventurers know what you know. And few, if any, wield weapons like you carry."

"So I've been around. So I know Redlin."

"And you can resist my magic and know about things few other humans have ever heard of . . . who . . . what, are you?" Vin asked forcefully.

Aaron's face contorted as he tried to put together what Vin was getting at. For the first time, he began to see how these many obvious clues fit together. He thought to himself, "I'm not sure what she's getting at but there's something there. I've been so preoccupied. It never crossed my mind to question him. Redlin said to follow him . . . so I did."

Peter's answer came slowly and with some reluctance. "I am Peter Zorich of the family Zorich. Named as the keeper of the Swords of Justice—Justifier and Vindicator. The ultimate judge and executioner. Long ago they were called Geminarex, the twin blades of truth and justice. For ten centuries we have used them to protect the weak and oppressed. We wield the Geminarex and defend that ideal with our lives." Understanding filled Vin's eyes as he spoke. Aaron was a blank. "I did not ask for, nor want, the responsibility. I have been given it by virtue of my lineage. When the last of my bloodline died, the swords and all that goes with them fell to me."

"What does that all mean?" Aaron asked naively.

"More than you or I will ever know. Just listen to what he says and learn anything you can boy. You'll never have a better teacher," she said with a tinge of awestruck admiration in her voice.

"Now you understand why I was chosen . . . why your magic doesn't work . . . why I am the way I am." Peter turned to Vin so she could see the coldness in his eyes. "My whole life was spent preparing for the weight of this duty and praying I would never have to carry it."

"How long have you had the swords?"

"Just over two years. As soon as I was given them, I headed into the northlands . . . to find Morgan before any of this began . . . before he became so powerful."

"Who else knows who you are and what you know?"

"None save Redlin, Permillion, and a few other of the ancient races."

Thousands of questions filled Aaron's head and raced to the front of his mind, all hoping to be asked first. Before any could be voiced, Peter raised his hand for quiet as he turned his attention to the road ahead. Three figures approached, each carrying a lantern.

Before any could be seen clearly, the one in front called out, "Good day travelers. Let us lead you home."

Peter responded immediately, "Only if home is warm and inviting."

"It is always that way for friends."

"Then lead us home." The figures stepped towards the riders. As they moved, Peter said to his companions, "These are Redlin's men. They'll take us into town. I'll go with them to the stables while you two go to the inn. I'll be right behind you." He dismounted and approached the figures.

Aaron and Vin dismounted and stepped off to one side. Peter gestured at them and one of the figures moved towards them with his lantern leading the way. Once the figure was close enough, they could see that most of their bulk could be attributed to a heavy brown cloak. Little more than the person's eyes were visible.

Soundlessly, the figure gestured for them to follow. Without waiting for a response, it moved off towards the lights of the town.

Peter said, "Go with her. She'll take you to the inn. Don't worry . . . they're here to help."

"What of our supplies? Our things?"

"Leave them with the horses. I'll have them brought to the room."

Both said "All right," at the same time and headed off in the direction that the woman had gone. After a long walk, they had come into the city of Phinn. The dirt path they had started on became a cobblestone road wide enough for two wagons to pass one another in both directions. Magical lights adorned the buildings and lit the streets so that the lantern became unnecessary. The streets were lined with shops and buildings of all types. Pedestrians filled both the sidewalks and streets.

As they walked, Aaron could see the top of the Grand Coliseum in the distance grow larger as it came closer. It drew him like a fragrant flower draws a bee. While he walked, he thought of the many stories of Konicker fighting in the pit. Even through the distraction of his recollection, he remembered the piece of advice Peter had given him. As he walked, he focused his attention on the things around and observed as much as he could without losing his guide or companion. His senses were delighted by the experience that was Phinn. Before he knew it, they were at the Dragon Head Inn and the guide had moved off into the crowded night.

Vin took him by the hand saying, "Let's go in and get something to eat. Peter will be along soon. We can talk while we wait. You can tell me your story."

The smooth cool feel of her skin coupled with her melodic tones gathered up his attention and drew him along as she moved into the barroom of the Inn. Even though he followed her like a puppy, he was still able to soak in the things he observed. The room he was led into could have been found in any tavern or Inn throughout the world. Vin sat them at a table amongst many in the dining area. Signs pointed towards other private rooms where gambling, drinking, or other forms of amusement could be found. As he sat and looked around, Aaron noted that the room was ornately decorated with gold and silver. He was immediately struck by the diversity of races and classes this one room held. Elves, dwarves and humans were all represented by both servers and patrons. Many other races he could not identify at first glance mingled in and amongst the rooms he could see. All of this paled in comparison to the most striking decoration the room had to offer. Over the largest bar, which consumed the wall behind him, he saw the giant yellow head of what he assumed was a dragon. He asked Vin, "Is that really a dragon's head? Is that why it's called the Dragon Head Inn? How did it get here?"

She smiled at his enthusiasm and naïveté. "Yes, it's a dragon's head. And yes, that's why this is called the Dragon Head Inn. It's here because Borac McPhinn, with the help of Redlin and some others, killed it."

"McPhinn was responsible for building the pit and much of the city, right?"

"That's right. But enough of that. Tell me about yourself. I know a little about you already. You're interested in the exploits of Max Konicker. You're somehow connected to Redlin. I'd like to hear about that. Just the fact that you're on this quest means you have things to share . . . things to talk about . . . a story to tell."

As Aaron was about to answer, the serving maid walked up next to him. She was a shapely human girl of no more than seventeen, with long blond hair and ice-blue eyes. "Hello, my name is Daria. What can I bring you?" Though her words were addressed to both people seated at the table, her attention was completely focused on Aaron.

He liked the attention and grinned confidently. "Bring me a leg of mutton and some ale." His voice was filled with assertiveness.

Daria turned to Vin with a questioning look in her eyes. "And for you?"

Vin said, "A peasant . . . I mean a pheasant, if you have it and some elven wine. Nothing less than 500 years though." She smiled just enough to show her teeth.

Daria returned the smile saying, "Of course. The food will be a few minutes. I'll bring your drinks right over."

Vin said, "No . . . you can bring them with the food. We want some time alone. Isn't that right, Aaron?"

"Well . . . I guess. Yeah sure . . . that's fine with me." He was not really paying attention to the conversation. Everything going on in the bar was much more interesting to him. He thought to himself, "Max Konicker has eaten here. He might have sat in this very seat and drank ale just like I'm going to. The pit is only a few feet away. I can't believe it."

The gentle touch of Daria's warm hand snapped him back to the conversation at the table. "I'll be back soon. Don't you go anywhere."

Suave was not something Aaron had ever mastered. He laughed stupidly. "I won't." He watched her move across the room back to the bar.

"What were we saying?" Vin asked trying to lead him back to the conversation. "That's right, you were going to tell me something about your exciting life."

As she spoke to him, he began to feel like a spotlight was focused on him and he liked it. "Now that you mention it, I do have some very interesting stories to share. Most of my life has been spent studying the use of weapons. I've been training for the quest . . . though I didn't know it."

Before he could finish, Vin raised her finger and put it across his lips to tell him to stop. "Shhh, it'll have to wait until later. I'm sure there are many things you can reveal to me in my room tonight." She brushed her fingers along his cheek softly and then drew them off his face over his chin. "I can't wait."

Aaron was lost in the enjoyment of the moment as Peter's voice intruded. "Good, I see you made it safely. Our things are upstairs. Aaron—you're staying with me. Vin, you're room's across the hall. Here's your keys." He extended a hand holding a large brass key towards each of them. Each took the key and put it on their belt. As they did this, Peter continued, "We should move to that table over there." He pointed at a table for eight in the corner. A slender but muscular human sat there by himself eating a meal large enough for five or six hungry humans. Peter started to leave, saying, "Follow me; let's go."

Aaron stood and followed behind Peter dutifully. His first impression of the man was that he seemed far too average to be of any importance or significance compared to the others in this room. Vin looked very annoyed by Peter's disregard for her, but followed indignantly. As they walked, Aaron asked with hopeful anticipation, "Are we going to kick him out and take the table. Stake our claim. Set up our ground. Make our presence known? He looks like a good target . . . not too tough."

Peter stopped abruptly enough so that Aaron walked into his back. He turned to the boy and stared in his eyes for several seconds. Though he was several inches shorter, Peter's closeness and sheer weight of presence made Aaron feel small. Placing his hands on either side of Aaron's neck, Peter said, "We need to have a long talk. What did I tell you to do when we came to town?"

Aaron could feel the sweat gather on his forehead and back. This was a test he had not prepared for. "Ahh, uhm . . . well . . . ehhem . . . you said . . . you said to . . . to watch and listen and basically, watch stuff."

Peter patted Aaron's left cheek and dropped his hands to his side. "Very good. Now how can you be watching if you're making your presence known? Then you'd be the one being watched, right?"

Aaron nodded dumbly as he said hesitantly and with a tinge of resignation in his voice, "Yes, that's right."

"Good. Now I'll give you another lesson. Use your powers of observation to tell me why you shouldn't kick that man out of his seat even if you needed to sit there."

Aaron looked long and hard at the man as he thought, "He's nothing special. He doesn't seem to have any weapons or anything I should be afraid of. He's eating too much. That's it! He has too much food. He must be waiting for a big bunch of people. Who knows what they'd be like." Clearing his throat, he said confidently, "I shouldn't kick him out because of what his friends might do. Even though he's no threat . . . small and unarmed, he has food enough for six. Also, he's sitting at a table for eight. Since I can't tell who he might be waiting for, I shouldn't be too quick to attack."

Peter smiled semi-approvingly. "At least that's a start. Remember, never underestimate someone. First of all, he's not unarmed. Second of all, his friends are already here, all around the bar. You can see him make eye contact with them every now and again. But you are right about him waiting for someone—he's waiting for us. That's the man we've come to meet. That food's ours."

Aaron dropped his head. "Oh . . . so that's why."

"Don't be upset. You did well enough but you still have much to learn. Just keep watching. Now go introduce yourself to Mr. Vanness and tell him who you are. Don't say anything about the rest of us."

Aaron smiled at the fact he had been given this important task. Turning towards the table, he stood tall and approached as confidently as he could. Once at the edge of the table, he said, "Hello sir. Would you happen to be a Mr. Vanness?"

"Why do you ask boy?" The man said in a guarded and evasive way.

"My party and I are looking for him. We have business with the man."

"Where's the rest of your party? You can't be all there is."

"Some are right behind me . . . others are around." Aaron thought that this was a clever answer and smiled.

Peter stepped up behind him and said in a friendly way, "Hello Vanness. We're going to join you for dinner. I hope you don't mind, thanks." Peter sat in a seat next to Vanness and gestured for Aaron to take the seat on the other side. As the boy moved to the chair, Vin stepped to the other side of the table and took a seat as well.

Vanness said, "Do I know you?"

Peter extended his hand and said, "I'm a friend of Redlin's. His agents have supposedly arranged things with you. I hope I'm not mistaken."

The man extended his arm and shook Peter's hand. Turning to look at the others, he said sarcastically, "Please make yourselves comfortable. I'm Vanness and I have what you need."

As Vin took her seat, she placed her journal on the table and opened it in preparation for writing. As she took up her pen, she said, "And what exactly do you have for us?"

"Just like a scribe," Vanness said condescendingly. "Ask your friends if you want information for free . . . come up with some gold if you want it from me . . . Azurine." Vin was startled by the response but before she could retort, he added, "I don't blame them for keeping things from you. Your kind are always trouble. Always watching; never getting involved." He turned to Peter to ask, "Where's the rest of your party? I thought there'd be at least one more warrior, a priest or healer and maybe even a sorcerer. A boy, no matter how big he is, and a scribe don't really cut it in the pit. You should know that."

Peter waved his hand as if to brush away smoke. "Don't be concerned about that. We can handle ourselves." He reached into a pocket in his belt and drew out the ring he had removed from the mind warrior in Hamiltanville. Showing it to Vanness, he said, "Just tell me if you have the items or know where I can get them."

Vanness snatched the ring from his hands and slipped it into his pocket. As he did this, Aaron grabbed at his other hand to stop him but missed. In a flash, Vanness had a dagger at the boy's throat. "Never lunge at someone, boy, unless you're prepared to fight. If you were a little faster, you might be dead right now."

Peter said, "Put that away. I'd hate to have to kill you before we finished our business. You can see for yourself he's just an apprentice. Leave him be and let's get this done." The cold sincerity of his tone caught the man's attention and let him know Peter was not someone to trifle with.

Vanness put the dagger down on the table. "First, I could only procure one of the items . . . the things you wanted were hot. It'll be in your room tomorrow morning. As for the rest of what you wanted . . . five powerful people have taken all the things you asked for. You'll have to fight for them or steal them yourself. I've arranged for you to be in the pit-battle tomorrow. If you win, you'll have everything you need. They're winner takes all, fight to the death matches. There's three of them back-to-back-to-back. I hope you brought a third along with you and a healer too. You'll need them." He smiled a nasty smug smile.

"Don't worry. How do we get on the rosters?"

Vanness dropped a leather pouch on the table. "Your guild cards, entrance fees, and other papers are in there. Just show up at the combatants' entrance of the Coliseum at first light. I've taken care of all the prep work—I assume you know the rest."

Peter shook his head 'yes.' "We can handle everything else. Are you sure the items will be in the Coliseum?"

"Absolutely—these fights are to the death. The winner of each is named a Pit Master and given the right to fight against the current Grand Master of the Coliseum."

"I understand. I'll deliver the rest of the payment in the stables later. Thanks for your help."

"It was a pleasure doing business with you." Vanness stood and gestured towards the table saying, "Please enjoy the food I ordered for you. It's all been paid for as part of your room. Enjoy." He nodded his head at all three to signify his goodbye, bowed, and left.

Once Vanness was gone, Peter began to eat hurriedly. He pointed to Aaron saying, "You'd better eat quickly and get to sleep. We've got a great deal to do before the battles tomorrow. I'll take care of all the preparations. You're going to have to fight in the pit. Are you ready?"

Aaron was shocked by the question. He had heard so much about the Grand Coliseum but never thought he would have the chance or the desire to ever actually enter it as a combatant. He said with some measure of confidence, "As long as you tell me what to do, I'll be ready."

Peter nodded approvingly. "I'll do my best to prepare you boy. After tomorrow, you'll be a man or the quest will be over for you."

"Don't worry about me. I won't quit," he said with a smile on his face.

Vin put her hand on his arm. Her voice was like that of a mother telling a young child about death as she said, "Aaron, you don't seem to understand. If you lose, you'll be dead."

Realization hit him all at once. His face became drawn and contemplative as his confidence left him. He spent the rest of the meal in silence thinking about what he should do while he ate what might be his last meal.

CHAPTER 17

Jeremy's sleep was restless. Sleeping in armor was new to him and not something to which he could easily adjust. Before the light of dawn was on the horizon, he was awake. After checking that Twig was safely asleep, he went outside the tent to stretch and take a breath of the morning air. He thought about what had already happened to him and what might be ahead. As he pondered his uncertain future, he felt the star around his neck shift.

After extracting the chain, he lifted it over his head and examined the star. The words on the back seemed to glow. Sitting with his back against a tree, he read them to himself. "Thrack . . . arrato . . . mambo, delivan . . . thrack, arrato . . . mambo, delivan . . . thrack, arrato, mambo, delivan." He put emphasis on different words and different parts of the words until he was sure he knew them. "Enough of that for now. What else can I do? I don't want to go anywhere and I can't make too much noise. I might wake Twig." As he looked around the small camp for another distraction, he saw Gallis' books. They were resting one atop the other just inside the entrance to the tent. He thought, "I wonder what's in them. She won't mind if I look, will she?"

Placing the star and its chain on the ground next to him, he leaned over and slowly edged closer to the books. With a finger on the binding and one on the pages of the bottom book, he slid them silently along the ground until they were out of the tent. Once safely in his possession, he picked them up and moved to a tree to examine them. He began by turning the leather-bound tomes over in his hands letting his fingers run up along their spine and other edges. They seemed like any of the others he had handled in his master's library. After a moment of debate and reservation, he opened the thicker of the two and began to read. The title read, as best as he could make it out, "Permillion Magic & Spell Casting." He leafed through the rest of the book making out what he could and letting the rest pass him by. Most of what he read, he recognized from watching lessons and seeing Twig and other apprentices practice. After an hour of browsing through the book, he decided, "This is a collection of beginning spells and exercises for young magicians." Though this book was interesting, he wanted to see what the other held. Closing the book carefully, he placed it gently on the ground as if it were a newborn.

The second book was much more interesting. Upon closer inspection, it was more well sealed than the first. Iron bands encircled it and it was enclosed by a riveted latch with no apparent keyhole. He recognized this tome as one from Permillion's private library which held the magician's most powerful and prized spells. After struggling with the problem of how to open the latch for several minutes, he muttered to himself, "Urr . . . I just want the thing to open. Open up. Come on." He tugged at the straps and fingered the clasp hoping to find some way to open it. All his attempts were unsuccessful. As he was about to give up, he saw Redlin's star resting in the dirt. Without any real thought, he picked it up, letting the chain fall around his arm. He brought one of the points of the star towards the clasp meaning to pry it off. As the tip of the star touched the latch, the lock sprung open with a click. Anxiously, he placed the star and accompanying chain in his lap. Once his hands were free of the amulet, he opened the book and read its title. "Momentous Magic of the Dragon Clan, by Elmo Patsy," was all he was able to decipher. The first pages read like a story. Though he had difficulty reading some of the words, he could make out enough to see that it was about the war amongst the eternal dragons.

"Help! Master no! Master, help me!" Twig cried in fear from inside the tent.

He flung the book to one side and stumbled towards the tent to see what was happening. In a desperate voice, he said, "Twig, what is it? Are you all right? What's wrong?" He dove into the tent prepared to face whatever had attacked her.

As soon as he entered, Twig threw her arms around his neck. In a frightened voice she pleaded, "Hold me. Don't ever leave me."

He could feel her shiver as he wrapped his arms around her and tried to console her, "I'm here. Don't worry, I'll always be here for you. I'll never leave you." They held one another for what seemed to him an instant and an eternity in the same heartbeat. Once she had calmed somewhat, he hesitantly asked her, "What happened?" with a hint of fear still in his voice.

"It was a dream . . . a nightmare. I saw those things, the guar, ripping the master to pieces. Then they shredded Gallis on their way to you and me. I woke up just as they were slashing me with their claws. It was awful." She shuttered. Pulling him close with a firm hug, she rested her head on his shoulder. She sniffled to hold back tears. "Please hold me. I'm so scared. It all just . . . I, I guess . . . it all just hit me. I feel so alone. Everyone I know and follow . . . my master . . . my teachers. They're gone—all gone." Jeremy could feel the tears trickle down her cheeks.

He tried to think of the perfect thing to say but he had little experience consoling anyone. "I'm here. They're not gone as long as you remember them. Be strong. Don't worry." All these things ran through his mind but seemed somehow wrong. He rubbed his hands gently across her back and said in a quiet consoling voice, "Shhhhh, don't' cry. It'll all work out." He ran his left hand up to the back of her head and began to stroke her hair. "I'll never leave you. We'll always be together."

Twig smiled and let her lips touch his neck. "Ahh . . . I like having you near," she said in a soft voice. His warmth and close-ness felt natural and good to her. "You make me feel . . . comfort-able . . . safe . . . like we're back at home, back with the master." He just enjoyed the moment saying nothing and hoping it would not end. As the first light of dawn lightened the sky, she drew in a deep breath and composed herself. "I want to get out of here. We should get going."

"Yes . . . of course." He resisted for a moment as she pulled away and then let her go. Being there for her had been all she needed to recover her strength.

"It's time to get back to the quest. We have a long way to go today," she said with an air of authority. "We should head straight through to Thwardscall with as little delay as possible." Softening her tone, she continued, "If you agree."

"Yes, that's, well, ahh . . . a good idea." He backed out of the tent saying with a smile, "I'll let you get ready while I tend to the horses."

She returned his smile with an awkward grin of her own. "Okay . . . be right out."

It only took a few minutes for Twig to get ready to ride. As Jeremy tended to the horses, she broke down the tent. Once she was finished, they worked together to repack everything aboard the steeds. Remembering Shane's advice, the two walked through the camp one last time to ensure nothing was left behind. As the looked around, Twig noticed Gallis' books lying on the ground. Jeremy's attention was quickly drawn to her as she pointed to them and called, "What's that?"

Realizing immediately what she was pointing at and, at the same time, remembering the amulet that must be with the two books, he rushed to pick them up. "Oh . . . sorry. Those are the books you took from Gallis. I was trying to read them." Bending down, he felt for the chain. "Here, let me get them for you. I probably shouldn't have even taken them. I'm sorry." He fumbled on the ground as if he were having trouble picking them up. She walked over towards him attempting to help. As his fingers touched the star, he wrapped the chain that held it into his palm and tried to pick it up unobtrusively. He handed her the simpler of the two books to distract her as she bent to get the other tome. Once her attention was elsewhere, he slipped the chain around his neck and tucked the star into his shirt. His heart raced and his mind was filled with the thought, "Please don't let her see or suspect. No one is to know I have this. Why did I ever take it off?"

Before he could berate himself anymore, Twig asked, "What's wrong?"

"Nothing . . . oh, well . . . I'm just embarrassed that I . . . I took the books and, read them." He dropped his eyes.

Stepping closer to him, she said, "Don't be embarrassed. I don't care if you read them. Actually, I'm surprised you can read any of it." Even as the words left her mouth, she realized how arrogant they sounded. Before he could answer, she added, "I mean, they're magical words and normally, you know, it's hard to read. I didn't think you knew how to read. I mean read magic."

He was so happy she did not comment on the star, he did not notice the arrogance in the statement or the subtle condescending nature of what she had said. "Yeah, you know . . . I just read bits and pieces to see what's there."

"How'd you learn . . . to read magic I mean? I'm sorry . . . I don't mean to sound so . . . so better than or above you."

"That's all right. I understand." Gesturing to the horses, Jeremy tried to change the subject, saying, "Let's get going. I'll tell you all about it as we ride, if that meets your approval. You're still in charge." He smiled and laughed playfully as he said this.

Twig joined in his laughter. "That's an excellent idea. Consider yourself my advisor." She moved to her horse and stowed the two books in her saddle bags. Jeremy knelt and gave her a hand up onto her horse and then mounted his own.

Pointing towards what he thought should be north and west, he said, "Let's head off that way. Once we come to the edge of the mountains, we'll just follow them until we hit Thwardscall."

"You're the woodsman and tracker. I'm in your hands."

"Only if that were true," he thought, remembering their embrace of a few minutes before. After clearing his throat, he said, "I'll be gentle, err, easy, uhm . . . careful." Shaking his head as if to clear it, he said, "Never mind."

Twig grinned a knowing smile. "Tell me how you learned to read magic."

He was happy she had changed the subject and rescued him

from his own awkwardness. "The master taught me when I was young. I would work for hours in the library. I put things back, straighten things, got things for the master. When I had free time after my chores, or the master was away on trips, I would practice reading the spells. I never thought I could be a great magician, but I wanted to know what was in the books. There were so many wonderful stories and things like that hidden in the midst of all the lessons."

"I know the feeling. Did you find anything interesting in Gallis' books? I didn't get a chance to go through them too much before I fell asleep."

"One was a book of magic lessons. Exercises, practice, tools and some simple pranks—even some things about staff users. I'd seen it all before in the master's library. The other was more advanced."

Twig broke in, "This one?" She raised the book bound with iron bands. It was once again closed and locked with the metal clasp.

Jeremy said without truly looking at the book, "Yes, that one."

"But how did you get it open? It's sealed with a magical binding spell."

The boy was caught and needed to think quickly. He could not tell her about the star but did not have another explanation. "I don't know. Gallis must have left it undone from when we were attacked," he put forth weakly. "I found it open. It must have locked when I dropped it to come help you."

Twig gave him an accepting shrug and gestured for him to continue saying, "Sorry to interrupt. Please go on."

He breathed a sigh of relief to himself as he said, "It had a story about Elmo Patsy, a staff using rune master and one of his quests with Max Konicker and some others. I've heard about some of that from Dirk Lancer and the master himself. That was back when I was studying to be a rune master."

She said with surprise in her voice, "You studied how to cast spells? Worked with the master?"

"I started. It was just before you arrived. I never went too far with it."

"Did the master make you stop so he could work with me?"

"No, not at all." he said hurriedly. "I had an accident with one of my spells. It took a long time for me to recover but master Permillion never told me I had to stop. I just never seemed to be able to get it right. While I was in bed, recovering from the accident, Dirk Lancer worked with me . . . told me stories. He would tell me of his travels around the world . . . of being a ranger . . . of hunting, and tracking, and being in the woods. Most of all, he told me about riding. That seemed so much more interesting than staying in the library and reading or doing chores. Once I was better or at least well enough to ride, I started training with Lancer in my spare time. I was never that great, but I tried to learn as much as I could."

"Ahh . . . now I understand. I'm impressed. You can read magic, and so much more. So, did Lancer teach you weapons other than the bow?"

"A little. I'm not nearly as good as you with any of them. I watched you train and practiced." She blushed slightly at this praise. After a moment's pause, he continued, "I always knew how to use a staff. As a rune master, I would have needed to know that to cast spells. Lancer showed me the basics of swords, daggers, knives, and a few others—even the ax. Mostly, though, he told me to use the bow. That's the weapon of a ranger."

"So rather than be a magician, or should I say, a rune master, you're a ranger." She said it in such way that he knew it was meant to be flattering.

"I'm not there yet. From the stories Lancer told me, I have a long way to go but thanks for the compliment."

There were a few moments of silence as they looked at one another. Their eyes told more to one another than their minds or body language might allow. Twig broke the silence first, trying to ease the tension that charged the air like lightning. "We better start moving. Why don't you tell some stories while we're riding.

I'd love to hear some of the things you read about or that Dirk told you. I had so little time for anything but my training and chores."

Jeremy thought for a moment and then launched into a story he had read, describing Androthy as a young journeymen. Twig listened intently and commented along the way. When the trail they traveled proved less difficult to follow and Jeremy's voice needed a rest, Twig read from her books of magic, trying to practice her new spell casting. After many hours, they finally came to the edge of the Blackspine. The day had passed into evening without either noticing. The enjoyment of each other's company had been enough to make the hours disappear like wax from a burning candle.

As dusk approached, they stopped to eat and stretch. Jeremy shot down several geese while Twig gathered wood and found a stream from which they could draw water.

Once they had finished eating, Jeremy said, "If you can make us a glowing rock or something similar, we can keep going. I think we'll be better off if we don't stop until we have to. I'm not tired and I would rather sleep in Thwardscall than out here where anything might happen."

"That's a good idea. As long as you think you can guide us at night, I can follow you. Remember though, I'm not nearly as good as you on a horse."

He shook his head and smirked. "I'll be here for you, though I doubt you'll need my help."

She looked around as he adjusted the horse's bridals and checked their saddles. After picking up and discarding several sticks and rocks, she finally selected a long slender branch which had fallen from an ash tree. Grasping it firmly with both hands, she cast the spell and watched as it began to glow with a brilliant white light. Handing it to him, she said, "This should last us until tomorrow."

Taking it, he said, "Good. Once you're ready, let's get going."

After one more long stretch and yawn, they both mounted their horses and headed out again. Darkness fell quickly in the dense forest they now rode through. Jeremy carefully picked his

way along being careful to find a safe way. Most of the time, they
followed barely visible paths and trails. Occasionally, they had to
backtrack because of a stream or canyon too wide to cross. Their
talk of earlier died down quickly and soon both were fighting to
keep awake and alert enough to ride. Eventually, even that was too
much for them to do. Twig slumped in her saddle as she slipped
into sleep. Jeremy continued on for a short while until he noticed
her horse had stopped. Though he tried to lead both horses, he
was too tired as well. Immediately he thought, "This is as far as
we're going tonight. I better put her to sleep and unburden the
horses."

As he dismounted, the suit of armor that he wore weighed
heavily upon his limbs. With a conscious effort not to wake his
companion, he worked at removing his armor. This was a new and
puzzling task. After wriggling and straining for several minutes, he
worked out of the suit and laid it to one side. Next, he unpacked
the bedrolls and laid them out. As gently and cautiously as he
could, he took her off her horse and laid her on the blankets. Like
a thief, he removed any items he could see that might disturb her
as she slept including her weapons. She did not stir. As the need
for sleep overtook him, he decided to take down as many of the
heavier items packed on the horses' backs before he collapsed. With
what was left of his strength, he released them from their burdens.
When he finished, he was at the point of total exhaustion.

Without thinking, he slipped into the blankets next to Twig.
His sudden motion roused her slightly but was not enough to
wake her. As he settled in for the night, she turned into him and
snuggled close. As he began to roll away, she wrapped her arm
around his side. Stopping, he returned the embrace. Quickly, he
slipped into a pleasant slumber.

CHAPTER 18

Thoughts of the impending pit battle and possible death ruined Aaron's appetite. His apprehension and concern only grew when he arrived at the room he was to share with Peter. When he entered, he saw a pile of armor and weapons under some of his other things that had been packed on his horse. Sitting at the foot of the bed, he sorted through his new equipment. Redlin had given him two fine sets of chain armor specially forged for his features. Along with these came a shield, bastard sword, and three matching helmets. Under any other circumstance, the boy would have been ecstatic to have received such gifts. They were better than anything he had ever worn or seen on the field of battle. Somehow, the situation he now found himself in made these gifts seem like an offering to a man on his way to the gallows. Just the sheer amount of armor seemed to suggest he would need all of it and more.

As he perused his things, he heard footsteps in the hall. His first thought was of Vin. As the door opened, he said, "Oh Vin, I'm glad you remembered to come get me."

Peter entered the room with a humorless expression on his face. "Sorry to disappoint you. You won't be seeing her tonight."

Peter's appearance had dashed that hope for the moment and what he said meant it would be longer than that. "Why not?" Aaron asked insistently.

"You need your rest; you need to be ready for tomorrow, and I don't trust her. I think she's a distraction at the least, definitely trouble, and, well, maybe she's a spy." The same cold expressionless look stood on his face as he listed each reason.

The last statement caught Aaron by surprise. "What do you mean a spy?"

"I don't trust the Azurine . . . and this one especially. We have too many things to worry about without her interfering right now. I could see her keeping you awake or worse, tiring you out. You need to stay focused for tomorrow."

"It's just another battle. I've fought in wars. I've killed men and beasts . . . warriors of all sorts." Though the words were brave, they lacked the strength and self-confidence of a pit warrior.

Peter took a seat next to him and said in a fatherly tone, "We need to talk." Aaron turned his head silently, acknowledging his presence but not really signifying anything more. Peter spoke anyway. "What you're being asked to do isn't easy. I know that. But it's up to us now. I'm not going to hide anything from you. We need to win both our pit battles. I'll fight first. Then you. I'll try and fight the third but if I can't, it'll be up to you . . . if you're able. If not, all is lost."

Aaron shrugged his shoulders and said, "I know. I'll do my best. I've fought before. I'll be ready." His tone was flat and unconvincing.

"I don't think you grasp the whole picture. By accepting, you're doing something few others ever would. This isn't just a pit battle. Only the champions are fighting. You'll be doing battle with nineteen killers who just want to see you dead. Each has been trained and equipped to win this pit battle. They'll all have magic and will stop at nothing to win . . . which means killing you. Some have ruled their local pits for years. Now they're here to stake a claim to the title of Pit Master and have a chance to face Shettfollufit—the Master of the Grand Coliseum. This is a winner-takes-all match. It's combat to the death. The winner takes everything that enters the floor of the Grand Coliseum. That's why we need to win. Redlin arranged this knowing to get the things we need form those fighting tomorrow. They'll never part with them and some wouldn't use them except in a battle such as this. We have to kill all the others to get what we need."

This monologue was not lost on Aaron. Everything registered. He was so overwhelmed, he could say nothing more than, "I understand. I'm ready."

"No, you still don't fully comprehend. Whichever one of us survives tomorrow will have to finish the quest. I'm making you an equal partner. You'll know everything I know. Whatever you were before, by accepting this challenge, you'll be a man—and an equal—in my eyes."

"It's not a difficult decision. I'm fighting. I accept whatever challenge you give me. I won't stop until I'm dead or we have the Slayer of Evermore and Morgan's dead."

These words were filled with the fire and conviction Peter knew would be needed to win. Putting his hand on Aaron's shoulder, he said, "I'm proud to call you a friend. Now there's much to do and you need to sleep."

Aaron turned to him saying hesitantly, "Since I'm to know everything, who, or what are you. What is the Geminarex? Why did Vin seem surprised but not really. I don't know how to explain it." He shrugged his shoulders to punctuate his confusion as he added, "Do you know what I mean?"

"I know exactly what you're trying to say. That's part of why I don't trust her. As for who or what I am. I'm the keeper of the Geminarex. The Geminarex . . . it's . . . well . . . it's hard to explain. More than fifty generations ago my ancestors forged, well, actually it might be more true to say created, the twin swords of justice and truth—the Geminarex. For over a thousand years, those in my bloodline and our loyal followers have used them to judge and maintain balance in the world. The magic that they hold and that which is bestowed upon the wielder is unparalleled."

"What about Slayer of Evermore?"

"It's difficult to say. None but Redlin and maybe Max Konicker know what the ax is capable of. Even so, I'd say the Geminarex is nearly its equal." Aaron tried with little success to hide his astonishment. Knowing all he did about the fabled powers of the Slayer of Evermore told him that the Geminarex must be extremely magical and very powerful. Peter continued, "The magic of the Geminarex is very unique. More than just enhancing abilities or physical characteristic like strength or intelligence, the swords carry with them the experiences of each of their users. All the knowledge that each Geminarex accumulates is stored with the swords. I know all that my ancestors knew. When I wield the swords, I know the ways of fighting that each knew; I can cast the spells that they once cast. I can even remember the judgments that they passed down and onto whom they rendered those judgments."

"Wow," was all an astonished Aaron could say.

"Then too, I know how each died . . . all the mistakes that each made . . . all the horrible decisions that each had to wrestle with as they came to their final judgment. Far too often, the Geminarex did not fight on the side of a just cause, but rather drew lines between two equally unjust sides of a conflict. Rarely has there been battles between good and evil . . . right and wrong. More often than not, blame is equally placed amongst the many parties involved. Judging is never easy and whatever the judgment, we're often despised. We sacrifice ourselves for the cause of justice."

"It must be difficult. Why do you stay?"

"It's my charge, my duty, and my responsibility. I've learned much from the wisdom of the swords." He looked thoughtfully at the boy. "I wish I could teach you all I know but too much of it comes with what I've experienced or know as the Geminarex. You need to learn honor, duty, pain, and most of all, sacrifice by living it."

"Can't I just wield the Geminarex and learn their secrets? Know what I have not yet learned."

"Only if I relinquish them to you. Once you've accepted them and all that goes with the Geminarex, you must draw blood. Then and only then will you become the Geminarex."

"And if you don't relinquish it?"

"You need to kill me and then take them."

"Has that happened before?" he asked with questioning surprise.

"Yes, several times but we always recaptured them."

There was a knock at the door as it swung open. "Are you all decent?" Vin asked as she stepped into the room looking around the opening door as she entered. "Aaron, I've come to talk with you. I wanted to finish what we started downstairs." She threw him a knowing glance as she lowered her eyebrows and pulled back her lips in a smile just large enough to reveal her teeth.

Peter stood and turned his back to Vin. Dropping his eyes, he looked at Aaron questioningly without saying anything. Aaron spoke through a yawn. "I'm very tired. There's so much to do before dawn." Shaking his head 'no,' he continued, "I think I'd better just stay here—get to sleep."

Peter smiled as Vin groaned with frustration. "Are you sure you can't spare a few minutes for me?"

Shrugging his shoulders, Aaron said in a matter-of-fact tone, "Sorry, warriors need rest and time to prepare."

She stepped closer to him extending her hand as she approached. "Are you absolutely sure?" Her voice took on a soft alluring quality that seemed to make it ring off of every surface around him and penetrate his mind. "I won't keep you too long. Just come with me for a short while."

Aaron could feel his resolve slipping away like smoke slipping through his fingers. He thought to himself, "Be strong. Be a man. Be a fighter. Say no, you don't want to go."

Even as these words echoed through his mind, they were met and drowned out by Vin's melody. "Come with me. Come to my room."

Aaron's body acted without direction from his mind that was still battling the charm she had woven. He slowly stood.

Vin moved her hand towards him but was blocked by Peter. He wrapped his arms around her and gave her a hug saying, "Time to go," in a loud voice. "Us men have things to do," he added as he gave her body a squeeze.

The sudden action and noise disrupted the spell. Aaron quickly caught himself as he fell back to the bed. Vin squirmed for a moment in Peter's arms. Realizing the futility, she stopped and stretched her neck up to put her lips next to his ear. In a whisper only he could hear, she said, "You should have let the boy come with me. I just wanted to add what he could tell me to the history of the quest. If he dies tomorrow, his story's lost." After a pause, she added in a sultry voice, "Or did you want to come to my room yourself and talk?"

Peter leaned his head down to whisper in her ear. "I thought you only wanted people you can control to join you in your room, you know, as company for a long night." His distrust and low opinion of her made his sarcastic tone unbearable to hear.

She drove her palms into his chest and pushed herself away from him. He let her out of his arms. Anger flared in her eyes. "I don't know what you think of me. I don't do that." The emphasis she put on the words struck Peter. "You need to learn manners . . . be civilized."

"If I'm wrong, forgive me. Either way, he needs to stay focused and have his rest, as do I. Talk to us tomorrow—after the pit. I don't care what happens once we're done."

Without acknowledging his words, Vin turned and stomped out of the room. Once she was gone, Aaron asked, "Why are you so distrustful? What do you see in her? It looks to me like she's trying everything to get to you . . . get your attention."

Peter came to the side of the bed and sat. "We know each other. Well, I know her. We met years ago. I joined a party she was part of and we got close. It was before . . . before I took the swords and changed. I don't think she recognizes me . . . even would remember me."

"Maybe you just don't want her too."

These words surprised the seasoned adventurer. "Maybe you're right. Being the Geminarex gives you wisdom beyond your years but far too much comes with that knowledge. I've learned to sacrifice friendships for control, security and survival. There's safety in being alone."

Aaron nodded to show he could understand Peter's position. "I'm sorry for that. I've not had to sacrifice friends, I just never had any. We're both alone, friend. We'll just have to depend on one another—if you trust me." These words were charged with as much respect and honor as the young king could muster. He extended his hand towards Peter without lifting himself up out of bed.

Peter shook it firmly. "You're right, but now you need to sleep while I get things ready." He released the boy's hand.

Nodding his agreement, he said, "Of course, but I needed to get some things for tomorrow."

"I'll take care of that. Just make a list and it'll be here in the morning." Leaning over, Peter picked up a satchel that rested at the side of the bed. After handing Aaron a piece of parchment and something to write with, he extracted a small leather pouch and placed it on his lap. As Aaron wrote his list, Peter opened the pouch revealing a collection of red leaves that shimmered in the dim candlelight of the room. Peter gingerly took one leaf. "Put this under your tongue. It will help you sleep for a few hours. When you awake, you'll be rested and rejuvenated."

"Just one more thing and I'll be finished." Aaron folded the parchment and exchanged it for the leaf Peter held out towards him, placing it in his mouth without hesitation.

Accepting the list with a nod, Peter said, "Now lie back and close your eyes. Before you know it, it'll be tomorrow."

Aaron did as he was told. Even as his eyes closed, he could feel a heaviness in his limbs. In a moment, he was asleep. After what seemed to be no more than an instant, he began to regain consciousness. As the haze of sleep dissipated from his mind, he heard the floorboards next to his bed creek. His mind raced. Without opening his eyes, he worked to gather more information. While trying to feign sleep, he thought, "What's happening? Is it just the effect of the leaf? Am I just being paranoid? Maybe this is a dream . . . or something else." As he strained with his ears and nose, he remembered Peter's words, "Trust no one." His thoughts snapped to a stand-still as he heard a click followed by a metallic slide come from the left side of his bed. He recognized this as the sound of a dagger being slid from a wrist sheath. "Assassins!"

Aaron knew he had only seconds to act. While sitting up, he threw the blanket that covered him up in a high arc over the left side of the bed. He hoped this would catch the assassin or at least his dagger. He continued his forward progress and turned it into a roll that carried him off the front of the bed. As his eyes opened and scanned the dark room, he saw nothing but the one figure covered by the bedclothes.

The figure exclaimed in a low voice, "No, damn it!"

The boy felt hands with sharp claws wrap themselves around his forearms. He yelled, "Help! Peter help me!" Even as he cried this, he pulled hard on his two arms to free them. There was a dull thud as two dark figures were thrust together. They spiraled off one another and at least one impacted the base of the bed.

As he looked in fear, the figure covered by the sheet cut itself free. To his horror, empty space was revealed as the sheet fell to the ground. A cold imperial voice emanated from the far corner of the room. "Kill the young warrior now."

Aaron stood clumsily and thrust himself backwards until he felt the wall at his back. He fumbled for the doorknob as he slid to his left along the wall. Finding it, he flung the door open flooding the room with light. For an instant, while his eyes adjusted to the sudden brightness of the magical orbs that glowed in the hall, he was able to make out the outlines of three different invisible creatures surrounding the bed. The figure who had issued his death order appeared to be a tall, slender, pale human standing off to one side. As he backed towards the opening of the door, the wall closed the gap and extinguished the light from the hall. He was trapped and blinded by the complete darkness. He tried to scream. "Peter! Where are you?" The words caught in his throat as if someone had stuffed a rag in his mouth. Nothing more than a whimper made it past his lips. His mind filled with terror as he felt invisible claws tear at his shirt. He sensed that magic was everywhere, but he had no idea what to do about it.

Flailing blindly with both hands, he tried to beat back the blows with little success. As he was about to cry out again, a vaguely familiar voice pierced the silence which had come over the room. "Boy, focus your mind on battle." The voice was too forceful for him to ignore.

After an instant of concentration, the terror faded as did the confusion that had overcome him. Taking a deep breath, he prepared for the fight. As his muscles tensed, he shifted from conscious thought to training and instincts. To his astonishment, light slowly filtered back into the room as the door reappeared. Narrowing his eyes to adjust for the light, he began to see the two figures that were trying to attack him. They were small wiry creatures that resembled elves except for the fangs protruding from their mouths and eight long thin fingers on each hand tipped with sharp claws.

Without thinking about what they were, he lunged forward knocking the nearest one down and landing on top of the other. Three quick punches hit the small creature's throat, collapsing its windpipe. The blows had such force, it did not have time to scream before its air supply was cut off and it died. Drawing blood had cleared the boy's mind completely. The heat of battle had driven out any spells that were affecting him. He sprang to his feet more agilely than might be expected for a man of his size. Before the other creature could regain its feet, Aaron pounced on the it with deadly force. His knee buried itself in the monster's chest knocking the wind out of it with a whoosh. Grabbing its head with both hands, he pounded it into the floor repeatedly until blood trickled from both ears. It was dead.

Even as Aaron let the body slip from his hands, it disappeared along with the other elf-like creature. His hands shot up to cover his ears as a high-pitched squeal filled the room. Lifting his head to scan the room, he saw Vanness kneeling over the body of a mind warrior near the window. The man who had seemed so ordinary now assumed a much more ominous appearance. Black armor made of lythrum covered his body. The magician's throat had been slit and a dagger driven through its temple. Even as Aaron tried to make sense of what had happened, Vanness searched the body of his victim.

Aaron frantically pressed for answers as Vanness removed items from the mind warrior's body. "Where's the others? What the hell are these things? Where's Peter?" Vanness stood gracefully and without effort. Aaron calmed as his mind cleared of magic. "What's going on? Where did you come from? Why are you here?"

The thief stood saying, "I hate mind warriors," without looking at Aaron.

Aaron insisted, "Answer me now!" He stepped towards Vanness aggressively.

Vanness said in a dismissive tone, "I'm just here to drop off the merchandise, not give you a lesson or answer questions boy." Gesturing to the dead body, he continued, "He's free. I kill them whenever I get the chance. I hate magicians who mess with your mind. All mind warriors need to be killed."

Aaron began his questioning again less assertively this time. "But what about?"

"Uhhh, shh," Vanness said as he raised his hand to quiet the boy. "I'm not paid to answer any questions, but if you have the gold, I'd gladly sit and talk with you. Otherwise, get out of my way." He glided in front of the boy effortlessly and silently.

Aaron grabbed at his arm to stop him. "Wait, you can't go."

With blinding speed his hand was snatched up and twisted behind the boy's back. The cold metal of a poisoned dagger touched his throat. In an emotionless tone, Vanness said, "I get paid a great deal to steal and even more to kill. If you touch me again without permission, I'll gladly take everything you have and leave your bloodless rotting corpse here for free. Am I understood?"

Aaron feared to even nod. He let out a squeak that could be understood as "Yes."

"I'm letting you go because the wizard burned your brain with his magic . . . made you see and do things you normally wouldn't. Besides, Zorich is your protection and he's paid me well tonight. Don't want to be on his bad side, you know." Light glinted off the edge of the dagger as Vanness withdrew it from Aaron's neck.

Aaron's mind fought with itself to make sense of what was happening. It was like he had just awoken from a nightmare to find himself still asleep. Though he swore he was completely awake, he could not make sense of anything. "What happened here?" He felt a needle prick his neck as he spoke. "What do you mean I'm protect . . ." Before he had finished his sentence, he had collapsed and was unconscious.

CHAPTER 19

As the sun reddened the morning sky, Jeremy was awaken by a shudder that ran through Twig's body but did not wake her. He could still feel Twig next to him as she struggled in her sleep. As his eyes adjusted to the light of dawn, he saw that she was still asleep. He mumbled to himself, "She must be dreaming again. What should I do?"

As he debated, Twig moaned. Without warning, she began kicking and punching at the air as she screamed with terror, "No! Don't kill him. Leave him! No! Die! Die! Die!" As her voice echoed through the woods, she threw her arms apart and spread the fingers of each hand. A bolt of lightning flashed from her left hand and struck a nearby tree sheering off its top. The stump burned as the splinters from the crown fell to the ground with a crash. At the same time, her right hand slapped the ground. A stream of flame sprang from each of her fingertips and cut deep furrows in the ground as if it had been plowed. All the trees and shrubs in the path of the flaming streams burst into flame and were quickly consumed by the magic fire. Startled by the eruption of magic, the horses ran off.

Jeremy stared in disbelief at the unfolding scene. His mind sputtered through his options, trying to come to a decision. "Should I wake her. I need to . . . to get the horses. I . . . I can't leave her. Can I wake her? Is it safe?" As he tried to decide, his chest tightened and his breathing became labored as his confusion and desperation increased. While he shook Twig, yelled in a loud voice, "Wake up! Wake up! It's okay. I'm here. Don't be afraid. You're safe."

As consciousness crashed in on Twig, she moaned. In a groggy voice, she said, "What's happening?"

Though she was speaking, Jeremy continued to shake her. As she became more coherent, he slowly released his grasp until it was nothing more than an embrace. "Are you all right?"

It took a moment for her to compose herself. As she looked around at the devastation, she turned to him and hugged him. "Oh, I'm so sorry. Did I hurt you? I had a dream. It was so real. I was so afraid you'd been killed." She wrapped her arms around him tightly pulling him in close.

Whatever thoughts had tried to form in his mind were completely lost as he felt her close to him. Her heart raced and he could feel it beat. As his lips brushed close to her cheek, he could taste the sweat that made her face glisten. He enjoyed her warmth and closeness so much, he pushed out everything but these sensations. The two young adventurers held one another silently reassuring each other. Both enjoyed the shared moments of vulnerability and, at the same time, strength.

Like background noose resolving into a voice, the repeated crackling of burning wood intruded upon their embrace. Jeremy looked up first and saw that the horses were gone. The forest around them was ablaze like a woodpile doused in gasoline. They reluctantly released one another as the two stood. He spoke quickly and with new-found authority. "We need to hurry. The horses are lost. Take whatever you can carry. We need to get away before the fire gets us." The two gathered what they could but it was not much at all. First, Jeremy reached for his armor. Almost instantly, he dropped it and moved to gather other more essential supplies. He grabbed his bow and quiver, food, and water. Meanwhile, Twig removed Splinter from its case. Shoving a sling that could hang on her back into a sack, she scrambled to find other necessities. As the flames grew more intense, she found the two books of magic and tossed them into the sack as well. There was no time to take anything else. The entire forest had begun to burn. The initial burst of magic had lit the nearby brush and trees like kindling in a fireplace. Now, all the underbrush and large trees where burning as well.

Taking her by the hand, Jeremy tugged her along behind as he moved. The fire found its voice and began to roar as he picked his way through the smoldering trees. "The whole stand will be burning soon. Let's go!" He started to run.

She followed closely. After frantically running for a few minutes, they came to a narrow slow-moving brook. Both jumped in and followed it downstream. After a short distance, the brook flowed out onto a large rocky plateau. Once the two were downstream enough for Twig to feel safe, she tugged at Jeremy's arm. In a breathless voice, she said, "Wait, hold on. We're out of the woods—we should be fine."

Fear coupled with the run made his breathing heavy and labored. Falling back onto the riverbank, he let the few things he had rescued from the fire drop beside him. As he released a long puff of air, he turned to look back at the forest. Reddish-orange flames shot up over the tops of the trees as thick black smoke billowed up into the morning sky. Twig sat next to him, letting Splinter and the sack she carried fall to her sides. As the sack hit the ground, the things inside dumped out onto the ground. She paid this no attention as her gaze turned to the ever growing fire. The two sat silently watching and listening to the fire that consumed trees a cluster at a time.

"You there. Are you all right?" The two adventurers turned to see who had called to them. A crowd of ten men came running up from downstream. They carried with them shovels, picks, hoes, and other farm implements. A tall slender young man was speaking as he ran. "We saw the lightning. Did the fire catch you? Is there anyone else with you . . . still in the woods?"

"No, we're the only two and we're doing okay now," Jeremy answered without standing.

All of the men except for the one who had spoken, ran to the edge of the forest and set to work building a firebreak. As the tenth man stopped to speak with Jeremy and Twig, five other men came up along the stream. This second group all carried axes and was led by a small stocky dwarf whose white hair and long beard showed

his age. "If you're well enough, I have to help stop the fire . . .
protect our village." Even as the words were leaving his mouth, the
man ran to help the others.

"Can you do anything to help?" Jeremy asked as he looked at
Twig helplessly. "There's really nothing I can do. I don't know
anything about fighting forest fires," he added meekly.

As the group of men with axes passed by and headed for the
interior of the forest, she said, "I'm not sure what I can do." Her
eyes skipped across the men working frantically with concern. "I
guess . . . since it was my fault. Since I started this, I should try
something." Standing, she surveyed the scene. As quickly as options would enter her mind, she would discard them. "No, no . . .
no, no, no, no . . . no." Whole classes of spells were contemplated
and then discarded with each no. Finally, she said, "Jeremy, I'm
going to try something that should work, but it will drain me. Be
ready to move in case it gets out of hand." As he stood, she closed
her eyes, focused her mind, and cast one of the most powerful
spells she knew.

He looked around and waited for something to happen. After
only a minute, he could feel the air around her begin to cool.
Slowly, clouds formed as the sky darkened above their heads. His
breath made cloud-puffs as he felt the bite of the cold that now
surrounded them. Snow began to fall. In less time than it took to
cut down one tree, she had changed the weather. Twig shivered as
she worked the magic.

It took all her effort to cast, shape, and control the magic that
was flowing through her. As the snow fell, the fire died. The spell
was working. She continued to concentrate until she could not
hold the spell any longer. The snow quickly turned to hail and
sleet. As her control of the magic slipped away, the temperature
fluctuated violently and the winds about them swelled. A tremendous bolt of lightning punctuated by a ear-shattering clap of thunder signaled the spell's end. Her body convulsed as she fell to the
ground exhausted. Jeremy took her in his arms and held her close.
Coldness enveloped her and seemed to draw in his own warmth.

As her temperature returned to normal, the snow stopped, the clouds dissipated, and the air grew warmer.

When Jeremy finally turned his attention towards the others who had come to fight the fire, he found that they had gathered around him. None seemed happy nor hospitable. The tall slender human who had addressed them before said in an accusatory tone, "So she's a witch . . . a sorceress."

One of the younger men said, "I heard her say the fire was their fault. They did it on purpose."

A grumble ran through the crowd. "Oh no, not spell casters," one man said. Others made similar remarks as they looked on in horror. With fear in their voices, several of the men said, "We need to stop them right now."

"Yes, we'll have to deal with them. Get them tied up." the leader replied as he shook his head.

The crowd began to grumble as they closed in. The blade of a shovel clanged off the back of Jeremy's head. As much surprised as hurt, the boy rocked forward and caught himself before he collapsed onto Twig.

As the shovel was brought back for another more decisive blow, the dwarf said loudly, "Stop! We take this no further. They'll come with us back to town. Their fate will be decided there." Everyone stopped what they were doing as if a time had been stopped.

Several men protested by saying, "What if they try something? We can't trust them."

The dwarf raised his hand saying, "Enough. The magician is spent. The boy is no threat. I'll take responsibility. Our lord will want to see them . . . speak with them. He knows magic and he wouldn't be happy to hear we acted without his consent." Glancing around the crowd, he made eye contact with each man. In a stern voice, he asked, "Is that right? Are we agreed?" All nodded their heads. Jeremy could see the fear that filled each at the thought of displeasing their lord.

Twig was in no condition to argue or explain herself. Jeremy knew he could not fight fifteen armed men, even if they were just farmers. More than that, there was no way he would leave Twig behind. They would have to make the best of whatever awaited them. Perhaps, the lord of the farmers' village could be reasoned with or knew Redlin. Keeping his eyes lowered, Jeremy said cautiously and with no pride or anger in his voice, "Please, we're headed to Thwardscall . . . to deliver a message for Redlin." The words had no effect on his captors. "We've lost so much already and she's in no condition to travel far." As two men grabbed him and forced his hands behind his back, he pleaded, "Please, let me carry her. Don't tie us up . . . I, I won't try anything. Really I won't. I promise."

The old dwarf said, "If you want boy, you can carry the girl. We'll hold your things. I don't trust you with them." He gestured for some of the men to take up the belongings that were strewn on the ground. Others tied Twig's hands and feet. Jeremy picked her limp body and draped her over his shoulder, taking care not to jostle her. She was so tired, she did little more than groan as he shifted her weight up over his back.

The two were led off to the village. As they walked away, Twig lifted her head and whispered weakly. "Be strong. As long as we're together, we'll be safe. Remember, I'm here. I'm yours and you're mine."

CHAPTER 20

Aaron felt his body convulse as consciousness crashed in on him. A bitter taste he did not recognize lingered in his mouth while he fought to rouse himself. In the distance he thought he could hear Vin speaking to him "Wake up. You're late. It's time for you to leave . . . get to the Coliseum." Though he tried, he could not clear his mind enough to even open his eyes. Mustering his strength, he tried to sit up. He failed.

"Where am I; what time is it?" he heard himself ask in a voice he could barely recognize as his own. His voice seemed to echo in his ears as if he were in a large cave.

Something warm and soft gently touched his lips. Suddenly his mind cleared and his strength returned. As he opened his eyes, Vin's face filled his vision. She was kissing him.

As he felt her warm moist lips caress his own, the bitter taste that coated his tongue was replaced with the sweetness of chocolate like that his mother would give him. He lifted his head and kissed. She pulled away and said, "Good, I've broken the hold of the potion." As she pulled back and stood, Aaron sat up in bed and looked around the room. "Get up. Everything's at the Coliseum. Peter's already fighting the first battle." Her words were tinged with firmness.

Sluggishly, he pulled himself out of bed, and looked around. "What time is it? What's happened?" He saw nothing in the room that he identified as his own. Everything was gone.

"It's almost midday. We couldn't rouse you. Peter's waiting. We must go." She took him by the hand and led him out of the Inn directly to the Coliseum. She seemed to know her way through the multitude of passages, entranceways, and guard stations that presented themselves on the way to the staging area for the pit battles. As they walked, Aaron kept quiet trying to clear his head and recollect what happened the night before.

Within minutes, she had delivered him to a small area in the stands at the edge of the floor of the Coliseum reserved for those who were to be battling and their entourage. "We're here. Peter's almost won." As Aaron looked up, he saw that a battle was in progress. Before watching the battle, he took in the immensity of the interior of the Grand Coliseum—something he had only heard stories of and read about. Immediately, he picked out the archers, guards, and mages. Next he scanned for the betting booths and food stands. Finally, he surveyed the hundreds of thousands of people watching the battle that was being fought just in front of him. Vin hit him saying, "Peter's winning. He'll be happy to see us when he's done."

The awestruck boy looked down at the floor of the Coliseum to watch the rest of the battle. Twenty-seven of the original thirty participants lay on the ground, dead, dying, or disabled. Old and new blood stained the floor and walls in so many places it was impossible to determine what belonged to who. The last three combatants fought in the middle of the stadium. Peter was clad in black chain that bore Redlin's flaming *R* emblem. In one hand was Justifier and in his other was Vindicator. He battled against a dwarf wielding a pair of war hammers and a human with a long sword and a shield. Both opponents wore black plate armor with helmets. Aaron recognized that both were using magical weapons and wore other enchanted armor and clothing. As he watched, he thought, "How much magic must they have to protect themselves? When Peter wins, it'll be ours. All that magic will be ours to keep." He surveyed the scene like a vulture circling the sight of a massacre.

Peter stepped towards the human as he swung down hard with Justifier. The shield that met the blow split, weakening the blow only slightly. The arm bellow was cleaved in two. Peter spun and brought Vindicator down on the stunned man while maneuvering Justifier into position to parry the Dwarf's blows. Vindicator found the man's exposed neck and bit deeply. As Peter pulled it back, the man fell to the ground dead.

The dwarf sprang backwards and threw one hammer at Peter. He tried to side-step but was too slow. It impacted his side with a crack. Peter crumpled to the ground bringing his swords together to stop the dwarf's other hammer that was spinning towards his head. The dwarf kicked at Peter trying to knock him over. Peter pushed back and brought his two swords together in a great semi-circle that ended at the dwarf's midsection. Both Vindicator and Justifier made contact, split the armor it met, and contacted flesh. Blood flowed from the dwarf's sides as he brought the hammer weakly down towards Peter's head. In a flash, Justifier had severed the hand that wielded the hammer. As Peter stood, the dwarf yielded. A bright yellow Y appeared on the dwarf's chest. This battle was over.

Even as the dwarf surrendered, stones were drawn back to reveal thirty entranceways that had been used by the combatants to enter the ring. Once the stones were drawn away far enough to expose the hidden passageways that led from the interior of the Coliseum, groups of antedates ran out from each to clear the ring. Some removed bodies and possessions while others cleaned debris and blood. Ignoring them, Peter immediately scanned the floor of the Coliseum for other targets. Once he was sure it was over, he looked to where Vin and Aaron were waiting. As he made eye-contact with Vin, she smiled and yelled, "Over here—we made it."

Peter sheathed his two swords and slowly walked to the edge of the stadium nearest them. They moved to the railing and leaned over so they could speak to him. Once he was close enough to be heard, both Vin and Aaron tried to congratulate him simultaneously. "Great job! Well done!"

He stopped them even as they started. His voice was weak but still had force enough to command them. "Stop," he said weakly as he cleared his throat. "No time." Pointing at Vin and motioning towards Aaron, he continued in a hoarse voice, "Take him down to our staging area. He needs to prepare. I'll meet you there." Not waiting for a response, he dropped his head with fatigue and trudged into the tunnel directly under them.

It took less than ten minutes for Vin to bring Aaron to the staging area in the bowels of the Coliseum. Peter was sitting in the room when they arrived. The room was little more than a space left empty within the rock walls of the structure. It had a table, two benches and several wooden cabinets. All the packages and sacks that had been in the room the night before now filled this tiny room. As Peter removed his armor, he spoke to Aaron ignoring Vin entirely. "There's much you need to know before you fight. We'll try our best to prepare you."

Without a word, Vin immediately began stripping off the boy's clothes and replacing them with special leather armor and then a suit of Redlin's chain that fit over it. "What's happening?" Aaron asked for what he felt was the thousandth time in the last two days.

Peter answered him slowly but without hesitation. "You and many others who were supposed to fight today were attacked by mind warriors last night. Luckily for you, Vanness happened to be delivering our items when you were being attacked."

"So that was real?" Aaron asked incredulously.

"Yes and no. Part of what you saw was the mind warrior's tricks. Other parts were actually assassins. Some of it was Vanness drugging you. I don't know what you think you saw or what you did see. That doesn't matter. You were attacked, knocked out, and we couldn't wake you this morning so I came to fight without you."

"What am I supposed to do now? Did I miss my chance to fight?" Aaron pressed.

"No, you fight next but this is the last match. They combined the three original contests into two. There's thirty combatants in each round.

Aaron's face dropped as he heard the words. "Thirty? Did you say thirty? "

"I'm sorry, yes." Peter looked compassionately at him. "I would have wanted you to fight first or at least watch me as I fought if I knew this was going to happen but we couldn't wake you, and I couldn't wait."

"I understand, what now?" Aaron said with conviction.

"Fight your best and keep your head. Don't break the rules of the pit and hope you get lucky. That's the best we can hope for."

Aaron was not encouraged by these words. "What rules are we using?" he asked more afraid than eager to hear the answer.

After removing his last piece of armor, Peter moved to sit next to Aaron. "It's vital you remember this, if you break these rules, the Coliseum guards will disqualify you immediately."

"What does that mean?"

"They kill you, usually by disintegration."

Vin gasped. Aaron said calmly, "But what rules are they using?"

"Anything goes except offensive spell casting. You can heal and use any magic contained in weapons as long as it isn't offensive. No fireballs, lightning bolts and the like."

"Easy enough," Aaron said sarcastically knowing he had no way to do any of that anyway.

Peter continued quickly, "If someone yields, they're out. If you strike them after they've yielded, or you yield and try to keep fighting, you're disqualified." Aaron nodded as his face showed his concerns. "If you fall unconscious, anyone is free to kill you. But, if you're able to recover and don't yield, you must fight to the death. You lose the right to yield. Other than that, everything's legal."

Aaron nodded his understanding as he said, "So much for the rules. Sounds like a standard champion's pit-battle."

Peter and Vin were surprised by this comment. Vin looked up from her work of attending to Aaron's armor and asked with obvious confusion, "Have you fought in a pit before? How do you know the rules?"

In a matter-of-fact tone, he said, "I studied everything Max Konicker ever did, including his fights in Redlin's pits throughout the world. I've been to pit-battles since I can remember . . . read about them . . . listened to bard's songs about anything to do with Redlin, Konicker, and the pit. I know far more than you might think. So Peter, what should I really know." A loud bell tolled.

Peter announced, "Better hurry . . . the fight's coming." Vin hurriedly affixed the last parts of the legging and handed Aaron two helmets.

Peter stood and looked over the equipment that filled the room. He took a pair of gauntlets from a pile and gave them to Aaron saying, "Use these. They give you strength, help your accuracy, and keep you from being disarmed. You can even catch other people's blows, though I wouldn't advise that." He put his hand on the boy's shoulder as Aaron put on the gloves. "There's not much I can tell you and too much you need to know. I'll try to coach you from the viewing box so stay close if you can. It won't be easy, I know, but it's the best I can do to help you make it through."

Vin asked, "What about the things you just won? Can't he have some of those weapons?"

Both men answered her together. "They're not ours until the end of the day's competition."

Peter turned towards Aaron and gestured at a chest near the door. "I put all your things in there, including Bloodlust. Don't use it unless you really need to. Control is more important than power in the pit."

Aaron moved to the chest and opened it. Immediately, he strapped Bloodlust to his back with its carrying harness. Next, he took a large backpack from the chest and examined its contents without taking anything out. "Everything seems to be here. I just need my rod and a spear; then I'll be ready."

Peter sifted through the piles of weapons and other items in the room and produced a metal rod that was a slightly taller than himself. From the same pile, he extracted a spear that was several heads higher than Aaron. Placing them together in his left hand, he passed them to Aaron. "These are the best we have. Is there anything else?"

Aaron shook his head no as a small girl came to the door. "I'm here for the combatant. Time has come for the tournament."

Aaron slung the pack on his back and picked up his extra helmet with his free hand. As he stepped forward to follow the girl, Vin said, "Good luck."

Peter patted him on the back saying, "Fight well my friend."

Aaron left the two without a word. He followed his guide to a small door in the side of the wall. Once he was through, he knew the tournament would begin.

In a gentle voice, the little girl said, "Step through the door and wait for the bell to toll. When you hear it, the stone behind you will begin moving. That signals the beginning of the tournament. Is there anything you wish to leave?" Aaron shook his head no without looking at her. "Good luck my lord." She opened the door for him and watched as he stepped into the tunnel that led to the floor of the Grand Coliseum.

Once he was inside, she closed the door. Aaron could hear a heavy bar fall shut locking him inside. His eyes fixed on the dim light at the end of the tunnel just in front of him. This was his moment to prove himself.

Questions raced through his mind in the seeming eternity that passed while he was waiting for the bell to toll. "Should I run out of the tunnel? Should I stay in? Do I fight? Defend? Wait? Act? React?" He breathed deeply to calm himself. "What would Konicker do? What would Redlin do? Peter? Cragmore?" Options raced through his mind. His confusion mounted as the anticipation and anxiety grew. Shaking his head violently, he growled. A calm came over him as his face set like stone. "The question is, what should Aaron Boewin do?"

Clang, clang, clang, the bell tolled as the wall at his back began to inch forward with the loud grinding of stone against stone. Aaron braced himself and ran out of the tunnel towards the middle of the Coliseum at full speed. After only a few steps, the roar of the crowd deafened him. Arrows and crossbow bolts from unseen combatants whizzed passed him as he ran. Though he felt the force of some impacting him, he did not feel the sting of the heads penetrating. Arrows had cut his flesh many times before but these did not. Rather than stop to consider why, he continued his run. When he was two-thirds to the middle, the first of the other combatants began to emerge from the tunnels looking for others to attack.

His run had put distance between him and all the others. Each entranceway stood about twenty yards apart. Each was now all but sealed by stone. His nearest opponent was more than a hundred yards away. Pausing for a moment, Aaron looked around for where Peter and Vin were stationed. He found them to his left a hundred and fifty yards from where he had emerged and easily that distance from where he was now.

His next thought was to scan the combatants nearest the box that contained his friends so he could assess those he would fight first. Two pairs flanked the box. The group to the left was a large human and an elf. To the right was a slender human or half-breed battling a dwarf. All were clad in various types of armor and carried an assortment of weapons that made it difficult for him to determine very much about them at all.

He decided to head for the center of the two groups and engage the first opponent to subdue their opponent. As he trotted towards Peter, he glanced around to see the other battles. Off to the far right, a giant crushed an elf under his war hammer while a half-elf shot at him with a crossbow. On the near left, a female barbarian hurled a dwarf holding an ax into two humans wielding swords.

Aaron felt almost invisible as he arrived at the far wall and put his things down. The nearest opponents were still fifteen yards away. He put the helmet he carried on the ground next to the wall and let the backpack slide down his arm. As he did this, he noticed that two arrows had hit the top and been caught in the heavy leather flap. After pulling them out, he opened the flap and then dropped the pack a few feet from the helmet. As he stood, he heard Peter's voice straining to be heard over the crowd, "Behind you!"

Instinctively, Aaron dropped the spear, and clutched the rod with both hands. Stepping back, he pivoted, and dropped to one knee. As he spun, he brought the rod up over his head, holding it with his hands spread shoulder width apart. There was a loud clang as an elven long sword hit the rod dead center and bounced back at the smallish figure wielding it.

Aaron's adrenaline was flowing and his senses were heightened as he engaged his assailant. There was barely enough time for him to glance at the scene around him before he was challenged by a flurry of slashes. Using the rod to block and parry, he regained his feet. From what he could see, several others had fallen already. The battles on his flanks were still being fought and so he assumed that this newest opponent must have come from some other part of the arena. As he focused on the battle in front of him, he heard Cragmore's words fill his mind, "Assess the enemy without bias."

As he defended himself, Aaron recognized that his enemy was a female and a mix of human and elf. More importantly, her armor was cut and she was bleeding in several places. In his mind, he went down the checklist Cragmore had given him as a boy. "Battered armor and shattered helmet. She's already weakened—good. That helmet won't stop anything." The elfish blade caught his left arm and hit flesh. "Damn, I'm thinking too much. Act and react. Instincts, use my training and instincts."

His first move was to disarm her. With a quick thrust and a one-handed spin, he drove the rod into her sword hand. With an elbow blow from his free arm, he knocked her back. The combination worked well. The sword fell harmlessly to the ground as its owner stumbled backwards. Aaron deftly picked it up and flung it back towards the wall behind him. As he did this, the half-elf sprang backwards and threw a pair of daggers at him. They hit his chest but did not penetrate his armor. Stepping forward, he pummeled her head with the rod. His blows hit fast and hard. The fourth blow made good contact, causing her to crumple to the ground. He drew back the rod but hesitated.

In a weak voice she said, "Stop, please stop, I . . . I." The elf drove a dagger up into Aaron's right thigh as he hesitated. It hit the chain and glanced off.

Peter yelled, "Don't hesitate until they say they yield!"

Before Aaron could react, there was a battle cry from his right. "Die by the hand of Reixor!" the large human screamed. He had killed his opponent and was running towards Aaron and the elf.

With a sweep of the rod, he knocked the dagger out of her hands and then brought it back into her side. She grabbed it and held it tight. Releasing the rod, Aaron turned and ran to pick up the spear. Meanwhile, the woman grasped the rod with both hands as Reixor charged up to her. With one downward slash of his sword, she was finished. As her body fell limp, he turned his rage towards Aaron. By this time, Aaron had been able to grab his spear and dug into his pack for a glass flask filled with a clear oily liquid.

Ignoring the boy's actions, Reixor charged at him. Aaron threw the flask at the man's chest. "I hope this works," he thought to himself in a disheartened tone. Reixor chopped at the flask with his sword, shattering it on contact. Shards of glass and droplets of liquid sprayed his body. As soon as the liquid hit him, metal and flesh alike began to bubble and fume. In a matter of seconds, the liquid had eaten its way through to his underclothing. Reixor's armor looked like cloth that had been eaten away by moths. Even so, the large man continued to charge.

Aaron charged at Reixor until the huge man raised his sword up to strike. Once he was committed to the attack, Aaron dropped into a crouch and braced the back end of the spear against his boot. The force of Reixor's own movement impaled him on the spear which drove through his weakened armor and lodged itself deep in the man's chest. As the spearhead dug in, Reixor brought his sword down on top of Aaron's head splitting his helmet cleanly. The force of the blow stunned the boy. Reixor's weight fell forward onto the teetering Aaron and the two collapsed backwards into a pile. The handle of the spear buckled and snapped with a loud crack as the spearhead was driven deeper into the chest cavity. The force of the fall finished the job the charge had started. Reixor was dead.

As the two hit the ground, Aaron's helmet separated along the cracked seam and fell away. Unprotected, his head rapped the floor of the Coliseum. His mind clouded. Consciousness slipped away as he felt the dead weight of Reixor settle in on top of him. As he struggled under the weight, he protested, "No, it's not fair. No, not this." He felt a trickle of blood flow from the top of his head. A pool of blood from Reixor's body began to form on the ground under him.

As consciousness abandoned him, the mistakes he had made ran through his mind. "I turned my back on the fight . . . stupid. I underestimated my opponent—unforgivable. I hesitated to kill because it was a woman—weak and worthless." Grunting he strained futilely against the weight that rested on him. His strength failed as his world darkened. "I was lucky enough to survive the mistakes." As everything went black he thought, "It can't end like this. I won't let it."

CHAPTER 21

Before Jeremy had taken a step, the leader of the farmers sent half the group on ahead to explain what had happened. Once they were gone, the march back to the village began. Fortunately for Jeremy, it was a not that far. As he came over the next rise, a tree-lined valley opened up before him. At the bottom, a cluster of modest homes sat in a clearing. On top of the far hill was a large keep surrounded by iron gates and stone pillars. As they walked, he asked, "Is that where your lord lives? Are we going there?"

"Yes." said the dwarf. Raising his voice, he continued, "Enough talking. Just walk."

"Yes sir," Jeremy said dutifully. He played the part of a servant well. The group passed the next hour in silence, as they trudged down the hill and up the next. Finally, they came to the gate of the keep. Two leather-clad guards with swords and crossbows stood in front of the gate which slowly opened as the party approached. The dwarf led Jeremy through a courtyard into the main building of the keep. The guards followed. Once inside, they made their way to a small windowless room in the interior. "Put her down," one guard barked. Jeremy obeyed.

"Take the girl and tie him down. I don't want to take any chances," the dwarf said as he gestured to the guards who had followed. One guard took Twig's body, while two others tied Jeremy into a chair.

After the long walk, Jeremy was happy to relieve himself of Twig's weight. Being bound was another thing all together. As there was nothing he could do about it, he simply resolved himself to the situation and sat. The guards used ropes to bind the boy's arms and legs to the chair. As the ropes were tied, the dwarf was called outside.

A slender human with dark skin entered and approached Jeremy. Four armed guards stepped into the small room behind him. All five carried swords and wore leather armor. The man spoke clearly and with authority. "Hello, my name is William. Lord Swinson wishes to speak with the sorceress. You'll stay here."

"I won't leave her," Jeremy protested.

"Then you'll die." William gestured to the guards. Four left with Twig while two flanked Jeremy. "Are you going to cooperate?"

"Yes sir." Jeremy said as William stepped up and raised his hand to strike. The boy watched Twig being carried away and knew there was nothing he could do. He thought to himself, "I'm nothing . . . worthless." He strained against the ropes as he asked, "Where are you taking her?"

William responded coldly. "To be questioned by our lord. He left your interrogation to me." He slapped the helpless boy and added, "It should be fun . . . I mean productive, for us." The two guards that remained in the room laughed knowingly.

Jeremy tried to speak before William struck again. "I'm . . . we're on a mission from Redlin. We have to get to Thwardscall. If you look around my." He paused and thought better of saying anything about the star and the other charms that hung about his neck.

William struck him again across the face. "I don't care," he said as the two guards looked on with smiles. "I'd just as well not hear anything from you. The master is interested in the girl . . . her magic and matters concerning Morgan's enemies. You're inconsequential." The air rushed out of Jeremy's lungs as a punch hit him in the stomach. "I don't even think he knows you exist. All his questions were about the magician . . . her things . . . her motives . . . her power."

Two more punches to the midsection made Jeremy shutter. He was already weak and the abuse was taking its toll. "What do you want from me?" he asked with the little breath that remained.

"Blood and enjoyment. We're bored and you're a good distraction." William's elbow crashed into his head dazing the boy. "Oh, stop talking and try not to scream too much. It might bother the master." Another elbow hit his head.

He could barely keep himself conscious as the blows hit him. He felt his hair being pulled up to keep his head straight as a fist drove into his face. Blood filled his eyes obscuring his vision. His ears rang and his head ached as he felt the gloved fist hit his face again. "Don't give up," he heard himself mutter.

"That's right boy, stay with us. Don't give up. It's more fun that way."

Squeezing his eyes closed, Jeremy remained quiet as William hit him repeatedly. Then suddenly, the blows stopped. The two guards hit the ground with a thud. A gravelly voice that Jeremy did not recognize said, "Fun's over little man."

As Jeremy opened his eyes and looked up, he saw a pair of crossbow bolts enter the left side of William's head. As he looked down at the guards, he saw that both were shot in a similar manner. Before he could lift his gaze, the shooter was behind him. A blade cut through the ropes even as he spoke. "Who are you?"

"Quiet boy," the man said in a hush. "It's me, Darvan. I'm part of Redlin's quest with you."

Jeremy breathed a sign of relief as he heard the name Redlin. He relaxed more as the ropes were cut away. "Thanks." As he got to his feet, his legs buckled and he fell back into the chair.

"Take it easy. You're pretty badly beaten up. You should rest. Then we'll figure out what to do."

"No, we need to get Twig." Jeremy tried his legs again and they still failed to hold his weight.

"She's just down the hall in the library, surrounded by at least ten guards. I already checked that out. That's why I took so long getting to you—sorry about that."

"No matter." Jeremy ignored his own well-being as his concern for Twig mounted. "What should we do?"

"Wait a few minutes." It was obvious that Jeremy did not like this answer. Darvan continued, saying, "Once you're ready, get into some armor. Then we'll go get the girl and get out of here."

Jeremy nodded as he said, "That sounds good." While Darvan watched at the door, Jeremy sat back waiting for his strength to return. "So where've you been? How did you come to find us," he inquired.

Darvan gestured for Jeremy to keep his voice down. In a whisper, he said, "Shhhhh, not so loud. I went to Thwardscall to scout ahead. It's full of Morgan's spies and henchmen. I came back to warn the party."

"That brought you here?" Jeremy asked as he stood.

Unconcerned with Jeremy's motion or his obvious distrust, the stalker continued, "No, I picked up your trail just north of Overton. It wasn't that hard to follow." His words were said coldly, but Jeremy could feel the brutal honesty they held.

"Sorry, I know Purple Dragons never leave the party." he said meekly. "When did you catch up to us?" As he spoke, Jeremy stripped off a suit of leather armor from one of the guards and put it on himself.

"I almost caught you in the woods near this village. Then I saw a fire ahead and had to detour around it. Once I found your trail again, you'd been brought into the keep so I came after you." He paused for a moment and then asked hesitantly, "Where's the rest of the party? While I was following you, I only saw the two sets of tracks. What happened to Gallis and Shane?"

"Guar . . . they attacked and almost killed Gallis. Shane took him back to Helexpa. He's going to join us in Thwardscall. We split up south of Overton and haven't seen anyone yet, until you."

"It's understandable. Morgan's assassins and trackers are all through the area looking for anyone who's heading north. Something big is going on in the Valley of the Dragons. I just hope we're not too late."

"Let's just worry about Twig for now." Stepping up next to Darvan, Jeremy continued, "I'm ready, let's go."

"You still stick out. Your face is too beaten to pass as a guard."

Jeremy's emotions swelled. "Then I'll have to pass as something else or not be seen or maybe, I don't know, maybe, or maybe," he hunted for a plan.

"Or wait here and I'll get the girl," Darvan put forth.

"No," he all but shouted. "I'm going to get Twig." The words had such conviction, the stalker did not even try to argue.

"Shhhh . . . keep it quiet or we're all dead." Realizing his outburst was wrong, Jeremy put his hand over his mouth. "Okay, I can be all but invisible. You stand out like a dragon in a town square. Unless we can hide your face, we'll be discovered."

"How far is it to where they're keeping Twig?"

"Not far . . . just down this hall in a large library on the other side of the keep.

"A library? Why not an interrogation room?"

"I think they want her to decipher some magic tomes . . . read things . . . explain her magic."

"We need a plan and quickly before they do something to her." Jeremy said desperately.

Trying to reassure the boy, Darvan said, "As long as she cooperates, I'm guessing she'll be safe, at least for a little while." As if to acknowledge what Darvan had said, Jeremy stared at him with pleading in his eyes as his mind tried to find a way to save her.

CHAPTER 22

Aaron's head ached as consciousness slowly returned. It was impossible for him to know how long he had been out. All that mattered now was that he was still alive. As he tried to move, he found that he was trapped under Reixor's body. With great effort, he turned his head enough to see that there were at least two battles still in progress to his right. Close by, a giant fought two humans while on the other side of the stadium, the female barbarian fended off two elves. Aaron struggled to free himself without success. As he did this, he sensed someone approaching from his left. The roar of the crowd had died down enough for him to hear footsteps just a few feet away.

Options ran through his mind. Nothing would give him leverage to help move the body that now pinned him. His strength was not yet fully returned. The gauntlets were not helping enough either. "Damn," he muttered in frustration. "Time's running out . . . only seconds . . . I'm trapped. I'm dead."

With all his might, he worked his right arm up and grasped Bloodlust's handle. Even as his gloved hand touched it, rage built inside him. "Give me strength." His chest swelled as he felt his strength increase tenfold. With a flip of his left arm, he tossed the dead body aside like he was removing a blanket. Blood stopped flowing from his wounds as they healed.

Once he was clear from Reixor's body, he stood with no hurry to his motions. A dwarf wielding two axes came at him with a flurry of blows. His attention, however, was drawn by a figure fifty yards beyond the dwarf. Irresistibly, Aaron's focus was drawn to and fixed upon a man-sized creature leaning against a far wall clutching his side. He was trying to bandage a leg that had been chopped by an ax. As Aaron watched, a bright yellow Y magically appeared on the man's chest. He realized that the beaten man must have already yielded to the dwarf. More importantly, Bloodlust knew that the disfigured being had Orcan blood in his veins. The ax demanded to be fed. Orc blood must be spilled. The creature must die.

Meanwhile, dwarf in front of Aaron swung both his axes with skill and dexterity. Unfortunately for him, however, this was no match for the raw force that Aaron now commanded. As the dwarf moved in to attack, Aaron stepped up and swung. Bloodlust's first hack removed the dwarf's left arm. Before he could do little more than scream, Bloodlust was brought back and through his side, knocking him into the wall in a large arch more than five times his own height. Even as the dwarf slid to a halt on the floor of the Coliseum, Bloodlust forced its wielder towards the orc. While coughing up blood, the dwarf muttered, "I yield."

As Aaron approached the half-orc, a yellow Y appeared on the dwarf's chest. The boy did not care. His entire attention was obscured by the rage he felt and the lust for the orcish blood that was only a few feet away. With each step, Bloodlust pushed him forward. "Kill the orc. Kill the orc. Kill the orc." The words kept running through his head. As he walked, another combatant approached him from the far side of the half-orc. His mind strained to regain control. "Kill the orc. No. I'll die. Kill the orc. No, the rules. Kill the orc." His thoughts were now words being screamed loud enough for the spectators to hear. "No, kill the orc. I'm in control. Kill the orc. No more orcs." As Aaron said this, he felt his rage subside. His strength disappeared as his mind cleared. Bloodlust was no longer in control. The blade felt heavy in his hand. As he looked up, he saw the man only a few feet away.

As best as he could, Aaron backed away to better his fighting position. The man wore leather armor and carried an oaken staff and a metal rod tipped with a long crystal blade. As he moved away Aaron thought confidently, "Even without the full force of Bloodlust, I should be able to win this battle."

In as confident a voice as he could muster, he said boldly, "Do you yield?"

His opponent laughed saying, "The great Tarreck never yields."

Suddenly, Aaron stepped up and swung down at the man. Tarreck ducked and brought the staff down across the back of the ax, driving it to the ground. Bloodlust dug a few inches into the floor of the Coliseum. Before Aaron could free it, the crystal tipped rod touched the ax blade. The metal became glass before Aaron's astonished eyes. Like tendrils spreading out from a fire, the magic spread out from the point of contact to consume the entire blade. Slowly, the magic worked its way up the handle towards the boy's hands. He released Bloodlust and sprang back away from the rod. Tarreck smirked.

In a condescending and disrespectful tone, Tarreck said, "Do you yield boy or should I crystallize you and everything you own?"

Unfazed by his opponent, Aaron took advantage of Tarreck's cockiness. Without warning, he dove forward and rolled. At the end of the roll, he sprang up at Tarreck who was still laughing. Both of Aaron's fists hit hard into the unsuspecting man's chest. Stunned by the blow, Tarreck fell back as he brought the rod towards Aaron's chest. Before the man could recover, Aaron twisted the rod from his hand and tossed it far to his right. Tarreck tried in vain to hit Aaron with the staff. The boy twisted it free and threw it to the side as well.

Aaron pressed his weight down on top of his opponent and held Tarreck's hands to the ground with his own. The man was pinned helplessly. Aaron asked, "Do you yield," as the man struggled underneath him.

"Tarreck never yields. You're as trapped as I am. It's a stand-off."

Aaron drove his head down into Tarreck's forehead and asked, "Do you yield?"

"Tarreck never yields." he repeated defiantly, continuing to struggle. This time it was followed by a wad of spit that hit Aaron in the cheek.

Aaron drove his head down into Tarreck's face a fourth time. With frustration showing in his voice, he asked again, "Do you yield?"

"Tarreck never yields." he repeated emphatically, continuing to struggle. He added, "I have a harder head than you boy. Just give up now."

"Ahh, I don't believe this. This sucks. What do I do?" Aaron asked himself as he saw the futility of his own position. "I can't just let him up. If I shift he'll free himself." There was a tremendous roar from the crowd. As Aaron looked around, he saw that the barbarian was coming his way. She had just killed the last of the opponents in the Coliseum. He only had a few moments to contemplate before the decisions would be made for him.

The barbarian turned over the body of the giant she had just killed, exposing a large two-handed sword. Picking it up, she tested its weight. Like an executioner coming to the chopping block, she swung it in front of her as she walked. Both men could hear her grunt as she trudged closer.

"This sucks," Aaron said again as he drove his head down into Tarreck's face and asked, "Do you yield?"

"Tarreck never yields." he repeated again and then added, "Besides, she'll kill you first. Then I'll be free to finish her myself." He stopped struggling and looked back at the hulk of a woman who was approaching.

Aaron's mind hunted for something to do. He ran through all the things he had read or been told about pit battles. There were only a few seconds before he would have to just run away. Suddenly, it came to him. He said aloud, "Redlin's body maneuver."

Tarreck looked at him with puzzlement and said, "What's that supposed to mean?"

Ignoring this comment, he waited for the woman to come within striking distance and raise her sword. As she drew it back, he threw his weight backwards without releasing Tarreck. He fell onto his own back and threw his opponent up. The barbarian brought the sword down and cut deep into the helpless man's back. "Ahhh ha, hahha," Tarreck cried out and then laughed. Smugly, he said, "That won't work either boy. Tarreck never yields . . . Tarreck never loses."

Aaron was too concerned with the barbarian. As the sword recoiled, he rolled off to his left. With a broad sweeping slash, the barbarian swung at both of her opponents. The sword caught Aaron on the back as he rolled, splitting both the chain and the leather armor underneath. He could feel the seam in his back start to ooze blood as he continued to roll away.

Tarreck fell back and rolled to the other side as the blade of the barbarian's sword came across at him. It cut deep along his left arm. As he rolled, Aaron could see the wounds clearly. In a matter of seconds, however, it was healed. More than that, Tarreck's leather armor was whole again. It had repaired itself. Witnessing this told Aaron that Tarreck had powerful magic on his side. He thought, "Gotta find a way to defeat him and survive the barbarian."

Aaron got to his feet and scanned the floor of the Coliseum. "Who's left?" As he looked around, he found that everyone else was dead or disabled. There were now only three—Tarreck, the barbarian, and himself. The crowds roared as the barbarian chopped at Tarreck. Aaron looked back to see that Tarreck had made his way to the rod and was beginning to fight back.

His back screamed in pain as he moved. All the other blows he had received were now starting to ache as well. Without looking at the fight behind him, he ran as best he could to his backpack. Once there, he looked back to see what was happening. Tarreck had crystallized the barbarian's sword. She was clubbing at him with her bare hands while he dodged.

Aaron thought to himself, "I'll only have a few moments to rest and then one of them will be on me again. I have to think." As he worked through the problem, he dug out a small leather pouch from his pack and extracted a dry bluish stem from inside. Putting it into his mouth, he sucked on it. The pain subsided and his strength returned somewhat. He glanced up at the battle, Tarreck had driven the crystal point of the rod deep into the barbarian's chest. With a twist, she screamed in agony and fell to the ground. It was only a moment before she was dead.

Withdrawing the rod, Tarreck turned slowly and confidently walked towards his last obstacle. The boy looked up towards Peter and Vin, hoping for help. They were standing at the railing trying to scream over the cheers of the crowd.

Until now, Aaron had not been close enough or aware enough to hear them. Keeping one eye on Tarreck, he turned his attention to their screams. Both yelled together, "No edged weapons."

Aaron nodded his understanding as he yelled back, "No edged weapons. Got it."

Vin yelled, "His amulet holds the magic."

"Amulet . . . got it." Aaron looked back at Tarreck who was sauntering towards him. He watched in disbelief as Tarreck confidently stopped and waved to the crowd. It was as if Aaron was already defeated. Unbeknownst to anyone, the wave was actually a signal to an assassin in the crowd. Looking back at Peter with questioning in his eyes, Aaron yelled, "What do I do?"

"He's regenerating."

"Regenerating?" Aaron knew what it meant but could not believe it. His mind struggled to deal with the new facts. No edged weapons . . . regeneration . . . powerful magic . . . extremely powerful magic." He turned to Peter and said again, "How do I kill him?"

As Peter began to answer, a large cloaked figure stepped up next to him. "You have to." As the words left Peter's mouth, the figure raised a dagger.

"Look out!" Aaron pointed as he screamed the warning. It was too late. Peter never got to finish his statement. The figure plunged a knife into the space between Peter's neck and shoulder. The Geminarex collapsed as blood sprayed the crowd. Vin fell to Peter's side as he lay prostrate on the floor of the viewing box. She drew out the dagger and tired to stop the bleeding. Aaron lost sight of them as the crowd crushed in and swallowed the entire box.

Once the dagger was thrust, the cloaked figure ran. Guards

swarmed the man as he tried to escape. The assassin refused to surrender as the guards cornered him. A flurry of arrows followed by a barrage of magical energy bolts ended the cloaked figure's life with a flash.

Aaron turned his attention back to Tarreck who was still slowly walking towards him carrying the rod. He had few options. As his destiny approached, he thought aloud, "I'll face this alone, like a man. This fight is until I win or I die." Taking a deep breath, he mustered his strength and self-confidence. "I'm on my own. This is my fight. No surrender. Aaron Boewin never yields."

CHAPTER 23

Twig awoke to find herself in a warm comfortable bed. The last thing she could remember was casting the spell to put out the fire. After that, everything else was a blank. Her first thoughts were of Jeremy. "Where is he? I hope he's safe. I wonder what's happened." As she pried her eyes open, she saw only the flood of sunlight from the windows that flanked her bed. The light was so brilliant, she had to squint until her eyes adjusted. As she was able to take in more of the room, it reminded her of home. Though sparsely furnished, it did not want for books. Every empty wall space was filled with shelves of books.

"Good, I see you've finally recovered my dear," a coarse voice said from the corner of the room. Once she had gotten over her initial surprise, she realized that though the voice startled her it was rather friendly. "I hope you're feeling better or should I say rested. You had quite a time getting here."

Twig strained to see who was speaking. The sunlight in her face joined with the shadows in the corner to hide all but the vaguest features of her host. "Who are you? Where am I? Where's Jeremy?"

"All in good time," her host said patiently. "I spoke with your young friend and now I need to speak to you."

"Is he all right? Can I see him?" Twig pleaded without realizing the emotion she put into the words.

"He's resting; Jeremy's doing fine. He misses you as much as you miss him. You'll see him soon but first we must speak."

"Okay," she said reluctantly as she settled back down on the bed. Though she could get up, she thought it best to conserve her strength until she might need it. "What do you want to talk about?"

"What happened to Androthy Permillion?"

The question surprised her. "I'm not sure. What do you want to know? The last time I saw him, he was sending us away as the guar came." As she spoke, the figure in the corner moved towards the bed. Twig saw the shadowy figure for the first time as he sat next to her. Though he could not have been tall enough to look over her shoulder, this venerable old man was at least twice as thick and three times as wide as her. Even so, she did not feel threatened. His entire visage seemed too cheery to be ominous. His rounded face and rosy cheeks almost glowed compared to the dull gray of his long hair and bushy beard. Twig thought he was human, though something about his eyes suggested to her that the old man had dwarven blood flowing in his veins as well. She said quite innocently, "Have we met? While traveling with the master, I've come to meet many of his associates. Were you amongst them?"

Her host let out a loud boisterous laugh that made his belly tremble. "Oh child, no. I stopped traveling fifty years before you were born and no one comes to visit me, until now." Gently, he patted her hand. "But all that will change very soon I'm afraid." His smile slowly faded and was replaced with a look of concern. "We have to get you out of here before we're overrun. That's why I need to speak with you. There's so little time and so much to know."

"What are you talking about?" She sat up as she searched for answers. "Who are you? How do you know so much? Did Jeremy tell you?"

Placing his other hand atop hers, he said in a quiet voice, "I'm Max Konicker. I'm the one you've come to find and unknowingly, you've led Thrack Morgan here as well." Shock overwhelmed her expression. She should have known. This is what she had imagined Max Konicker to look like. "I'm so sorry; we didn't know."

"It's all right my dear but now I need to know some things. I need to prepare."

"Of course, whatever I can do."

"First, where were you headed?"

"Thwardscall . . . to find you."

"Alone?"

"No, the rest of our party's meeting us there."

"Where are they?"

"Some went to Phinn . . . others returned to Helexpa after Gallis was wounded."

"Who went to Phinn?"

"Meldrin led Peter, Jack, Aaron, and Vin there."

"And back to Helexpa with Gallis?"

"Just Shane."

"Very good, what about the ax? Where did you get Splinter? And do you know what magic it holds?"

"Your ax? Redlin gave it to us." She replied quickly. She continued, "As for its magic, we were told nothing."

In a dismissive tone, Max sputtered out, "Oh, of course, that's good. I know what it does and that's enough." He shifted on the bed and put his hand on the side of her head. "What of the spell books? Are they yours?"

"They belong to Gallis but I was reading them after he was wounded by the guar."

"Yes, that makes sense. Can you open the bound one?"

Without thinking, she said, "No, Jeremy got it open last time. I didn't know it was locked."

"Of course, I understand now." Max gestured to an empty space in the middle of the room and said, "Bring the boy." He suddenly stood. As he moved away, the entire room changed before her eyes. In a flash, the sunlight disappeared and soon after the windows were gone as well. The bed melted away and was replaced with a heavy wooden chair. Rather than lying comfortably, she was tied down. As she scanned the room, she saw a table off to her left. Splinter and several books rested upon it. Along with Max, ten other figures slowly appeared, filling the room. The shelves of books seemed to be the only thing that remained constant.

As her eyes focused, she could see that all the new people in the room were leather-clad guards. Even Max had changed drastically. Rather than a chubby, friendly-looking man, he had become a pale dark-haired magician in robes. As she tried to make sense of the scene, she thought, "A mind warrior . . . he must be a mind warrior." Before she could think or do anything more, her mind went blank. All her thoughts were drawn down into a deep dark well and left to drift. Her spell casting was useless. The mind warrior had cast her mind into an oblivion of thought. As the room around her faded away, Twig screamed aloud. The darkness closed in. "What do I do? Master never told me of this." She felt her limbs grow cold as she was consumed by the impenetrable darkness.

The sound of a door being thrown open drifted to her from far off. Voices raised and lowered, but the words were all but lost to her. As sound faded she heard Max say, "The boy . . . it's . . . get . . . go now." Then nothing but a long pause accompanied the darkness. Again she heard Max's voice. "Invisible . . . someone's invisible."

Then there was silence. Blackness covered everything. She grew colder. With all her strength of will, she tried to muster a flame to warm herself. Nothing happened.

Androthy's voice spoke from somewhere deep inside her. "All magic comes from within. Focus and drive back the outsiders."

A shiver ran through her as her teeth began to chatter. "Yes master." The words helped her mind to focus. "Fire, fire . . . think of fire. The heat . . . the light . . . fire . . . white hot burning fire." Darkness receded as she saw her skin begin to glow. Flames licked along her limbs and spread out like the tongue of a serpent flicking at the air. As the fire spread, light returned to the room. She was wining the battle for her own mind. With a sudden flash, her mind was clear.

Twig saw the scene before her with perfect clarity. There was a thud as the robed figure hit the floor next to her. As she looked over at him, she saw three crossbow bolts sticking out of the back of his head. "I hate mind warriors," Darvan said quietly from somewhere behind her.

The room was full of commotion. At first glance, she saw several guards lying motionless on the floor with bolts in their heads as well. Then she noticed two of the guards fighting with one another just in front of her. It took a moment before she finally realized that one of them was Jeremy. Immediately upon seeing him, her mind snapped into focus. She said aloud, "He's come to rescue me." A smile crossed her face. The fight did not last long. As she looked on, Jeremy was hit in the chest. She cried out, "Oh no, Jeremy! Look out!" Her warning came too late. With a quick sideways blow, the guard knocked him unconscious. He then raised his sword to finish the helpless boy.

The fire that once kept her warm in the darkness exploded out of Twig. Rage mixed with her other emotions to give it power. The ropes that held her disintegrated as fire spread out from her like the rays of the sun. The flames stretched out for a few inches in front of her and then exploded into a ball that shot forward. The guard was consumed. It passed through him leaving only a puddle of metal where his sword once was. All else that was him was incinerated.

Everything in the room except Jeremy caught fire. The fireball continued on its path unimpeded by furniture, people, or even walls. As it traveled, it completely disintegrated everything in its path. Moreover, anything flammable on either side was set ablaze.

Twig watched as the ball of fire cut a long cylindrical tube as tall as she was through the entire keep. As she looked on, the chair under her fell away. The intense heat of the fire had turned it to ash. After picking herself up, she ran to Jeremy's side and tried to rouse him. Miraculously, the fire had not touched him. Screams filled the air as the entire keep began to burn. She bent and kissed her rescuer. His eyes opened as a wide grin filled his face.

Darvan stepped up behind them saying, "Come on, we need to get out of here. This place is coming down around us."

Without question, she nodded her agreement saying, "Grab the things from the table." As she got to her feet, she pointed at the space were the table had been. Now it was little more than charred firewood. The books and Splinter lay on the floor amongst the ashes. "You get the ax, I'll gather the books." She did not wait for an answer. Quickly, she grabbed the sack and threw all the books she could find into it.

Darvan said, "Got it," as he moved to find the ax. It took him only a minute to find it. Without thinking, he grabbed hold of the metal handle with both hands. Instantly, he released it and jumped back screaming in agony as the flesh of his hands sizzled. As he scrambled to his feet, a tremendous crack came from above. Looking up, he saw a rout iron chandelier heading towards him. The support beam from the ceiling had given way. He dodged to one side avoiding the chandelier. Even so, the beam hit his midsection, pining him to the floor. With one of the main supports gone, the room began crumbling down around them.

Jeremy rushed to Darvan's side. With panic and fear in his voice, he said, "This place is falling apart. We've got to get you out fast." With all his strength, he pushed at the timber. It did not budge.

Twig moved to the ax saying, "Watch out, I'll use Splinter."

Jeremy and Darvan yelled to her together. "No, stop!" The words halted her. Darvan continued, "It's no use. The handle's too hot to hold. You'll never be able to wield it.

She stared at Splinter. Her frustration showed as her voice faltered. "Uhhh . . . there has to be a way . . . just has to be." She began to reach for Splinter again and felt the heat radiating off the metal.

Darvan said calmly, "There's no time. Leave me before we're all trapped."

Jeremy pleaded with her, "Leave the ax and help me. Maybe together we can move it."

She came to his side and the two pushed against the timber. It did not move. "What do we do?" she asked Jeremy.

He put his hands on her shoulders and said, "Can you use your magic . . . move the timber . . . get him out?"

"I can shrink him."

"I'll be crushed."

The panic in Jeremy's eyes worried Twig. "Can you lighten the timber? Move it over? Change it to something else? Stop the fire?"

"Yes but there's not enough time." she said hopelessly. "We'd all be dead before I could finish the spell."

"Just go! I don't want your magic." Darvan yelled. The two looked at one another and knew they would not leave him.

Twig said, "We need something fast."

Jeremy looked into her eyes saying, "Send him somewhere, anywhere that's not here. The master did that in no time. Can you?"

She nodded 'yes' and began the spell immediately. Touching Darvan, she cast the spell.

"Be careful . . . be safe." he said as she worked the magic. As he felt the magic begin to affect him, he yelled, "I'll meet you in Thwardscall."

The two young adventurers watched as the stalker slowly disappeared. As the beam settled to the floor with a creak, the two turned to one another. Twig said, "We're on our own again."

Jeremy nodded, saying, "And we need to go. Grab the books."

She did as he said while he removed his shirt. Using it like a pot holder, he wrapped the leather top around Splinter's handle. It was still hot, but bearable. The two came together at the round opening where the ball of fire had crashed through the wall. Together, they ran through the cylindrical path out of the keep. Neither said anything more until they were well on their way to Thwardscall.

CHAPTER 24

The crowd in the Grand Coliseum hooted as Tarreck approached Aaron. Ready or not, the fight was coming to him. The boy quickly gathered up his things and moved to where his rod was laying. The move put twenty more yards between him and Tarreck. Cragmore's advice replayed in his head. "Running isn't the answer, it's easier to be hit in the back," he thought as he moved away from Tarreck. "The extra distance gives me time to think. I need a plan." Something came to him as Tarreck closed the distance.

First, Aaron gathered the nearby weapons and piled them with his own things. He now had two dwarven axes, an elven sword, two throwing daggers, a knife and a two-handed sword along with his own rod. The backpack would make the difference—he hoped. As he looked at what he had gathered, the words, "No edged weapons," rang in his head. He checked on Tarreck who was still a good distance away and moving slowly.

His opponent smiled as he saw the frantic look in Aaron's eyes. "Don't worry boy, I'll make it quick but not too painless." Saying nothing, Aaron quickly stripped off his chain armor and tossed it into a pile off to his left. He moved the rod next to the pile of metal. "Don't give up boy, the audience wants a show." Tarreck turned to the crowd and elicited loud cheers.

While Tarreck played to the crowd, Aaron took a large sack and two flasks from his backpack. Quickly, he poured the contents of the flasks into the sack and tossed them aside. After dropping the sack, he dropped the knife into his backpack and slung the pack on his back. Finally, he put the second helmet on his head. He was ready.

Speaking softly to himself, he said "All I need now is Tarreck's overconfidence and some luck." His voice fell to a prayerful whisper, "I hope this works."

As Tarreck turned back to Aaron, he said, "Enough of this. I need to dispose of you so I can prepare myself. Do you yield boy? You know you can't win."

"No." Aaron said meekly hoping to appear weak. He dumped the contents of the sack on the ground. A large net made of rope and steel fibers dropped to the ground in a lump. He skillfully unwrapped it and spread it out in preparation for throwing it. With a single fluid motion, he tossed it towards Tarreck. It landed three feet short of its mark.

Tarreck laughed. "Hahah . . . good try. You almost came close to hitting me," he said patronizingly. His tone betrayed the utter disregard he had for Aaron. Apprentices where spoken to with more respect. "What's next, a bucket of water? How about some fruit or a fish." He laughed a heartily. "It would go well with the net." His sarcasm was not lost on Aaron nor the crowd.

Next, Aaron moved to the pile of weapons as Tarreck stepped around the right side of the net and continued his slow advance. As he rounded the net, Aaron tossed the two axes haphazardly at him making sure to pass them to his right side. They whooshed passed Tarreck with no effect. "Oh no," he said with feigned fear in his voice. With as desperate an expression as he could muster on his face, he frantically tossed the two swords. They tumbled towards Tarreck and landed a few feet in front of him.

Halting as they bounced erratically around, he watched them taking care not to be hit. Once they had come to a rest, he said contemptuously, "What's next, your armor?" He stepped up to the elven sword and moved the rod towards it. As he was about to touch it, he said flippantly, "Why bother?"

Aaron looked at the scene he had set up. He mustered every bit of strength and conviction he could find and prepared to fight. As he took a deep breath, he heard a mix of Peter's and Cragmore's voice echo in his head "You're ready. Now execute." An instant later, his own voice added, "And pray it works."

It was time to fight. He threw the two daggers at his opponent's midsection. They hit the mark. Tarreck doubled over from the impact but did not seem to feel the pain. As he drew them out, Aaron prepared himself. First, he draped the leggings of his armor around his neck so that his chin faced the crotch and the pant legs hung over his back. Once that was in place, he took the sleeves of the torso section in his right hand, letting the chest area hang to the ground. A murmur ran through the crowd as he worked. None had ever seen something like this before. Moreover, no one could fathom what the crazed boy might be thinking. Once he had a firm grip of the chain, he picked up his rod and ran towards Tarreck screaming, "Death to you and death to me."

The scene seemed so odd to Tarreck, he stopped and shook his head in disbelief. He was just passed the net and five feet beyond the swords. This was exactly what Aaron wanted. "You're insane," Tarreck said glibly. "I'll be doing you a favor by killing you." He raised his rod and braced himself against the charging boy.

Instead of charging through his opponent, Aaron stopped short. Using the armor in his right hand like a ball and chain, he swung at the crystal blade of the rod. Tarreck reflexively stabbed at the metal armor. When the chain made contact, Aaron released his grasp and let the arms wrap themselves around the blade and rod. Within seconds, the entire top half of the rod was encased in glass. Before Tarreck could fully understand what happened, Aaron caught up his own rod with both hands and hit Tarreck square in the chest. The glass-encased rod was knocked free and fell to the ground harmlessly. Tarreck looked around stunned. This was not supposed to be happening.

Aaron drove his rod into Tarreck's chest sending the man stumbling backwards. As the blows hit, Tarreck turned to catch himself and look for another weapon. He saw the swords laying on the ground and reached for one. Aaron's rod caught him in the back of the legs sending him sprawling onto the net. As he hit, he felt the thick black slippery oil that coated it. His hand fumbled for a place to catch hold so he could regain his footing. As he struggled,

Aaron hit him in the back with the rod keeping him down. The oil, combined with the barrage from the rod made it impossible for him to get up. Moreover, his continued struggling entangled him in the net. "This can't be happening," Tarreck exclaimed with frustration mounting in his voice.

Aaron used the rod to flip the net over onto his opponent. Even as he become more and more trapped by the net, Tarreck maintained his air of superiority. "Go ahead boy, keep trying. What can you do to me?" The plan was working well. Dropping the rod, he grabbed the leggings from around his neck. Throwing one leg of the armor over the entangled man, Aaron rolled the net over and grabbed the loose leggings. Tarreck grabbed at him without success. The combination of the net and the armor acted like a straight-jacket. His hands were pinned at his sides. Tarreck said insolently, "Now what? Are you going to ask me to yield? Perhaps you'll starve me to death. Or wait for me to fall asleep." He sighed indignantly as he continued, "Uhhh, you can't hurt me boy—give it up."

Aaron smiled at these comments, knowing the fight was all but over. He retrieved the two swords and returned to Tarreck's side. Peter's words played in his head as he moved, "No mercy! No mercy. No mercy." Rolling the bound man over with a flip of his foot, Aaron looked down at the helpless man and realized Tarreck had no idea what was about to happen. "Do you yield?"

His opponent smiled. "Tarreck never yields . . . Tarreck never looses." He shook his head arrogantly. "Those swords are useless. Your rod is useless. This net can't hold me forever. It's another stand-off. Eventually, I'll get free."

"So be it." Aaron barely noticed the deafening crowd noise as he worked. Raising the elven sword over his head, he took careful aim and brought it down with all the force he could muster. It hit just to the left of the net. The blade pierced through the leggings and penetrated a few inches into the floor of the Coliseum.

"You missed me boy. Try again."

Silently Aaron took up the two-handed sword and repeated

his actions. This time, however, he hit just to the right of the net again piercing the leggings and driving the sword several inches into the floor of the Coliseum. His confidence swelled. The battle was over. "I ask you one last time, do you yield?"

"Tarreck never yields. Tarreck never . . ."

Aaron cut him off and in a cold matter-of-fact tone said, "Then you die. You pompous egotistical fool." He slipped the backpack off and put it next to the net. Taking the knife out, he knelt next to Tarreck. Like a surgeon, he carefully cut away a few strands of the net near Tarreck's neckline.

Though helpless, Tarreck still jeered at his captor. "Now you're cutting me free. That knife can't hurt me. Haven't you realized that you can't win boy. Give up."

Ignoring what Tarreck said and the calls for action from the crowd, Aaron methodically worked the knife around the leather armor until it hit the cord that held the amulet around Tarreck's neck. With a sharp tug, he lifted it up and cut it at the same time. Tossing the knife to one side, he used his fingers to grab the ends of the strap. Carefully, he worked the amulet from around his opponent's neck. Leaning back, he dropped it into his backpack, and extracted a small metal case from inside. From the case, he removed a piece of flint. "Remember Tarreck, you were killed by a boy. No magic . . . no weapons . . . just a boy." Standing, he ran the piece of flint along the blade of the elven sword causing a shower of sparks to rain down on the netting. The oil flashed and began to burn. He continued speaking as he turned and walked away. "Killed by a boy you underestimated and dismissed . . . just a boy with a piece of flint and a splash of lantern oil."

As Tarreck realized what the true nature of the trap was, he began to scream. Fire consumed him before he could say anything but "No!" The entire oil-soaked net caught fire and began to blaze. The magical leather tried in vain to repair itself as it was incinerated. Tarreck's magic could not save him. He was neither cut by edged weapons nor bludgeoned by blunt ones. Fire was consuming him and stealing all his precious air.

As his body was burned, the crowd cheered. Aaron raised his hands victoriously. While slowly turning in a circle, he took in the scene. He told himself, "I'm the master now. All this is mine." For that moment, there was no quest, no outside world, no Redlin, no Konicker, no and no Peter. There was only Aaron Boewin, Master of the Grand Coliseum. He was the center of everything. Falling to his knees exhausted, he listened to the crowd cheering as the stones were pulled back to allow the attendants came to clear the ring. Whatever else might happen, this one moment belonged to him alone.

CHAPTER 25

While Aaron battled, Peter was brought to a place of healing within the Coliseum. The place was more like an operating room than a chapel but those inside were both priests and doctors. Benches lined the walls. Six long wooden tables filled the middle of the room. Most notable of all was the mix of smells that assaulted all who entered the room. Some were sweet and others pungent but most could only be recognized as death.

Vin leaned over the only occupied table. Around her was a cluster of bearded men wearing ceremonial robes. In her hand she held Peter's pale limp hand. Peter lay motionless on the table. Blood oozed from a deep gash cut in the right side of his throat and shoulder. His skin looked gray like the marble of the walls. Crimson stained his shirt from the collar to his waist.

Vin pleaded with the healers, "You have to do more. Help him." Before she could say more, Aaron stepped up behind her. As he took in the scene of Peter's torn body, Vin turned to him and put her arms around his midsection. "Oh, you made it." She was genuinely relieved to see him. Without looking up, she continued, "The healers stopped the bleeding but he's been poisoned. They can't close the wound." She raised her eyes to Aaron who still stared at Peter's body. "They say he won't live passed sunset."

"What about magic," he asked solemnly. "Can't the healers cast a spell?"

"Their magic doesn't work on the Geminarex. His own magic protects him." She sniffled, holding back tears. "He's too far gone to help himself. Even if he wanted to tell us what to do, he can't speak." Arching her back slightly, Vin leaned back and looked at Aaron. Tears streaked her cheeks. "We're all helpless. He's going to die."

Aaron pulled her close and hugged her trying to be supportive. "Don't give up. There's still time."

"But they've tried everything. All their magic was used up. They're spent." He could sense the dejection in her voice. She had already resigned herself to Peter's death.

"There's still one thing left." After placing his hands on her arms, he pushed her away and asked, "Where's the swords—the Geminarex?"

"What, they're there." She pointed to a space under the table. "But we already tried that. Their magic is gone or he can't use it in his condition." Her voice fell to a low disheartened tone. "It's no use."

He looked into her eyes saying, "I told you, don't give up. It's time to save Peter and set him free."

Bending down, he picked up the Justifier. Holding it, he bent over and put his lips next to Peter's ear. In a whisper he said, "My friend, it's time for you to let go of your duty, Your time is finished."

A gurgle came from Peter as blood trickled from his mouth. As he tried to speak, his head moved slightly to signal his dissent. In a barely audible tone that was less than a whisper he said, "No."

All crowded in though none could hear the exchange. "You have no choice. I know what I am asking. I want this. I truly understand what I'm asking for. I'm the only choice, my friend . . . your only hope now." Aaron said with conviction. He pressed his cheek close to Peter's as he continued, "Please, let me do this. It's what I want. It's what I need. It's what I've been waiting for."

After a long pause, Peter nodded 'yes' ever so slightly. Vin pressed, "What are you talking about?" When she received no answer, she put her hand on Aaron's shoulder and said, "Stop wasting his strength. Leave him alone."

Aaron drew Justifier out of its sheath and raised it up saying, "I know what I am undertaking as I draw you and your brother. I will be the keeper of the Geminarex."

As he said this, all those in the room except Vin stepped back from the blade. She tugged at his arm trying to stop him. Frantically, she yelled "What are you doing? Leave him alone."

Ignoring her, he touched the edge of Justifier's blade to Peter's forearm. A thin line of blood appeared as the blade cut like a razor. Instantly, Aaron's mind filled with more knowledge than it could handle at one time. Suddenly, his awareness of everything—his history, his surroundings, and, most of all, himself—was changed forever. In a calm tone, he said, "I am the keeper of the Geminarex. I now wield Justifier and Vindicator, the twin swords of truth and justice."

Vin exclaimed, "Stop! You can't be the Geminarex, Peter will die." Peter smiled as he turned his face to look at her.

Swiftly and more dexterously than he had ever moved before, Aaron bent and took up Vindicator. After removing the second sword from its sheath, he crossed the blades on Peter's chest saying, "To the unjustly slain, I return life. To those who have been wrongly attacked, I bring justice—morta, nova, erratteh." The swords glowed a brilliant white as he spoke the words. Peter's wounds closed and the color returned to his face.

Though he could not speak, Peter slowly moved his hand up to the chain around his neck and tore the Purple Dragon from it. Lifting his arm, he stretched the charm out towards Aaron. Once Aaron took it, Peter settled back and closed his eyes. Vin looked around confusedly. "Aaron, what's happened? Is he all right? Are you all right?"

Aaron looked passed her at Peter and said coldly, "He just needs rest now. I know him now. He's kept more from us than I could've imagined. Take the things we won today and return to Helexpa. If there's a problem, the healers can deal with it."

"What about you? Where are you going?"

"I must finish the quest I started. That means I must go to Thwardscall. I just hope I'm in time."

"In time for what?"

"To keep the others from their deaths." Turning to her, he said, "I now know all Peter knew . . . felt . . . thought. Stay with him; he needs you and the others need me. He knew you in his past . . . but that's no concern of mine now." Before she could fully comprehend what he was saying, he turned to leave.

While still looking at Peter, she called to Aaron. "What do you mean knew me? What else has he kept from us? What's in Thwardscall? What's so important?" Her questions spilled out as she struggled to understand all information. It was all happening too fast.

He stopped at the door but did not turn. In a grave tone he said, "Thrack Morgan's in Thwardscall. Slayer's in Thwardscall. My quest's in Thwardscall. Redlin made Morgan think that Slayer would be in the pit . . . so he would wait for us. He needs Slayer and wants us dead. Peter can tell you the rest." Aaron lifted the purple dragon Peter had given him as he stepped out the door. "I vowed to recover Slayer—it's in Thwardscall. Get it or die trying . . . that's my quest."

CHAPTER 26

Once Jeremy and Twig were clear of the keep, they headed up into the edge of the Blackspine. After a time of hard climbing, they reached a summit where they stopped to rest and gather themselves. The sun was setting as they looked across the valley that stretched out in front of them. Neither had said much while they were walking. Fear and exhaustion had worked together to keep them occupied and silent.

Jeremy spoke first as he scanned the horizon for signs of Thwardscall. Calling to Twig, he pointed at something off to the north. "I think that's Thwardscall . . . about a day away."

Twig squinted her eyes and peered off into the falling night. "I think I see it." As dusk turned to nigh, the lights of Thwardscall begin to glow.

"Let's rest here and move on in the morning, if that's okay. I'll try and find some food and you can start a fire."

"All right, I guess . . . a fire would be nice and I am hungry. Just be careful."

His first move was to dump out the sack and put the books safely under a tree with Splinter resting on top of them. "I'll be right back." Smiling, he added jokingly, "I expect a nice fire when I get back." She chuckled as she frowned with feigned disapproval. Rustling through the underbrush, he moved off into the darkness.

As he moved out amongst the bushes, Twig gathered sticks and branches for a fire. In a few minutes, she had a good sized pile built up with enough set to the side to last the night. With a flick of her finger, she created a flame and lit the fire. It caught quickly and began to burn. She settled down next to a large oak and leaned back. Taking up one of Swinson's books of magic, she began to read by the rapidly disappearing daylight and the flickering firelight.

Jeremy returned with a sack full of berries and edible roots. She was so involved in her reading, she did not hear him until he was on top of her. After putting the sack down, he settled in next to her as he said, "What's so interesting?"

"Oh! You startled me." she said with a start. They both leaned back resting against the tree. Relaxing, she continued, "It's nothing. Just another book; it's about casting spells and that stuff." Closing the book, she put it down next to her and moved closer to Jeremy.

"You don't have to stop on account of me. I'm happy to just sit and rest. I'm tired." He stretched his neck and then put his head back so it rested on the tree.

"That's okay, it's getting dark and I'm tired too." Though they had been together all day, this was the first time she had stopped and actually looked at him. Shadows from the fire danced across his face. Even in the poor light, she could see the concern on his beaten and bruised face. She noticed a bit of blood that had collected just below the corner of his mouth and dried. Wetting the index finger of her left hand with her tongue, she leaned over to look at his face more closely. Using her moist fingertip, she gently brushed away the dried blood. In a tender voice she said, "Thank you for saving me and, well, I'm . . . I'm sorry . . . I . . . it's, all my fault. You . . . this, all this should never have happened . . . I'm sorry."

He brought his right hand up and put it atop hers. In an equally soft and tender voice, he said, "No . . . don't be sorry . . . you saved me."

"If not for me . . . well . . . you wouldn't be here . . . you should've left me . . . been far away, long ago."

"I'd never . . . I couldn't even think of leaving you . . . I'd follow you . . . I couldn't forget you . . . couldn't be without you."

She blushed as her wiping became more of a touching and caressing. Her finger played over his cheek feeling its smoothness and its warmth. "Thank you . . . that means a lot." He took up her other hand in his free left hand. She giggled with nervousness as he leaned in closer. Slowly he tilted his head and kissed her. As their lips met, both sighed. She returned his kiss as he wrapped his arm around her. Everything felt natural and as it should be. After a long moment, the kiss ended. The embrace lasted for a few moments longer and then the two sat back.

Jeremy spoke first, saying, "Now what?"

"We go to Thwardscall," she replied.

"I meant about us . . . this isn't the time for . . . well, you know, us." They both laughed.

"Go to Thwardscall and get a room," she said as she kissed his cheek.

Embarrassed by her response, he smiled a wide smile and shook his head happily. "Okay, but I didn't mean that . . . I, oh, I mean . . . I don't know. It's not the right time for any of this." Shaking his head, he continued, "I'm just so confused."

"I don't know what to say . . . we're on a quest . . . we're on our own and we're . . . well, together . . . with one another but still all alone . . . on our own." Lacing her fingers into his, she took his hand in her lap as she continued. "I don't know what's going to happen but I know I love you . . . that's enough. I'm not leaving you and I hope ..."

Before she could finish, he interjected, "I love you too and I'd never leave you either."

She kissed him. "Thank you . . . I needed to hear that. But I don't know . . . I don't think, well . . . I . . . we . . . can't control that."

"We'll be okay . . . I know it." He tried to sound as positive and confident as possible.

"I'd like to believe that but, well, we're who knows how far from Thwardscall . . . we have no supplies . . . one ax and a bag of magic books. Even if we make it, who knows if anyone else will be there to show us what to do. Our quest might be over whether we want it to be or not." She dropped her head. "I just don't think we'll be able to do it by ourselves . . . even if we want to."

With his free hand, Jeremy reached into his shirt and produced the star. "This is all we need to complete the quest."

She looked at it curiously. "What good is a star? Is it a magical direction finder?"

"Better than that." With it still around his neck, he pushed it towards her so she could see it more closely. "Redlin gave it to me . . . it will be the guide to our contacts in Thwardscall. There's a code and then we'll be told what to do." He hesitated and then sheepishly continued like a guilty schoolboy revealing a well kept secret. "I'm not supposed to show it to anyone until we get to Thwardscall but you're different. I want you to know about it . . . so you'd know we're still all right."

She took hold of it gingerly and examined it. "Does it do anything? Is it magic?"

"I don't know. I was only told what to say and when to say it. Other than that, I'm on my own."

Snuggling into his side, she squeezed his hand. "I feel better now that I know but there's still . . . still so much to worry about."

Jeremy hugged her and brushed her hair with his palm. "Shh . . . it's nothing we have to worry about now. For now, let's just forget everything but us. We'll worry tomorrow . . . tomorrow we'll go to Thwardscall . . . tomorrow."

She put her head on his shoulder. Closing her eyes, she said, "I'm so tired and you feel so warm and comfortable. I wish we didn't have to go. I don't want tomorrow to come."

Kissing her softly, he said, "Neither do I." Moving as little as possible, he put more wood on the fire. With that done, he wrapped his arms around her to keep her warm. Closing his eyes, he breathed in her fragrance and tried to remember everything he could sense. He feared that this might be the last night they ever spent together.

CHAPTER 27

Vin stood and stretched as Peter dismounted while three other horses futilely foraged for something to eat nearby. All the horses were packed with the things won in the Coliseum the day before. After riding for half a day, Peter had decided to stop as much to rest as to avoid the constant questioning from his companion. Though she had tried repeatedly to get him to talk, Vin had not been successful. The scowl Peter now wore was the softest expression that adorned his face the entire time he had been with her. As consciousness had come to him, so did his current mood. It had not lessened now that they were returning to Helexpa. Until now, she had been patient. The time for waiting was over. "Talk to me," she said firmly as she put her hand on his forearm.

Ignoring her, he freed himself from her touch. "Let's just go." He moved to remount his horse.

Vin quickly put a hand on his arm to stop him. "Why won't you talk to me . . . tell me what's wrong . . . explain what happened . . . why Aaron left . . . tell me anything at all."

"Because I don't want to . . . at least not right now."

"I could make you," Vin said coldly but then thought better of it. "But I wouldn't do that to you." she added apologetically.

"I'm glad to hear that and I'm sorry." He relaxed slightly and turned to look at her. "You have to understand or maybe you can't. I've lost my . . . uuhhh, I can't explain."

"You lost your what . . . your power . . . your what?" she pried without pressing.

"Too much and not enough. I . . . oh, I just . . . its too hard to explain." He stopped his horse. "I'm free but I have no honor . . . the boy took my burden and left me with nothing but . . . oh, never mind."

"No, don't stop." As she heard herself all but yell these words, she softened her tone. "Please talk to me. I want to listen and help you."

"You just want another story . . . something to occupy your mind and your time." His words were harsh and biting and meant to be that way.

A surge of anger swelled inside of Vin. With obvious effort, she quelled it. "If I wanted a story, I could have followed the boy. I was worried about you. Please, let me help you."

"Like you helped me before. I guess this time's different." he blurted out like a scorned lover.

"What do you mean, this time?"

Turning to her, he drove his gaze deep into her eyes. "Do you remember a boy named Jonathan. It was many years ago, on a quest to the lost kingdom of Granthenor, to find the magic machine."

After no more than a moment, she nodded her head and responded, "I remember. I think of him often. We fell in . . . had a. . . . were close. What does that have to do with this and you and Aaron? Did you know him?"

Peter saw immediately the pain of her memories and that her emotions were real. "What can you tell me of the boy and the quest?"

"I don't see what this has to do with anything. It's a painful part of my life—my past."

"Please, humor me. It's important, if you really want to help."

She began hesitantly, "I had joined a group as you said. I was enthralled by one of the young men. He was so different than the others. We would talk for hours on the journey. It was more than just his story. We became friends . . . and much more. But then it all ended when we came to Granthenor. Our party was destroyed and Johnny was killed . . . crushed by one of the stone guardians of the city. We tried to fight them off and save those who were left, but it was no use. An elven mage grabbed me and the healer and transported us back to Stalliac with a spell. The lost city was lost again. I drove it from my mind"

Peter shook his head slowly. "Did you love him . . . Johnny I mean?"

Though she was silent for a few moments, her expression betrayed her true feelings. Slowly she answered him saying, "As much as any Azurine can love another." As she recalled all this, she struggled to hold back her tears. "Those Azurine sent to travel amongst the world are forbidden to become involved in any way. Ours is the role of scribe . . . our duty to record. We rarely reminisce about our past and never become involved in the adventures of the present."

Peter could see she truly felt the loss. Putting his hand on hers, he said, "I'm sorry . . . it's been so long." He bent and kissed her tenderly

"What do you have to be sorry for?"

"I'm sorry for waiting so long . . . for hating you and resenting you."

Vin looked at him with perplexity as she tried to understand what he was saying to her. "Why would you hate me?"

Taking her face in his hands he stared into her eyes. "Look deep into me. see what is there behind the Geminarex, the battles, the years since we first met." She returned his gaze searching his stare for what he spoke of. As she looked, he continued, "It's me . . . I'm Johnny . . . Peter Jonathan Zorich."

Her face went slack as she looked at him in disbelief. "That's impossible," was all she could say as she continued to search for familiar in his face.

"It's not impossible, it's really me." He wiped a tear for her cheek as he continued. "I was pinned under the rubble of the building but not killed. When I dug myself out, everyone was dead or gone. It took years for me to recover and then make my way back to civilization. I searched for you, but it was no use. You were gone. Soon after, my brother was killed. It was then I decided to take my place as the Geminarex. With that, my thoughts of you were lost amongst those of the thousands of other loves that had been lost by those that came before me."

"Why tell me this now? Why did you wait? And what does this have to do with Aaron and the others."

"I couldn't be sure you'd remember or want to remember me. I couldn't let it interfere with the quest. Now I'm free from my oaths and without the Geminarex, all my thoughts are of you. When Aaron became the keeper of the swords, he knew all I knew. At that instant, he was me and then he assumed my burden as he took my purpose. He freed me from my responsibility, my oath, my every obligation. But I was left with nothing to hold on to but my memories." He shook his head in disgust. "And I'm happy for that and I hate myself for being happy." Shaking his head, he continued in a soft dejected voice. "You say you want to help, but I don't know what can help me now. No one knows or can know what I've been through . . . what I've lost . . . what I still have to lose."

She wanted to say something to help, but had no idea what the words should be. In a consoling tone, she said, "Don't hate yourself. I know what you were.. what you are. It was his choice . . . his decision. He did it for himself and for the quest. It was the only choice. Saving you brought you back to us . . . to me."

"But he got more than you or he could imagine and I lost more than I could have ever thought. I'm empty. My life has nothing but the fleeting memory of you and my failures."

A puzzled look swept over her face as she tried to understand what he was saying. Though hesitant to ask questions, she had to probe deeper. Cautiously, she asked, "What have you lost? What did he find out?"

"More than I can relate to you. You wouldn't understand."

"Stop saying that!" she heard herself scream in her own mind. In a soft persuasive tone, she said, "No, tell me all of it. Let me hear for myself. I'll understand—trust me like you once did." Her subtle charm worked.

"I'm vulnerable . . . weak . . . confused . . . I can't see all that I did yesterday. I don't know all that I knew a day ago. It's as if a huge part of me has been torn away leaving the rest to scramble and pick up the pieces. I'm a different person . . . less, much less a warrior, far less a man. I'm lost . . . set adrift . . . dishonored . . . disgraced. I have no home and no purpose."

The honesty of his words touched her. Though she had heard thousands of stories in her life, Peter's was more alive for her. As he opened up, she felt herself being drawn in as she had years before. It was as if she had a need to know not just a want. "Uhuh . . . go on," was all she said as he continued.

"When Aaron took the swords, he knew all my intimate secrets . . . everything that I knew, that was only mine to know." He ran his head over his face as he spoke. "I guess I should be honest with you. It's the least I owe you now."

She looked at him to try and read his expression. It had never crossed her mind that he could be dishonest. "What more do I need to know? What else have you kept from us . . . from me?"

Taking a deep breath, he held it for a second and then released it in a long slow exhale. Everything around them seemed to linger in silence waiting for him to begin speaking. "Redlin and I had worked out the scheme but it all went wrong when I . . . when he . . . when all this happened to me."

"What are you talking about? We have all this." She gestured to the things packed on the horses. "Was there something we missed?"

"No . . . none of this was that important. All this . . . all our efforts are just a diversion."

"What do you mean?" Her genuine confusion softened the emphasis she was putting behind the question. "What plan?"

"Our whole quest was . . . is a distraction. Redlin needs generals can use these weapons to fight Morgan but he mostly needed time. Time we've given him."

"What about Thwardscall? The others were headed there . . . to meet the envoys and get the Slayer of Evermore." Fear and concern tinged her voice as she spoke.

"Thwardscall is infested with vermin working for Morgan. Redlin knew that. He sent us there so the city wouldn't fall. It's a suicide mission. Morgan's forces are already beyond Thwardscall and pouring into the Forbidden Lands. Redlin needed time to move his armies north and catch Morgan's troops at the narrow part of the valley."

Slowly, she began to realize what had been happening. "What about the others . . . about Aaron? Slayer . . . is it there . . . is it real? You and me? What about the Purple Dragon code . . . our quest to Thwardscall?" Her words sputtered out as she tried to ask all her questions at once.

He continued speaking without trying to separate out the multitude of questions. "Redlin used the others to delay Morgan's actions. Once there was a chance Slayer was in the city, he'd have to stop his advance and search the city. Redlin counted on that. He wanted it to seem like he was desperate and we were his only hope."

"But is it there . . . Slayer I mean?"

"Yes . . . Max Konicker is waiting in Thwardscall for the signal. One of Redlin's spies told him that Morgan devised a spell powerful enough to locate Konicker and the ax but not pinpoint it. That's when he sent for me and told me his plan. It was bad from the start. Permillion didn't arrive . . . then Helexpa was attacked and the allies were killed. I should've stopped then, but Redlin said it could still work. All he needed was a week . . . everything would be . . . just a week." He turned his face to her and said, "I knew how important it was to stop Morgan. That's why I went along with it . . . with the deception."

The words hit like knives. "Why me? I'm not part of any of this."

"Exactly. I was afraid you'd see through it but Redlin said you were a vital part of his plan . . . necessary for its success. I didn't tell him about our past and when you didn't recognize me in Hamiltanville, I kept it to myself."

"What about the others?"

"They're capable and expendable. The children wouldn't ask questions and the others owed Redlin their lives. He kept modify-

ing the scheme but the goal was always the same—get to
Thwardscall and let Konicker know that Morgan was watching . . .
waiting. None knew what was to happen but it wouldn't have
mattered. They were all sworn to Redlin. Konicker couldn't get
Slayer to Redlin without help."

"How could you let that happen? How could you not tell
them? You sent them off to die. What happened to you?" None of
her feelings or emotions were hidden now. None of her words were
softened to spare him.

"That's why their quest was for Slayer of Evermore, not for the
weapons. That was my quest and I..."

She cut him off saying, "That's no excuse. You'd have been
better off just killing them. Morgan will torture them . . . if they
even make it that far."

"I know. That's why Aaron left. He went to stop the others . . .
to save them. His oath was to get Slayer. That's what he's doing.
He knows the plan. He knows Morgan is waiting for them to
reveal where Konicker is."

"I thought you said Morgan wanted to kill them . . . capture
them . . . whatever. How do I know what's the truth? Everything
you say . . . it's all suspect. How could you have been the keeper of
the Geminarex? Truth, justice . . . what happened to you? How
could the man I loved have changed so much?" She shook her head
in disgust as she looked at him.

"We're all prepared to die for the cause. Redlin needed the
weapons I'm bringing. He told me to train the boy. I did both.
Aaron learned more here, from me, than, than he . . . oh, never
mind . . . you won't understand."

"Stop saying that." Frustration showed in her voice. "I
understand too well."

"No you don't . . . none of this would've happened if not for
you."

"What?" she exclaimed in disbelief. "How's this my fault?
Because I left you?"

"No. It was an Azurine who helped Morgan find Slayer . . .

who told him of Redlin's weaknesses . . . who brought about all this. An Azurine started this for a story or revenge or something."

"It wasn't me. I never did any of that," she retorted defensively.

"It might as well have been you. A copy of your writings were turned over to him. Everything you know, he knows too." She was speechless. Turning to her, he said, "You ask how I can stand for truth . . . for justice. I can't . . . I never wanted to. The duty . . . the obligation . . . all that is the Geminarex, it was given to me to carry . . . forced upon me when my brother was killed by Morgan. I ran to it to escape my thoughts of you just like I ran to the quest to escape my destiny—the Geminarex." He shook his head and paced as he searched for words. "Ahhh . . . it was Morgan . . . he . . . the whole thing . . . it had to be stopped . . . killed, destroyed or millions of innocents would be slaughtered." He leaned in close to her and accentuated his words. "I say slaughtered not just killed. He wipes out entire villages to show his power . . . hundreds were sacrificed to summon Thazul and his demons. Whole towns leveled to clear his way. The beast, the barbarians, and all his followers are cruel vicious monsters." He leaned back and tried to calm himself. "I spent two years of my life—from the instant I received the swords until Redlin called me—tracking Morgan. I saw all the destruction . . . all the pain. There is no justice if Morgan wins . . . if Morgan lives." His voice faltered as he dropped his head. "I sacrificed myself to stop him and now I've even lost that. I trusted Redlin when we said Morgan would wait if we fought in Phinn . . . if we went to Thwardscall. I had to believe him . . . I wanted to. I don't know what to trust . . . what to do . . . where to go. In the end, I'm lost and worthless."

As much as she wanted to be angry with him or hate him, she could not find those emotions. Her heart ached to see him in pain. She stepped up next to him. "You did what you had to do." Putting her hand on his shoulder, she cast a charm to ease his worry. "Don't worry, it'll all be better soon. I'm here."

He smiled at her and said, "Thank you for being here."

"Why didn't you follow Aaron? We could've caught him . . .

stopped him?" She tried to distract him with the question while the charm worked.

"He knows everything I knew and more. He now has perfect recall of everything he's ever read or heard."

"So, why does that matter?"

"He pledged to secure the Slayer of Evermore. That's his quest—he gave his oath. Now he knows it lies in Thwardscall. My quest was to give Redlin time and get him these items. That's my quest. Once he knew these things didn't matter to him, he left." Exhaling loudly, he looked off at the eastern edge of the mountains. "I'm still bound by my oath . . . what little that's worth. I gave my word I'd get these to Redlin." Gesturing to the packed horses, he continued, "Once all this junk is delivered, I'm free. Then, and only then, am I free. I can hunt Morgan and I will." Turning to her with a tear in his eye, he added, "It's the least I owe Aaron." Lowering his head and turning away, he returned to his horse and mounted. "Let's go. It's late and we still have a long way to go if we're to make it to Helexpa tonight." With that, she mounted and the two rode off.

CHAPTER 28

Jack and Shane sat across from one another at a side table in an empty dining hall deep inside Helexpa. Though brightly lit and large enough for hundreds of giants to feast comfortably, the room seemed confining and ominously forbidding now that it was empty except for the two bounty hunters. Each man stared at his breakfast, not sure if it was better to eat it or push it aside. Neither was in the mood to eat. Shane broke the silence first. His voice echoed off the ceiling as he spoke. "So why do you think Redlin's kept us here . . . I mean for so long? I wanted to head right back out but, well, he said to stay."

"So you did . . . without worrying about it?" Jack said sarcastically. "Now you're tired of waiting and need me to get us going again," he added with a smile.

"Well, I didn't see you so eager to leave after riding that monster into here." Shaking his head, he continued, "Ahhhhh . . . you've been here as long as I have—big man. All you do is play with that scaly fireplace."

"What're you trying to say, little man?" Jack asked his friend kiddingly.

"Well, I guess, if I were you, I wouldn't be saying I was the one doing stuff . . . getting us moving . . . least not around here." Shane hit Jack with the back of his hand. As he continued, "You're too lazy to get us going anywhere."

In a distracted, searching tone, he asked, "So did Redlin tell you why we're supposed to wait for him here?" He prodded at his food and added, "I thought, maybe, it was something about us getting back on the trail . . . track down the others." Raising his voice slightly, he suggested, "Or maybe even Morgan."

"Nope, didn't hear a thing," Jack said flatly.

Seeing no reaction to his first line of questioning, he asked, "How's it going with the monster? Any progress?"

"He's doing well. I've been able to ride him around pretty expertly if I do say so myself and his name is Quinx, not the monster."

"Growing attached to the little guy are you big man?" he said jokingly.

Jack did not appreciate the humor. "Shut up Shane; just shut up. At least I'm doing something, not just waiting for my bumps to heal and worrying about when I'll be let out." Jack's tone shifted from sarcastic to a more serious harsh indictment of his partner. "So how's that leg doing anyway?"

Before Shane could answer, Redlin entered the room and in a booming voice announced, "We've much to do. Come with me." He waited as the two scrambled to their feet. Jack moved quickly across the room as Shane limped slightly on the leg that had been hit by the guar. As he came up behind Redlin, the half fire-giant asked, "How's the leg? Guar cuts can be deadly."

He turned his head slightly and stared at Jack as he answered. "I'm fine. I was lucky; it was only a small puncture—only one of the claws."

"Good to hear. I need as many fighters as I can get. We're moving out today." Both Jack and Shane smiled to one another and each knew all was forgiven. Redlin led them through the halls of his castle, occasionally stopping to let the other two catch up. The journey ended at a small private sitting room far to one side of Helexpa where few outsiders were ever allowed. After opening an ornately carved iron door, he gestured for the two to enter, saying, "Please come inside. I need to discuss some things with you before you leave Helexpa." Both entered and looked around. Once they were inside, he closed the door behind them and barred it from the inside with a huge slab of metal too large for anyone but himself to move.

As best as Shane and Jack could tell, this was a private meeting room. Eight large plush high-backed chairs that looked extremely comfortable were arranged around a small table in the center of the room. An open hearth fireplace filled the far wall. A fire roared in it filling the room with a bright orange glow. Immediately upon entering, the two bounty hunters noticed Darvan sitting on the far side of the room. He rested uneasily in one of the two chairs that had a view of the door. Off to one side, a slender male elf stood rigidly at attention. He was young for an elf and wore the clothing of a royal page. A bulging black satchel was strapped across his shoulders and hung down passed his knees. Jack stepped forward and Shane followed him into the room.

Redlin moved passed them saying, "I wish the circumstances of our meeting were different . . . very different but they're not. There's too many problems to deal with and not nearly enough time." He moved to the seat next to Darvan. As he walked, Redlin gestured towards two of the other chairs and said in a powerful and commanding voice, "Please take a seat. I've no time to waste." He sat. While Redlin settled back, the page took up a position behind and to his right.

Shane limped along behind Jack as he made his way to an open chair and sat down tensely. As they headed for a place to sit, they both realized that there were others present. Peter and Vin waited quietly in a pair of adjacent chairs across from Darvan and Redlin. As they sat, Jack summed up their feelings by muttering under his breath, "Oh no, this can't be good, not good at all."

Redlin did not wait for anyone else to speak. "Forget about everything that's happened. Ignore anything you might have heard or been told before. The only thing that matters is what I'm about to tell you." He leaned forward. Everyone leaned towards the center of the circle of chairs. In a confidential tone, he said slowly, "Morgan is waiting in Thwardscall." There was a long pause as his words sunk into the minds of his audience.

Vin broke the uneasy silence. "Does he know about . . . about Thwardscall? Why is he?"

Redlin cut her off, not bothering with tact or decorum. "Don't talk—listen." He softened his tone and continued. "We've all been

talking too much . . . planning too much. Now its time to act."
His eyes scanned clockwise around the room. Stopping at each
person in turn, he paused for a few seconds to make eye-contact
before continuing. "As far as I can tell, Aaron's at least a day's ride
away from Thwardscall right now but riding there fast. He knows
all we know and maybe more. He's in good shape, but on his
own." He glanced back to Peter as he said this. "The other two—
Permillion's group—they're nearer, but exactly where is anyone's
guess and they're on foot. I'm more worried for them, but there's
little we can do now." His eyes shifted to Darvan who nodded yes
casually. "Gallis is almost healed but he won't be of use to anyone
for a while yet. The guar made sure of that." Everyone nodded
their understanding. Redlin looked at Shane and asked, "How's
the leg? Are you well enough?"

Proudly Shane answered without hesitation, "I'm ready. My
life is yours Lord Redlin, No task too great."

"Good, I might need it." No one as much as smiled. Redlin
continued without pause. "Jack, how's the beast?"

"Quinx is strong and healthy and he trusts me. I can ride him
anywhere, I think." He glanced over to Vin and caught a glimpse
of a smile that passed over her lips.

It quickly disappeared as Redlin continued. "How well can
you fight from his back?"

"As well as you need. I'm . . . we're a good team."

"Good enough; be ready to leave for Thwardscall tonight."
Redlin stood, towering over the others who had to crane their
necks to keep eye-contact with him. "My plans are working well.
Morgan's in Thwardscall, his armies are in the just moving out of
the Valley of the Dragons, and Slayer of Evermore is still just out
of his grasp. Tonight we move; tomorrow we strike."

Turning to the page, he stretched out his hand. The elf replied
silently by taking five scroll cases made of bone out of the satchel.
He handed one to each of the seated individuals. Redlin turned
back and began to speak. "Take these, read them, and decide what
you will do on your own. I hold you to no oaths . . . no promises.

But now, I ask you for your help as a friend. I've wagered my life, the lives of my armies, and my allies but you have done all I asked and now you must choose for yourself." He crossed the room and turned just as he reached the door. "Forget about the others— Aaron, Jeremy, and Twig—they're on their own now. We've all been charged with a greater task. We are going to fight the war against Morgan and I need every one of you. If you choose to come with me, then outfit yourselves and be ready to leave by nightfall. Most of my armies have already gone north. My wizards will send the rest soon and then we will go. Morgan must be stopped. He can't leave Thwardscall alive." Redlin effortlessly slid the metal slab back and opened the door. "Read the scrolls . . . take the payments inside. Then do what your heart tells you is right. I must prepare for the battle."

As Redlin paused, Peter lifted his hand. In it he held the engraved card that Redlin had given him years before. "Redlin, my friend, you hold me to no oaths but I hold you to yours. You owe me a favor and I'm calling in your marker."

Redlin nodded once saying, "Read what it is I want and then come to me. I will honor your request, whatever it might be."

As he was turning to leave, Vin asked, "What is it you want?"

In a quiet fatherly voice, he replied, "I want you to make a choice. It's all in the scrolls. Once you've decided for yourselves, my page will take you wherever you wish. I hope and pray you'll choose to join me. If you do, the next time I see you it will be on the battlefield. I only pray that we are all still alive." Lowering his head humbly, he added, "If you choose to leave, live well and thank you. If you choose to fight, fight well and be remembered with those who stood at my side against Morgan. If it is your fate to die, then die proudly and with honor." With that, he turned and walked away. An eerie calm silence fell over the room as all those sitting there looked at one another saying nothing.

Jack acted first. Opening his scroll case, he poured out the contents on his lap. A magnificent diamond necklace fell out. Paying it no attention, he dug inside the scroll case with two fingers to pull out a rolled piece of parchment. As he read it, the others followed his lead opening and reading their scrolls as well.

Each case contained a valuable piece of jewelry and a small piece of parchment just like that in Jack's case. All the messages were the same. The paper read, "Follow me to save the innocents or save yourself. The choice is yours to make."

CHAPTER 29

Warmth from a fire greeted Jeremy as he awoke. Hunger that had not seemed so important last night, loomed much larger in his mind now. Opening his eyes, he looked around for Twig. He found her a few feet away reading the books of magic near a small fire she had built. Next to her were two chunks of tree bark which she had used as dishes for the food he had collected. One was mostly finished while the other was heaped high. As he rustled around, she turned to him and said, "Good, you're awake. I thought I'd let you sleep while I built a fire and set out our breakfast." She gestured to the full plate saying, "Come have some food."

Sitting up, he shook the sleep from his head and rubbed it from his eyes. "Thanks. Food's a good idea but we should probably get moving. With Thwardscall a day or two away, we should head out as soon as possible." Moving closer to her, he took up the plate of food. "But, well, that's just my suggestion; you're still in charge."

She laughed out loud. "Okay, if you say so but when we get to Thwardscall, you're the one with the directions. Then, I guess, you're in charge."

Smiling, he nodded his head slowly. "Okay, when we get there, I'll take the lead but you still make the decisions."

"Well then, get up, eat your breakfast, and let's get moving. It's getting late."

As Jeremy picked up the plate and ate, Twig put the few scraps of food they had left over into the sack with all the magic books. Once he was finished, he picked up Splinter saying, "I'm ready, can we go?"

Throwing the sack over her shoulder, she began walking down the side of the hill. "I'm already going. Come on, catch up."

After putting Splinter on his shoulder, he headed down the hill after her. He did his best to keep the ax balanced as he bounded along dodging tree roots and small shrubs that seemed to pop up and throw themselves in his way. When he finally caught her, he asked, "Why are you so full of energy? You seem almost giddy."

Shrugging her shoulders, she said, "I'm happy. I liked waking up next to you without anyone around to bother us. It was nice for once not to be . . . I don't know . . . it was nice and those books I read . . . they were great."

Her words pleased but confused him. "I'm more worried than happy," he put forth. "I don't know what's going to be waiting for us in Thwardscall and I can't seem to do anything right these days."

"Nonsense, everything is going to be fine. You have the star and you've been doing wonderfully so far." She put her arm around his waist and added, "Now stop thinking about that. I'm in charge and I say to stop so you have to stop."

In an unconvinced tone, he replied, "Okay, I guess you're right. You're the boss." Trying to change the subject, he asked, "So what was in the books?"

She perked up at the question. "Besides the two from Gallis, I got three from the library." She let her arm slip down from around his waist and take up his hand. "So anyway, these book are all about magic. A lot of it I knew but some was new. One told all about casting the offensive spells . . . control, accuracy, shaping . . . all that stuff. It was great. Another told a story of Morgan and our master. The third had a chronicle of the great battles of the past three centuries. All described strange magic and spells I never knew existed. I don't know If I could ever cast them; they seemed tough."

As they headed down out of the hills onto the floor of the valley, they could see the vague outline of Thwardscall in the distance. "It'll be a while before we're there. If you can read while we walk, I can lead you. It's probably a good idea that you get them read as soon as possible."

"That's a great idea. I can read to you while we go." She tugged at his hand as she added, "Just don't walk us into any trees or ditches or anything."

"Okay, we'll be in Thwardscall in no time." He let her hand go as she took the sack off her shoulder. Reaching inside, she felt around and extracted a red velvet-covered tome with ornate golden artistry on the cover. Before she could replace the sack, he grabbed it saying, "Give me that, how do you expect to read and hold my hand with that on your arm?" She did not argue. He hooked the sack around the handle of the ax so that the whole thing balanced on his shoulder like a seesaw. He used his free hand to steady and adjust the ax which teetered slightly as he moved.

Opening the book, she said, "Looks good, let's go." She slipped her hand in his and waited for him to move them forward. Once he had taken a step, she started reading.

The time passed quickly as Thwardscall grew more clear on the horizon. Except for a few stops to change books, the two waked continuously until they were at the outskirts of the city. It had taken longer than they expected to reach their destination. The sun was setting as they reached the first buildings of Thwardscall. As they passed the city limits, Jeremy could feel the star he wore begin to tingle under his shirt. "We should put these things away and I should hold Splinter. It's all up to you now," Twig said as she reached for the ax on his shoulder. Removing the sack, he handed it to her. After dropping the book in, she gave it back to him.

He handed her the ax and slung the sack over his shoulder. "Okay, now I can do my part but I'm not sure exactly how to go about it."

"What're you supposed to do?"

"Say thrack, arrato, mambo, delivan, to someone. I'm not sure who."

"Well, let's hope they know to come find you or you'll be saying that a lot and we'll confuse a lot of people."

They laughed together and started into Thwardscall. All those who lined the streets could see their wide eyes and lack of direction. If not for Splinter, they would be choice marks for robbers, thieves, and swindlers. The ax, however, kept those types and many other good people at a safe distance.

From what they could see, the city itself was simple. Two and three story wooden buildings lined the dirt streets. Merchants sold their goods in stores as well as in stands. A number of meager homes made up most of the buildings at the southern end of town that they now entered. Before the two could get more than a few steps beyond the first building, a young shabbily dressed boy stepped up to them with a smile on his face and a scroll in his hand. In a salesman's voice, he said "Hello sir, would you like to buy a map of our fine city? My father draws them himself and they're very accurate and they're not very expensive."

"Thrack, arrato mambo, delivan," Jeremy said as he looked at the boy.

Undaunted by the words, the boy said, "I'm sorry sir, I don't speak that language." He looked at Twig and said again, "Would you like to buy a map?"

She responded in a sweet tone, "I'd love a map but we've nothing to buy it with unless you'll trade."

The boy said, "What did you have in mind?"

Jeremy looked at her oddly and asked, "What do we have to trade?"

She whispered to him confidentially, "I'll think of something. The map will be very useful. We should get it."

Pointing at the ax, the boy asked, "Do you have more magic like that in the bag? Anything small would be fine. Magic's worth a great deal."

Jeremy said cautiously in a whisper, "What're you thinking? We can't give him anything we have, especially for a simple map."

"Don't worry. Just give me the sack."

Obeying, he took the sack off his shoulder. She took it and put it on the ground. Kneeling next to it, she picked up a small palm-sized stone, making sure the boy could not see. She reached into the bag and pretended to feel around with her hand searching for something. Squeezing the rock, she concentrated and cast the spell.

"Here it is. I think you'll like this as a trade." She produced the stone and held it out towards the boy.

"It's a rock?" he said skeptically. "What's so magical about a rock?"

It was her turn to be a saleswoman. In a soft confidential tone, she said, "All you have to do is say the magic words and the stone will glow bright enough to light a room."

"What's the words?" the boy asked anxiously.

"First, let's see the map." He handed her the scroll. Spreading it open, she examined it. "It looks quite good." As she spoke she showed Jeremy the map.

He nodded his agreement, saying, "Yes, it's very nice."

"Now the magic words, what are they? Tell me." The boy could barely contain himself.

"Just touch the stone and say, light up stone, and it will. But you need to be careful not to use up all the magic too quickly. Watch." She extended her finger and touched the stone saying, "Light up stone." The stone began to glow with a brilliant white light. After a moment, she touched it again saying, "Be dark," and the light of the stone disappeared.

The boy was amazed. Ecstatically, he said, "Thanks!" and ran off into the city.

Jeremy turned to her saying, "Well, now we have a map, but still no place to go."

"That's okay, at least now we won't retrace our own steps. We can see where we're going even if it isn't leading us anywhere."

As they were about to set out into the heart of city, the small boy came running back followed by a slender man wearing a black cloak over leather armor. Before they could do much more than take in the scene, the out-of-breath man was next to them. The boy spoke directly to the man, saying, "These are the travelers . . . the ones you said you're looking for. They have magic."

The man looked over the two. His eyes stopped on Splinter. After handing the boy a gold coin, he looked at Twig and said, "You carry the ax. Do you know of Redlin and the Forbidden Lands?"

Jeremy broke in saying, "Thrack, arrato, mambo, delivan."

Surprised, the man turned to him and said, "Good day messenger. Lord Konicker awaits the true arrival." Jeremy reached into his shirt and produced the star. Relieved, the man continued speaking immediately. "Thank goodness you've arrived. I'm Earl. Put that away and follow me."

Jeremy dropped the star back into his shirt and took up the sack. He and Twig followed behind Earl through the busy streets of Thwardscall. The entire time, Earl checked behind them to see if they were being followed. After walking through many streets, they came to a narrow avenue filled with taverns and shops. Much of the walking seemed to be in circles. Finally, they stopped in the middle of this block at a five story building. A sign in front read, "Dragon's Tooth Inn." Earl said quietly, "We're here." Twig and Jeremy looked to one another for support and guidance.

Earl pushed through the double doors of the inn into a small entranceway with halls leading off to the left and right with a large barroom directly ahead. He gestured for the two to move to the right as he checked behind them one last time. Once they were all safely inside, he made his way down the long hall to a small private room in the back of the first floor. Earl moved ahead of them and hit the door with a gentle play of his knuckles—tap, tatap, tap, wrap. He ended with a loud knock and swung the door open. With his two followers close behind, he stepped into the room saying, "I'm back. Here's the ones Redlin sent—at least the ones that made it. They have the amulet." After a moment, he added, "And your ax."

An elderly man and two half-elves waited inside seated around a table. On it rested a plate of food and two full cups of water. There were no windows or other doors in the room. Both the elves held crossbows pointed at the doorway. As the group entered, the elderly man stood. He did not come up to Twig's chest but had to be at least three times as wide as her. His craggy scarred face showed his age, even though his well-defined muscular body could have belonged to any young warrior. The old man extended his hand towards Twig and Jeremy and said cordially, "Please have a seat. You can eat and drink if you like." Each one in turn shook his hand and sat at the table. Jeremy let the sack fall to the ground as he took up the glass and drank it. Twig sat more slowly and carefully. She placed Splinter on the table in front of her as she settled into the seat. Taking the cup, she sipped the water.

Everyone watched as the two nourished themselves. After taking his seat, the elderly man, looked at Splinter closely. After a moment, he leaned forward and said, "I'm Max Konicker and, I can only assume, you've come for my ax."

CHAPTER 30

As dusk approached, few people remained in Helexpa. Wearing a suit of Redlin's finest armor, Peter paced in the same courtyard he had left only a few days before. He contemplated his future as he waited for a wizard to arrive. His head snapped around as the door opened. It was Vin. Sighing softly to himself, he said, in a dull emotionless voice, "What do you want?"

Showing her concern, she replied, "I thought you'd left already without talking to me." She crossed the courtyard to where he stood. "I couldn't find anyone. I didn't know if they'd left. If you'd left. if I was the only one still here. When I stopped in to see Gallis, he told me you were here, waiting for a wizard. I was worried about you." As she approached, he turned away. "Where is everyone?" She joined him as he began to pace. "More importantly, where are you headed?"

Slowing his pace to a directionless stroll, he looked up at the sky. His voice was weak as he began, "Shane left as soon as he could find a magician to send him. When I pressed the wizard for where, he finally broke down and told me—Destin an elven stronghold deep in the Blackspine." Shaking his head, he sighed and added, "Uhh, I don't know what that means but I guess he had enough of the fighting. The guar hurt him pretty badly, whatever he might have told everyone, I could see it in his eyes. He was tired . . . hurt . . . used up." Turning around, he walked slowly in the other direction and continued to speak. "Jack left soon after Shane and he took Quinx . . . headed up the valley. No one knows what he's doing either." Vin gently placed her hand on his arm. "Darvan disappeared and no one has seen him since we were all together this morning." He put his hand atop hers and stopped his walking. "I guess that just leaves you and me."

In a tender caring voice, she said, "And what about you and me? What are you going to do?"

Moving his hand up to her cheek, he caressed it softly. "There is no you and me . . . no us. There's only Morgan . . . the battle. I'm going to kill Morgan. Morgan's in Thwardscall . . . the Dragon's Tooth Inn. It's the only place I know I can find the others and find Morgan." Fighting back his emotions, he finished his statement, "Redlin owed me a favor and I called it in. I'm going."

"Then I'm going too." She turned her head and kissed his hand softly.

He shook his head no. "I don't want you there . . . anywhere near Thwardscall. This is a time for warriors and wizards. Subtlety is lost in a war of this scale. It's time to kill and time to die . . . not a place for you." He leaned in and kissed her. "I don't want you to come to Thwardscall . . . to follow the fight . . . to go after Morgan. Someone has to survive in case I . . . we . . . all of us don't come back."

A tear ran down her cheek. "Don't say that . . . you're coming back . . . we're coming back. I'll be at your side. We'll fight together." She hugged him so that he thought she'd never let him go. He returned the embrace. "You can't leave me. I won't let you."

In a sad mournful voice, he said, "My destiny's in Thwardscall. I have to go and go alone. Please try to understand . . . don't follow. I need to regain my honor. Avenge my brother . . . destroy Morgan for more reasons than you could ever know. But more than that, I need to know you're safe. None of those other things will matter if you're not safe." He took her by the forearms and pushed her back. Without letting her go, he leaned in and kissed her. "I just wish things could be different, but they can't." He kissed her again and then slid his arms around her and hugged her tightly.

Though she tried to speak, she could not find words. As she searched for what she wanted to say, the door to the courtyard opened and a cloaked figure entered. In a deep resonating voice, he said, "I've come to send you off but we must hurry. The others are leaving soon and I have much left to do." He moved to the stables and opened the door. "Get your horse and I'll start the spell. When I tell you, walk through the doorway and you'll be in Thwardscall."

Peter kissed Vin one last time and said, "I must go. Be safe and remember me. I'll always remember you." He hugged her once more and left for the stable.

"Goodbye and be safe. I . . ."

Peter entered the stables and took his war horse by the reigns as she hunted for words. It was packed with enough supplies and weapons for four people. As the wizard cast the spell, Peter stood patiently in the center of the stable just a few feet inside the doorway. Vin watched as he looked back at her.

A mist gathered at the threshold of the doorway. The wizard yelled to Peter, "All right, the spell's done. Walk into the mist."

He mouthed the words "Goodbye Vineta Azurine. I love you," as the wizard gestured for him to move forward. He stepped into the doorway. Even as the mist came up and slowly enveloped him, he could see Vin watching him. When her image was almost gone, he saw her begin to weep.

Then, the scene shifted and he was standing in a street surrounded by the city of Thwardscall. His stomach knotted as he fought back the urge to vomit. The shock from the trip coupled with the emotions of seeing Vin for the last time crippled him for a few moments. He fell back and sat down on the dirt street. After regaining some of his composure, he looked around to see where he was, exactly. Pausing for a moment, he conjured up the picture of Vin in his mind. It helped clear his head. He heard himself saying, "I wish it could be different but you know it can't. Push it from your mind. Concentrate or you'll find yourself dead. Morgan's here somewhere. Focus." Unfortunately, he knew it was not that easy. Vin had touched him in a way he did not know he could be reached. It was impossible for him to forget that.

While he dealt with his queasiness and emotions, he looked around. Now that it was dark, the torches that lined the streets were burning, throwing an orange light bright enough to see by. Hanging only three doors away from where he sat was the sign for the Dragon's Tooth Inn. The street was empty except for a group of figures huddled in the street outside the door in front of him. Every other storefront was closed and seemingly abandoned. At first glance, Peter could tell little about the figures in the street. They seemed to be waiting for someone while they talked. Something about them bothered him. With effort, he got to his feet. Taking care not to draw too much attention, he hitched his horse to a nearby post and dug through his equipment. After a minute, he found what he was looking for—a Dragonthorn case. Placing it on the ground, he opened it. As the lid raised, a bastard sword, a pair of throwing daggers, and a black leather belt were revealed. The sword was the most impressive by far. Its blade was engraved with intricate designs and inlaid with gold. Its pommel and hilt were encrusted with gems. The word HAVOC was emblazoned on both sides of the blade. A flaming *R* was beautifully carved at the point where the blade and handle met the hilt. Peter thought, "I hope Redlin didn't exaggerate the power of this weapon. I'll need its help."

As Peter touched Havoc's handle, a deep but friendly voice spoke in his mind. "Don't worry master, I'm all you could want and more."

He quickly released the sword. "What? Did it just talk to me?" Peter was stunned. He had heard of the power of Redlin's magic but would've never expected to hold a weapon that could possess enough magic to speak. Even the Geminarex only guided actions. Carefully, he removed the belt from the case and put it on. He added the sheath from the case, clipping it to his belt. With reverence and respect, he picked up Havoc and slid it into its sheath. It seemed to rest there as if it had been specially forged for him.

"Thank you master. I'll serve you well." It responded as he put it at his side.

"Your welcome," he answered unconsciously and then added, "I can't believe I'm talking to a sword." After adding the daggers to the belt, he closed the empty case. Next, he unpacked a mechanical hand crossbow. Though it looked like any other larger crossbow might, it was small enough to fit comfortably in his hand and weighed no more than a dagger. Runes were carved along both sides of the handle. After checking to see that everything was in good working order, he loaded in one of the cartridges which contained five bolts ready to be fired in rapid succession. The bolts it used were no larger than darts. Each was made of lythrum and had a feathered tail made from the scale of a dragon. The tips were honed to needle sharpness that could pierce even magical armor. He clipped the small crossbow and three extra cartridges to his belt. After one last check of his equipment, he turned towards the inn. He was ready.

Slowly, he walked along the street. When he was within ten feet, he could tell the creatures at the door were not human. A closer look and one sniff told him that they were knarves. There were five of them just waiting there—three with their backs to him and two facing him. With only a glance, he knew there would have to be a fight. Stopping, he took hold of the crossbow and raised it, taking aim at the knees of the three with their backs to him. With five rapid jerks of his trigger finger, he had emptied the cartridge. Reflexively, he snapped it back onto the belt and reached for the daggers. Two knarves crumbled to the ground before realizing they had been hit by his bolts. The third pivoted towards him but caught the fifth bolt in the leg. He stumbled back and tumbled over onto the ground. Once the last two saw what was happening, they charged at Peter screaming something he could not understand. The two daggers were drawn and thrown in one smooth motion before they had taken a step. The dagger hit one of the knarves in the center of head. An instant later, the other dagger buried itself in the throat of the other victim. The fallen knarves tried to scrambled to their feet. Peter closed the distance to his enemies quickly. As he walked, he drew Havoc and raised the sword, wielding it with both hands. "Die!" he heard the sword say quietly in his head as he yelled it aloud. In one tremendous slash, he cut through the three knarves as if he were cutting through air. All three fell to the ground dead. He sheathed the sword. As he replaced it, he saw the daggers had returned to the belt without him calling them.

Even as the last gurgle of the knarves' lives sputtered out onto the dirt street, a group of beasts rounded the corner led by two humans. Peter counted twenty knarves, some guar, and a stalker. His eyes were drawn to the men that he immediately recognized as mind warriors. "I hate mind warriors," he said indignantly. Looking behind him, he saw another similar group approaching. He was surrounded. Just then, the door to the inn was shattered into a million splinters as the body of a dead dwarf was thrown through it from inside. A large human quickly followed. Peter raised his sword and prepared to strike. As the human rolled to a stop and tried to regain his feet, the sound of heavy footsteps came from inside the inn.

A familiar voice yelled, "Stop, it's me!" as the figure on the ground stretched his hands up to catch the blow. It was Aaron. He was hidden by a long robe and hooded cloak. The Geminarex were at his side in their sheaths. As he got to his feet, three hulking figures emerged from the doorway, one after the other, each larger than the last. As they came into the torch light of the street, Peter recognized them as grundlers, beasts that were half orc and half giant. Though stupid, they were loyal, obedient, and unimaginably strong. Moreover, they could be sent anywhere without question. These were Morgan's enforcers. The smallest had to be at least seven feet tall. As Peter looked around, Aaron grabbed the dwarf and hurled his body at the legs of the leading grundler. It caught him at the knees and knocked him down slowing all three as they stumbled over one another.

Peter's shock could not last for more than an instant as all three groups converged on his position and pressed the attack. "Talk later. Now we fight." He backed away from the door trying to better their fighting position.

Aaron stepped back from the doorway following his lead, say-

ing, "You're right, my friend . . . though it's good to see you here
alive." As he saw the scene outside for the first time, he said, "I
hate mind warriors."

As Peter shifted around and jockeyed for position, he said,
"Good to see you too and I'm sorry . . . sorry for everything. If we
survive, we'll need to have a long talk—a very long talk."

"When we survive, then we can talk all you want my friend.
For now, just fight." Aaron drew Justifier and Vindicator.

The doorway of the Dragon's Tooth Inn was like the opening
of a beehive. Knarves and grundlers swarmed Aaron and Peter. The
mind warriors conjured a thick mist that seemed to flow in from
everywhere around them. As the knarves began to attack, the
grundlers regained their feet. Peter and Aaron stood back-to-back
ready for the attack. Aaron raised the swords together and pointed
them at the mind warriors yelling, "True sight." A brilliant white
light flashed and the mist disappeared. "That won't last long. We
need to get to them."

Peter stepped forward and slashed at the first grundler with
Havoc. "Blink . . . get behind them. Get to the mind warriors. I'll
take the others."

"Right!" Aaron said as he looked in the direction of the mind
warriors. The two vile wizards had taken up positions just on the
other side of Peter's horse. From there, they cast their spells and
directed the fighting. A stalker and four guar waited at their side.
Aaron blinked his eyes as he fixed the position behind them in his
mind. Instantly, he was there. Each of his swords was driven into
the hearts of one of the mind warriors, killing both instantly. As he
drew out the swords, the guar turned and attacked.

While Aaron dealt with the mind warriors, Peter faced the
other beasts. He kept giving ground until he was across the street
from the doorway to the Dragon's Tooth. With his back to the wall
of the shop, he could limit his blind-spots and protect his back.
Most of his enemies, including all the guar and grundlers, ignored
him and entered the Inn. Even so, he had more than enough knarves
to keep him busy. They came at him in groups of five and six. As

one was felled by Havoc, it seemed two more took its place. His best attack was to parry and slash with the mighty sword. The knarves' blades were inferior, snapping like toothpicks under the blade of a hatchet. Armor and flesh split at Havoc's touch. However, despite his best effort, Peter could not gain ground. There were too many of them coming. He was cut, bumped, and nicked by claw and sword alike. Though no one blow could hurt him severely, when added together, they would take their toll. As the bodies began to pile up around him, Peter was pushed off to his left further and further away from Aaron. Knarves continued to attack even though more than a dozen of them had fallen to Havoc in only a few minutes.

As Peter fought off the onslaught of so many, Aaron dealt with his few. With the mind warriors killed, three guar sprang at him while the stalker moved towards the doorway to the inn followed by the last guar. Even with the help of the Geminarex, and all his skill, he could do little more than hold them off. With his back to the wall of the storefront, he worked to keep from being cut. If they drew blood, he would surely die. Block and parry was all he could think of. He caught glimpses of Peter fighting across the street as he passed under a torch. Aaron knew he had to try something or be killed. He fixed his eyes across the street. As the guar sprung, he blinked. All three hit the wall hard, as he appeared across the street. One stayed down while the other two turned and glided through the space that now separated them from him. He lifted Justifier and Vindicator saying, "Strike to the heart of my enemies." With a snap of his wrist, the swords flew across the street and buried themselves in the chests of the guar. The beasts fell to the ground dead. Opening both of his hands as if to show he was holding nothing, he said, "Geminarex, return to my hand." With a flash of white light, the swords were back with him.

Quickly, he crossed to the last guar as it struggled to pick itself up off the ground. Impacting the wall had broken several of its bones. As it writhed in pain, Aaron drove Justifier into its neck killing it. As he drew out the sword, he looked to Peter and the others in the street. More than twenty knarves lay dead around Peter while at least that many still pressed in on him. Everyone else was gone. He assumed they had entered the Inn. As he took a step towards the shattered door, another group of people came around the far corner of the street. Nine very large figures surrounded a smaller figure like body guards. Each of the larger figures appeared to be human. All of them wore full plate battle armor that differed only in color—the five in front wore blood red while the other four were dressed in blue. Helmets that looked like the face of a dragon encased their heads and completely covered their faces. Each carried an assortment of weapons that would have been enough for two warriors. Upon the chest-plate of each was Morgan's crest, a demon riding a dragon. As they passed near a torch, Aaron could make out the figure in the middle. He was a tall slender human with a long white beard. It took only seconds for him to realize who it was. His jaw dropped. In a dull, disbelieving tone, he said, "It's Morgan. It's really Morgan. He's here and he's mine."

The final battle had begun.

CHAPTER 31

"You don't look old enough . . . I mean . . . well, you're still alive?" Twig fumbled through what she was saying, still trying to make sense of the scene.

Meanwhile, Jeremy had taken the star off the cord around his neck and placed it on the table. As he pushed it towards Max, he said, "This is yours, I think. Redlin gave it to me and told me to say the words; the ones I told Earl. After that, I don't know." He shrugged his shoulders and looked around the room. He was met with cold stares from Earl and the two elves.

Max chuckled. "I can't believe you're the ones who made it to me. Don't get me wrong, I'm impressed." He shook his head incredulously. "I'm just surprised that two as young as you would undertake the quest and see it to its end." He leaned forward and looked at Twig, as he slipped the star around his neck. "Enough of that. To answer your question, if it was a question, I'm older than I might look. It's the dwarven blood in my veins. Trust me, I'm old and I can feel it." His gaze shifted to the boy. "Thank you for the star. I haven't seen if for many years. It'll work to nullify Morgan's magic and help us in the fight. My time's short; I'm just here to pass on my ax—Slayer of Evermore." He picked up Splinter and examined it. "Whose is this? I mean, who did Redlin give it to?"

"It's mine," Twig said promptly as if she had been called on to answer a question by a teacher. "Redlin gave it to me."

"Are you a magician?

She nodded 'yes' as she said, "Almost. I know all the master has taught but I do not yet have my own name."

"I understand but you use magic and wield weapons. You're the one to carry Slayer." The shock on her face was obvious to everyone. He continued without letting her regain her mental footing. "Redlin must've had his reasons. I'll give it to you."

As she looked on, Max took a chain from around his neck. Hanging from it was a miniature replica of the Slayer of Evermore. Placing it on the table, he slid it towards her. "Is that mine?" she asked naively.

"Yes, take it. It's the key to the battle. You need to get it to Redlin and . . ."

As he was speaking a tremendous crash sounded just outside the door. An instant later, the door to the room was knocked off its hinges by a grundler. In a dull stupid voice, it yelled, "In here," as it stepped into the room.

Before it moved again, the two elves had shot it in the head with three bolts each. It stumbled forward and fell flat on its face, dead. Behind it stepped up another grundler and a guar. Earl stepped forward and drew out a pair of mechanical hand cross-bows as Twig turned and pointed her finger at the grundler. A pair of bright white energy bolts flew from her outstretched finger and pierced the grundler's eye sockets. It fell back dead, pinning the guar to the floor. Earl and the two elves moved forward closer to the door as another grundler and two knarves came down the hall.

Max stood and grabbed Splinter. "We're trapped and surely out-numbered. Take Slayer . . . head south. Once you meet up with Redlin, he'll know what to do. He'll be waiting." He lifted Splinter without effort and chopped at the wall yelling, "Split," as it hit. A four inch gash was cut into the back wall of the room from floor to ceiling. He repeated the action again a body width to the left. Again a large gash was cut in the wall from floor to ceiling. Drawing the ax back a third time, he swung it with all his might yelling, "Splinter," as it flew. When Splinter made contact with the wall, it lived up to its name. The wood between the two gashes was instantly turned to splinters which filled the store next to the inn. There was now another door out of the room.

Jeremy and Twig had been so intent on watching and listening to Max, they had not paid attention to the fight behind them.

As they looked back, they saw a stalker, two guar and too many knarves to count battling with Earl and one of the elves. The other elf was mortally wounded. Now they could see down the hallway. It was filled with creatures waiting to overrun the room.

Max yelled, "Come on, they'll hold them for us. I need to get you out of here." He crossed the store and hacked at the far wall yelling "Splinter." The wall shattered into a million small splinters. A hole large enough to let them pass was created around where Splinter had contacted the wall. Max turned and ordered the two behind him, "Come on! Move it!" Both young adventurers moved quickly, focusing all their attention on the orders coming at them. "Get outside and go south. Slayer . . . the chain I gave you . . . it's the key."

As Max helped them through the hole, he looked back at he oncoming beasts. Twig put the chain around her neck and tucked it into her shirt. She asked, "Aren't you coming?"

"No! I'll try and hold this place as long as I can. I need to keep them from catching you. I'm sure they'll be more on the street but hopefully, they won't know it's you. Go now! If you wait too long it'll all be lost." Max turned and chopped at a knarve who had made it to the hole in the wall.

"Goodbye," Twig said sadly as she grabbed Jeremy's hand and led him outside like a lost child. As they reached the street, they saw the mayhem. Both stopped at the doorway, staring at the scene. Aaron was half way between Twig and Peter walking towards the far end of the street. As they turned their attention to where he was going, they saw Peter fighting for his life. Though he had killed more then thirty knarves, the beasts seemed to keep coming. Even now, he was surrounded by five and four more were approaching from the far end of the street. Buildings and Peter's horse obscured everything else they might see from the cover of the doorway. Jeremy looked to Twig for guidance. Both were confused and lost amongst the turmoil.

Max's voice erupted from behind them. "Move out from the doorway. We're being overrun." Before they could react, he pushed them through the door forcibly. As the two stumbled into the street, Max cut away the building supports with Splinter. The front of the store collapsed, sealing everyone else inside for the time being. While Twig and Jeremy tried to gather themselves, Max stepped into the street and looked around. Instantly, he recognized Morgan. In a stern voice he commanded, "Go, take the horse . . . leave. Ride south towards Redlin and his men. They're waiting on the plains outside the city. I'll keep Morgan here, at least for a little while."

The collapse of the building had stopped Aaron's movement and drawn the attention of everyone on the street. Even as Max took his first step towards Morgan, Aaron began to speak. What started as a whisper to himself, quickly became loud pronouncements. "It's Max Konicker. He's here. Max is here with Slayer. He's come to fight Morgan." Aaron watched as Max approached. Once he was side-by-side with Konicker, he turned and walked down the street keeping pace with his idol. Not seeming to notice the boy, Max continued his slow walk towards Morgan. He glanced over at Peter who was now only a few feet in front of him and off to his left. With a signal from Morgan, all four of his blue guards moved out from his back and drew weapons as they walked up the street. Ten knarves and two grundlers made their way out of the inn. Immediately upon reaching the street, they attacked Max and Aaron. The dozen beasts were little more than a momentary distraction for the combination of the Geminarex and Konicker. Aaron could not contain his happiness as he saw himself fighting next to Max. Even as Justifier and Vindicator cut down his enemies, his only thoughts were, "I'm fighting with the greatest warrior ever and he has Slayer of Evermore. We can't lose. Morgan will die."

While the others fought, Twig and Jeremy looked on like spectators at a sporting event, lost in all the commotion. She took hold of his hands in her own, saying, "If Morgan's here, I need to help. I'm the only magician they have."

He protested, searching for the right words. "No, you can't.

Staying is bad. You need to do what we were told. We need to go . . . get out of here. Redlin needs Slayer. That's our quest." He tugged at her trying to pull her away.

She said resolutly, "No, I'm in charge—I'm staying." Without answering, Jeremy moved to Peter's horse and took a longbow from the packed weapons. As he searched for a quiver of arrows, she said, "What are you doing? You're leaving. I need to know you're safe. I can't be worrying about you. You've got to go."

"No! I'm a Purple Dragon and my place is with you. I'm not leaving. We fight together and I'll give my life for you. I'm not leaving and I'm not afraid." Finding a quiver, he took it and slung it across his back.

Twig placed her hands on his cheeks saying, "I can't cast spells if I'm worried about you. We'll go together." He smiled, thinking he had won. "I'm sorry but you'll be safe at home. I should've done this long ago." She kissed him. Her lips stayed with his for a few seconds. As her lips drew back from his, the boy slowly disappeared from view. Her spell was cast and he was transported home. "I'm sorry but you'll be safe now." Her head dropped as she sighed. A tear ran down her cheek. "Goodbye my love, goodbye." Shifting her focus to Morgan, she gathered her strength. The confusion and concerns that churned in her head settled as she composed herself and looked towards the battle.

Meanwhile, in the mounting disorganization and confusion of the street, Peter was able to cut down the beasts that remained. With the appearance of Max, he was of no great concern. Though he knew his anonymity would not last long, he was happy for the rest. The beasts had exhausted him and beaten him badly as well. Breathing deeply several times helped him clear his mind and prepare himself for the second round of the battle. After regaining his breath, he yelled to Max, "Don't go further. Let them come to us." As if they were of one mind, Max stopped. Seeing this, Aaron stopped as well. Peter called to him, saying, "Aaron, remember your quest. You're not here to battle at Konicker's side. You're not here to kill Morgan." He let the words sink in before continuing.

"Go to the girl. Go help Twig. She's behind you. Go now while there's time." Shaking his head 'no,' he tried to ignore what he was hearing. As Aaron looked to Max, Peter said, "Take my horse and get out of here. This isn't your fight." Peter moved out into the street hoping to draw some of Morgan's fury. "That's right Morgan, the boy isn't here to kill you, I am." Raising Havoc and swinging it in a circle over his head, he pointed the blade at Morgan as if to say, "I'm coming for you."

Without looking away from Morgan, Max said, "He's right boy, this fight isn't yours." He raised his free hand and pointed towards the oncoming guards. Aaron paused as Peter's words replayed in his mind. "My quest . . . Max Konicker . . . Slayer," he thought with anguish and indecision. Not wanting to believe the thoughts that were beginning to from in his own mind, he looked pleadingly at Max. "This is my chance, my one chance to fight with Konicker . . . to kill Morgan . . . to see Slayer of Evermore in action." As the thoughts ran through his mind, Max cast a spell.

The street filled with bluish light as a forked bolt of lightning sprang from Max's outstretched hand and sped towards Morgan and his men. The electricity vaporized the fallen bodies of the beasts that were unfortunate enough to be on the ground. As the bolt reached the blue guards, it seemed to dance over and around them without effect. Once it was passed them, it continued towards Morgan. When it finally hit the second group, it simply dispersed with harmless sparks and some crackling. Max put both hands on Splinter and drew it back ready to strike at the first guard who came within range. This test told him that, at this range, his magic was useless.

Immediately, Aaron knew something was wrong. His mind searched through the wealth of knowledge at its disposal. "Max cast the spell. He didn't use Slayer. That's not right. The men . . . the creatures . . . they were untouched . . . protected . . . immune." As his mind wrapped itself around these facts and tried to rectify the discrepancies, he reexamined the scene in front of him. Backing away from Max, Peter, and the advancing guards, he took a closer look at the ax Max was wielding. As if his eyes had just been opened, he saw that the ax was not Slayer. Words rang in his head like church bells. "That's Splinter. He's not using Slayer." Shaking his head as if waking from a daze, he jerked his head around looking at all the different groups on the street. As his gaze passed by Twig, he stopped and focused on her saying to himself, "I must find Slayer . . . help Twig. She's the quest. She was with Max. She must know." As he started moving towards her, he yelled, "Good luck, my friends. Good luck. Kill Morgan for me." He sheathed his swords and ran to where Twig waited.

During all the movement and action, Twig had watched, trying to make sense of what was happening. As if there was a commentator within her, she heard a voice in her head replaying all that was happening. "Max stopped his attack. Peter's not attacking or moving. Aaron's running away and he has Peter's swords, I think. Morgan's not casting spells. Max is but they're not having any effect. It's all too strange. It's like everything is crazy and I don't belong." She watched as Aaron made his way down the street towards her. "I want to stay . . . to fight with the others but I don't know. Everything's confused. I just don't know." She gathered her strength and prepared to cast a spell. The problem she faced was what spell to cast. Her words found a voice as she began thinking aloud. "Obviously lightning isn't effective. What about my other spells?"

Before she could run through her options, Aaron yelled to her with such force, she thought he must have been someone else. "Take the things down off the horse—we're leaving."

Despite his authoritative tone, she protested. "No! I'm not going anywhere."

"We have to leave. The others . . . all the rest . . . they've died so we can get away. Max and Peter, they're sacrificing themselves . . . giving their lives for the quest . . . to stop Morgan. We need to leave. You're the key to Slayer."

The words hit her like punches. She had never thought of the others that had died to let her live. As she looked at Peter and Max preparing to fight, she realized what was happening. She muttered "Max . . . Peter . . . they know there was no chance. They're dying so I can live." She stood listlessly in the street unable to do anything.

"Don't just stand there, get the things off the horse. There's no time. They won't last long against Morgan's men." He drew a dagger and cut loose all the weapons and other supplies on the horse.

Twig protested, "How can you leave? We need to stay . . . to help. They'll all be killed."

"I know, that's why we're leaving." His tone was forceful and unwavering. Grabbing Twig by the arm, he pulled her towards the horse. "Climb up. I'll ride behind you."

"No. Who put you in charge?"

"I'm the Geminarex now. Remember the quest . . . to get Slayer to Redlin. You're the key. Now let's go before they sacrifice themselves for nothing." He saw his words were not persuading her. Leaning in close to her he said, "Are you going to let Permillion's death and the death of all the others go unpunished. We can't kill Morgan without Slayer—he's too powerful. If you fight him here, you'll die and all this will be for nothing."

As the words sank in, her face went blank. An image of the last time she saw her master filled her mind. Shaking her head, she climbed aboard the steed. Grabbing the reigns, he dexterously mounted the horse as if he had been riding it for years. Both glanced back at Morgan and the two warriors one last time. There was a loud thwap as Aaron slapped leather onto the back of the horse's neck to speed it down the street.

Even as the two escaped, the first of Morgan's men reached their companions. Max struck first. Chopping with Splinter, he hit the chest plate of the leading man. Though it knocked the blue-clad warrior to the ground, the blow did not penetrate the armor. Even as Max drew Splinter back, the other three warriors were on him. Weapons flashed and Max was hit from three different directions. Striking with Splinter a second time, he yelled,

"Shatter!" as the blade made contact with the guard to his right. The man screamed in agony as he fell to the ground. His body was riddled with cracks as if it were a pane of glass that was hit with a rock. Bluish blood seeped out of all the cracks as the creature writhed on the ground. The two remaining warriors closed in on Max as he tried to strike again. It took only a few hits by each of them to finish Max Konicker. As they attacked, Morgan examined the scene more closely. Suddenly, he realized what was wrong. Pointing at Twig and Aaron, he yelled, "He doesn't have the Slayer! Stop the others. They must have it. Get them!" Before the remaining two warriors could act, Max threw Splinter towards the guard on the ground. It hit ineffectually and landed on the ground harmlessly. As the two healthy guards moved down the street, he threw himself at them with all his remaining strength. As each of his hands made contact with one of the guards, he yelled, "Stone!" A marbled, gray stone layer formed on his hands and flowed out over their bodies. As they tried to move, it consumed them. In a matter of seconds, they were granite statues.

Before Max could stand, a sword pierced his lower back. The last blue guard had driven his long sword deep into him. Blood rushed out of him like rainwater pouring down a hill. His strength waned as his life ended. With his dying breath, he said, "Strike," and raised his hand to point at his killer. A beam of energy leapt from his finger and penetrated the helmet of the guard. Max fell to the ground dead as the killer stumbled back, leaving his weapon stuck in the ground through his back. Max Konicker was dead.

CHAPTER 32

Until now, Peter had been all but ignored by Morgan and his men. All that changed when he stepped into the middle of the street and slashed the last of the blue warriors. Havoc's blade sliced through the dragon helm as if it were paper and split the warrior's head into two equal halves. As the blade was withdrawn, he heard Havoc speaking in his mind. "That's no man; it's a dragonseed. Beware master. These aren't normal enemies. Use all my power. kill them all. Kill them all!"

"Be quiet," he grunted as he shook his head. After seeing the battle with Max, he was sure these things were not human. "Havoc can't be right. If these things are dragonseed, I've no hope."

"They're dragonseed," the sword instead, "And I'm your only hope. You're too weak without me. Use me. Bring havoc."

Still trying to ignore the voice in his head, he said deliberately as if emphasizing a simple point to a child, "All I need to do is delay them . . . slow them down so the others can get away." His resolve weakened as he doubted himself. "I can't kill dragonseed. I don't even think I could slow them down."

Havoc's words boomed in his mind. "I can! I was built to slay dragons . . . kill wizards . . . destroy whole armies. Bring havoc to hopeless battles. That is my calling. Use me—bring havoc."

Peter grunted as he tried to clear his mind again. It was becoming harder and harder to separate his thoughts and think clearly. After checking on his two young companions one last time, he thought, "Redlin said cast the spell. I hope I can give them enough time. I'm their only hope now." Staring at Morgan, he knew he needed to do something drastic and do it quickly. While he watched the old wizard, Morgan spoke quietly to the guards that surrounded him. An eerie calm came over the street filled with death.

In a cold scratchy voice Morgan called out, "Don't fight us. You'll just perish. We'll leave you. Just put down the weapon and let us take it and the ax. That's all we want. We don't need to kill you." He accented the word need in such a way that Peter felt a shiver run up his spine. His tone was condescending and so superior that Peter almost felt like a the wizard's apprentice.

At that moment, he decided to take a chance and, perhaps, buy some time for his friends. In a slow deliberate tone, he said loudly and with confidence, "I've not come to surrender, I've come to kill you. I am Peter Zorich of the family Zorich, the holder of the Geminarex. I know you and I know the dragonseed you have with you. You killed my brother and I've come for revenge. I wield Havoc, one of the ancient weapons forged to slay dragons and wizards of the past centuries." He watched the wizard's eyes as he spoke these words. For the first time, Morgan faltered allowing his face to show concern. The red warriors shifted uneasily as Peter continued. "I slew this dragonseed without effort. Soon you'll all follow. I know you. I know your weaknesses. We, the Geminarex, have killed many more powerful than you." The anger and uneasiness of the entire group grew. "Come face me if you dare. I know where Slayer is. I know what you are. I'm here. Come if you can—if you dare."

Though he was truly afraid, he did not show it. Havoc's words boomed in his mind. "They will kill you. I'm your only hope. Let me bring havoc. Bring havoc. Bring havoc! Let me bring havoc!" The words repeated over and over in his mind. Concentration and focus were impossible.

Without a word from Morgan, all but one of the guards advanced toward Peter. Each drew a two-handed sword as they moved forward cautiously. The last guard knelt down putting his hands on the street. After rolling his neck in a clockwise circle several times, he craned it back and emitted a horrible groan. Before Peter's eyes, his neck began to extend as his face stretched and widened.

The plates of his armor elongated and turned to scales. What were once human legs became the thick scale-covered hind legs of a red dragon. His hands transformed into claws. Once the transformation was complete, the dragon all but filled the street and was at least as tall as the two-story buildings. Havoc was correct. All these guards were dragonseed magically hidden in human form. Morgan climbed up onto the back of the dragon as it spread its wings preparing to fly. Peter had no time left. This was something he could not have imagined. Now, Morgan could just fly away and catch the unsuspecting riders with ease.

The words "Bring havoc," still echoed in his mind. The four red guards were just beyond the reach of havoc now. He had to act. His mind searched for something to do but all he heard was, "Bring havoc, bring havoc!" With all his might, he drove Havoc into the ground as he somehow knew he should. The sword was ruling his actions now. As loudly as he could, he yelled "I bring you Havoc!" As he said these words, the sword began to glow a fiery reddish-orange.

Everyone except Peter froze in their positions, not sure what was happening. Peter dove towards Splinter and grabbed it. As he did, the ground began to rumble. Cracks radiated out from Havoc's blade in all directions. Those cracks under the guards opened into large fissures, swallowing their legs. While the dragonseed worked to free themselves, Peter regained his footing. Taking care to avoid the cracks, he moved dexterously to Morgan and the dragon.

As he approached, the dragon shifted trying to avoid the cracks as well. When Peter was close enough to strike, the dragon reared its head back and breathed out a stream of fire. The flame enveloped him even as he dove to the ground to avoid it. His entire body tingled as the flame passed over him. Luckily, his armor had absorbed much of the fury of the dragon's breath. but the charred remains of his armor was now useless as protection. Having survived, it was Peter's turn to strike. Morgan tried to spur the dragon into the air before Peter could make contact. As best he could, Peter rolled forward and brought Splinter up over his head aiming the blow at the joint that connected the dragon's wing to its body. Splinter buried itself deep into the scaly side of the beast almost severing the wing. The dragon rolled away from the blow in pain, throwing Morgan off its back. The wizard fell hard landing face-down on the far side of the street. As the beast rolled, it kicked at Peter with its front claw knocking him off to the side.

Meanwhile, Havoc glowed even brighter as a mist gathered around it. Working feverishly, the four guards struggled to free themselves. They yelled to the dragon, "Brother come help us, we're trapped." Ice began to form on the ground around Havoc and radiated out along the street. Rivers of mist flowed into the fissure, wrapping themselves around the lower halves of the four guards. Each cried out in agony as ice crusted on their armor. "The mist is frozen hell. Melt it our brother." Once the mist filled the fissure, it solidified into ice.

The dragon paused momentarily to breath fire onto its trapped brothers. It had no effect. As if in response to the attack, the mist billowed into a cloud that rapidly grew in size. Soon, the entire street around Havoc was filled with the frozen cloud. Small icicles began shooting out of it in all directions like arrows from a thousand archers. Windows shattered and wood splintered as the icicles destroyed the nearby stores. The flying ice riddled the four trapped guards cutting them to pieces. As the cloud expanded, Peter began to feel the bite of the cold himself. The words, "Bring havoc," were still being quietly muttered in the back of his mind. Though he was far from the sword, he could see the cloud approaching. The fissures looked like the tendrils of a giant octopus stretching out along the street. The main cloud had already engulfed two of the dragonseed and was rapidly moving up the street. The red dragon spat flame at Havoc one more time. Immediately, the fury of the storm shifted in the beast's direction.

Small shards of ice hit Peter as they rebounded off the dragon. Working his way around the flailing parts of the monster, he hunted for Morgan. As he moved further from Havoc, the voice in his head diminished. Havoc's cloud had billowed four stories high as it overwhelmed the struggling dragon. The ice finally took its toll. Thousand of dagger-like icicles lodged themselves amongst the scales of the beast as it labored for breath. Its face was white with ice as it collapsed to the ground.

Even as the dragon fell, the ice storm enveloped it obscuring it from view. Off to one side, Peter saw Morgan hobbling away. "Stop!" he reached for his crossbow. As Morgan looked up, Peter fired all five bolts at the wizard. Every one hit, sending him sprawling to the ground. With what strength he had left, Morgan rounded the corner. The ice that had crusted on his robes and his hair shattered as he hit the ground. Far off in the distance, four men dressed in black waited. Morgan waved weakly to them. At the signal, all four ran to his aid. The old wizard was hurt.

"I only have one chance," Peter said aloud as he resolved to finish the fight. Closing the distance between him and Morgan as fast as he could, he loaded the last cartridge into the crossbow. Raising it and aiming in the direction of the approaching figures, he yelled, "Die!" Not caring where the bolts hit, he threw the crossbow away and drew both daggers. Rounding the corner, he prepared to strike. Morgan had regained his feet and was leaning against the wall for support. Only a a short lunge separated the two as Peter struck. With an upward thrust, he drove both daggers into the throat of the helpless wizard. Morgan died without even a murmur. After the body slumped to the ground, it began to shimmer and change shape. Before his eyes, the old wizard disappeared. In his place was a pale man dressed in the same clothes that Morgan had been wearing. Suddenly, he realized what had happened. "I hate mind warriors."

Spinning, Peter prepared to face the figures coming at him, but it was too late. They were on him before he could react. Two swords slashed his back between his shoulder blades. His armor split and blood gushed from the two deep furrows that were cut into his back. The force of the blow knocked him forward into the wall of the building. As he tried to turn and face his attackers, they cut him repeatedly. Pain riddled his body. With his back resting on the wall, he used the daggers to block the swords as best he could. His strength was leaving him as the blood ran down his legs and gathered at his feet. Scanning the street, he saw that his attackers were humans. More importantly, his bolts had killed one of the four—a mind warrior. "I hate mind warriors." He yelled, "Disintegrate!" and reached out at the three attackers.

All jumped back as one exclaimed, "Watch out! Don't let him touch you."

Peter laughed to himself for a split second. In one fluid motion, he threw both daggers at the two figures standing to his left while he shifted right. Both daggers hit their marks, knocking the two backwards. With a sharp blow to the wrist and a twist of his hand, he disarmed the third attacker. The stunned man stood defenseless as Peter slashed him across the face and then drove the blade into his midsection. The man collapsed taking the sword with him.

Though the daggers had hit, they had not killed the targets. Both men pressed the attack. Peter's fingers fumbled for the daggers. As his fingertips played on the belt, he felt the metal of the handles. His strength was failing. In desperation, he drew and thrust them at the faces of his assailants.

One of the attackers fell back with the dagger in his eye. Unfortunately for Peter, the other dagger had missed its mark. A sword pierced his abdomen. For the first time, Peter knew he was going to die. As the blade was drawn out, he slid to the ground along the wall. A crimson stain marked where he had stood as a pool of blood gathered around him on the ground. Weakly, he reached towards his killer with his left hand while he waited for the knife to return to his belt. As the sword came down towards his head, he tried to trip his attacker. At the last second, he felt the handle of the dagger. Pulling it out and raising it, he deflected the oncoming blade. As the figure tumbled to the ground, Peter drove the dagger down into his killer's calf crippling the man.

There was a loud crash from off to Peter's right. Buildings all around began to collapse under the constant pounding of the ice storm. The ferocious storm seemed to continue to grow in strength as the size of the cloud grew large enough to consume whole buildings. With the last of his strength, Peter drew his other dagger and drove it into the forehead of the prostrate warrior in front of him. Having finished his work, he rolled over onto his back and looked up. "I failed but at least the others are away—I hope."

As his vision clouded over and grew dark, he saw a familiar face hovering over him. It was Vin. "Don't die," she pleaded as she scooped up his head and put it in her lap.

He smiled, saying, "At least my last dreams are of a beautiful woman . . . one I loved."

"No my love, I'm really here and we are together until the end."

Blood seeped out onto the ground from all of Peter's wounds as his breath became short and labored. "Goodbye."

"No, it can't be goodbye. Hold on. Don't give up. I won't let you die." The terror and despair in her voice made her words a broken stream of syllables. "The Azurine know much and you will be saved. Your life can't end." These words slipped from her lips as Peter slipped away.

He closed his eyes as the world grew dark. The last thing he felt was the gentle rain of warm teardrops hitting his cheek as his body grew cold and stiff.

CHAPTER 33

Though it was night, lights shined everywhere, illuminating the entire valley. The sounds of battle and death filled the air. As Aaron and Twig rode out of Thwardscall onto the vast plains, they could see that the battle they had just left was not an isolated incident. Morgan and Redlin had brought their two armies together for one great conflict. Normally, a speeding war horse with a pair of riders would have drawn attention. However, on this night, none would even notice them as they passed. As the two rode, they saw many dying or dead warriors from both sides who had fled the battle to die in peace on the side of the road. Aaron drove the horse hard, heading south until he reached a rise with a small group of trees. Once safely inside the cluster of trees, he brought his horse to a halt and dismounted. In a surpassingly gentle voice, he said, "We need to let the horse rest and sort out a few things. I need to speak with you."

"Of course," Twig answered. Climbing down, she asked, "What's happening? What's happened to you? I thought . . . I mean . . . why didn't he . . . what should we do?" Trying to sort out the jumble of words and thoughts, she looked off towards the battle that raged to the south and east. Large flashes lit the night sky as dragons and wizards exchanged spells throughout the entire valley "The battle's started and I have the key to Slayer. Max said bring it to Redlin but who knows where he is."

There was a sudden flash as Aaron drew Justifier. The blade glowed brightly, showering the nearby trees with light. Stepping up close to her, he said in a confidential voice, "There's far too much I need to tell you and far too little time."

"Tell me what I need to know so I can understand what's

happening. I don't need everything but I don't want to be lost either."

"Peter gave me the swords; he was dying. I know everything he knows and all that I ever saw, read, heard, or was told." He put a hand on her arm adding, "And everything any of the wielders of these swords ever knew."

"Everything?" she asked incredulously.

"Yes, everything and so I know that our quest was as much to decoy Morgan as to get Slayer."

"So that's why Morgan was in Thwardscall."

"No, he wasn't. That wasn't Morgan." A look of shock consumed her face as he spoke. "The mind warriors and seeing Max Konicker clouded my mind . . . blinded me to the truth. Once Peter called to me, everything cleared. Then I saw the fight for what it was, just another bluff. Morgan is leading his troops south to face Redlin. Redlin is heading north to meet him. We need to find Slayer and join the fight. I know I can get to Morgan, with your help."

"Then let's go." She turned towards the horse. Where do we go to get the ax?" She stepped towards the horse as if to mount it again.

"Just wait a minute. You're the one with the key." He put a hand on her elbow to stop her. "Tell me, what did Max say?"

"Let me think. Not much." As she spoke, she worked her fingers along her neck, hooking the chain that hung there. Catching it, she lifted Max's chain up over her head adding, "He gave me this and said it's the key to the battle or getting Slayer or something. Whatever it is, he said it was mine." After fully removing it from around her neck, she extended it towards him. It seemed to glow in the light thrown by the swords.

Immediately, Aaron's face showed his shock and surprise. He stuttered and stammered like a nervous schoolboy. "That . . . tha . . . that's, that's." He pointed in disbelief as she looked on, baffled by his reaction.

"That's what? What is it?"

"That's Slayer of Evermore!" he exclaimed with a mix of shock and excitement.

"I assumed it looks like this. It's a replica, right?" she shrugged her shoulders slightly as she asked honestly, "But why is that so shocking." Her head shook as her confusion mounted.

Shaking his head emphatically, he said with certainty, "No, that's not a replica. That's Slayer of Evermore." He stretched out his hand hesitantly as if he was afraid to touch the ax.

"What are you talking about? This can't be it. Slayer was . . . is . . . it's supposed to be big . . . powerful. How can this puny thing be Slayer?"

Prying his eyes from the ax, he looked up at her to explain. He began, "This is just one of it's many powers. Redlin enchanted this weapon with more magical abilities than anyone could imagine. The ax can cast more spell than most journeyman magicians and with more force than ten accomplished sorcerers." Twig examined the amulet more closely, still refusing to believe her companion could be right. "There's a story of how Max wore Slayer around his neck into a meeting where no weapons were allowed. No one would've suspected it to be anything more than the amulet that it appears. They were wrong. It can fit in the palm of your hand or be too large for a giant to wield with both hands. More than that, Slayer shapes itself magically to fit its wielder." Aaron's enthusiasm was rivaled only by his knowledge. As she listened intently, he continued his story, "If you've been given it, then you are the one to wield it. Set your mind to it and the ax is yours to command. Be careful though, it's a powerful force and it will try and drive you. It's not an easy thing to control." He spoke in a grave tone as he finished his explanation. "Like magic, it is a difficult and dangerous thing to control. Slayer has a mind of it's own and is more power than you have ever felt. Only Redlin and Max have been able to claim it as their own until now. You must become the master of Slayer of Evermore."

She mumbled "No," as her head shook to show her disbelief. Dumbfounded and all but speechless, she stared off into the darkness. It was as if she had found a secret admirer for whom she had been longing all her life yet did not know about until moments before. Her lips voicelessly formed the words, "The Slayer of Evermore is mine." Irresistibly, her eyes were drawn to the glowing edges of the tiny double headed ax that so many had sought for so long. "This is my destiny?" Her mind struggled to accept what she had been given. "I am the Slayer of Evermore."

Kneeling in front of her, Aaron lifted his eyes to her and said, "As holder of Slayer of Evermore, I'm yours to command." Lowering his eyes, he put Justifier at her feet. "Just tell me what you wish."

She removed Slayer from its chain, letting the chain fall to the ground. The ax felt heavy in her hand. The words, "Slayer of Evermore be mine," played through her head. Her lips moved and the words flowed out as if she had not actually said them herself. Instantly, the ax glowed more brightly and grew before their eyes. After a moment, she held an ax that was perfectly balanced for her to use with either one or both hands. Slayer resembled Splinter except for the words written across the blades. There was a long metal handle, connecting a pair of large double-headed ax blades. A short spike extended outwards from the end of the handle like the tip of a pike. On one side of the two blades she saw the word SLAYER. Letting the ax handle spin in her grasp revealed the other side to her. The word EVERMORE glinted with its own light as the ax glowed brightly pushing back the darkness around her. The letters O and F were carved into the spike and were colored with a bloody crimson tint. As the ax grew, the two could see that runes and intricate carvings covered the entire handle and parts of the blade. She recognized some as magical incantations. Still others were obviously words but she could not decipher them.

Throughout the transformation, Aaron had remained silent, simply staring at what happened. Once it had finished its growth, he said, "I can tell you of its powers . . . what I know from the stories. None but Redlin truly know what it can do completely."

"First, get up. You're not my servant." She extended her hand as if to say rise as she continued, "Then you can tell me what it is fabled to be capable of." She swung Slayer effortlessly through the air testing its weight and feel. With the first sweep, she felt like it had been forged especially for her hands. "I need to know all I can so we can join the battle . . . so we can kill Morgan."

Aaron replaced the Geminarex in their sheaths and stood. He smiled as he saw her wielding Slayer. "Anything I know, you'll know. And I'll fight at your side when you face Morgan. But we'd better hurry. Morgan has already begun the battle."

After picking up the chain that had held Slayer, she moved towards the horse saying, "Then we'll ride. We can make the plan as we go. From the sound of it, the battle isn't far off, but that doesn't mean Morgan's close." She mounted the horse. With Slayer resting on her lap, she gestured for Aaron to climb up.

He nodded his agreement saying, "We should head due east and try to get behind Morgan."

"That sounds dangerous. Are you sure that's a good idea?"

"No, but if we head in any other direction, we might be ambushed or overrun." He moved to the side of the horse and added, "If we head directly at Morgan's lines, we can shoot right through. They won't expect that—I hope."

Her eyes opened widely. A battered man stumbled towards them. What was left of his armor hung on his bloody body more as a hindrance than as protection. When he saw them, he stopped and stared at Aaron. The light from Slayer was no brighter than firelight but it revealed enough of Aaron's features for the man to recognize him. In a weak, raspy voice, the man said with surprise and respect, "Lord Boewin, thank the gods you're alive. We thought you'd been killed." Before he could say anything more, he collapsed, falling face down on the ground.

Aaron drew Justifier and shed light on the lone figure. It was Deans. Quickly, he ran to the man's side asking, "What's happened? Please, we must know."

Twig dismounted and joined Aaron at Deans side saying, "We need to heal him?"

Lifting his head, Mark said, "No, don't waste the magic, you'll need it." His words came slowly as he labored to suck in a breath. "The dragons . . . Morgan's monsters . . . the barbarians . . . they were too much for us." Blood oozed from his lips and dotted the ground. "Ahh . . . Morgan's dragons and Redlin's wizards killed one another. The rest of us didn't stand a chance . . . our minds . . . they . . . we couldn't . . . It was horrible. We were . . . it was . . . I was lucky to get out alive." Coughing, he swallowed hard and took in a breath. "Redlin sent us north. Morgan pulled in his flanks to push south. We're all but lost. Hundreds of us are retreating this way being beaten down as we go." He struggled to speak but nothing else came.

Aaron looked at Twig and said, "Morgan's using mind warriors."

They looked one another and said in unison, "I hate mind warriors."

From out of the darkness came the noises of others moving away from the battle. Standing, Twig said, "We'd better go."

"Of course," he agreed. Placing a hand on his lieutenant's back, he said, "You've done well. Rest here and do your best to survive. Your fight's over."

As Aaron stood and made his way to the horse, she asked, "How good a horseman are you? My magic can direct us towards Morgan but you'll have to guide us in the dark."

In an honest tone that lacked arrogance, he replied, "Quite good. I'll find the camp." After sliding Justifier back into the sheath, he mounted the horse.

"Then we head east and search for Morgan." In a forceful commanding tone, she said, "Let's go." With no more than a thought, she bid Slayer to shrink back to the size of a charm and replaced it on its chain. Slinging it over her head, she moved to the horse and mounted.

Aaron eased the horse out of the trees and headed it across the valley. As he rode, Twig closed her eyes, concentrated, and cast a spell to sense Morgan's magic and his mind warriors. With that, they were off to find Morgan and end the quest once and for all.

CHAPTER 34

Ribbons of scorched earth scarred the landscape of the valley as if flowing water had cut deep groves in the rock floor. Bodies of slain warriors from both armies were strewn everywhere like debris left by a tornado. As dawn rapidly approached, the two armies regrouped and awaited the final conflict that was to inevitably come with dawn. In his encampment at the front lines of the battle, Redlin convened his war council. All those who could still lead their men into battle were gathered around to hear him speak. Even after a day of battling and being beaten by all types of spell, weapon, and beast, Redlin still commanded the respect and admiration of all gathered. The giant towered over the assembled mass of warriors. His armor gleaned as if it were new. Strapped to his back was a two-handed sword he had forged especially for his size and incredible strength. Taking hold of the handle, he drew out the mighty sword. Its entire blade was covered with carvings and magical words. In the center on both sides was carved the word FINALITY. As the blade glinted in the pale firelight of the small torches, the crowd cheered.

With one smooth powerful motion, Redlin drove the blade deep into the ground and released it letting it remain in the earth like a crucifix. In a powerful yet somber tone, he began, "Two days ago, our scouts met the first of Morgan's armies. His dragons looked forward to feasting on our bones. His beasts thought to take our women and burn our homes. His barbarian allies wished only to kill us and destroy our magic." A grumble ran through the crowd. Redlin raised his hand high as he added with force of certainty in his voice, "Today, their dead bodies litter the battlefield." The crowd cheered and hooted. As the noise died down, he continued,

"Our magicians killed their dragons, and shattered their hoards. Each of you led your troops into the fray and killed them as they ran. All fought valiantly and I'm proud to say I was there to see them at my sides. I'm proud to call you comrades in arms." The gathered mass cheered again. Redlin gestured for them to calm as he spoke over the cheers. "Our task is not yet finished. Many have died to give us this opportunity. We must avenge them and finish what was started. Even now Morgan gathers his troops not to attack but to protect himself. He is afraid." Again the crowd cheered and Redlin tired to quiet them. "As we speak, the Geminarex and the Slayer of Evermore head south from Thwardscall." A murmur ran through the crowd when the two names were spoken as if they were magic words that assured victory. "My agents in Thwardscall have cast a powerful spell that will be renewed at dawn. It has conjured an ice storm that now consumes the city and seals the valley. Morgan and his troops are cut off from retreat and reinforcements. If he uses his remaining magic to flee, his armies will scatter and be destroyed. If he stays, we'll kill him and all that stand with him. He is trapped." The entire crowd stood and cheered loudly. Turning towards his tent, Redlin raised his hands for quiet. In the voice of a general, he said, "You have your orders. Prepare your men. We attack at first light and don't stop until Morgan's head rolls on the ground and all his armies are little more than stories told to our children." The entire assembled mass cheered. Over the roar of his army, Redlin yelled, "Go prepare your men; first light comes soon."

As the troops moved off, Redlin returned to his tent. Seated at a table waiting were Gallis and Jack. The two looked over a map of the valley that covered the tabletop. As Redlin entered, both looked up. Each showed signs of the wear from the day's battle and their night's work. Jack was covered in open cuts and bandages while Gallis looked as if he had not slept for a week. As Redlin entered, Jack said, "That was a powerful speech but what's the truth? If you were that confident, we wouldn't be here now."

Gallis nodded weakly showing he agreed with Jack's sentiment.

"I've used all my strength to do as you asked but I can't say I know what you plan now that you know where Morgan is waiting."

Dispensing with any pleasantries or formalities, Redlin spoke his mind. "All of that posturing was as much to rally the men as to distract Morgan's spies. I sent Darvan to find Morgan and assess his strength. I sent you to know his encampment. Were you successful? Have you pin-pointed his position on the map?"

Gallis replied, "I think so. It was more difficult than I could have imagined. I kept us hidden as best I could as we traveled. The search went slowly especially in the dark. It took most of my magic, but we found him and Thazul."

Jack broke in, saying, "I was busy trying to keep Quinx steady and avoid being spotted."

Redlin cut off the discussion and focused on Gallis. "I know it was difficult. Flying a young dragon invisibly in the dark while avoiding stalkers, demons, and the like isn't easy but you made it. Tell me what you saw."

Jack's jaw dropped as he said, "Demons? What demons? Nobody said anything about demons. What demons?"

Gallis responded to Redlin without acknowledging Jack's question. "Darvan was right about everything. Morgan's personal guard is still surrounding his camp. He has at least a dozen dragonseed that I could recognize. I thought I saw a triad of mind warriors as well. The entire encampment is protected by more beasts than I could count. Luckily, I didn't notice any stalkers or barbarians anywhere near him."

"What about the demons," Redlin asked with a note of concern in his voice.

"Thazul and his minions are leading the armies. I think Morgan is using him as a general to keep the forces in line."

"What are you talking about? I didn't see anything. At least nothing like that. Just some tents . . . maybe a few people. How did you get all that?" Jack pressed for answers as if the others were keeping a terrible secret from him.

Redlin turned to him saying, "You should know what you're

being asked to face. Morgan's magic is powerful enough to summon demons. That's why the beasts and the barbarians call him Thrack Morgan. In their language, it means Morgan—Master of Demons."

Gallis added, "You're neither magical nor elven so you wouldn't have seen anything I saw—no dragonseed, no mind warriors, and definitely not Thazul. Especially not from that height and in the dark."

Taking a moment to grasp what he was hearing, he asked with hopelessness in his voice, "What're we supposed to do against a demon and his minions?"

"Nothing,' Redlin said confidently, "I'm going to go after them by myself. All you have to do is drive my forces towards them."

"Easy enough," Jack said sarcastically.

Leaning over the map, Redlin asked, "Where are they?"

Gallis pointed to a small hilltop saying, "That's where Morgan is; about half a day's march from us." Moving his finger along the map, he continued, "His armies are all along here and Thazul is with them."

"Good, that's perfect."

"How's that perfect," Jack interjected. "What is it you're planning?"

Redlin sat and leaned in close, lowering his voice to a whisper. Both Jack and Gallis leaned in as well, listening intently. "I'll tell you all I know and be honest with you. Our victory lies in your hands." A grave look crossed both men's faces as Redlin continued, "Neither the giants nor my other reinforcements have arrived yet. I've called out all my armies and my allies to the battlefield. All my wizards are spent but at least they rid the skies of the dragons, except for Quinx. Most were teachers not adventurers and so they'll not recover for days. Those gathered here are all we have to fight with. There's nothing else I can do." Looking into Jack's eyes, he added, "Morgan's armies aren't equipped to fight a dragon and so you're my perfect general."

Jack asked hesitantly, "What about Morgan and his dragons?"

Placing a hand on Jack's forearm, Redlin said confidentially, "They're his personal guard and won't leave his side. Thazul is the only thing you need to worry about. The demon will lead the armies to stop you. I need you to lead my forces directly at Morgan's camp and draw Thazul and the others away." Redlin pointed at the map as he spoke. "You're to head right at him using Quinx to attack as best you can. Can you do that?"

After a long moment of soul-searching, he said, "Yes, of course but where are you going to be? Why can't you lead the men yourself?"

Placing his other hand on Gallis' forearm, he looked at the elf saying, "Because once you've drawn Thazul and the army away, Gallis will send me directly to Morgan."

Both Gallis and Jack were shocked by the words. Redlin was going to fight Morgan and his private elite guards himself. Gallis spoke first in a hesitant sputter. "But you . . . well . . . that's not right. You'll be killed. You . . . Morgan's . . . it's insanity." Jack nodded his speechless agreement as Gallis spoke.

In his general's voice, Redlin said, "It's the only way. If I kill Morgan, Thazul is banished, the beasts scatter and the barbarians will flee. Morgan must be killed." As all three looked at one another letting the words sink in, a page came to the door of the tent. "Lord Redlin, the men are assembling. Dawn is upon us."

Redlin stood and looked towards Jack. "I've already told the men that they're to follow you. I hope you'll accept the command."

"Of course, anything you ask Lord Redlin. It's my honor to lead your army."

Turning to Gallis, Redlin said, "Rest here for now. Once the army's marching, I'll return and you can send me." With that, Redlin stepped out of the tent followed closely by Jack. Gallis watched them leave and put his head down on the table to rest. The camp was filled with busily working warriors organizing themselves into ranks.

Upon exiting the tent, Redlin moved to the men that were gathering while Jack headed off to prepare Quinx. As Jack reached

PU

the young dragon, he heard someone yelling to him, "Well, big man, looks like this monster is doing well by you." As Jack turned back, he saw Shane standing inconspicuously off to one side.

Smiling, he said, "I thought you were gone forever or at least until the battle was over. Where've you been?"

"No way big man. Couldn't let you have all the fun. I just went to get some friends to even up the odds."

Jack's face showed his surprise. "You brought the Foresters? I thought they never left the valley even when it was flooded."

"Them and others too. This was special and they all owed me." Shane stepped up and patted Jack on the shoulder saying, "I'm glad I made it back before this all got finished. Who do I report to anyway, to see what I'm doing?"

"Actually, I'm in charge, for now. How many are you?"

Shane laughed out loud. "You're the general. Redlin must really be in trouble or is it that you have a dragon. That must be it."

Jack grumbled and repeated his question. "Enough, there's no time for that. How many are you?"

Shane sensed the urgency in his voice and the seriousness of his statement. He gestured to the woods behind him saying, "I've brought all the Foresters and some others too. We number nearly nine hundred—all with bow and sword."

"Excellent. Lead them up the flank and just keep behind me. I'll be the one flying in the air." Jack smiled and chuckled. "It's good to see you again my friend. I hope we can talk about the battle tomorrow and many years from now as well." With that, Jack mounted Quinx and spurred the dragon into the air. He watched as Shane disappeared into the trees. As he stared at the forest below, he could make out the tops of hundreds of silver-helmeted warriors amongst the trees. Immediately, Jack realized that his friend had delivered the elite elven guard of Stalliac, the most skilled archers of Corinan. Bringing Quinx around in front of the army, he waved to the lead men and settled to the ground. In his most impressive voice, he said, "You all know what to do. We fight today until we have killed Morgan and shattered his armies." Spurring Quinx back into the air, he waved his hand, to take command of the army.

The march north to find Morgan's armies was not a long one. After a short time, the two armies came together and the battle began. Once the army was off, Redlin returned to his tent. After several minutes, he heard the first battle cries from the distance and saw a blast of fire fill the morning sky. Waking Gallis, he said, "It's time."

The elven wizard said, "I wish I had more time. I don't know how well I can cast this spell."

"Do your best, then rest and join the fight when you can." Redlin checked all his weapons and then placed a helmet upon his head. "I'm ready."

Gallis brought his hands together letting his fingertips touch. After a few moments of intense concentration, he began the spell. Placing both hands on the giant's chest, he said, "Find yourself at Morgan. Find yourself at Morgan . . . at Morgan . . . at Morgan." Redlin disappeared as Gallis collapsed to the ground in a heap. His magic was gone and his strength with it.

CHAPTER 35

Aaron drove his war horse due east for most of the night while he explained everything he knew about Redlin's plan, Slayer of Evermore, and Morgan to Twig. Long before the approach of dawn, she could sense her magic failing. It was not that she was loosing her strength, but rather Morgan and his mind warriors were blocking it. She said to him quietly, "It's Morgan. he's thwarting my magic . . . stealing it. We must be getting close."

"Just stop. Save your strength for the fight. I haven't seen a guard all night. I think something big's happening." Putting a hand on her shoulder, he added, "I'll be fine on my own. I can use my powers to find him now. Lean back and rest, if you can."

Nodding her agreement, she leaned her head back on his chest and closed her eyes. "How do you know so much?" she asked as she settled back.

"Three days ago, I became the Geminarex. In that instant, I knew all that had come before me. I spent the journey from Phinn to Thwardscall exploring it . . . myself . . . everything. There's so much I never knew . . . we were never told."

Even as he spoke, she began to fade off into sleep. As much talking to himself as her, he continued, "I had much to learn about myself . . . about the world . . . about magic. Even now I don't know what I should . . . what I'm free to say to you. At first, I was outraged, then depressed. Now, all that's left . . . I'm . . . I guess I understand. I'm the Geminarex and that means I know and I am resolute." Tiredness overtook her and she was asleep as these words drifted over her. As she slept, he carefully picked his way over, through, and around the many small hills that filled this part of the valley. The entire time he though of the battle that waited for him somewhere in the darkness ahead.

Soon after sunrise, smoke and the sounds of battle began to rise from the south. A short while later, as the two riders came up along a small rise, Aaron saw Morgan's encampment on a hill in the distance. Immediately, he brought the horse to a halt and woke Twig. With the scene laid out before them, the two could now see that all but a handful of Morgan's guard had left to join the southern lines. Just visible on the horizon was a dark figure atop a dragon. Pointing to the speck, Aaron said, "That must be where the main battle is happening. It looks like Redlin's armies are advancing this way." Dismounting, he slowly walked half way up the next rise.

After sliding down from the horse, Twig edged forward and carefully surveyed Morgan's camp. She was not as interested in the battle as in the wizard's view of it. Though she could have shot an arrow to Morgan from where she lay, a deep ravine ran between the hill they stood on and Morgan's position. "This won't be easy," she said as much to herself as to her companion.

Aaron turned to her asking, "What do you think we should do? We'll only have one chance at this. I figure surprise won't last long or count for too much but it might get us to Morgan."

She tried to clear her mind of the muddled thoughts that filled it. Thanks to the mind warriors she was deprived of her magic. Even so, she could still look to the focus of her warrior training for some comfort. It felt strange. "I wish I knew what to tell him," she thought. "I'm not a leader, I'm not even an adventurer or a journeyman wizard." As she edged closer to the top of hill, she raised her hand to silence Aaron and gestured for him to move closer. The distinct ringing of swords came to them from nearby. Until now, these sounds had been lost in those of the far-off battle.

Flashes of reflected sunlight played across the hillsides as the two saw what was causing the noises. Both Aaron and Twig knew immediately that there was no more time to think. They could see Redlin's profile as he battled valiantly. The earth around him was scorched and the bodies of countless grundlers, guar, and other beasts were strewn across the landscape. Finality had burnt, battered, or sliced them to death as he fought his way towards Morgan. At least six dragonseed guards now surrounded him, pressing their attack against the weary warrior. All used swords and shields as they pushed Redlin down the slope away from their master. Half way up the hill stood two groups of three wizards a short distance apart. Two of the six wore red and gold robes signifying their standing as grand masters of illusion. The others wore silver robes and carried staffs. At the top of the hill, Morgan stood and watched surrounded by a half-dozen more guards and two figures that neither of the two could identify.

Twig felt Aaron slide back away from the edge. As she continued to watch, she could hear his armor rattling. With some hesitation, she slid back and turned to see what he was doing. As she turned, he extended a bare hand to help her up, saying, "There's not much time. Redlin can't hold them off for long. As long as the mind warriors are there, magic's useless and he probably can't even see who's attacking him." As she stood, he handed her the gauntlets he had been wearing. "Take these. They'll help you wield Slayer."

Shaking her head, she said, "But, what about you?"

"Just take them. There's no time for arguments. Slayer's the only weapon that can damage Morgan now. He's been protected magically. None but the most powerful weapons stand a chance. You're the only one. You can get Slayer to Morgan and finish him." As she took the gloves and put them on reluctantly, Aaron removed Tarreck's amulet from around his neck. "You'll need this too. It'll protect you from poison, edged weapons and anything thrown at you."

She took it without even attempting to disagree and placed it around her neck. "Thank you. But even with these things, can we get to Morgan?"

He fixed his eyes on hers and said, "We can't—you can." Though she knew he was right, she was still surprised by his statement. Before she had a chance to say anything, he continued, "I'll help Redlin while you ride up the hill to Morgan. Forget us, we're just a distraction." As he spoke, he could see her doubt.

Putting his hands on her shoulders, he added, "I'll go after the mind warriors. Once they're dead, we'll be able to use our magic. Get to Morgan. Use Slayer to kill him. That's the quest—the only thing that matters now."

Shaking her head 'no' she said, "But you'll be killed. Redlin will be killed. I won't be able to . . ."

He raised his voice stopping her. "Morgan's killed millions. He killed my men . . . my only friends." Twig began to nod as he continued, "Cragmore . . . Peter . . . Max . . . Permillion . . . even your family. They all sacrificed themselves so we would have a chance. Don't let their deaths be for nothing."

A cold rage filled her as he said this. "I'm not letting anything happen. It's not me . . . it's." She wiped at her cheek as a tear welled up. "No, that can't be. Androthy . . . my family, it's not fair."

He wrapped his arms around her to comfort her and said in her ear, "I wish things were different but we don't have time for this." Releasing her, he patted her shoulders and continued, "Redlin's dying and the battle will soon be lost. We need to stop the mind warriors and you need to kill Morgan for your master . . . for your family. For everyone he's hurt . . . killed. For everything he's done." Drawing Justifier and Vindicator, he stepped over the hill and peered down at Redlin as he battled. Without turning to Twig, he said, "I'm going. Do what you must."

In a powerfully commanding voice she said, "Stop." As she continued, Aaron felt as if Cragmore had suddenly appeared and was speaking to him. Her words were those of a general not a scared girl or a wizard's apprentice. "We must make Morgan think I am a powerful wizard. One so powerful his mind warriors have had no effect. He cannot know I have Slayer until it is too late. Slayer can cast spells but few will be useful. I know powerful magic . . . Gallis' magic, but I can't use it until the mind warriors are dead. Can you still use the magic of the Geminarex?"

He was taken aback by her tone and her words. Slowly, he answered, "Yes, of course. Just tell me what to do."

Kill the mind warriors as you wanted to, but make it seem like the magic comes from me. Do whatever you can. We'll loose surprise but gain confusion."

He nodded as he began to understand her plan. Without looking back at her again, he drew his swords saying, "Whenever you're ready, master Twig."

She tucked Tarreck's amulet under her armor and extracted the chain that held Slayer of Evermore. Slipping her hand through it, she took it off and wrapped it around her finger so that Slayer rested comfortably in her palm. The two stepped over the top of the hill and looked at the scene before them. Redlin was down on one knee and two guards were closing on him. The lifeless bodies of at least ten of the dragonseed guards were strewn around him as he fought off the advance of the others. Twig pointed Slayer at them and thought to herself, "Fireball."

A large reddish-orange ball of flame as wide as Redlin erupted from the spike at the top of Slayer and shot towards them. As the spell was cast, everyone looked up. The ball of flame hit the two dragonseed closest to Redlin, knocking them backwards as it set the entire field ablaze. Even before the ball of fire hit, she had raised her hand up and cast another spell. This time a bolt of lightening leapt from her hand and sped towards Morgan and his men. With a wave of his hand, Morgan dispelled it, causing it to dissipate into little more than a wash of sparks. She patted Aaron's shoulder as if to say, "Your turn." He responded by saying to himself, "Geminarex, give me strength and fortitude." As these words were uttered, his muscles bulged and he seemed to grow in size. As the magic flowed into him, he fixed his vision on the two grand masters. As he said, "Strike to the heart of my enemies," he threw both swords. Justifier and Vindicator glinted in the morning sun as they soared through the air towards the mind warriors. Not wasting any time, he shifted the focus of his vision to a point just behind them and blinked. In an instant, he was there and had enough time to watch Justifier and Vindicator pierce the heart of the two eldest mind warriors just in front of him. As the other four cloaked figures looked at the far hilltop in confusion, he said "Geminarex, come to my hand." There was a bright white flash as both swords transported themselves from the bodies of their victims to his hand. The befuddled mind warriors had moved towards Aaron to take cover from the attack only to find themselves at the mercy of his blade.

With two quick slashes the last four mind warriors were cut down like so much tall grass. There was another bright flash from the top of the hill as Twig sent a stream of magical arrows from Slayer down towards the guards surrounding Redlin. As Aaron surveyed the scene, he could see that ten guards were still battling with him. He maneuvered to his left to put himself between these men and the path he hoped Twig would soon come riding along. Killing the unsuspecting mind warriors had been easy, but killing dragonseed would be a much more difficult task.

Two guards moved towards him as the rest closed in on Redlin. There were eight or nine on the ground between himself and Redlin but it was difficult to tell which were dead and which were simply wounded. His only thoughts were of the battle. "What to do if they rush me . . . if they?" He shook his head to clear his mind. "No, I'm the Geminarex . . . mind warriors. They're still in my head eroding my control." Knowing there was no time to be confused, he said loudly, "Vindicator, clarify my mind." As the words were spoken, he felt the magic flow from the sword into his body. As if a weight had been lifted, he found it easier to concentrate. While the two guards approached him, he glanced back at Morgan one last time. One of the unidentified figures seemed to sprout wings. Immediately, he recognized it as a demon. Though it was no taller than himself, it was at least twice his width. Its skin was the color of molten lava. Coal-black razor-sharp claws tipped its finger and identically colored fangs protruded from its mouth. One large horn jutted backwards from the top of its head. With all his breath, he yelled to Twig, "Morgan's summoned a Mazor demon to dispel offensive magic . . . to protect him." Looking back to the fight in front of him, he thought to himself, "I hope she heard me."

Returning his attention to the battle, he watched as two swords buried themselves into Redlin's sides. Charging forward, he yelled, "No!" The two guards nearest him were stunned by his exclamation. With a flurry of slashes and thrusts, he reduced them to little more than pieces of bloody armor. Seeing this made the others step away from Redlin and angle for position on their new opponent. Without thinking of strategy, Aaron ran to Redlin's side and touched him with both swords saying, "Heal." Redlin's wounds closed and the flow of blood that had been running from them stopped as if a faucet had been shut.

He had saved Redlin, but now he was surrounded. Three different attackers hit him with their swords. With all his might, he struck back trying to block and parry the blows as they came. Though his blows made contact, he was still outnumbered. Redlin had left him six and he had only been able to kill half of them. For each one that fell, another took his place. His toes felt the warmth of his own blood gathering in his boots. The pain of his wounds seemed a distant reminder of the battle as he struck at his attackers with both swords. The magic was all but gone now and he had no way to heal himself. All his efforts now were a result of his desire and inner strength. As the last three of Morgan's guard closed in on him, he said, "I'm not going to die here. I will not give in . . . not give up." He felt his legs buckle as he tried to step into his thrusts. The magic from the Geminarex was used up and the strength it had given him was gone.

At that moment, his instincts took over. Throwing both swords, he cried, "Geminarex, strike to the heart of my enemies." The two guards in front of him were thrown back forcibly as Vindicate and Justifier buried themselves deep into the chests of the two men killing them instantly. As Aaron moved towards Redlin, the third guard drove his sword into the small of Aaron's back. The blow knocked him to the ground. Rolling towards Redlin, Aaron took hold of Finality and moved it with all his might. The giant-sized weapon moved slowly and clumsily through the air as he yelled, "Die!" The surprised man jumped back as the sword sliced across his midsection drawing blood. The weight of the sword and the awkward position made it difficult for Aaron to do much more than let it fall on the far side of his body. Releasing it, he said, "Justifier come to my hand." With a flash, the sword appeared. As his attacker tried to stand, Aaron dove at him with the last of his strength, driving Justifier into the man's neck. The blade cut deep and the guard rolled backwards—dead. Releasing Justifier's hilt, he collapsed to the ground next to Redlin.

As he labored to breathe, Aaron could hear Redlin straining to speak. As he tried to stand, he found that his legs were stiff and unresponsive. He pulled himself closer and put his ear next to Redlin's lips. "Kill the mind warrior," were the only words that Redlin could say.

"I did. They're all dead." Aaron responded dumbly as his mind lost focus. He though to himself, "Why isn't Redlin healed? I healed him. Why can't I move? What's happening?"

His mind refocused as Redlin put a hand on his forearm. "No, the one . . . by . . . next to . . . Morgan." the words were coming slowly and with much difficulty. "At Morgan's side . . . by the demon . . . a mind warrior." After drawing in a deep breath, he continued, "Kill that one."

Aaron's legs had lost all feeling. "I can't move. Why can't I move?"

"Poison blades . . . para . . . lyzing." Squeezing Aaron's arm tightly for emphasis, he said, "Hurry . . . before . . . it's too . . . late." Each word was said amongst a long exhausting breath. Pushing the boy away, he said, "Kill him!" with his all the effort he had left.

The push rolled Aaron over so he could see Morgan at the top of the hill. The robed figure stood a few feet from Morgan in plain view. The demon had gone after Twig and so had the guards. Three were headed down the hill towards his position. He thought to himself, "Only three." As he reached out for his swords, he found it difficult to breathe. His arms were still free but the rest of his torso and lower body were all but useless. The paralysis was creeping up his spine and he knew he would soon be as stiff as any corpse. He said to himself, "Vindicator, come to my hand." With a flash, the sword was in his hand. Craning his neck back, he focused his vision on the point between the legs of the mind warrior and blinked.

In an instant, he was looking up into the eyes of the robed figure and saw a beautiful woman staring back at him with astonishment. Even the shock of seeing a women at Morgan's side did not make him hesitate. The mind warrior watched as he thrust Vindicator up into her midsection. There was a horrible scream followed by a gurgle as the blade drove upwards through her abdomen, stopping in her left lung. Crumbling to her knees, the mind warrior gasped for air. Releasing the handle, Aaron's arms stiffened. The mind warrior's robes draped over him as her limp body fell on top of him. While the paralysis consumed all but his face, he felt her breathing stop as the life ran out of her.

Each breath was more difficult than the last. He could hear Morgan yelling orders and trying to cast spells. His only thought was, "I've done it. The mind warriors are dead." As his eyes closed and darkness came over him, he thought of Twig, "I hope she can do it. I know she can kill Morgan. She must kill Morgan."

CHAPTER 36

Atop the hill, Twig watched anxiously as the battle unfolded below her. When Aaron had killed the robed figures, her attention had been split between the battle and Morgan. As Aaron continued the fight, she had waited expectantly for her magic to return. She was disappointed. Nothing changed. Before much else could happen, Morgan gestured and strained with concentration. Her attention focused on the wizard as she worked through the spells he was casting to try to determine what was going on. "Summoning, alteration, charm, so much . . . far sight." Shaking her head, she said, "Uhhh, what now?"

As if in answer to her question, Morgan's guards charged down the hill as the Mazor demon unfolded its wings and glided across the spaces between the hills. As it approached, Twig could see it clearly. In the distance, she though she heard Aaron yelling to her, but her mind was working to remember anything about the demon that approached her. "Think—you read the master's books. They told you what to do." As the demon game closer, she eliminated all but two classes of demons. "It's a Mazor or a . . . a . . . a Bellintine, but which is it." She knew both were highly resistant to magic, were minions of more powerful demons, and neither could be easily killed. They looked almost identical but were totally different. She was sure it could be killed, but it would take the proper spell.

Looking down at Slayer she thought about what spells it still contained that might be useful. As it came up over the top of the hill, she pointed Slayer and cast the spell. A blizzard of grayish-white icicles shot out from the tip and covered the demon. Within seconds of touching its skin, the ice melted and disappeared. She exclaimed, "Ahh, Mazor, total destruction—disintegrate it or die." The words came out of her as a chant from the days when she had memorized the proper spells to use from the books in her master's library. Now she had to put it to use.

Before she could do or say anything else, the demon was on her. It took only one slash of its powerful claw to knock her back and cut her deeply. Tumbling backwards, she rolled down the hill until she lost sight of Aaron, Morgan and the rest of the battle. Regaining her feet, she dodged the demon's claws as it pounced. A powerful flap of its wings sent it up away from her reach. It hovered for an instant and then dove down again. She rolled to one side just in time to avoid being hit. It was far too quick for her to do much more than keep away from it. The time had come to use Slayer as more than a spell book.

With no more than a thought, Slayer of Evermore was transformed into a throwing ax. As the Mazor swooped up and dove down again, she threw Slayer. The spinning blade cut through the left arm and wing of the demon as easily as it had sliced through the air. The beast shrieked in agony as it tumbled to the ground in a heap. Black ooze with the consistency of cold syrup dripped out of the slice in the Mazor's arm. Grunting and spitting, it put its undamaged hand over the wound. Twig watched as the flow of blood stopped and the arm repaired itself. Folding its wings behind it, the demon came at her on the ground.

She thought, "Of course, Mazors regenerate—destroy them or die." The demon closed in giving her few choices. Behind the demon, from the direction of the main battle, Twig saw what Morgan had been summoning. Twenty grundlers led by a stalker on horseback charged towards her. In a matter-of-fact tone, she said, "Enough of this, Slayer come to my hand." With a flash, the ax had returned. A thought transformed it from a small thing that could be thrown into a two-handed battle ax. The demon was not deterred by the appearance of Slayer of Evermore. Lowering its head, it charged. Twig was not prepared for this and had to jump in order to clear herself from its path. Its horn just passed her right side as the demon's shoulder caught her and drove her backwards. As the demon turned to come back at her, she thrust forward with Slayer burying its tip into the Mazor's chest. She yelled, "Disintegrate." Magic flowed from the ax as the Mazor broke into a thousand small shards and then disappeared.

As the demon ceased to exist, four bolts from the stalker's crossbow dug into her side. Screaming, she clutched at them and tugged them out of her flesh like she was puling weeds from a garden. After drawing them out, Twig turned her attention to the hoard that quickly approached. Her first thought was to deal with the stalker. As Tarreck's amulet healed her wounds, she brought Slayer up over her head. The grundlers where ten yards away, but she focused her attention on the flank of the Stalker's horse far behind them. With all her might, she drove Slayer down yelling, "Rumble!" Slayer cleaved the earth. As it made contact, the spell was cast and a fisher split the ground and ran up the hill to a point beyond the stalker. Though only a few inches wider than the blade at the near end, the spell opened a chasm that was wide enough to swallow the Stalker. The movement knocked all the grundlers to the ground causing several to fall into the widening hole in the earth. As she withdrew the ax, the ground closed, crushing the stalker and four of the grundlers. Six more found themselves partially trapped.

Without waiting for the rest to make it to their feet, she began to revolve Slayer around her head. A wall of flame formed around her and expanded out. Once the flame had reached the ground, she brought the ax forward and spun the tornado of fire out towards the grundlers. As the fire touched them, their clothes burst into flame while their skin charred. Twig moved sideways backing away from the remaining grundlers.

When the tornado had run its course, only six grundlers remained. More importantly, she saw four of Morgan's guards coming over the top of the hill towards her. Most of the spells in Slayer were gone and the wounds from the Mazor had not been healed by the amulet. She knew they would not heal without magic. The time had come for her to be a warrior. Calling on Slayer, she said,

"Heal me. Give me strength . . . all your power." This was far more than she had hoped for as she felt its magic remedy all that was wrong with her. Slayer had given her all its magic. Her body grew as her muscled felt the power of ten giants.

The grundlers were first to fall. They had neither weapon nor skill, only strength. This was no match for the empowered Twig wielding Slayer. The blade cut across the oncoming beasts knocking them back forcibly. Twig slashed and chopped relentlessly as they tried to recover. In a matter of moments, all were reduced to lifeless bloody chunks. As the last grundler fell, the first guard was already attacking. Spinning to face him, she tried to think what to do. Pain rippled through her abdomen as the guard's blade cut her. Force and instinct overtook thought as she swung the ax down on his head like he was a spike being driven into the ground. Slayer's blade split his helmet and continued on through his body stopping just above his belt. Before she had withdrawn the ax, her cut abdomen sealed itself and the pain dissipated. The show of power stopped the other three guards before they could attack. The furthest one turned and began to scramble back up the hill as the others looked on dumbfounded, unable to decide whether to fight or flee. Two slices of the mighty ax solved their dilemma. The first slash severed one guard's right leg beneath the knee, knocking him to the ground. As the ax came back through the other guard, it cleanly removed his head. His lifeless body fell at her feet as she looked back at her first victim. He squirmed away from her clumsily.

At that instant, she truly enjoyed the battle. Until now, fighting had always been training for and secondary to magic—nothing else. Now that Slayer was driving her, she felt its power. With all her might, she brought the ax up over her head and came down on the helpless guard writhing on the ground. The blow cut him in two like a piece of firewood being split.

The last guard had made it half way up the hill by the time she could turn her attention to him. She moved slowly after him not caring to hurry. Suddenly, her mind filled with the presence of magic. The haze lifted and she was again a magician. Though the strength and resolve of Slayer still remained, she no longer felt the forceful desire to do battle. Pointing her left index finger at him, she concentrated. A bright white bolt leapt from her finger and caught the fleeing figure in the back of the head. He fell forward and slumped to the ground with a smoldering hole piercing the back of his helmet. She quickly moved up the hill and made sure he was dead by driving Slayer down on his neck, severing his head.

With that done, she said, "Now, I kill Morgan and finish the quest." Looking to the south, she could clearly see the front lines. Redlin's armies were pushing north as Morgan lost control over many portions of his armies. Off to the east, she could see the banners of the kingdom of the giants and the Dwarves. Recognizing them as allies of Redlin, she thought, "Reinforcements. Morgan may flee soon, especially if he knows his demon is dead."

Peering over the top of the hill as carefully as she could, Twig scanned for Morgan and her companions. Only Morgan was visible. He was busy casting spells to help his army and recall his demons. There were no sounds of fighting anywhere nearby. Inching forward to look for Redlin and Aaron, she caught a glimpse of Redlin's body resting motionless on the ground. Sliding back away from the edge, she said despairingly. "They must be dead. It's up to me now." For the first time in her life, she felt truly on her own. She was no longer a follower, but a leader and the master of her own life.

Focusing her mind, she concentrated and cast the spell. Slowly, her body shifted shape and she transformed herself into a replica of the Mazor demon. Morgan would easily see through any illusion she could cast. The transformation would be difficult to maintain, but as long as she concentrated, it would work. Spreading her wings, she rose up and floated into the air using Slayer's flying levitation spell to help her keep aloft. As Morgan saw the demon drift up over the hill, he grinned. When he saw that it carried Slayer of Evermore, the grin grew into a wide smile. She could see that in his mind, he had won. Turning to the south, he returned

JAMES M. LIPUMA

to his conjuring, paying her no more attention. Hovering behind him for a moment, she drifted to a rest just behind the old wizard.

For the first time, she could see him clearly. He was human, with, perhaps, a bit of elven blood somewhere in his heritage. Magic had extended his life, but even so, he looked haggard and old. She saw no weapons or even magical staves, rods, or wands. Rings adorned all his fingers and she thought she could see an amulet under his silken robes. From what she had observed, Morgan cast spells with gestures and incantations. Somehow, he did not seem to be as formidable as his reputation had suggested. At this point, he appeared to her as more of a frail old man than a malevolent mastermind and killer. As she stepped towards him, he spun around suddenly. With his left hand, he drove a dagger deep into her stomach. As the blade penetrated, he grabbed Slayer with both hands and ripped it from her grasp. Stumbling back, she said, "Nullify," and then clutched at the dagger.

"I wasn't fooled. Your magic didn't work."

The transformation reverted as Twig's mind filled with pain and rage. Withdrawing the dagger, forcibly, she clutched it tightly in her hand. Her chest burned as she yelled, "No!"

Morgan laughed. "Sorry young one—you lose. I have your ax and I've finished you in the bargain."

She controlled her rage as the pain subsided and the wound healed. Focusing on the ground at his feet, she concentrated and cast the spell. In an instant, solid rock liquefied. What was firm ground became a pit of pebbles, quicksand, and mud. Morgan dropped in and was covered up to his shoulders. Without shifting her focus, she cast another spell and the ground turned to granite trapping the wizard. As he struggled, he tried to cast spells, but much of his magic was gone. "What have you done? Who are you?"

"I am the wizard Nella of the family Monterack. Student of Permillion . . . and now, Slayer of Evermore." Morgan's eyes widened with recognition as she told him all he needed to know. She continued confidently, "When you took Slayer, you sealed your fate. It was the thing to steal the magic from your rings."

Morgan pleaded with her as he struggled in the ground. "Don't kill me. I have Permillion . . . your family. I can save them."

Her heart stopped for an instant as the old wizard spoke these words. "What! What do you mean?" she asked with disbelief.

"Thazul holds their souls in his realm. It's our bargain. If you kill me, he is banished and they're lost. Free me and I'll command him to return them to you. I'm lost without my magic and no threat to you." His soft tones tried to charm her as he continued to plead his case. "Please? What can I do?"

Indecision plagued her. Her mind seemed to yell to her from a far off place. "I'm never the one to decide. I'm the follower. The one to be trained—the apprentice." As she wrestled with her choices, the dagger slipped from her fingers. Her eyes scanned the battle field below for signs of Redlin's armies. The dragon that had been hovering in the southern sky was gone. Though many still fought tirelessly, hundreds of thousands of other torn bodies littering the field as far to the south as she could discern. Turning, she looked back towards the place where Aaron and Redlin had fought valiantly against Morgan's guards. She saw Redlin laying prostrate on the ground motionless. Aaron was nowhere to be seen. Surveying the area carefully, she walked around until her eyes picked up the bottom half of his body trapped under the mind warrior.

Pushing the dead mind warrior off to the side, she tried to rouse Aaron. He was alive, but far off. Having no magic left that could help him, she slipped Tarreck's amulet off of her neck and placed around his. Though she was not sure it could heal him, this was all she could do for him now. She looked into his eyes for guidance and strength. Staring into his mindless depths, she searched for any help he might give her. As if in answer to all her questions, she heard herself say, "The quest . . . the quest . . . kill Morgan. That's the quest." She did not need to hear him speak the words in order to know he would simply remind her of the oath of the Purple Dragons.

By this time, Twig had walked away from Morgan. In a quiet

voice, the old wizard began reciting a chant to free himself. "Thrack terra mota . . . terra mota. Thrack terra mota . . . terra mota."

Before he could finish, she pointed at him and yelled, "Silence!" Though his lips moved, no sounds emanated from them. Struggling in vain against the stone encasing him, Morgan screamed to make himself heard. Nothing helped. Her spell had robbed him of the last bit of his magic—he was completely trapped.

In a cold quiet voice, she said, "I'm a Purple Dragon. We're all Purple Dragons. My oath was to kill you. Thazul will be another quest." Walking slowly, she approached with a look of determination in her eyes. Lifting her left arm high in the air, she thought, "Slayer of Evermore, come to my hand." With a flash, the ax appeared in her outstretched hand. Bringing it back behind her, as she thought, "Death to my enemy," and drove the ax down on the helpless wizard. As it made contact, there was a clap of thunder that boomed through the entire valley accompanied by a bright orange-yellow flash that filled the sky.

Turning towards the battle, Twig let the ax slip from her grasp and fall to the ground. From the top of the hill, she could see the battlefield spread out in front of her. Without Morgan's magic or the leadership of Thazul and his demons, Morgan's armies broke ranks and retreated in disarray. Jack led the remains of Redlin's army forward driving the beasts and barbarians up the valley before them. Shane and the Stalliac archers rained arrows down on the flank of the fleeing armies as the giants pressed in from the opposite side of the valley. Morgan's armies were defeated. They had won.

Dropping her head, she closed her eyes and thought of Jeremy. "I want my home and my Jeremy. My quest is over. Thazul is banished. Morgan is dead."

AFTERWARDS

So ended the quest for the Slayer of Evermore and with it our story. However, much was still left undone. With Morgan dead, his armies fled into the vast wastelands of the north. Redlin's allies, led by Shane and Jack pursued the hoards north as far as provisions and their resolve allowed. Those who remained behind returned home to declare the victory and heal. In the calm that followed this great battle, all paused to rest and plan for the future that seemed bright and promising once again.

This, however, was but the beginning of our story. Many great adventures were to come and are recorded in our hallowed archives. Thazul still held many souls in his realm and had minions positioned throughout Moniva awaiting his instructions and his return. The mage master Nella, formerly Twig, was to claim her throne, restore the fallen heroes, and return those to power who had been supplanted. Her love Jeremy found himself across the continent at Permillion's home. With Lancer, he would return to Twig's side and help her free fulfill her destiny. Aaron and Redlin, though fallen were neither lost nor forgotten after the great battle. These and many other events of that time are chronicled by others of our clan.

Most important of all, the future of the clan Azurine was forever changed that day. As Peter Jonathan Zorich, lie on the streets of Thwardscall, Vineta Azurine, the scribe, vowed to use the knowledge of the Azurine to save her love or forfeit her life trying to restore his life. Moreover, she pledged never to stand by as others fought the battles of the world. In time, this vow has brought a new age to our clans and a new challenge to all those who have come after her. Those quests, her stories, and her life with Peter are all things that we know well and that are not to be told here.

Morgan is dead, the Slayer of Evermore is found, this quest is over, and the story ends.

The End

NOTE TO THE READER

I hope you have enjoyed "Slayer of Evermore." This is the first of a series of stories related to Twig and the rest of the adventuring party described in this book. Many of the other characters, including Redlin and Max, have many stories of past adventures to share. However, the next story relates to the quest for Thazul. If you have questions or comments regarding this book and its character or would like to make suggestions about the quest for Thazul, you can e-mail the author at the address listed below.

SlayerOfEvermore@yahoo.com

Printed in the United States
48306LVS00002BA/172-183